I0760501

Praise for What the Wind Brings

"A triumph!" ~ Cecelia Holland, author of the Corben Loosestrife series

"What an incredible novelist does well is make a reader see the world from a different perspective. Mr Hughes does an exceptional job of that in this book. *What the Wind Brings* has ships, slaves, arquebuses, swords, jungles, and monks. It also has a good dose of indigenous magic that plays an integral part of the story. With this book, you will be drenched in humid jungles and steeped in rarified, mountain air while immersed in cultures and histories we should all know more about. A finely researched, detailed story that will touch your heart and make you realise, yet again, that while we may bodily beat each other down, we can't stop our spirits from rising. If I was ever lost in a jungle, I'd want Expectation to find me." ~ NE White, sffworld.com

"Beautifully immersive and the historical details are incredibly well drawn; the amount of research that went into this is evident on every page. Engrossing and enlightening." ~ Anwen H

"What a journey you take reading this book. You feel like you are there back in ancient Ecuador, and living out the brutal existence portrayed. I found myself fearing for my life. The spine-tingling, edge-of-your-seat storyline will keep you up all night." ~ Siouxanne M

"Sensational!" ~ Candas Jane Dorsey, author of *Black Wine*

What the Wind Brings

Matthew Hughes

Pulp Literature Press

Pulp History is an imprint of Pulp Literature Press.

Library and Archives Canada Cataloguing in Publication

ISBN: 978-1-988865-15-7 (hardcover) ISBN: 978-1-988865-18-8 (numbered edition)
ISBN: 978-1-988865-16-4 (trade paperback) ISBN: 978-1-988865-17-1 (ebook)

This book is a work of historical fiction.

Cover art: *De Windstoot*, Willem van de Velde the Younger, 1707
Cover design: Kate Landels
Interior design: Amanda Bidnall
Map: Mel Anastasiou

Published in Canada by Pulp Literature Press
www.pulpliterature.com

This book is dedicated to the memories of two women
who inspired me to become a writer:
Eileen Rafferty, my mother
and
Ruth Eldredge, my Grade 12 English teacher
They each left a lasting mark on me

Esmeraldas
Cayapas
Niguas
Esmeraldas River
Niguas
Campazes
Andean Mountain Range
Yumbos
Quito
Traditional Territories of Northern Ecuador

One

Expectation

I was in the spirit house, meditating on breath. The men of the village were in the men's house, where Pidi had called a meeting to discuss something to do with the crops. The women were in the women's house, brewing corn beer and making jokes about each other's husbands and children, but keeping an eye on the men's house across the central open space.

I did not go to the meeting; I was not a man. I did not go to where the women were gathered; I was not a woman. Besides, I knew that Pidi would come to me in due time. He was staunch for the proper ways of doing things, despite all that had befallen us and the other towns of the Nigua nation in the years since the Spaniards had passed through.

I returned to my meditation. I had been thinking about breath a great deal lately. Now it was time to consult my guide.

Under my predecessor Pallu's tutelage, I had learned how to control my breathing, to channel and focus the life force so as to perform acts that were impossible for the untutored unless they took the mushrooms called "the openers," as the men did in some of their ceremonies. But the openers brought them only dreams—though sometimes those dreams could be of serious import—instead of truly opening the doors to the upper and lower worlds.

I could climb or descend into the other realms without openers, simply by regulating my breathing while repeating the secret words that Pallu had taught me after he took me into his keeping. After he prevented Manda, the father of Pidi, from dashing my infant head against a rock because of my ... discrepancy.

Thus I had chosen today—the signs were auspicious—to go beyond meditating, to go down into the lower world and seek wisdom from my guide. Thus I was sitting cross-legged in the spirit house with my back straight as Pallu had long ago taught me. I fixed my vision on the central post, the axis between the upper and lower worlds, and took charge of my breathing, slowing it gradually, until my abdomen and chest would scarcely have shown movement had anyone been in the spirit house to see it.

The interior of the house grew brighter, one of the signs that I was becoming detached from the middle world. The blond wood of the axis post began to glow with a golden light, telling me that I was nearing the threshold of the channel to the upper world. I reached without looking for the small wooden bowl and took two small sips of the clarifying tea, then set it down and continued to concentrate on my breathing.

The tea began to work within me, opening the ways. I felt my pulse throbbing in the seven parts of my body. My torso became a great hollow tube, extending from my buttocks to the inside of my mouth, but I kept my lips tightly sealed to prevent my inner parts from rushing out; if I let them escape I knew it would take a long time to recover them. Gradually, the pressure ebbed away while the glow grew brighter and moved to envelop me, until my view of the spirit house was completely suffused by the light and I saw only gold, with the usual rim of blackness at the edge of my vision. The Old Deceivers hissed and chattered at me from the darkness, but I had long since ceased to give them any heed.

Motionless, I waited for the expanding light to absorb me completely. When I was sure I was surrounded by its warmth, I let a portion of my innermost self seep from one nostril and make contact. A lightness filled my chest and I felt as if I could float up to the thatch above me, to fly out the smoke hole and perch on the roof—it was a better perch than Pidi's for listening in. But I resisted the urge and called instead on the one who guarded and advised me.

She came, as always, in the form of a monkey eagle, her feathers grey above and pale below, showing bands of light and darkness as she spread her wings then closed them. I offered my own courtesy and a greeting. She turned her head and looked at me from one golden eye.

She did not speak; she never did. But I felt her presence within me and knew that she waited for me to begin the conversation. I spoke in my spirit voice that none but she would hear, "I have been thinking about breath. And life. And fire."

The word *mystery* formed in my mind.

A great mystery, said my own voice, though I knew it was speaking for her, *woven through the world.*

Consider the wind, my inner voice said, *and what it brings.*

It was a thought that had already passed through my mind a number of times. The wind was like breath, but none knew where it came from, or where it went. Did something breathe the wind? If so, whose breath was it? Or did it breathe itself? These were old questions, never answered.

But the guardian had spoken of what the wind brought, which was a new consideration, and now I said, "What does it bring?"

The answer came not in words but in a sense of sudden motion. I was rising up as if I were a monkey seized in the eagle's claws, though I felt no pain and knew I would not be harmed; it was not the first time I had flown like this.

We climbed through the leafy canopy, as I had often seen such birds fly in the forest, their short, powerful wings finding holes and pathways among the branches. Then we were out in the open air and still rising. Far off to the east I could see the forested hills climbing to the blue mountains, obscured today by overcast. To the west was the sea, as grey as the sky, the line where one met the other made invisible by rain. We passed over the ruined town the old chief—Manda, Pidi's father—had led us away from in my childhood, when the spotted sickness came again. Then we flew on, out beyond the horizon, out to the deep sea where our men used to sail on balsa rafts, trading with towns three and four days' sail away—towns that were all gone now.

We flew through rain and out into sun again. The water turned blue, marked with snails' trails of currents. But now, farther out, I saw something I had never seen, though I recognized it from descriptions I had heard: it was a ship of the Spaniards, rounded at one end and squared-off at the other, with tall posts from which great swatches of pale cloth hung motionless in a windless calm. Unlike a canoe, its hollow spaces were roofed over with wooden planks, and on them were the first Spaniards I had ever seen.

I saw them with the bird's eyes, sharper than any human's, and the image became even clearer as my guardian tipped one wing and glided down towards the scene. I saw that the Spaniards were of two sorts. There were many of the pale ones, like those who had come to our town wearing metal over their puffed-out clothing, carrying swords and the wood and iron things that smoked and shot deadly fire. How did they get fire into iron, I wondered, and my thoughts went along that path until my guardian returned my attention to what was beneath us.

As well as the pale men there were dark-skinned Spaniards, men and women, walking in a circle, each with a hand on the shoulder of the one in front. Hupuka and the other men who had been taken to carry burdens had spoken of these dark Spaniards. In the high country they were common. Some were labourers, grubbing and carrying, and not just for a period, as the Quechua speakers were forced to be for months at a time; the lowest of the dark Spaniards were worked all the time. But some were craftsmen and seemed to have some license to decide for themselves how their days would go, whereas a few others were no different from the pale Spaniards—these wore armour and carried weapons; they swaggered and caroused and beat the Quechua speakers, just like the others.

These circle-walkers were not the swaggering sort. They were clothed in tatters and went barefoot. And they were watched by pale Spaniards who held swords and spears and those terrible spear-axes our men had seen do murder. Two more Spaniards stood on a raised platform at the rear of the vessel, and these held long objects of wood and iron from each of which a thin trail of grey smoke rose into the air. That caught my attention, but my guide had other interests. She tipped a wing and slid lower through the air.

A pair of pale Spaniards were hauling buckets of water from the sea and throwing them on the circling dark ones, I supposed to clean and cool them. But that was not what my guardian wanted me to see.

As I looked where she looked, I saw a dark face glance up and stare right at me. He was not one of the circle-walkers, though. He was young, dressed in the padded, tightly fitted clothes that some of the paler ones wore, the sleeves ridiculously filled out. He wore shoes with squares of bright metal on them. I could see his eyes blinking as he sought to focus on me.

Now my guardian's gaze shifted again, and I saw another dark-skinned man, though this one was not looking up. This one was mature, had wielded power, and in his expression I saw rage and dignity mixed. Unlike the others, he had both hands on the man before him, and his wrists were circled by dark metal bands joined together. I knew that those hard eyes did not see the man in front of him but watched scenes that played out like shadows on the wall of his mind.

Once more my guide's attention moved on, and I found myself seeing the face of a woman who walked behind the angry man, her face still but her eyes no less deep in thought than the man whose shoulder lay under her hand.

Then we were spiralling up into the air, the ship shrinking like a toy. We flew towards the eastern clouds. The voice spoke in my mind again: *what the wind brings.*

A moment later, I was back in my body, the glow fading around me. I was shaking and chilled, as I often was after returning from the upper world, and my mouth was dry and foul from the tea. Near me was a calabash half-filled with corn beer. I took a mouthful, rinsed it around, and spat it through the gaps in the floor. Now I drank properly, my throat narrow and normal again.

I waited until the shivers subsided and rose, stiff in my joints for all I had still not yet seen thirty rainy seasons. I went to the door and descended to the open space.

Only a short time had passed. The men were still in their meeting. A rack of poles served as a ladder up to the door of the men's house. I waited at the bottom and made the gesture that courtesy required. I could see some of the men seated in the common space within, passing around a jug of beer. One of them glanced down and saw me.

"Expectation is here," he announced.

I heard Pidi's voice say something, then the man near the door looked down at me and said, "You are not needed this time."

I inclined my head and went back towards the spirit house. I had only briefly considered telling them about the ship and the pale and dark Spaniards. Clearly, the vision was important, but I would need to dwell upon it for some time before I could understand what it all meant. And what the wind was bringing us.

*T*wo

Alonso Illescas

Today the sea is flat, stretching away to the west like a dancing floor of green marble, veined and figured, until it meets a line that does not really exist yet is strong enough to demarcate world from sky. Yesterday, the wind blew fitfully from the south and made the ocean dance to its arrhythmic medley. The heavily laden galleon tacked continually, making scant progress as it alternately slanted towards the dense, forested shore with its strip of white beach then turned and beat its way out to sea again.

But today *La Virgen* has scarcely moved a furlong since the offshore wind died in the morning watch, like the last breath of a dying man, leaving ... nothing. The sails hang inert, with not so much as a baby's fart to fill them. The expression is Mendoza's, speaking to Esquivel, the Basque mate, a moment ago. And now the stitched canvas actually billows a little backwards as the northbound current carries the galleon along against the resistance of the moist, dead air.

Alonso would like to know what is going on now as the captain and the Basque confer on the other side of the raised afterdeck, both of them staring fixedly at the south-western horizon. They must see something that eludes Alonso's unsailorly gaze, because some quality in the flat line has energized the two men. Mendoza is asking the mate a question, and Esquivel is tugging at the filthy ruff that rings his neck above the sweat-stained doublet. It is a habitual gesture; Alonso has seen him do it whenever the mate feels that responsibility is being thrust upon him. Esquivel will never be a captain, he thinks; he is a man always in need of someone to tell him what to do. He would make a good slave, Alonso is thinking, and then he turns the thought on its head and examines its other end. Does that mean that I am a bad slave, since I enjoy having a wider scope?

The captain has come to a decision, and now the mate is moving to carry out his superior's will. Esquivel is charged with energy now that the thinking has given way to doing. His shouts bring men running to the mid-deck, where *La Virgen*'s two boats are tied down. Hands untie and loosen the ropes on one of the boats, and in seconds it is turned right side up, revealing the oars stored beneath the thwarts. More shouts, all in Spanish but in half a dozen accents—Genoese, Venetian, Greek, even red-bearded Irish—more ropes, more coordinated bustle, and the boat is efficiently lowered over the rail to sit lightly upon the sea. In even less time, the second boat is in the water, and seamen are jumping down, seizing the oars. They row towards the bow, where their shipmates cast heavy lines down to them to tie to cleats on the boats' transoms.

Soon, Alonso sees the two boats pull out ahead of the galleon, the men at the oars bending and straightening in a slow rhythm, the wooden blades biting into the green-marble water, the thick, corded hemp tightening, spraying drops that sparkle in the sunlight as it lifts from the sea. Other seamen are brailing up the sails, and now *La Virgen* is turning, slowly, in a wide arc towards the open sea.

Alonso looks east to where a thin smear of green marks the unnamed land. Between the port city of Panama and the even newer port at Lima lies a realm of impenetrable jungle and muddy rivers that the Pizarro brothers have won from the barbarians for the glory of His Most Catholic Majesty, Philip of Spain. Alonso approaches Mendoza and says, "*Señor* Captain?"

Mendoza's back is to him. He looks south-west, squinting.

"*Señor* Captain?"

One of Mendoza's shoulders twitches beneath the heavy cloth of his doublet, but he does not answer.

Alonso speaks softly. "Why are we turning north-west? My *patrón* was very clear. The cargo is needed urgently in Lima."

Mendoza says something Alonso cannot hear, then half-turns his head and says, "A storm is coming. There is no shelter on this shore. We must have sea room."

Alonso looks at the horizon then up to the sky, which is blue and innocent of clouds except for some high wisps far out to sea. He is not sure what to say, and so he says nothing. Things were clearer before they left Panama. *La Virgen* had been built for the Illescas in Nicaragua in the shipyards of the Gutierrez brothers, a trio of shipwrights from Seville brought to the New World by the Illescas family. Don Alonso, Alonso's *patrón* and namesake far away in Seville, had seen that whoever owned the ships would control trade to the new and growing southern markets.

The Gutierrezes established a shipyard on the western coast after hauling their tools and necessaries across the isthmus by mule and on the backs of *Indios* conscripted by a conquistador turned *encomendero*. Don Alvaro Illescas, eldest son of Don Alonso and manager of the family's trading establishment on the sugar island of Hispaniola, needed the galleon to take a mixed cargo south to the port at Lima. There the goods would be unloaded and carried up into the highlands, where the newly arrived viceroy was consolidating the *Audiencia* of Quito amid the spoils of the victory over the still-restless savages.

But two days before their intended departure, Don Alvaro had been struck by one of the fevers bred by the foul, damp air that hung over the raw city. He had called Alonso to his bedside, where he lay pale and sweating, while a priest who had training as a physician prepared to open a vein in his arm.

"Alonso," he had said, "you are young, but you must see the cargo to Lima."

"I will do it, Don Alvaro."

"I will send a letter with you to Jorge Estebar, our factor. He will deal with the authorities. Besides, the cargo is all paid for."

"Very good, *patrón*."

"But you must see it safely through. Sailors are thieves. Do not let them pilfer from us."

"I will not let them."

"And keep them away from the black women. They are not for the pleasure of Mendoza's sailors."

"I will sleep in the hold."

"Good. If any give you trouble, tell Captain Mendoza. I have already spoken with him."

The priest had cut the vein then, bringing a grunt from Don Alvaro and a spurt of thick blood that dripped from the elbow and into a wooden bowl that an attendant held, its inner surface stained dark. The sick man's face grew even more pallid. He reached with his unencumbered hand to take Alonso's, and the contrast of their skins, white over black, was stark. "Until you reach Lima, *you* are the House of Illescas. Act accordingly."

"I will not fail you or your father."

Don Alvaro blinked, and it seemed to Alonso that he would say more. But then a kind of haze passed across the man's eyes. He sank more deeply into the soaked bedding, ripe and rank with the iron smell of his sweat. The priest-physician put the fingers of one hand to the patient's wrist, while the fingers of the other brusquely fluttered to shoo Alonso from the sickroom.

***La Virgen* moves sluggishly behind** the straining boats. Mendoza still watches the western horizon, now dead ahead of the bow. Nicaragua's coastal galleons are made mostly of cedar, not like the hardwood ships built in Manila for the trans-Pacific trade. She rides lightly on the water even though she is heavily laden. When her sails are filled with wind, the ship progresses to the accompaniment of a concert of her own noises: creaks of stays, tympanies of snapping canvas, the rush and gurgle of bruised water along her sides. But in this calm, there is no sound save for the shouts of the coxswains in the towing boats, calling the rhythm of the stroke.

The heat is stifling, the air so thick with moisture that, with every indrawn breath, Alonso can feel its weight settle into his lungs. The six passengers—two merchants and their wives, a blacksmith, and a cordwainer—have come up from their cabins where they spend most of their days so as to avoid contact with the crew. Sailors are the lowest of the lowly, ranked down there with foreigners, and foreign sailors are doubly unacceptable. Alonso sees the passengers pull their sweat-soaked clothing away from their torsos, their faces red and dripping. The wife of one of the merchants wears a green gown stained dark down the back. Her husband notices Alonso and says something to his colleague. A brief glance in Alonso's direction, then both turn their backs and usher their wives farther forward.

Below decks, the stifling heat must be worse. Alonso crosses the aft deck and approaches the captain. "*Señor* Captain, we should bring the Africans up."

Alonso always refers to the twenty men and seven women as 'Africans'. Don Alvaro and the crew of *La Virgen* usually call them 'the blacks', or 'the slaves', or 'the Moors'. It is important to Alonso to make a distinction, to draw a line between him and the people below his feet: they are of Africa; he is of the House of Illescas. He does not know what the sailors call him. He does not mix with them, nor do they approach him.

The captain is watching the horizon again. "Not today." Without taking his eyes from the horizon, Mendoza gestures towards the boats, full of his men, and says, "Who will watch them?"

"*Señor* Captain," he says again, "it is very hot."

"Let the blacks sweat. The storm will break the heat."

Alonso looks west. He sees no sign of a change in the weather. The high wisps of clouds are as faint as forgotten scars against the bland blue. He wants to argue with the captain, feels sure that Don Alvaro would not accept such a rebuff. But Don Alvaro is a hundred leagues to the north, and Alonso has already seen Mendoza order a one-eyed Greek sailor branded on the cheek for stealing from the food stores, blue smoke wreathing the end of the iron as the man screamed and fought a useless fight to escape the hands that held his head hard against the mainmast. Besides, it is not just the Africans Alonso is concerned for.

The merchants and their wives move farther towards the bow as Alonso descends the short stairway to the mid-deck. The main hatch is open, at least, though no air will be circulating in the sweltering space below. He stands at the top of the ladder, looking down into the darkness. The hold is a square of almost liquid blackness against the glare of light that freezes the deck. The smell of pigs' droppings rises, sharp and almost sweet. Usually he cleans the animals' pen while the Africans are on deck. He does not mind the noisome chore; indeed, the pigs are Alonso's pride. But he does not like to do it under the eyes of the Africans.

The hold is deep, and Alonso must descend to the lowest of three decks. For all it rules the deck above, the sunlight does not seem able to penetrate far. Alonso reaches the bottom of the ladder and stands in a twilight. He looks up, and now the hatch is so charged with brightness, he finds it almost strange to think he has just come from there. The glare brings water to the corners of his eyes. He has to suppress a sneeze.

The pigs rustle in their soiled straw, one of the flap-eared sows making throat sounds that combine a snuffle and a string of grunts. Their triangular pen, just forward from the ladder, is made of rough boards nailed to the ship's ribs and to a post that supports the deck above. There is no gate, because the animals will not leave their sanctuary until *La Virgen* reaches La Portete. He strips off his much-patched doublet, rolls up the sleeves of his worn cotton shirt, and climbs over the top board. He reaches for the wooden pitchfork, nudging the animals with the toe of one brass-buckled shoe.

Usually they react to his arrival, rubbing against his shins, snuffling at his scent, talking to him in their throaty pig voices; but today the terrible heat, which fills the hold as if it could burst the ship's sides, has rendered them torpid. Still, as he always does before mucking out the piss-soaked straw and lumps of pale excrement, Alonso stoops to scratch the young boar behind his ears, the beast's bristles stiff under his fingers. The pig grumble-grunts in pleasure, and one of the sows lifts her nose and makes a sound that could almost be a word. From behind him, deeper in the aft part of the hold, he hears a man's angry voice, a woman's softer tones, the words indistinct. Alonso does not turn to look that way.

He has known the pigs since they were month-old shoats on Hispaniola. "These will be the first swine to reach the newly conquered territories," Don Alvaro told him, "where they will breed multitudes. You are old enough now to have some responsibility, so these will be yours to care for on the journey. Feed them and keep them clean."

"I will, *patrón*."

Don Alvaro quirked his mouth, as he did when he was about to say something that he didn't mean to be taken seriously. "Years from now, when the new lands are thick with swine, you can say that you were the father of their nation."

Alonso smiled. From another man, it would have been mockery. But Don Alvaro was always kind to him, almost like an older brother. "Yes, *patrón*."

Now he scrapes the soiled straw to the edge of the pen, nudging the somnolent animals to move them, until the floor is clear. Then, with the side of a foot shod in the red leather shoes that were Don Alvaro's until they grew too scuffed and faded, he pushes the bedding under the lowest slat of the pen. He climbs out, goes towards the forward end of the hold, and returns with an armload of fresh straw, its dust tickling his nose, its sharp ends prickling the skin under his jaw. He throws the straw over the pen's top board, then makes two more trips until he is satisfied the animals are well provided for.

And, through all of this, eyes watch him from the shadows. Now Alonso must turn and make his way into the darker part of the hold, to the strong grid of thick, interlocking beams of timber. The beams extend from the floorboards to the joists that support the deck above, braced by iron brackets. Behind the barrier, the Africans sit or lie on the bare wood, as prostrated by heat as the pigs. Most are in their prime years, the men dressed in cast-off shirts and breeches, the women in simple cotton shifts, all of them barefoot.

Some of them watch him approach. Others sit with their heads bowed and their eyes on the wood between their feet. The older woman, Miriam, who sometimes smiles at Alonso, lies on her side, her knees drawn up and her brown hand beneath her cheek, her eyes closed. Anton, the one Don Alvaro warned Alonso about, sits where he always sits, beside the chequered bars, the back of his large head leaned against the ship's side, his eyes never leaving Alonso. As the young man nears the cage, Anton rises to his feet, a sudden burst of motion, surprisingly fast and smooth for such a big man. The fetters on his wrists and ankles clink unmusically.

"Stop," Anton says. "You are unclean."

Alonso's step falters, but he comes forward again, showing the light-coloured palms of his hands. "No," he says, "my hands did not touch the filth, only the fork and the buckets."

"The beasts are unclean, and you are unclean from touching them." Then he says some words that Alonso does not understand, though the sound of them stirs a faint almost-memory. Somewhere, in the far-back reaches of his mind, he must have heard words with that kind of rhythm. But he does not try to put flesh on the ghost; whatever it was, it is now all past and gone, nothing to do with Alonso Illescas, trusted by one of the great men of Seville, named for him at his confirmation. He focuses on the matter before him.

"The captain will not let you on deck today," he says. "His men are in boats towing the ship. There is no one to watch you."

Miriam has sat up. "Our water is almost gone," she says, "and the slop bucket is full."

Alonso can smell the reek from the bucket where the Africans relieve themselves, even though it has a tight-fitting wooden top. Usually, one of the sailors brings it up on the same rope that hauls up the pigs' soiled straw.

"I will tend to it," he says.

"First wash your hands," says Anton. "You are unclean."

Alonso's impulse is to stand on his dignity, but Miriam's hands make a small motion, a gesture that combines with the expression on her face to ask him not to make an issue of the big man's words. Anton does not see the exchange. His head is reared back, his eyes fixed on Alonso.

The young man sees a solution. "Very well," he tells Miriam. "I will wash after I have dealt with the slops bucket." He looks at Anton. "You do not mind if my unclean hands touch that, do you?"

The glare that comes back at him is so intense it strikes him almost as a physical blow. Alonso can see a rim of white all around Anton's brown irises, and the man's wide nostrils flare.

Discomfited, Alonso must look away. *He hates me,* he thinks, surprised at the depth of the ill will he sees in the man's aspect. He does not look at Anton again, nor at Miriam, but busies himself with the logistics of getting the slops bucket out of the Africans' enclosure without opening the gate. Don Alvaro made it clear, before the ship left Panama, that Alonso is never to open the heavy padlock that connects the chain that holds the door closed, unless armed men are in position, matches smouldering.

"Some of these slaves killed men and women on Hispaniola, cut their throats and opened their bellies," the *patrón* said. But, though some of the ringleaders of the slave revolt were made examples of, burned with hot irons and whipped to tatters with lead-weighted cats, the rank and file were too many, and too valuable, to waste; a healthy slave is worth four hundred pesos in Lima. They would be shipped to the newly conquered lands, where it would do them no good to run away; the savages would catch them and kill them as if they were true Spaniards. In Peru, the former rebels who had fired the sugarcane fields of Hispaniola would go into the mines and work to repay the cost of transporting and feeding them. They would go into the cracks in the ground where the *Indios* had dug for silver and gold, and they would never come out.

"Bring the bucket over to the hatch," Alonso tells Miriam, not looking at Anton.

Miriam and a thin woman with a corded neck—Alonso thinks her name is Juana—push the full bucket across the deck to where a portion of the latticework of beams is hinged so that it can swing out and upwards. Miriam keeps one hand on the top of the bucket, so that it cannot come loose and splash filth on them. Alonso kneels and fetches from inside his shirt a set of keys that hang from a cord around his neck. He takes the smaller of two similar keys and unlocks the padlock that secures the hatch's latch to a stout iron ring countersunk into the decking. He lifts the wood out of the way, and the two women shove the bucket though the gap.

A moment later the slops bucket is clear of the gap, and Alonso closes and relocks the hatch. For the next few minutes, he occupies himself with his chores, getting a rope, fastening it to the tub that contains the pigs' straw, climbing the ladder, and hauling the tub onto the deck. The container is heavy but he enjoys the physical effort, enjoys being usefully employed, having nothing to think about but pulling hand over hand, leaning out to make sure the rim of the tub does not strike the edge of the hatch and cause the contents to tip. He empties the straw over the side, noting that he does not have to check for wind to know which side of the ship to go to—the air is as still as death, except for the faintest breath from forward as *La Virgen* creeps over the featureless sea to the coordinated splash of oars.

Alonso returns the tub to its place, squares away the fork, then leans over the top of the pen, his belly pressing with painful pleasure on the top board, and gives the pigs a last round of ear-scratching affection. He turns towards the Africans' enclosure, and again Anton's glare strikes him as an almost physical blow. Alonso drops his eyes to the slop bucket and does not look up again until he has its weight in his grip and he is walking bent-legged to set it under the hatch. Then comes the business of tying the rope and climbing the ladder, and the even more careful hand-over-handing that brings the bucket onto the mid-deck.

Again he concentrates on correctly carrying out the task. The bucket must go, lidless, over the side to sink into the green and lose its contents, then be hauled back up, emptied of seawater and, if necessary, plunged back in again until it is clean. Alonso has seen it done by a sailor and imitates the procedure perfectly.

As he hauls the bucket out of the sea for the third time, and his examination finds it clean, he feels a stronger stir of air across his cheek, cooling the sweat on his neck. He turns towards the galleon's bow and the air comes fresher, a breeze that is even now growing strong enough to be called a wind. The men in the boats are rowing back towards the ship. Others on the foredeck are hauling in the dripping cables, walking them into coils, while the Basque mate shouts orders from the mid-deck, urging more speed as he disparages the men's mothers for their choices of mating partners.

One of the boats clumps alongside, bringing a fresh spate of profanity from the mate as Alonso takes the sea-scoured slops bucket below. He leaves it beside the grid of timbers, then goes to the scuttle—a barrel of fresh water lashed to a strong post forward in the hold—ladles water into a shallow bowl, and makes an ostentatious show of laving his hands and forearms.

From above his head comes the thud of bare heels on wood, more shouts from Esquivel, the clatter of the boats being brought aboard and stowed. Captain Mendoza's voice says something Alonso cannot make out, though the tone bespeaks urgency. From the scuttle, the young man fills a tarred leather bucket—not the one he used to water the pigs—and carries it to the enclosure. The Africans have their own wooden cup to drink from, taking turns.

Under the continued assault of Anton's eyes, Alonso unlocks the hatch and passes the water bucket through to Miriam. The others are stirring now, hands reaching for the cup. Alonso pushes the slops bucket through the opening then relocks it.

"What about food?" says Miriam. Her voice is soft, the question empty of any note of demand. A lyrical accent sits behind the Spanish words, like a face behind a half-slipped mask.

"I will see about it," Alonso says. The Africans are fed corn bread in the mornings and gruel in the evenings. But the supplies that were supposed to last them to Lima are running low. The bad winds and currents have kept them north of the Rio Esmeraldas, a long way from their destination. Alonso has heard the captain talking about putting in to one of the small bays along the shore to get food and water from the barbarians.

A sudden downdraft of cool air comes through the hatch, cutting through the womblike swelter of the hold. At the same time, the deck tilts. Alonso automatically compensates for the motion, as he has done ever since Don Alvaro brought him aboard an Illescas ship tied near the family's river house in Seville and told him on the first day out on the Atlantic that he had a seaman's legs.

Anton also shifts his balance. The wooden cup has come around to him, but he pauses with the water halfway to his lips, and his eyes leave Alonso and go to the square of light high overhead. It is not so bright now. The glare is muted, then it comes back in full brightness—but only for a moment before it dims again. From above come more shouts and thudding footsteps, and now there are new sounds: the creaking of ropes and stays, the snap of canvas.

Anton is listening, his eyes moving back and forth as if to follow the motions of crewmen moving about on the deck above, as if he can see through the multiple barriers of wood. The African's gaze returns to Alonso, not full of anger and outrage now, but still hard. When he speaks, his accent is stronger than Miriam's, and he makes no attempt to disguise that he is issuing Alonso an order, and that the big man has given orders before.

"Boy, when the storm comes, you will be down here. With us."

Alonso finds he is nodding his head, responding to the ring of command, but he recollects himself. "Don Alvaro has made me responsible for you," he says. "I will do as he would wish. And I am not a boy."

Anton's expression dismisses the rationale. "You just be here," he says.

Alonso makes no response. His unthinking deference to Anton makes him vaguely guilty, as if he has betrayed Don Alvaro and the House of Illescas. He turns and leaves the Africans, climbs the ladder to the deck. His midday chores finished, it is time for him to eat—hot beans and cornbread, the sour wine that the sailors drink, maybe some cheese today if he can find a piece that hasn't gone mouldy.

But when he puts his head out of the hatch he sees no queue of hungry men, bowls and mugs in hand. The passengers have fled to their cabins beneath the aftcastle. The decks and rigging are flurries of motion, hands and bare toes gripping tarred ropes as sailors swarm above, setting free the topmost sails, half-reefed. Other men are lashing down the two boats, now returned to their places on the mid-deck. Another gang comes, carrying the double-canvas-sheeted cover for the main hatch, and they do not stop to give Alonso time to go back down the ladder. He ducks his head as they position the cloth over the hole, and hears their hands moving at speed to fasten the loops of rope that line its edges to cleats set in the deck's planking. Almost no light comes through the canvas. Alonso hears a shout of anger from below, followed by startled squeals from the pigs. He descends, deck after deck.

The descent is dangerous. The ship has begun to buck like an outraged mule. It plunges and falls, and every few moments the hull sustains a blow as if from a giant's hammer. He arrives on the lower deck, where the pigs scent him and make noises he takes for friendship. He gropes his way to where he knows flint and steel and tinder wait behind a board nailed to the inner hull. There is a stub of a tallow candle and eventually he has it lit. He sees the pigs rustling in their pen and makes noises to soothe them. The Africans are only eyes against the darkness and the sound of someone retching from seasickness.

He hears Anton's voice, harsh, anger conquering fear. "What is happening?"

"A sudden storm. The wind is pushing us hard."

"Which way?"

Alonso has to think. "Back the way we came. The wind is always against us."

Anton makes a noise deep in his throat, a thinking sound. "Is there enough food?" he asks. "What about water?"

"I don't know. The captain does not like to talk to me."

"Make him!"

"How?"

"This ship belongs to the Illescas. He is a hireling. You are the family's man aboard." Anton pauses, then says, "Man," again, as if to himself, as if it is a near absurdity.

Alonso has turned away to put the candle stub into a bracket so he can find where he stored his rolled-up bedding. "What does it matter to you?" he says, over his shoulder.

"It matters," Anton says. "Find out and tell me."

Alonso has had enough. He blows out the candle, and stretches out on his unrolled pallet.

Anton's voice comes from the darkness. "Do as I tell you, boy. Speak to him."

"Maybe I will speak to the captain about having you whipped."

"Be careful, boy. There was a house slave on Hispaniola— "

Miriam speaks. "Enough," she says. "Alonso will speak to the captain because he has sworn to look after us."

Anton grunts, but Alonso speaks over him. "That is true. Now let us just try to get through the storm. Sufficient unto the day— "

Now it is Anton's turn to drown him out. "There was a priest who would come to the plantation and fill our ears with false scripture. Do you know what I said to him?" When Alonso does not reply, the harsh voice from the darkness says, *"Allahu akbar!"*

"I am going to try to sleep," Alonso says. He lays a folded blanket over his head but he can still hear the contempt in Anton's laugh.

Alonso does sleep after a while, even dreams, but the tossing of *La Virgen* wakes him. The dream runs away like a trickle of water into dry earth, leaving only a darkness: the shape of something he cannot grasp. He strains for it, but there is only the sense of coming out of light and into gloom, and a voice speaking softly. He can almost recapture the words, for they were words, though now they are only sounds in his mind. They drew him towards comforting warmth, a room, a roof, a woman's hand reaching towards him.

The pigs stir and snuffle nearby, and their sounds mingle with the fading syllables in his dreamer's ear. Perhaps that is all it was, the animals making their noises, his mind weaving them into a fantasy.

The deck is hard and still in motion under him. Sleep seems to have retreated to a distance, a long swim back. He refolds the blanket into a pillow for his head and lies looking up into the blackness above him. Anton's voice comes out of memory: *This ship belongs to the Illescas ... You are the family's man aboard.*

He has been given the Illescas name, christened Alonso after the head of the family. But he is not really one of them. If he were, the captain and the crew would bow their heads when he came on deck, would address him as *vuestra merced*—your grace—and answer his questions with respect in their voices.

And yet he is not one of the crew, either, though he sails with them and has responsibilities here between the decks. He does not speak as they do; he frames his words in a good Castilian accent while they use the slippery consonants of the docks and the odd patois of the sea: a language of their own, fashioned from half a dozen dialects of seagoing Spaniards and mixed with the purely foreign vocabulary of Basques and Greeks and Italians. He suspects that, in his hearing, the sailors make themselves deliberately unintelligible, putting up a barrier of argot to keep him outside their world, ever the stranger at their gate.

Yet neither is he one of the Africans. They are even more strange than the sailors, though his child's eyes must have seen the same sights as they have. Alonso has been told that he was born in Cabo Verde, the Portuguese slave-trading entrepot off the west coast of Africa. Don Alvaro has told him of how he was bought as a little boy, how his name then was Enrique, and how he did not speak all the time he was on the ship that brought him to Seville, nor for months after—until one day it was as if a door had opened in his mind, and he began talking in simple Spanish.

From then on, he ceased to be a kind of family pet. Don Alonso had come and looked at him, towering over him in the doorway of the kitchen where Enrique slept by the fire. "We will make him a good Christian," the man had said, lamplight from the hallway making a halo about his head.

There had been tutors, even a fencing master. Little Alonso had read books, mastered a merchant's mathematics, learned weights and measures and all the ways the goods in which the Illescas dealt ought to look, feel, smell, and taste. For two years, he had accompanied Don Alvaro everywhere, carrying a tablet of smooth wood and a stick of hard, dry charcoal to make notes of anything the young master told him to record.

And yet, and yet ... he did not eat with the family but with the servants in the kitchen. He did not speak before he was spoken to. He walked a step behind and kept his mind on the business of the Illescas.

He is a functionary, well treated but entitled to the name he bears only on sufferance. He was raised to his anomalous position by grace and affection, but he knows he will keep it by being useful. He does not mind the requirement; he enjoys being useful. It is his place.

But it is a place unique to him. He is neither a Spanish merchant nor a sailor nor an African. Nor is he Enrique nor whoever he was before he stopped speaking whatever language he spoke with his mother, whom he does not remember save as a fleeting memory of a dream: a voice, a hand, a curve of a cheek in the dimness beyond the low doorway, always fading as he seeks to recapture it.

THREE

ALONSO ILLESCAS

The storm has blown through the night, but the dawn brings calm. When sailors peel back the cover from the hatch, Alonso comes on deck to see the sea scarcely ruffled, the wind once again fluttering from the south. They are far out to sea now, no sign of land in any direction. The ship tacks and tacks again, trying to inch its way south, but the storm has pushed them back a week's sailing, perhaps more.

This Alonso learns when he ascends to the deck atop the aftcastle and overhears Mendoza talking with the mate. He clears his throat as he approaches them. "*Señor* Captain," he says, "have we enough food and water to reach Lima?"

The captain gives him a sideways glance and makes a brushing motion with the fingers of one hand. But Alonso has been thinking about the question Anton asked and has to admit that there is a concern. The Africans must reach Lima in good condition. It has also occurred to him that if rations run short, the sailors will surely want to eat his pigs. He cannot allow that.

So he speaks again to Mendoza. "*Señor* Captain, I am responsible for the cargo. Don Alvaro has told you this."

Mendoza passes a broad hand over his face, his eyes swollen with fatigue. Alonso realizes that while he slept fitfully on the heaving deck beside the pigpen, the captain has probably not closed his eyes in twenty-four hours. Still, the young man's responsibilities are plain.

He stands before Mendoza, politely attentive, even deferential, but he stands there.

"If Don Alvaro had not waited three weeks before giving us our sailing orders," Mendoza says, "we would be only a few days from Lima now."

"He was ill. He hoped to recover."

Mendoza waves away the argument. "We are still north of Guayaquil," he says. "We have lost time and distance."

Alonso knows that Guayaquil is one of the new port cities struggling to establish themselves amid hostile savages. There is a river with a barbarous name that leads to the highlands then onward and upward, a long uphill trek to Quito. There are never enough mules, so the *encomendero* often assigns *Indios* to carry the loads. Many of them die in the thin air they climb into.

But Alonso's concern is for his duties. "We are going to Lima," he says.

"Right now, we could not make Guayaquil or Portete," the captain tells him. "We have not the water. Nor the food, for that matter." He laughs without humour. "But we will not starve before we die of thirst."

Alonso feels a shiver that has nothing to do with the coolness of the early morning. "What will you do?"

The captain blinks and sighs and waves to where the land lies invisible below the eastern horizon. "There are places where rivers come down to the sea. There are *Indios* who will sell us cornmeal and fruits."

Alonso's eyes move from the captain to the east and back again to Mendoza. The shiver has somehow gone deep into his innards. "I am told the barbarians on the coast are wild savages—cannibals, even."

Mendoza makes a dismissive gesture. "There is a wide and shallow bay called San Mateo with creeks running into the sea. The *Indios* there are called the Niguas. They are milder than those farther south, and many have died from the pox. Plus we have weapons, armour. There will be no trouble."

"How long before we can be there?"

The captain looks at the sky, the horizon. "Two days if God gives us the wind. More if we have to row."

In the end, they have to row the last day. The inconstant wind finally dies just as the coast comes in sight. Mendoza brings out his prized Portuguese astrolabe to shoot the sun at noon and makes calculations with a stick of charcoal on a board. "San Mateo," he says, pointing eastward with his chin after checking and rechecking his figures, and sends Esquivel forward to tell the men in the boats that fresh water and good food are just over the horizon, which the sailors down on the face of the sea cannot yet spy. A half-hearted cheer comes up from the rowers, and they bend their backs to draw the oars again and again and yet again.

The Bay of San Mateo is wide, a shallow bite out of the forested shoreline rimed with a strip of white sand. The remains of a wooden jetty extend into the water, not far from a sizable creek, but Mendoza does not take the ship in close. He knows that between the shore and the open sea lies a reef that would tear out *La Virgen*'s fragile bottom. He orders the anchor dropped and calls in the towing boats.

The men who come up on deck are burned dark by the sun and near exhaustion after rowing since dawn, but after allowing them a brief rest in the shade and as much of the ship's foul water as they care to drink, the captain orders Esquivel to break out the ship's cutlasses and matchlocks. There are also a few pieces of chest-and-back armour and a battered morion with a dented crest that Esquivel puts on his head.

Empty water casks are brought up on deck, ready to be lowered into one of the boats, but first Mendoza will send eight armed men ashore with just one cask.

The passengers have come on deck and crowd the rail along with the crew. The merchants want to go with the scouting party.

"At your own risk," says Mendoza, eyeing their frowning wives as if to assess their potential for launching lawsuits.

"We have our swords," says one of the two, his hand going to the brass hilt of the good-but-not-excellent Toledo blade hanging from his belt.

Mendoza shrugs and cocks his head to where Esquivel and the armed sailors are clambering down rope ladders into one of the boats. The Sevillians follow.

Alonso watches the rise and fall of the oars as the boat pulls towards shore. Halfway there, Esquivel signals a halt, peering over the bow into the water. He orders the men to row parallel to the reef for several yards before he calls for the boat to turn again towards the beach.

Alonso hears Mendoza, watching from the aftcastle, swear softly under his breath. While all else aboard are seeing the scouts ashore, Mendoza turns and scans the sea to westward, shading his eyes against the descending sun. After a long moment, the captain shrugs and turns back to watch the shore party land on the beach.

The men under Esquivel run the boat's bow up onto the sand and leap out to haul it farther out of the sea's grip. Alonso sees the mate issuing orders, leaving two men with matchlocks and lit matches to guard the boat, and sending two of those armed with cutlasses to wrestle the cask out of the boat and roll it to the nearby creek. The rest he leads along the waterway, across the bright sand, and into the green darkness under the trees.

The minutes stretch, with nothing for Alonso and those on the ship to see but the pair of sailors guarding the boat and their two shipmates using buckets to fill the cask. Occasionally, these two look towards where the creek disappears into the forest, but whatever they see or hear causes them no concern.

More time passes. *La Virgen*'s shadow lengthens towards the land. Finally, Esquivel and the armed party come back onto the beach. Esquivel raises one hand then shakes his helmeted head from side to side, a slow exaggerated gesture. Mendoza signals that they should come back to the ship. That takes a while, because the heavy water cask must be lifted into the boat and stowed. By the time it is being hoisted onto the galleon's deck in a cradle of ropes connected to a block-and-pulleyed line anchored on a middle-mast spar, the sun has touched the horizon, and, with the astonishing speed characteristic of these latitudes, night takes charge of the world.

The merchants and the sailors returning from shore have brought more than water. They share out plantains, tree fruits, pineapples. There is a deserted Nigua village not far inland, Esquivel says, its neglected gardens overgrown but some of its untended trees still bearing.

"Good," Mendoza says. "Tomorrow, we will take what is there. The next day we will see if we can find where the barbarians have hidden themselves. They will have bread and meal and dried foods. We can also shoot some fresh meat."

Alonso brings some of the fruit down to the Africans and has one of the sailors lower a bucket of fresh water. He strikes flint against steel to ignite a little flame in his tinderbox and uses it to light the stub of candle. When he delivers the scant share of the bounty from the scouting expedition, Miriam gives him a smile, but Anton takes the slice of pineapple with an upward jerk of his head. Now Alonso crosses the deck to see to the pigs and slips the young boar a hoarded piece of fruit; he hears a harsh sound from behind him.

This afternoon he cleaned and fed the animals and removed the slaves' slops bucket. There is nothing more to do now but lie down and sleep. But when he pinches out the candle flame, Anton's voice comes from the darkness, wanting to know what will happen tomorrow.

"You will go ashore," Alonso says. "Some of you, at least. You will pick fruit and fill water barrels."

"What is the land like? Is there forest? Is it thick with trees or thin like on Hispaniola?"

"You will be watched by men with firearms. You cannot escape. Besides, the barbarians will catch you and eat you."

Anton snorts. "Will you be in charge?" he says.

"You are my responsibility."

The sound that comes from the darkness is not quite a word, but it manages to express disrespect, amusement, and anticipation. It is a lot of weight for one syllable to carry, Alonso thinks. He resolves to surprise Anton by not including him in tomorrow's trip ashore.

But in the morning, it is Alonso who is surprised. Mendoza overrules his decision to keep Anton in the ship. "He is strong," the captain says, "and there will be much work to refill our water. I will assign one man with a matchlock to watch him closely and to shoot him if he puts a foot wrong."

"I do not want him shot," Alonso says. "I want him delivered safe and healthy in Lima. I have sworn to Don Alvaro."

"And I have contracted to bring *La Virgen* to port with her cargo intact and her passengers healthy. It is not you Don Alvaro will take to court if we do not make a good voyage. You may look after the cargo and your precious pigs. I will decide those matters that concern the well-being of the ship."

The landing is a complicated operation. While the Africans are brought up onto the deck, blinking in the sunlight, Esquivel and four armed sailors go ashore. Then the slaves are ferried, a few at a time, to the landing place. Two more matchlock men stand in the stern of each boat, their weapons ready. When all the shore party have landed, the rowers go back and forth with casks for the watering, and heaps of baskets and buckets for the food gathering.

Esquivel designates the work parties and gives their assignments: six of the black men to fill the water casks and bring them to the waterline, where they will be loaded into the boats and rowed out to the ship; the rest of the slaves to go into the overgrown gardens and gather food, under guard and directed by Alonso; the sailors to go through the abandoned orchards along with the two merchants and the pair of artisans who have also had enough of being shipbound—that will put them between the Africans and the forest. Esquivel himself and one other man will go deeper into the trees and look for meat—the Basque has an old crossbow, his grandfather's, and swears he can hit anything he can see at fifty paces.

Anton is one of the six left on shore; Mendoza has insisted on that. He is still in manacles, although before they left the ship, Esquivel ordered his ankle fetters struck off by one of the slaves, who is a blacksmith. Anton watches Alonso organize his other charges into two gangs, men and women mixed together, each to be watched by two sailors armed with matchlocks.

Alonso selects the members for each gang with care. Some of the Africans have bonds to each other—there are three couples, and two of the women are very close to each other—and he makes sure to place those who have attachments in different gangs. They are more likely to try to run if they can do so together.

He feels Anton's gaze on him as he makes his decisions and looks to see the other man regarding him with sardonic amusement. When their eyes meet, Anton puckers his lips in a mocking kiss. Alonso fights his first impulse—to look away—and stares at Anton. *I am doing my duty,* he tells himself, *as I have sworn.* Finally, the slave gives him another derisive smile and turns to lay hands on one of the empty casks that must be rolled to the creek. Anton pushes the curved wood and sets it moving, singing what sounds to Alonso like a traditional Spanish dock worker's song but in a language the young man does not know.

Esquivel and the sailors have gone ahead into the forest. Alonso follows, leading his Africans along a trail that runs beside the creek. The track has become overgrown in the years since the Niguas abandoned their town and moved deeper into the forest. The sailors ahead of him cut back the vines and suckers that erupt from the trees, and pull up the saplings that have taken root in the once-clear ground.

The derelict town stands in a clearing that is now being filled in by the power of vegetative persistence. It was stockaded, but the walls of upright logs now lean at lazy angles, and the gates of tightly woven wicker hang open. They must go through the town's hundreds of houses to reach the gardens and orchards beyond, winding their way among serpentine streets that are little wider than Alonso could span with outspread arms. Yet he does not feel hemmed in, because the houses are built on stilts, the floors higher than he is tall, their walls made of woven withies, the roofs of bundled grasses tightly packed. Looking through the stilts, he can see almost from one side of the town to the other.

Alonso would like to explore, to climb one of the ladders that lead to the open doors and see how the godless barbarians lived. But his responsibilities outweigh his curiosity, and so he turns and walks backwards a few steps, urging his Africans to hurry along. They go no faster; if they did, they would overtake him. He turns and leads the way again, but now he feels more foolish than duty-bound.

There is an open gate on the far side of the town, and beyond it lie garden plots returning rapidly to forest. The woodland beyond, thick with trees of all different colours and textures and conformations, has been sending out creepers and seeds to recolonize the soil the Niguas had usurped with fire and stone axes and wooden hoes. Among the new-sprung vegetation, the domesticated plants have struggled to keep their once-protected places.

"Spread out," Alonso says. "Collect anything that looks as if it can be eaten." He has no idea what the farmers who once lived here might have eaten. He has seen pineapples and avocados and knows that maize is everywhere in the New World, though the stands here do not appear to have reseeded themselves; the few dried stalks remaining lean in their rows like starved soldiers, and many of their fellows have been climbed and pulled down by dark-leafed vines.

The Africans are poking about among the remains and finding things to fill their baskets. Alonso looks doubtfully at some tubers being plucked from the soil below the rampant vegetation. Perhaps they are the *papas* he has heard about: the barbarians in the highlands were said to grow many different varieties; they may have had ones that flourished here on the coast. He also sees manioc, a tuber that is ground into flour. It is a slave food on Hispaniola.

The sun is well up now, and the damp heat smothers the gardens. Sweat breaks out on Alonso's brow, and he can feel rivulets running down his back and chest and sides under his cotton shirt. There is no shade here, though there is some in the orchards beyond, where the sailors are stripping the trees bare of fruit and amusing themselves by throwing unripe specimens at each other.

And there must be deep shade in the forest, he thinks, but the darkness under the closely packed trees is not inviting. It is not the comforting darkness of a familiar room at night, in a familiar house in a familiar city. It would not do to close one's eyes in that forest, even in the day; something, anything, might lurk among the shadows, lying unseen though only at arm's length, crouched with twitching limbs behind a bemossed trunk or a screen of leaves until the moment it hurls itself at you, all claws and teeth and yellow, feral eyes.

He looks away from the forest, up into the sky. Against the overcast, he sees a bird hovering high up, its wings spread and motionless. He remembers a bird he saw, days ago, when they were out at sea and the Africans were walking in their circle. It came down low, and he had the strange sense it was not just looking at him but studying him in particular, until it flew away. It is difficult to keep today's bird in focus, because it is as pale as the grey behind it, and it slips in and out of view as if it were a recurrent mirage.

Tilting his head so far back causes the muscles in the back of Alonso's neck to spasm. He looks instead to where those for whom he is responsible have kept on working, one hand going up to knead the tension from his nape. Despite the heat, he feels a sudden coolness on his face. For a moment he is prepared to chide himself for letting his fears get to him, but then he realizes that the chill originates from the outside: a breeze is blowing from the sea, drying the sweat on his brow, ruffling the loose fabric of his slashed sleeves.

He has felt this before, he knows, and as the meaning of the memory breaks over him he hears a distant whistle, shrill, blast after blast. And it, too, is coming from the sea.

Esquivel comes out of the forest, crossbow in hand, a quarrel still in its slot. He is shouting at the sailors, making angry shooing gestures with his free hand. The seamen drop their baskets and turn towards the town, and as they come through the gardens they are shouting in turn for the Africans to move ahead of them. The matchlock men who have been guarding the slaves now add their own shouts, gesturing with their heads and their weapons.

"Back! Back to the shore! Hurry, you sons of whores! Drop that! Leave it! Move!"

The sailors are with them now, and they have drawn their cutlasses, holding them two-handed to push with the flat of the blades against the arms and backs of the blacks.

"What is it?" Alonso asks the nearest sailor, but his only answer is a curse and a shove with the cold steel of a cutlass.

"Your mother's quim!" the man says and shoves again, hard enough to make Alonso stumble, then plants his hard-soled, bare foot in the young man's side.

Alonso scrambles to his feet and runs. They are all running now, Africans and sailors mixed, through the stilted town, out the shoreward gates, down the path, through the trees, along the stream. They burst out onto the beach in a mob, and for a moment it is all confusion until the Basque mate arrives and begins issuing orders.

"Separate them!" he shouts. "Sit them down, over there. You, you"—he addresses the two with matchlocks, then another pair with cutlasses—watch them!"

Alonso is pushed, along with the people he has just been in charge of, towards an open stretch of sand well clear of the tree line. He sees Anton and the water detail being directed by Esquivel to get the loaded casks out of the boats, under the watch of the remaining two matchlock men. Anton does as he is ordered, but his gaze keeps moving, from the men with guns, to the gabble of sailors on the beach, to the slaves sitting under guard, and to the guards themselves.

Then Anton looks out to sea and, when Alonso follows his gaze, he sees the cause of all the commotion: out to the south-west, the horizon has disappeared under a wall of grey while above it, clouds are roiling and piling. He looks back to Anton, now being marched at gunpoint with the other men from the water detail to join the men and women sitting around Alonso. His face is an icon of anticipation: the tightening of the jaw, the smile that betokens no humour, the hard glint as of polished metal behind the eyes.

Anton sits at the front of the group, legs crossed, arms loose on his thighs, the chain of his manacles dangling to the sand. He turns his head and looks at Alonso, and the humourless smile widens a little. Then he turns back towards the sea, where Esquivel and the sailors have piled into the boats and are rowing for *La Virgen* with frantic speed. The six left on shore, four with matchlocks and two with cutlasses, surround the slaves but keep a distance. They can't help looking away then back again, from slaves, to ship, to the blackening wall rushing towards them across the sea.

The bay is full of chop now, the blue water going green as accumulating clouds block the sun, the wind whittling the waves to white spikes. The hiss and suck of the surf rolling up the beach and sliding back into the sea grow louder, and Alonso feels flecks of spray hit his cheeks as the breeze strengthens and begins to gust.

He stands up, and one of the sailors points his weapon at him. "Don't be ridiculous!" Alonso says. "I am an officer of the ship, in charge of the cargo!" He gestures at the sitting Africans. "In charge of these!"

The sailor is nervous, looking to Alonso, then to the slaves, then to his shipmates. It occurs to Alonso that he should have learned the names of more of them.

The moment is broken when a sailor standing behind them all says, "*Jesu Maria!*" and points towards the sea. The horizon is a black bruise now, rushing towards them. The men in the boats have rowed to the galleon's bow, where sailors aboard are throwing down the towing cable. Alonso can see the captain on the aftcastle, shouting orders, though no sound carries to shore above the increasing bluster of the wind.

The boats turn towards the sea and the oars dig into the waves as the anchor clears the water. The ship begins to move a little seaward. But then Alonso hears a soft curse from one of the sailors. It is too late. The wind against *La Virgen*'s bows is stronger than the muscles of the rowers in the boats. Mendoza is gesturing again, and the anchor rattles back down into the water.

The boats turn back towards the ship, but now the waves are man-high and rising, tossing the small craft like bugs on a shaken blanket as they try to come about in a half-circle. One of them, with Esquivel at the tiller, completes the manoeuvre, but the other boat is met broadside by an outsized wave. The green-and-white cliff rises up and up, relentlessly tilting the boat, tipping the sailors in it to the downward side until the leeward gunwale slips under the water. In a heartbeat, the boat capsizes, flinging men and oars into the water. They flounder, grasping for anything that floats, even for each other, and then the next wave comes and drives most of them under.

Esquivel's boat has made it to the side of the galleon, where the sea is now heaving against *La Virgen*'s bulging curve. A rope comes down from the deck and a sailor in the stern of the boat catches it, but before he can make it secure to a cleat, a surge of water sucks the boat away from the ship and capriciously slams it back into the cedar strakes. The man clings to the rope, his feet braced against the boat's gunwale, while another sailor grabs for the free end. Another wave lifts the boat stern first—almost vertical—and the small craft slides down the green incline that is carrying it towards the shore. The man holding the rope now dangles against the side of the ship, the sea lifting him and dropping him. He struggles to climb, but the next wave surges to cover his head and hands. When the trough appears, the rope hangs empty.

The storm drives Esquivel's boat towards the beach, wind and waves combining to give it momentum. Alonso can see the mate in the stern, his hand on the tiller, mouth open in a shout. The sailors are trying to get their oars in the water, but there is not enough time. The boat encounters the reef while deep in a trough, and the vessel comes apart as if it were made of matchwood. The men go into the water, and the sea smashes them into the unyielding coral.

Alonso hears a shout, a scream, a cracking sound, and then there is only the wind and the surf, each rising to its own roar. Out on *La Virgen*, crew and passengers are struggling to get the spare anchor to the bow. Even Mendoza is lending a hand. But the deck is pitching on the rising waves; the heavy iron drops, and Alonso hears a scream that is torn away by the wind as the squall now races in from the sea—as if everything up until now has been a hop and a skip, but now comes the jump. The line of impenetrable rain sweeps across the bay and over the ship, and instantly all sight and sound of her are lost. There is only the howl of the wind, the lash of the rain, and the bone-numbing chill descending from the upper sky like an invisible angel of death.

And now Anton moves. He erupts from the sand, his arms raised high, his wrists as widespread as the chain will allow, and comes chest-to-chest with the cutlass-armed sailor in front of him. He drops the chain onto the back of the man's neck and slams the sailor's face into an upraised knee. The sailor falls forward and Anton crosses his wrists with a sharp jerk. Alonso can hear the crack of bone even above the sound of the storm. Then Anton is crouching, the cutlass in his hand, facing the man with the matchlock.

The smouldering length of hemp has sputtered out in the downpour, and the sailor is reversing the weapon to use as a club when Anton's cutlass opens his throat. Anton turns to find another guard to kill, but several of the other Africans, the women as well as the men, have thrown themselves at the sailors, bearing them down, wrestling their weapons from them. As Alonso watches, the big bearded one who had pushed him in the garden is borne down to his knees and onto his back by the weight of three men and a woman, the latter throwing herself onto the arm that ends in a fist now gripping a cutlass. A moment later, Anton arrives, finds a clear space in the melee, and drives his sword into the man's open mouth.

When he looks around for more sailors to kill, he finds none. The other three guards are down, one with his brains knocked out by his own matchlock. Two of the Africans are dead, a third lies on his back, his hands trying to keep his pale intestines from spilling out of the diagonal slash that opened his stomach. He is talking to his insides as if a reasonable tone will help in his efforts, but he is getting sand in the gaping wound. Anton goes to the man, looks down at him. Alonso sees no expression on his face as Anton puts the point of his weapon against the wounded man's throat and leans his weight on the pommel.

All of the killing has taken less than a minute, and the squall continues to lash at them. Anton is giving orders, shouting to be heard over the wind. "Gather up the weapons and get into the trees! Don't show yourselves!"

The surviving Africans—they are seventeen men and seven women—turn their backs to the wind and do as they are told. Alonso finds himself alone as they all move away from him, all except Anton, who stands not three paces away, regarding the younger man through the cold, lashing rain. Only now does an expression animate the larger man's features: the look of a player who has just thrown an unlikely winning combination of dice across a tavern table and wants his opponent to know that it was always going to work out this way. He comes forward, not hurrying, the cutlass loose in his grip.

Miriam is between them. "No," she says, putting a hand on Anton's chest.

She is an ineffectual barrier. He says nothing, keeps moving, and she must walk backwards.

"We will need him," she says.

Anton stops and looks down at her. "For what? To tell us what to do? To feed the swine?"

"He knows things we do not."

The wind is dropping, but the rain continues to drench them. Anton blows a puff of air from his lips, and tiny droplets fly. "What things?"

Miriam does not rise to the challenge. Her voice is calm, her tone reasoned. "He has been inside the houses of the ones who speak and are listened to. He knows who has power and who can influence power."

Anton shrugs and lifts the cutlass. "Here is all the power that matters."

"And when they come with soldiers? Because they *will* come, and with soldiers. How many will that kill before they kill you?" She raises her hand from his chest to his cheek. "On Hispaniola, we had swords and matchlocks. We even had horses and armour. But they had them, too. More than we had. And they had cannon that shot chains and nails. Remember?"

Anton wipes the rain from his face and makes a sound in the back of his throat.

Miriam says, "What we didn't have on Hispaniola was one like him." She hikes a thumb over her shoulder. "He knows how they think, what they value, what they don't. We need to know those things. And he will tell us."

Alonso sees Anton look past the woman at him, the cold eyes weighing him, considering him. "Is that true, boy?" Anton says. "Will you tell us what we need to know?"

Alonso thinks of Don Alvaro convalescing in Panama, of Don Alonso waiting for news in Seville. He thinks of all he owes them: his life, which likely would have ended in barracoon fever in Cabo Verde, his education, his rise to a position of responsibility, his very name. Then he thinks of how far away they are, of all the miles of sea and forest between him and them, of Anton leaning his weight on the pommel of the sword. A voice speaks in his head: *be useful*. "I will," he says.

"Because you want to?"

"Because I must."

The older man makes the throat sound again. But when he speaks, it is to Miriam. "You will be responsible for him. If he betrays us, if he runs away …" He shows her the point of the sword, inches from her eyes. The rain has washed away the blood, and the steel is slick and grey.

She says nothing, but looks past the sword into his eyes.

After a moment, he lowers the weapon and shifts his gaze to Alonso. "My advice: keep yourself useful."

The squall dies almost as swiftly as it arrived. The wind drops and the rain slackens, and Alonso can see once more beyond the diminishing surf. As the sky begins to clear, he sees *La Virgen* broadside against the reef, her decks steeply canted, one of her masts splintered and leaning against a now-tangled web of rigging.

Heavy rolling waves are coming into the bay, lifting the ship against the coral, grinding it against the unyielding hardness. When one surge brings her higher, Alonso sees a gaping breach in her side, cargo shifting around as the sea washes in and out of the hole, crates and barrels spilling out to be smashed as the mass of the galleon crashes again into the reef. He can see bodies in the water. One of the merchant's wives is recognizable by her billowing green gown. There is nobody on the decks.

Anton is watching, too. He says, "We'll need to make a raft." He studies the ship's plight for a while longer then makes the sound in the back of his throat and turns towards the tree line. "The logs from the stockade," he says.

"No," says Alonso, which earns him a sharp look. But he meets Anton's gaze and says, "Farther up the creek"—he turns his head to nod with his chin in that direction—"I saw the remains of a balsa. We can repair it."

Now Anton makes a different noise. "So you *can* be useful," he says.

Alonso shrugs and meets his eyes. "I must."

The log raft floats easily over the reef. Anton stands in the balsa's centre, legs spread to balance against the surge of the waves, though they have dropped now. Four of the men have come with him and Alonso. "You," the big man tells Alonso, "will look in the captain's quarters. I want maps. And in the passengers' cabin."

"Yes," says Alonso. "And I want to see if my pigs have survived."

Anton's eyes seem to grow too large for their sockets. "Forget the pigs! They are unclean! *Haram!*" he peers at the younger man. "Do you know what that means?" And when Alonso shakes his head, Anton says, "It means forbidden! You do not eat them, you do not touch them, you do not breathe the same air!" He shakes his head. "Did your people teach you nothing before the slavers took them?"

Alonso cannot answer. The nine years of his life before Don Alonso took him from Cabo Verde are as grey and amorphous as the sky above them. "I don't remember my . . . people."

They are nearing the ship. The hole in her side is immense. Her masts are gone, a tangle of spars and rigging draped over her aft quarter. Bodies float in the water, their clothes ripped or missing altogether, their flesh torn in strips by the sharp coral, their limbs broken by the battering waves and flopping with a strange looseness. Small fish are feeding on them, and Alonso sees a great dark shadow pass sinuously beneath the raft.

There is a constant mix of sounds to the scene: the slap and ripple of waves against the seaward side of the hull, the creak and groan of timbers, the crash and bash of floating cargo inside and outside the ship, the cries and quarrelsome squawks of the gulls that have landed on the floating dead and set to work with their beaks. Some kind of crow is up in the rigging, raucously complaining. Its voice sounds different from the crows of Seville, as if it speaks a different bird language. He looks but does not see any floating carcasses of his pigs. Then he peers into the breach in the hull and sees their pen, still whole and awash with seawater flowing in and out as the ship rocks on the waves. Their bodies are rolling within its confines. His eyes cloud with tears and he looks away.

It is too dangerous to attempt an entry through the breach in the hull. The men paddle to where the collapsed rigging trails in the water. They make fast the raft then swarm up the ropes and onto the canted deck. Anton seizes Alonso's shoulder and roughly pushes him aft towards the aftcastle. "Maps," he says, and his face dares the younger man to argue.

The door to the companionway that leads down into the aft cabins hangs open. Alonso makes his way along the rail then scrabbles on all fours up the sloping deck until he can seize the door and pull himself up and into the opening. Negotiating the companionway's slanted steps is tricky but he manages a careful descent.

Ahead of him is a closed door. Behind it is Mendoza's cabin, running the width of *La Virgen*'s stern. To left and right are passenger cabins; the doors to the ones on the elevated side of the ship are open, those on the downward side are closed. He pulls himself up into the first cabin. It is dark, but he finds a chest strapped to iron rings bolted to the deck. He undoes the buckles and opens the lid, sees clothes and a capacious leather wallet with a shoulder strap. When he digs beneath, he finds flat wooden cases with brass catches that he undoes to reveal a set of tools, sharp pieces of steel with wooden handles. Their late owner was the cordwainer. He carries the wallet to the light of the doorway and finds that it contains letters of recommendation and an introduction to a man named Obregon in Lima.

Alonso slings the wallet by its strap over his neck and shoulder. He slides down to the open doorway and out to the bottom of the companionway once more. He faces two closed doors, a narrow space between them. He stands on one door and pulls the other up, throwing it back. The space beyond is dark, and he hears water moving lazily as the downward side of the tilted ship grates against the reef.

The open door throws some light into the space, showing a sheen of water that fills the cabin almost to the lip of the doorway. A man's body is floating face down, the neck bent at a lethal angle—one of the merchants, by his clothing. Everything loose in the small space has slid into the seawater. Alonso perches in the doorway and feels with one hand down to elbow depth, but finds nothing. He will not go into the water. The thought of the floating corpse brushing against him makes the hairs on his neck rub against his shirt collar. He shivers.

The second merchant's cabin is as dark and flooded as the first, but empty. The ship is listing farther now, and Alonso has to close the second cabin door so he can stand on it and open the door to the captain's quarters. The tilted space beyond is lit by the stern windows, and the sea has entered here as well, but more than half of the cabin is dry.

A narrow bed is built into the wall on the high side of the space. Strapped into it is Captain Mendoza. The left leg of his hose has been cut away and a sharp fragment of bone protrudes from a shattered shin. At first, Alonso takes him for a dead man, but as he braces himself in the slanted doorway, Mendoza's eyes open.

He blinks at Alonso for a long moment as if he is not sure of seeing reality. Then he speaks, his voice a croak in a dry mouth. "Who's left?"

"Us," says Alonso.

The captain is not too weak to show anger. "Which us?"

"Us," Alonso repeats. "The Africans."

"No crew? Not even the men I left on shore?"

"Dead. All dead."

Mendoza closes his eyes, whispers, "Mother of God." Then he takes a wavering breath and gathers himself. "You have to help me. The ship is breaking up."

"I don't think they will let me," Alonso says. The captain is like a figure out of memory, a ghost from another life, faint and fading into the limbo of Alonso`s past.

"You must!"

"It is not for me to say anymore. My life is in their hands."

There is a sound behind Alonso, and Anton is looking past him through the doorway. He and the captain eye each other silently, and then the heel of Anton's hand strikes Alonso's shoulder. "Maps," he says.

"What about the captain?"

"What about him?"

Alonso enters the slanted space. There is a double-doored cupboard on the upward side of the cabin, between Mendoza's bed and the stern windows. He crabs his way towards it, scarcely able to keep from sliding down into the rising water. As he passes the captain's bed, the injured man pulls his gaze away from Anton and regards Alonso with wordless contempt.

"I am sorry," the young man says. "There is nothing I can do."

He reaches the cupboard and opens one of the doors. Rolled charts and a leather-bound book try to slide out, but Alonso is alert to the possibility and seizes them. But Mendoza's astrolabe falls to the tilted deck and slides into the water. For a moment it is a gleam of brass in the darkness, and then it is gone.

Alonso finds more pages and rolls in the other half of the cupboard; he stuffs them into the leather worker's wallet, tucks it under one arm, and struggles back to where Anton catches him by his bicep and pulls him through the doorway.

"Come," says the older man. "We need to hurry. The ship will not last much longer."

He propels Alonso towards the companionway, now tilted at more than a forty-five-degree angle so that they have to use the side of the steps as a ramp to get back onto the deck. They slide down to the rail, which is now almost under water. The balsa, laden with crates and chests, is moored to the fallen rigging, the men aboard looking apprehensively at the creaking mass of timber that *La Virgen* is rapidly turning into.

Anton takes the stuffed wallet from Alonso and directs him to scramble down to the raft. He follows then casts off. The men paddle the raft over the reef and towards the beach. Alonso looks back at the ship, sees it heel farther over. The waves pushing it onto the reef are gentle, but they are relentless. He hears the sound of wood breaking and thinks of Mendoza, strapped into his cot, seeing the water rise towards him.

Anton does not look back. After a silence he says, "Your *haram* beasts," and waits for Alonso to turn to him. "Dead, all dead."

Alonso looks back at the ship, grinding itself into flotsam on the unyielding coral. Then he turns and watches the approaching shore. Again the world has divided into two halves: behind, the sunlit wreckage of the ship with all its dead; ahead, the darkness under the trees and a new life—if he survives.

Four

Expectation

I was sitting in the shade cast by the spirit house, idly listening to the women gossiping, when young Pablillo ran past, shouting, "They've come! They've come again!"

The women in the central open space stopped their knitting and corn grinding and watched the teenage boy race past them to the ladder at the foot of Pidi's hut. Pablillo was so excited he forgot to make the gesture that everyone must make when addressing the chief. Instead, he shouted up into the dark opening at the top of the ladder, "They're back! I saw them!"

Pidi had been sitting just inside the doorway as he often did so he could listen to what the women said as they worked. It was a good way to keep in touch with what was happening among the people—what they liked and didn't like—before anything was formally brought to his attention. It gave him time to think about how he would respond, which was not a bad quality in a peace chief.

Now he put his head out and used his stern, calm voice to tell Pablillo to settle down and stop shouting. "I will come down," he said, "and then you will tell me."

His head disappeared, and there came a lengthy pause before Pidi re-emerged. He had taken the time to put on his regalia of feathers and shells and take up his spear, the obsidian-headed one—the stone had come from far to the north—with the three fringes of coloured feathers on the shaft. That told the men, who had by now gathered in the open space, that their headman considered the situation to be of serious concern and not an occasion for village gossip.

Pidi came down the ladder without turning his back to the people, which caused some of the women to murmur to each other. He spoke to no one in particular, saying, "We will go to the men's house." Then he looked at Pablillo, the boy dancing from foot to foot with repressed excitement. "You will come."

He led the men to the large, long structure with two doors, one facing east, the other west. He sent Palapcha, the oldest of those assembled, up the ladder to pull aside the woven mat that blocked the east entrance. Only after Palapcha had come down again and offered his courtesy did Pidi ascend the ladder. He disappeared into the men's house, followed in order of precedence by those men of the village who were present.

Pablillo stood at the base of the ladder, waiting to be invited up. He was not dancing anymore; instead, he shivered in his excitement and I thought he probably wanted to run to the stockade and relieve his bladder. But that would have offended the dignity of the headman and all the other men waiting above. The least consequence would have been a cuff on the ear; worse would have been if Pablillo's public name—he was almost old enough for the naming ceremony—preserved the urination incident forever.

Kucha, the youngest of the men in the house, now leaned out the doorway and beckoned Pablillo to climb up. I saw the boy's arms tremble as he went up on all fours. He paused to swallow in the doorway, made his courtesy at last, and went inside.

I waited a little then rose and went out into the open space. I could hear the hum of voices from the men's house. The women had withdrawn to their own gathering place, their children sitting on the ground outside, though a few of the older boys were standing at a respectful distance from where the men were talking.

I went to the foot of the ladder at the men's house and waited. It was a matter of protocol. We had worked it out before Pallu had died of the sickness that causes headache and fever. My predecessor had explained it to Pidi's father—old Manda—and the others. "The men's house," he had said, "is forbidden to women; but Expectation is not a woman."

The old chief had looked at me askance. "But she looks like a woman, and she is not a man."

"She is both man and woman," Pallu replied. "Thus she is neither."

The old chief had wrinkled his brow. He was a peace chief. His responsibility was to deal with matters of crops and shares and to adjudicate disputes among the people. This was not the kind of question he was accustomed to decide. He asked Pallu, "Do you tell us that no evil will befall us if she ... or he ... is admitted to the men's house? We want no trouble with the ancestors."

Pallu had shrugged. "No evil that would not have come on its own," he said. "As for the ancestors, I have spoken with them. They sent Expectation to us. They did not say why, but they did it for a purpose. In time we will know what that purpose will be, and we will be glad of it."

And so the issue was settled, and I attended sessions in the men's house with Pallu. After he left to join the ancestors, I went on my own. But to mark the fact that I had never been initiated into the men's culture—how could I be if I was not a man?—I always paused at the foot of the ladder and waited until my presence was noted. Then I climbed and entered quietly, taking a seat beside Pidi.

The chief had told the men what Pablillo had told him, and had repeated the news to Manga and Pi, who had been netting fish in the river and came late to the conference. I arrived as he was finishing the second telling. When he was done, I put my hand out, palm upward and resting on my crossed legs, as a signal that I had something to say.

Pidi noticed and said, "Expectation will speak."

I told them that I had flown with my guardian and seen the ship when it was at sea. "A wind is coming," I said. Even as I spoke, the breeze that had been flowing through the west door towards the east where we sat suddenly swelled in strength; some of the men looked sideways at each other then at me. "Now it is here," I went on, "and it is bringing us more Spaniards. Some of them are the dark kind that we have heard about in the high country and down the coast but have not seen on our land before. My guide showed them to me and let me know that it is a matter of significance."

I paused to let them digest that part then said, "We know that their ships sometimes do not carry enough water and food, and they put in at places like our old town to forage or even to trade for what they need. That may be what they are doing here now."

I paused again and heard expressions of relief. I let that go on for a few moments before saying, "Or maybe not. If they are just stopping for supplies, why would my guide have shown them to me?"

And now the faces were worried again. The wind was still rising, eddies of air entering the men's house through the open door though we were sheltered by the forest and the stockade. "It may be," I said, "that the storm will break their ship. We have heard of that happening in other places. If so, they will want to walk to one of their towns. That means they will want to make us carry their possessions."

Pidi asked if anyone had anything to say. Hupuka said, "I do not want to carry their goods. They paid us with whips and kicks."

"Worse," said Pi. "Some they kept in the highlands and sent down into the earth to dig for silver. I fear my brother is dead in the cold dark ground."

Some of the other men said much the same thing, and those who did not speak showed that the feeling was universal. When all had spoken, Pidi gave his judgment.

"We will take the canoes and the balsa upriver then go into the forest until the ship has gone. The women will stay. They do not take women for carriers."

He looked at me to see if I had anything more to say. I had a feeling that hiding in the depths of the forest might not deal with whatever the wind was about to bring to us. It was blowing stronger now, and the sky was turning black. I said, "They won't come until after the storm, if they come at all."

The men went to their houses, calling to the women to help them prepare. Soon they were streaming towards the creek that led to the river, carrying their bundles. They put the canoes in the water. The creek was too small for the balsa, which was large enough to hold twenty men, but a group picked it up and carried it downstream to where the creek met the river. They stepped aboard to sink their long poles into the slime. Their arm and back muscles strained as they kept the balsa against the bank and prevented the sluggish current from carrying them down towards the sea.

The wind was lashing at the canopy above us, twigs and leaves spiralling down and being swept away in the sudden gusts. Now the rain came in a rush, so heavy that it soon penetrated the thick mass of vegetation and stippled the surface of the river with a myriad of intersecting rings. Pidi was shouting orders from the bank until he saw that all the canoes had been accounted for. Then, with considerable dignity, he stepped onto the raft and positioned himself in its centre. He spoke a word, and the men with poles shifted their stances and began to move the lightweight craft upstream. The canoes, loaded with men, paddled after.

The women and children watched from the shore as the flotilla faded from view behind the pelting rain. Pablillo had not been invited to go with the men, but now he saw himself as the senior-ranked male. He gave unnecessary orders as we made our way back to the village, sounding remarkably like a squeaky-voiced Pidi, telling the women to do what they would have done anyway, so as to appear as if he had taken charge.

Then he looked at me and, before he could exercise his new-found authority, I beckoned him. He came to where I stood, his chin up. He was a little taller than me—I had stopped growing before he was born—and it seemed that he thought now might be the time to try to alter our relative status.

But I have a way of looking at people that makes them reconsider rash plans. Pallu told me I had had that ability even as a child, and he was not surprised when, after I had made my first foray into the upper world, I returned to tell him that my guardian was the powerful grey bird that hunted monkeys and sloths through the forest canopy.

Now I told Pablillo that I wanted to hear what he had seen. I led him to the spirit house and gestured for him to climb up. He had never been sick as a child and so had never been in the spirit house before; he looked about with a mixture of curiosity and trepidation. I let him sit on one of the stools, which flattered him, and I gave him some corn beer weakened with a little water, which pleased him greatly.

"Tell me from the beginning," I said.

"I was in the forest near the old town," he said.

"What were you doing there?"

He looked embarrassed and said, "Oh, just looking around."

I surmised he had gone there to masturbate. He was at that age when his testicles had descended, but he was still too young for the older women to take an interest. "Never mind," I said. "What did you see?"

"I heard them first," he said, "shouting and coming up the canal to where the balsas used to load. There were a lot of them."

"How many?"

He flashed his palms at me, opening and closing his fingers four times; then he looked into his memory and said, "Maybe more."

"What did they do?"

He looked inward at his memory and said, "The ordinary ones went to the old orchard and began gathering fruits. The dark ones were digging up roots in the gardens. Some of the ordinary ones stood watching them. They had the big knives."

"*Espadas,*" I said. I used the Spanish word. I had learned as much as I could from what Hupuka and the other men who had gone upcountry had been able to tell me.

"Yes, and some of them had the smoking things that kill at a distance."

Arcabuz, I thought. I had heard that word, too. "What else?"

He thought. "I could hear others still on the shore. I think they were putting water in big gourds, the kind made of wood."

That fitted with what I had heard of other ships. Last year, two of them had stopped in a bay north of here, in the territory of our friends, the Cayapas. A Cayapa trader had told us of it. The Spaniards had given knives and axes and painted pots and something that sounded interesting: a round, flat object encased in wood that reflected better than the stillest water. When someone breathed on it, the breath became visible for a little while. I would have liked to see that.

But now I asked Pablillo, "Was there more?"

He thought for a moment, then said, "Yes. Some of the ordinary Spaniards were coming across the orchard. They had smokers, but one of them had a bow that was attached to a stick."

I had heard of those weapons from Hupuka and others who had gone with the Spaniards. They were not like our bows that shot lightweight arrows with tips smeared with the poison that came off the skin of frogs. Instead, the bow sticks shot a large, heavy dart, or it might have been a small arrow, with great force. A wicker shield that would stop a breath-blown dart or a light arrow was no more defence than a butterfly's wing.

"When I saw them coming towards me," Pablillo was saying, "I slipped deeper into the forest and ran to tell the people."

"You did well," I said. "You may have saved us from bad things." I gave him a little more diluted beer, and he grinned as he took the wooden bowl. He drained it and smacked his lips.

Outside, the rain had slackened and the wind was dying. I made a decision. "Pablillo," I said, "I want you to stay and make sure everything is well here. I will go and see what is happening on the shore."

"Be careful," he said. "I have heard the smokers are deadly."

"The rain may have put them out," I said. "But I will take care not to be seen."

I went warily along the path to the old town. There was no need for silence, since the forest was alive with the sounds of trickling water and the cries of birds and the indignant complaints of monkeys that did not like to get wet. Still, I approached bends in the trail carefully, peeking from concealment to make sure the way was clear before moving on. I came to the place where the forest met the abandoned tilled land. The weapon Pablillo had mentioned, the bow on a stick, lay on the trail, a dart beside it.

That was odd, as if the man who had carried it had thrown it down and left in a hurry. I crept down the trail to the tree line and looked out into the open. I did not see what Pablillo had seen. There were no Spaniards of either colour between the forest and the town where we had lived when we were sea traders.

The gardens and orchards were empty, though I saw baskets half-filled with overripe papayas and plantains, and farther on I found abandoned collections of manioc and *papas*. The storm must have caused them to rush back to their ship, I concluded. Powerful as their vessels were, I knew that they were far less manoeuvrable than a balsa and could not simply be floated to a beach and carried up on shore until the bad weather passed.

I went back up the trail and picked up the bow weapon. When I touched its polished wooden stock it spoke to me, as certain objects sometimes will. The message was not in words but in a quiet blossoming of a thought behind my eyes: *keep this.*

It had a leather strap running its length, doubled and held by a buckle of metal. *Such casual wealth,* I thought, *to use metal where we would use a thong.* I slung the thing over my back and took another long and careful look into the orchards and fields. I saw nothing between me and the old stockade. Crouching, trusting the diminishing rain to hide me, I went out into the open.

The old town, too, was empty. I crept through the houses and peered out through a gap in the stockade near the gate. There was activity on the beach, scarcely visible through the screen of trees. Then, off to my left, I saw men—all of them dark and in rags—carrying pieces of the old balsa that had lain there for years. They took them down to the shore then went back for more.

I needed to know more. I crept along the inside of the stockade to where some of the timbers were leaning at angles, and slipped out through one of the spaces. A short run across open ground brought me to the screen of trees, and I slipped through them until I came to the beach. I lay down on my belly and edged my head and shoulders out until I could see along the tree line to where the dark Spaniards were busy.

I saw bodies, both kinds. I saw dark men and women using creepers to lash together the balsa logs, making a small raft. When I looked seaward, I saw one of their great ships broken on the reef that parallels the shore. The waves were grinding it against the coral, making a moaning sound like some huge wounded beast, with here and there the crack of breaking bones. A hole gaped in its side, and things slid around in the wet dimness.

I watched as they finished the raft. Then, the waves having slackened, six of them poled it out to the ship. I could see that one of the dark Spaniards was in charge: the big man with huge hands and a head like a gourd, the one whose eyes had been filled with anger on the ship. His hands were still linked by metal, but a sword encased in leather hung from a belt around his thick waist. He was talking to the man who had looked up when I was in the spirit bird's keeping, the one dressed in the padded clothing and the tight cloth leggings. They were arguing, but the disagreement was quickly resolved when the big man shouted and the smaller man bowed his head.

They passed over the reef and reached the ship, tethering the raft to the mess of ropes and pieces of wood that hung over the side and into the water. All but two, including the big man and the young one, scrambled up the trailing debris, made their way across the slanting deck and disappeared from view. After a while, some of the men appeared in the gaping hole in the ship's side; they passed bundles and boxes back to those on the raft. When it was well loaded, two of those who had been inside swung over to the balsa, cast off the tether, and let the waves carry them shoreward.

I saw none of the pale Spaniards on the ship, though some of the corpses near where the raft landed were of that kind. I watched as the dark ones unloaded the raft and went back for more. Then I drew back into the trees and thought about what I had seen.

Hupuka and the other men who had gone up-country had told of the dark Spaniards who worked without pay or choice or limit to their indenture. These were that kind. That is why they had to march in a circle while the Spaniard with weapons controlled them. I wondered if that were part of their religion; what I'd heard of it sounded very strange. The one who had looked up at me was not one of the ragged kind, but all the rest were, including the angry man and the older woman.

It came to me now what it meant, that the pale Spaniards were all dead and the dark ones were castaways on our shore: they would not need Nigua men to carry their burdens. These people would not want to walk the shoreline all the long way to the nearest Spanish settlement, nor would they want to follow the river up into the highlands where the Spaniards were spreading through the Quechua speakers' towns. If they encountered the pale ones again, they would be made to work without rest and march in a circle.

They're not going anywhere, I thought. *They have nowhere to go.*

The raft was being poled out to the ship again. I saw the big man up on the flat top of the vessel, which now sloped sharply towards the sea. He had braced himself against a length of wood that had ropes attached to it and was shouting to the men in the raft. He did not look angry now as his chained hands lifted over his head a long, thin object: dark wood and some metal that gleamed in the newly returned sunlight. He shouted again, his voice harsh and triumphant, brandishing the thing with a pumping motion. The men on the raft replied in kind.

They manoeuvred to where the mess of wood and ropes trailed down into the water. One of them set down his pole and scrambled up into the clutter midway between the big man and the balsa. He reached and took the object carefully from the leader, passing it to one of those on the raft, who put one end to his shoulder and sighted along its length, saying something with a laugh.

The man above stooped, picked up another thing, and passed it down. Then two more. He followed with two cylindrical boxes and a leather bag that looked to be heavy. All of these the men laid reverentially on the balsa logs—except for the cylindrical box, which one man held high against his his chest.

It must not touch water, I thought, and wondered if it was in some way sacred to the Spaniards. I had heard some snippets of information about their gods and rituals, though I discounted most of what I'd heard as nonsense.

The men on the raft didn't wait for a full cargo. Their leader shouted again, gesturing to the shore, and the one in the ropes scuttled back down to the balsa. They set the ends of their poles against the reef and pushed off towards the beach. When they came into the gentle surf, the men they had left on shore splashed towards them, taking the long objects and carrying them to the land, again making sure they were well clear of the water. And again, one of them raised the thing to one shoulder and looked down its length. He made an explosive noise, and they all laughed.

I knew that laugh. It was the same sound our men used to make when they talked about killing the Campazes, when the head-breakers used to come north to raid our land. *Those are the weapons,* I thought, *that the Spaniards call* arcabuzes.

The raft was going out again. They would be busy for a while. But, no, the man who had carried the round box was talking to those on shore, pointing inland, first towards the creek and then up the beach to where I lay watching. There was some discussion, and the issue must have been settled, because they became busy with the weapons and with the cylindrical box, which they carefully pried open.

I wished I had my guide's eyesight to see more clearly what they were doing, but they sat around the box, and it looked as if they were carefully taking handfuls of black earth out of it and pouring the stuff into small wooden bottles that came out of the cloth bag. When the bottles were full, they hung them from leather straps like the one that supported the leader's sword. One of them stood and held the *arcabuz* upright, then poured the black earth from a bottle into the end of it. I wondered if the black earth were some kind of tinder, better at catching fire, the way metal is better than stone. I would have liked to examine some of that black stuff, to hold it in my palm and blow on it.

I continued to watch closely. This was clearly a group of men readying themselves for the hunt or for war. Yet I saw nothing that spoke of the ritual involved in the taking of an animal's life or the moving of an enemy from the middle world into one of the other realms: the price to be paid, the powers to be propitiated, and the risk borne by those who killed without observing the proper forms.

The circle around the box of power—surely it was such—broke up. Two of the men with the new weapons turned towards the stream; two more turned my way. I very slowly drew my head out of view, wormed backwards through the trees, then rose and ran as fast as I could for the gap in the stockade. I raced through the dead town, across the old fields and the orchards, then into the forest, the bow weapon still strapped to me, bouncing so that its heavy butt struck the small of my back with every other step.

I ignored the pain and did not stop to rearrange things. I ran down the trail that paralleled the edge of the abandoned orchards, but I avoided the stream, taking another path that led me into the village. I came to a halt in the open area. The women were gathered in their usual fours and fives, doing their usual jobs, the absence of the men making no change in their dawn-to-dusk lives.

That change would come when no one met in the men's house to take their evening meal. The women would dine alone in their place, along with the children, as they always did. Then they would go to their individual quarters for the night, but no husbands would come to their wives, and no bachelors would make soft sounds at the feet of the ladders that ascended into the huts where the young women sat and heard the whispered comments of their mothers and aunts.

Tonight, someone else would be coming, and there would be no soft sounds. Standing in the open space, the women's and children's eyes on me, I called for Pablillo, keeping my voice low. He came from somewhere, again trying to be the man of the scene, but his face was a question.

"Gather the other boys," I said. "Take them upriver and find the men. Here is what you must tell Pidi."

I had him memorize four simple statements, making him repeat them back to me until he was word-perfect. His expression was an unbalanced mix of excitement and fear. As he rehearsed the four messages for the last time, I had the strong impression he would rather have gone out to the stockade wall and urinated.

Finally, I sent him off on his mission. Then I turned to the women, who had clustered around us as I gave Pablillo his instructions. "Mothers," I said, "here is what we must do.

Five

Alonso Illescas

Alonso realizes he must have been in the ship longer than he thought. He sees a pile of boxes and bundles on the beach, and four of the African men are leaving the site, one pair to follow the stream and the other going north on the beach before disappearing into the tree line. They are wearing swords and carrying matchlocks, with bandoliers of powder bottles slung across their chests.

The raft is coming out to the ship again. "They had better hurry," Alonso says to Anton. Though the waves have slackened, the tide is running towards shore, and the ship is fragmenting. The crunch and crack of breaking timbers and shattering coral are audible over the continuing shrieks of the gulls and the harsh comments of the crows. The deck tilts another couple of degrees towards the reef.

Anton says, "Get out on the ropes. And keep those maps dry." While Alonso does as ordered, the big man cups his palms around the sides of his mouth and shouts to the men on the raft. "Come on, we're sinking!"

Alonso looks down through the wreckage of the rigging. The water is clear, and he can see the slope of the reef as it disappears under the shadow of *La Virgen*. Pale shapes move languidly in the dimness, and it takes a moment for him to realize that they are the bodies of the crew. The big, dark shape passes again at a leisurely speed; he has no doubt it is a shark.

He thinks for a moment of the captain, strapped helpless in his cot. By now the water may have risen to take him. They had left the cabin door open. Even now, fish might be investigating the torn flesh around his broken shin.

He knows he should be moved to pity. The captain did not like him, but they are fellow Christians, and Jesus urged compassion even for one's enemies. Alonso discovers that he is not feeling any strong emotion. It is as if the events of the past few hours have used up his store of sentiments or driven him beyond his usual perspective, refashioning him as an unmoved observer not only of the world and what the others were doing in it, but even of himself.

It feels as if he has become a small creature on a vast territory, seen from above as an insignificant speck of life. He remembers something the Illescas family priest said once about God viewing the death of small birds. *This,* he thought, *must be how He views us: as little things creeping about, crashing into each other to cling or clash as our natures dictate, all looking very much the same from His perspective.*

But then the ship settles again, and the foot that Alonso has placed on a short length of rope between two longitudes of the rigging sinks into the water. He gasps, pulling it back as if the sea is boiling, and suddenly he is thrust back into himself again. The raft is still beyond the reef, the men having a harder time driving it out now that the tide has turned.

"Come on!" Alonso shouts. "She is going down!"

Above and behind him, Anton swears at the men poling the balsa, making reference to their ancestry having included apes and hyenas. His vocabulary is graphic, and the word he uses for their mothers' sexual organs is one Alonso has never heard.

The raft arrives. The men do not tether it to the wreckage, because the litter of wood and cordage is dipping deeper into the water. Alonso jumps to the balsa, the leather satchel tight to his chest, and is caught by the Africans. One of them—is his name Battista?—says something to another, who takes hold of Alonso and pulls him towards the centre of the raft so that there is room for Anton to leap aboard. The one who catches Alonso laughs.

Anton says, "Get us to shore. Something is happening."

Alonso looks where Anton does. Two of the men who went inland with matchlocks are now coming back onto the beach. One of them is waving two-handed to the raft.

"Faster," Anton says.

"A footprint," the man on the beach is saying. He is a small, sinewy fellow, his skin not much darker than a Moor's, who sometimes talks to himself in a language that uses clicks and pops. He sets the butt of his matchlock on the sand and lets its muzzle lean against the crook of his elbow as he holds up two index fingers a few inches apart.

"Not one of the sailors," Anton says.

"No," says the matchlock man. "Too small." Alonso remembers this one's name now: Poquito, for his stature. "Wearing a shoe, but not like an officer's. No heel."

Alonso can see Anton thinking. The crew went barefoot, their soles hardened by wooden decks and rough hemp. The Basque mate wore shoes, but with a well-defined heel that could be heard striking the deck planks as he moved around the ship.

"A woman," Poquito is saying. "Maybe a boy. Running, I think."

Anton nods, taking counsel with himself. He looks at the screen of trees that shelters the old town from the sea wind. "So they didn't go too far," he says, mostly to himself.

He looks at the pile of cargo they have brought out of the ship. Tools and iron ingots, plus some good steel—the drowned blacksmith's goods—some cured leather, bales of woollen cloth, a bundle of swords and another of sailors' pikes, a cask of salt. Another of rum. And, of course, the powder and lead shot for the matchlocks.

Someone has found the blacksmith's tools from *La Virgen*'s hold. Anton signals to a man almost as big as he is—Juanito is his name—and they go to where a rock is exposed in the tree line. When they come back, Anton's wrists are free and he is carrying his fetters. "Put them with the pig-iron ingots," he says. "They may come in handy."

Rubbing his wrists, Anton looks at the sky over the sea. The sun is sinking behind a bank of clouds that hangs over the horizon. He nods as he comes to a decision.

"We will carry all of this into the town, find the biggest building, and store it there. Then we make the building defensible as best we can. If we get through the night with no trouble, tomorrow we look for the savages. If their women or children have been spying on us, they won't be far away. We will find them."

Alonso is waiting for him to say something more. But Anton has stopped talking, and his mind has turned to whatever pictures he is seeing in his large round head. The other Africans are picking up pieces of cargo, turning towards the trees.

"What happens after we find them?" Alonso says.

Anton's head turns slowly Alonso's way, the eyes giving away nothing. "We'll see," he says. "Now pick something up and carry it. Do you think you are still somebody special?"

Alonso does not answer. The big man has raised a question that will need some thought. He shifts the satchel he is still carrying so that its strap crosses his chest then stoops and picks up cask of the salt, its weight solid in his two hands. He turns towards the trees.

"Wait," Anton says then steps in front of him. "Follow me."

They pass through the trees and into the open space. Beyond is the derelict stockade and the open gates. Men and women are carrying burdens into the town, setting them down in an open space just within the gates. Anton arrives, Alonso close behind. Hands fisted on hips, Anton surveys the collection of huts on stilts.

"We need something bigger," he says.

Alonso says, "There are larger ones at the centre of the town."

Anton grunts and sets off down the winding passage between the huts, Alonso at his heels. *I am following him like a dog,* the young man thinks. But what can he do? Anton hates him, is keeping him alive only because he might be useful. Surely, the leader of the Africans cannot read the maps in the satchel Alonso carries, nor can any of the others. And what Miriam said about knowing the ways of the Spaniards—that is true.

So I will be useful, he thinks. The Africans are the property of the Illescas. Alonso's duty is to protect them until such time as he can make his way to Lima and tell Don Alvaro what has happened to *La Virgen* and its cargo. Then he can guide an expedition back to this place, with soldiers and chains, to put things right again.

It is a comforting thought, even though a part of him disputes the likelihood. He cannot imagine making his way through the jungle to Quito and down to Lima. And to walk down the coast probably means death by starvation or at the hands of savages. He has heard the Campazes, south of here, eat their captives. Now, as he follows Anton and sees how the big man's wide shoulders move as he strides down the alleyways, he can't help noting the contrast between his own fear and the confidence that shows in the African's every motion. *He must have been like this in the hills of Hispaniola,* he thinks, *playing the general. Until they came and got him.*

Patience and more patience, he tells himself. The time will come.

They pass between two huts, and suddenly there is a wide plaza before them. Its dirt floor has been pulverized into dust by generations of hard-soled feet, dust that has been turned into mud by the storm but is now drying fast. The open space has the shape of a long ellipse; at either end is a long building on stilts, each with wide ladders reaching up to open doorways. Their palm-frond roofs have taken damage from storms, but the walls of plaited withies look solid, as do the thick vertical poles that support the floors.

Anton gestures to the structure on the right. "That one," he says and marches towards it. He climbs the entrance ladder, hand and foot, and Alonso sets down the salt cask to follow. The building is capacious inside, one long open space except for the far end, where woven mats have been hung from the rafters to enclose a partitioned area. The rafters and the timbers of the walls are lashed together with creepers and leather thongs. There are no windows, but another wide door stands open at the far end.

Anton stamps a heel against a floor of split planks covered over with rectangular mats of tightly woven grass. The floor does not give. "Good," he says. He turns and calls to the men and women who have followed him, bearing their burdens. "Bring it in, all of it. Miriam, show them where to stack it."

He goes down the steps, moving lightly. Alonso understands he is seeing Anton in his element. He watches from the doorway as the big man issues orders: sending some of the Africans back to the beach to bring more cargo; telling others to begin tearing down huts on the rim of the plaza and to bring the more substantial timbers to the big house. "We'll block the doorways. And we'll build barricades down below so no one can get at us from underneath."

Anton turns and sees Alonso watching him. "You," he says, "bring the maps. I want to know where we are."

The ground is dry under the big house, and there is still light enough to see. Alonso unpacks the satchel. There are folded charts of individual harbours: he recognizes Panama City and thinks that another represents the cove in which *La Virgen* met her end. Anton has no interest. He seizes a larger scroll of heavy paper and unfolds it, places rocks at the corners to hold it flat against the ground. It is a map of the coast between Nicaragua and the country south of Lima.

Anton squats and studies the chart. It is marked with place names, more inland than on the coast. Lima is prominent, and Cuzco in the mountains. Rivers run down from the uplands.

Alonso has been standing, bending over to see. Now Anton puts a hand on the back of the young man's neck and pulls him down to his knees. "Where are we?" he says.

Alonso runs a finger down the line where sea meets land. "The captain said this place was called San Mateo," he tells Anton. He finds it and points. There is a circle with a simple rendering of a house in it. "That is this town. The river here," he says, indicating a delta to the north, "is called Esmeraldas. I think the whole area is called that."

"There are emeralds?" Anton says. "Mines?"

Alonso does not know. "Don Alvaro did not think so. He thought the savages told stories to make us go inland and leave them alone."

"Us?"

Alonso does not respond to the question. He points to a large bay well south of San Mateo with a wide inlet cutting north into the land. "Here is Guayaquil," he says, "the only big town between here and Lima."

"Soldiers?" Anton says, his gaze fixed on the map.

Alonso struggles to remember what he was told. "Maybe some," he says. "The savages to the north of Guayaquil are very fierce. They are called the Campazes. They have already attacked the town and killed many people."

"So they are south of us, between us and the soldiers?"

"Yes."

Anton makes a noise in his throat, continues to study the map. "What about the savages here, where we are?" he says after a while, pointing to the bay Alonso has called Portete.

"I think they are called the Nigua. Don Alvaro said it meant 'chiggers,' the little insects that burrow into your skin if you sleep on wet leaves."

"Fierce?"

"I don't think so. We—the Spaniards—used them for porters and sent some to the silver mines in the mountains. They got sick with the measles and the viruela."

"Weak," says Anton. He looks out at the derelict town. "They have left this, gone to hide in the forest."

He refolds the map, looks at the two leather-bound books Alonso found in the captain's cabin. "What are they?"

Alonso takes one, opens it. It is full of handwritten notations interspersed with numbers. In places, there are drawings: irregular lines that look like seacoast, sometimes with islands and what might be rocks; from some of these, straight lines have been drawn, often at angles to each other, with numbers beside them.

"I cannot read it," Alonso says. "I think it is in Basque."

"Look at the other one," Anton says.

It is the same. Each page identical to its counterpart in the other book.

"Rutters," says Alonso. "Pilots make them to find their way. He made one for himself and one to sell."

Anton tilts his head to one side and back again. "Maybe someday we'll sell one." The men and women he sent to break up the nearby huts have been bringing back the materials. Anton tells Alonso to repack the satchel and take it up inside the hut. "Give it to Miriam and tell her I said to keep it safe."

He goes into the plaza and begins directing the fortification of the big house. The doorways will be blocked, and one end of the understory will be walled with piled timber—in case, Anton says, anyone tries to get under us and make a fire. He also tells four men to take matchlocks and pikes and to station themselves in one of the huts on the east side of the plaza.

"If we are attacked, you wait for my signal. First, shoot into them but don't bother to reload. Drop the guns and attack with the pikes." He rubs a hand over his scalp. "Just in case they are not as weak as we think they are."

Alonso has found Miriam directing the storage of their goods upstairs in the big house. He gives her the satchel and Anton's message. She nods and he turns away, but she calls him back. She hands him a scabbarded cutlass and indicates the three women who have been rearranging cargo against the wall.

"Take them," she says, "to where we gathered the food before the storm. They are afraid to go alone." She smiles. "Be careful you do not cut yourself."

It does not occur to Alonso until he is descending the ladder that he has been given an order by one of the Africans he used to be in charge of—and a woman at that—yet he has obeyed without thinking.

He leads the three women through the abandoned huts towards the inland gate. *I will think about it later,* he tells himself. But he finds himself thinking about something similar as they reach the overgrown fields: how Anton has changed since the wreck of the ship. Alonso first saw him when the recaptured slaves were marched across the isthmus and put aboard *La Virgen* while it was provisioning for the journey. His first impression was that this was a dangerous man. Anton was filled with rage as an egg was filled with meat. The deep creases in his brow, the rigidity of his body, the way his head would snap around at any sudden noise—he was like a tortured beast on a chain, straining, eager to break the links and leap upon his tormentors. The rage remained throughout the voyage south. Alonso saw it in the way Anton moved when the Africans were forced to climb up to the deck for exercise, dancing under the muzzles of the crew's matchlocks. He felt it like a physical blow whenever the African glared at him through the bars of their cage.

And now … now it is all different. The rage that was so frightening has become another kind of energy: directed, purposeful, even …

admirable. Alonso remembers a day in his adolescence when the Illescas went out *en masse* to one of Seville's great plazas to see Don Fernando Alvarez de Toledo, the Duke of Alba, ride by with his retinue. The nation's greatest general, sent by the King of Spain (who was also the Holy Roman Emperor) to crush the German heretics, was returned in triumph and had come to visit relatives in Seville.

The Duke's countenance was lean and stark, with a nose like a Moorish sword and a beard forked into two sharp tines. The crowds cheered him, and many knelt and crossed themselves when he passed, crying out that he was God's soldier. The Duke gazed straight ahead, and Alonso thought the beams that came from those dark, deep-set eyes must have the power to pierce oak and stone—certainly to penetrate to the heart of any man who came under their stiletto gaze.

And now he realizes that Anton has acquired the same posture, the same incisive gaze, the same air of being not only in charge but born to the rank. He reassesses his impression of the man. *He is not playing at being a general,* Alonso thinks. *He is one.* All that time as a field slave and a prisoner was an error. The Spaniards should have struck off his chains, given him a sword and a horse, and set him at the front of a column of conquistadors.

The women are gathering the baskets of fruits and tubers abandoned when the ship's whistle sounded. There are more than they can carry back to the big house. Alonso says, "Bring them all to the gate then take them in a few at a time."

They do as he says. He wonders if it is because his order makes sense or because they still have the habit of obedience. While they work, he crosses the field with the vegetable plots and goes into one of the orchards. There is fruit on some of the trees, old and wrinkled, and more on the ground. Little of it looks appealing to Alonso's eye, even after the weeks of near famine on the ship. But it will be better than the salt pork, which must have been almost rancid before it was salted, that was his daily fare during the last days of *La Virgen.*

He is not quite sure what to do with the scabbarded sword. He has no belt, and it is heavy and cumbersome to carry. Don Alonso allowed him to learn the art of swordsmanship in Seville, but the weapon the younger Alonso used in the practice hall was lighter: his instructor favoured the newly popular rapier with its slim, straight blade and hemispherical hilt.

Alonso takes a grip on the cutlass and assumes the stance he was taught: right foot forward, left to the rear and turned at right angles to the line of the body, right arm fully extended. But the blade is so heavy that he cannot maintain it for more than a few moments. The point begins to droop and drags his arm down with it.

No finesse, he thinks. *No finding the flaw in the opponent's disposition and slipping through the gap. This is a weapon of brute force, of battering down resistance by main strength.*

It is yet another part of his training that will not serve him under his new circumstances. If he faced Anton in a duel with cutlasses, the big man would have him de-limbed and filleted in no time.

He imagines the way it would go and shudders. It cannot be. Anton is the leader. Alonso is a remnant of a world that the Africans have left behind, have escaped from. It makes no difference that he never truly fitted that abandoned world, either. Here and now is all there is. Indeed, tonight or tomorrow, they may have to fight the savages whose leavings they are gathering. Alonso shudders again. In that event, he will not be sorry to be directed by Anton.

He is approaching the place where the orchard ends and the forest begins. From the gate of the old town, the forest looked like a solid, unbroken wall of green cut through with black and brown. Now, as he nears it, he sees that it is a riot of differences. Alonso has seen forests in Spain, oaks and pines, the individual trees differing only in their details. Here he must be seeing ten different species of tree, perhaps twenty, just within the scope of his vision, which takes in only sixty or seventy feet of the tree line. Black trunks and several shades of brown, one or two that are grey; rough bark and smooth, and some that appear to be peeling; leaves that are round, spear-pointed, multi-lobed, each with its own tint of green.

And out of the forest comes a constant, multi-toned soundscape: rustlings and whisperings as the sea breeze finds its way among the tangle of branches and twigs; bird calls and animal cries, some soft, some loud; and when he moves closer still he hears the sound of light, scattered rain—the storm's leavings, still working their way to the ground from the canopy high above.

In there somewhere, he thinks, Poquito found a footprint—a woman's or a child's. The savage who made that print moves in the forest like one of its own, at ease, at home, unfazed by its bewildering disordered variety, its cacophony of snarls, howls, and chitterings.

Will I ever be at home there? he thinks. The very thought of entering into that alien world sends another shudder through him. *So easy to become lost, to wander and weaken, helpless, alone.*

He hears distant voices. The women have returned. One of them says something, too far away to make out the meaning, and the other two laugh. Alonso looks through the orchard and across the field to where they stand by the gate. They have been looking at him, or at least in his direction, but now they bend and take up more baskets and sashay through the gate, laughing again.

They were laughing at me, he thinks, *because I was their master's underling but still above them. And now I have been brought down, while they have been raised up to freedom. It may not last, but for now they have a place in the world, however precarious, and I have none. And my non-place may be even more precarious than theirs.*

He must be useful, he knows. He should not just wait for opportunities to be of help, especially to Anton, but look for them at his own initiative. He did that when he told Anton about the wrecked balsa raft. He would keep an eye open for other contributions he could make to the well-being of the group. *At least,* he thinks, *until the soldiers arrive to round them up again.*

He walks back to the garden plots, the heavy sword resting against his shoulder. The farther he gets from the forest, the easier he feels.

Night falls fast. Though Alonso is no longer surprised by the sudden transition from light to darkness in this latitude, it nonetheless feels wrong that there is no twilight. The day goes as if God has blown out a candle.

He is in the big house with most of the Africans. The women have been cooking a meal. Strangely, there are no hearths in the huts; the savages cooked on campfires out in the open, although there are small roofs over the fire pits to keep off the rain. There were no pots or utensils to cook with until someone investigated the partitioned areas in the two big houses and found shallow bowls of various sizes as well as some pots that once contained some kind of beer, now dried to powdery residue.

"They must have eaten communally," Alonso offers as an explanation. "Like monks."

They are seated in the big house, passing around bowls of roasted tubers and raw fruits, sliced and cubed. Everyone eats with fingers except Anton; he has commandeered a knife from the leather-working tools Alonso found on the ship. He uses it to spear pieces out of a small bowl that he has filled from one of the larger. It rests on the floor in front of him.

"They are savages," says one of the men, a thin-chested young fellow whose name Alonso has not yet learned. "Their ways are strange."

The scene is lit by tallow candles brought from the ship, the candles lit by tapers from the cooking fires and the fires lit by a flint-and-tinder box someone found in *La Virgen*'s galley. The discussion around the circle remains on the subject of the missing Niguas. Why did they abandon the town? Sickness and Spanish slavers is the consensus. Did they have gold? Maybe, it is agreed: the ones up in the mountains paid, as a ransom for their chief, a roomful of gold.

"And then the Spaniards strangled him anyway," says Anton. "Remember that when Spaniards offer you terms." He chews a mouthful of a root that is still fibrous after lying in the ashes of a cooking fire all evening and nods in agreement with something he has left unspoken.

Alonso speaks again. "Don Alvaro told me that some of the forest tribes leave gold in the graves of their chiefs. Perhaps we should look tomorrow for a graveyard."

Anton throws the young man a considering look. "We will have other chores tomorrow." Then he looks pointedly around the circle in a way that says he is issuing an order. "Right now, gold is useless to us. There is nothing to buy. We will acquire what we need by other means." He selects a piece of fruit, spears it, and chews it thoughtfully.

After the meal, as the bowls are being collected, Anton gestures to Alonso with a flick of the head that says, *follow me*. He leads the young man back to the partitioned room, where the satchel containing the rutters and map are now stored. He brings a candle, and by its light Alonso unfolds the map again so that the African can study it.

"Did your master tell you where the savages find their gold?" he asks after poring over the chart.

Alonso has to think. "In the mountains there are mines," he says after a while. "Some produce gold, but more are for silver. In the lowlands, the gold is found in streams, washed down from the uplands."

"Look at the map," Anton says. "Are any of the mines marked?"

The mountains are marked with rows of chevrons. Alonso looks closely at the markings in that part of the map. The printing is small and faded, but he can see the names are not Spanish. He points to some of the places. "These are towns from before the conquest. They still have the names that the savages gave them. These exes ..." He indicates three places. "I think they may be mines. Give me the candle."

He brings the light closer, peers at the faint markings. "Yes," he says. "Here it says 'mine' and 'silver'."

Anton makes a noise in his throat. He traces the line of the big river to the north of the abandoned town. It climbs towards the chevrons but does not pass near any of the silver mines; all of them are in the south-east and south-west, many leagues away.

Anton's finger taps at the nearest mine. "What distance is that?" he asks Alonso.

There is a compass rose and legend in one corner of the map. The young man consults it and makes a calculation. "At least forty leagues," he says.

Anton makes a calculation of his own. "Four days' march."

Alonso sees an opportunity. "More," he says. "The air is not rich up there. It is hard to get a good breath. People grow tired quickly and move more slowly."

Anton looks at him. "You know this? You have breathed this poor air?"

"No, but Don Alvaro has been there. He told me."

Anton makes the throat noise again. Then he tells Alonso not to speak of any of this to the others—not the gold, the mines, the river, the air. He refolds the map and puts it away. "Understood?" the big man says.

"Understood." As he follows Anton and the candle out of the little room, the young man is feeling as if he has laid a small area of solid footing that he can stand upon. It is a comforting feeling, but at the same time he wishes he could leap far beyond this dark house in a dead town to land lightly like a fencer in the courtyard of Don Alvaro's house in Lima, safe and sure again.

The night passes with no sign of the savages. Anton has divided up the hours of darkness into watches, assigning pairs of men to take stations at each end of the big house and telling the couple he is sending to the small house to take turns, two hours at a time. Alonso takes his turn with Poquito, watching from behind the barrier that now blocks the rear entrance of the big house. At first, they do not speak as they look out upon the bare ground lit by a half-moon that has risen over the forest. But as the shadows recede and the scene brightens, Poquito says, "Look at each patch of shadow. Get to know its shape. Then if the shape changes, you will notice. That is how you keep watch in the night."

Alonso thanks him for the advice and tries to follow it but has trouble even delineating the shadow-shapes until the hunter says, "Do not look straight on, but from the corners of your eyes. They see best in the dark that way."

Alonso tries to do as the other man counsels, without much success. "It is hard," he says.

"It's easier when there is something moving," Poquito says, "though I prefer it when nothing does."

At the end of their watch, Anton comes and Poquito reports that nothing has happened. The big man whispers to two other shapes in the darkness, a man and a woman, who come to take their places. As he rises from where he has been crouched behind the barricade, Alonso hears a soft sound nearby.

"What's that?" he says.

Anton is immediately alert, looking out into the moonlight.

"No," Alonso says. "It was inside, with us."

Anton cocks his head, listening, then moves swiftly to where a hanging screen of woven reeds, barely visible in the small glow of moonlight, closes off the partitioned space in the long building. He pulls aside the screen and goes within. Now come shouts and grunts, the sounds of blows, and a sharp slap followed by a woman's cry. A man, unidentifiable in the dimness, comes stumbling out of the enclosed space, bent over, his hands scrabbling on the floor as he tries to prevent himself from falling. Another slap, and a woman comes after him, hurrying towards the front of the house. She passes through a shaft of moonlight coming through a gap in the roof, and it is enough illumination for Alonso to see it is the one who made the other two women laugh when they were gathering food.

Anton's voice is low, but the menace is unmistakable. "There will be no coupling until we are on sure ground. If any of you, man or woman, can't live without it, you can go into the forest and live like beasts. But you won't be part of what we do here."

There are some grunts of approval from the sleepers who have been awakened by the tumult. The house begins to settle again, and Alonso looks for a place to lie down. But Anton taps him on the shoulder. "Go to the other house," he says, "and make sure they are awake."

Alonso climbs over the barricade at the front door and makes his way across the moonlit plaza to where the four men are stationed. A few paces from the hut's ladder, he hears a voice say, "What?"

"Anton sent me to check on you."

"We are doing what we are supposed to," says the voice from the darkness. Alonso turns to go back and hears lips smacking in an exaggerated kissing sound, followed by laughter.

Is that what they think of me? That I would kiss the rump of whoever is set over me? Yet there is some truth in it. As he crosses the open ground, he lets himself feel he is Anton's trusted lieutenant. But is that how the big man sees him? After all, it was Alonso's sharp hearing that picked out the fornicators. Now another thought intrudes: perhaps Anton sent him out into the open because, if the savages shot darts or arrows into him, it would be a small loss.

No, he thinks as he clambers up the wide ladder and slips over the barricade into the big house. *I am useful.* He remembers the dead sailors on the beach. *And that is not a bad thing to be, considering what Anton offers as an alternative.*

In the morning, Anton leaves six men and the women to guard the supplies in the big house. He leads the rest, including Alonso, to where Poquito found the track. It has been raining in the forest all night, the canopy sending down what it caught during the storm, and a trickle of water along the trail has all but obliterated the footprint. But the tracker finds it and points with his chin, saying, "That way."

The trail they follow leads to the stream and turns to follow it. Anton divides the men into two groups. "Stay separated. If one group is shot at, the other goes into the forest and flanks those who are doing the shooting."

They move off, Poquito leading the way, looking for a new sign. He finds it after a few more paces, a heel print in mud that is drying faster where the stream creates gaps in the canopy. They do not have far to go before they find a place where the bank of the waterway is an expanse of bare earth. The tracker points to scrapes and gouges in the mud and says, "Canoes." He pauses to examine the ground. "Seven of them."

Now he squats and studies some patches more closely, turning his head from side to side. Finally, he goes to his hands and knees, lowers his head, and squints sideways at the ground. He grunts to himself and stands.

He tells Anton, "Several men put the canoes in the water during the rain. There were women and children, too, but they did not go. Their tracks lead that way."

He walks over to a large fern growing next to a black-boled tree. He pushes aside the fronds, and behind the spreading plant is a trail. Even Alonso, crowding forward with the others, can see footprints.

Anton has been taking it in. "So the men went upstream and left the women and children"—he gestures along the trail—"to go that way?"

"Yes," Poquito says. "There will be a village."

Anton makes his thinking noise. "And they want us to find it, don't they?"

Alonso is thinking, too. "A trap?"

"A distraction, at least," Anton says. "While we're busy … organizing things, the men come with spears and clubs. The canoes are gone upstream, but maybe they haven't gone far."

"They may have gone to hide when they saw the ship. The Spaniards used to make them carry heavy burdens upcountry."

Anton shakes his head. "The footprint Poquito found was made after the storm sank the ship. They must know we have no wish to rejoin His Most Catholic Majesty's empire."

He pauses to consider, then says, "Two groups, as before. Everyone with an *arcabuz*, check your powder is dry and your match is smouldering." He glares at them, making sure he catches each man's eye. "But no one fires except at my command!"

He waits until the order has been acknowledged by everyone who holds a matchlock, and waits again until powder and matches have been checked. "I will lead the first group," he says. "Alonso, with me."

They brush aside the fern and enter the forest. The usual maelstrom of sounds envelops them. It is worse here than by the big town, because a troop of monkeys has taken up residence in trees along the trail. They shout and hoot at the men, and fling filth. When it hits, the men curse. Alonso ducks his head between his risen shoulders and wishes he had a hat.

The village is not far from the stream, no more than two hundred paces. It is a miniature of the abandoned town, complete with a stockade and a central open space where two larger houses face each other, though these are smaller than the one in which Alonso spent the night. The plaza is surrounded by the same huts on stilts, with ladders leading up to open doors. Everything, Alonso notes, is in better repair.

The gate is made only of plaited reeds and tree limbs the thickness of a man's arm, and it hangs open. Beyond is a semicircle of open ground with a wide walkway leading to the plaza. In the middle of the plaza, a crowd of women and children stand waiting, watching them approach.

Alonso studies them as he follows a pace behind Anton, the men around and behind him with their firearms and pikes at the ready. The Nigua run to shortness and squatness, with moon faces and long, straight hair parted in the middle. He sees women of every age, from young adolescents to wrinkled crones, and children of both sexes. The oldest boy is no more than twelve years.

The women wear lengths of cloth—it looks to be dyed cotton—wrapped around them from just below the armpits to below the knees. Wooden and bone pins hold the material together. Alonso sees no gold or silver. Two of the mature women also wear mantles of woven fabric over their shoulders and pinned in front. As he comes closer, Alonso sees decorative stitching in some of the garments. The neck of one of the mantles has a border of tiny bird feathers, blue and green and yellow.

The Africans enter the central plaza watchfully. Anton tells the men in his group to spread out and keep watch on the huts. When the second contingent arrives at the gate, he orders them to face about and watch the path they came along.

There is silence in the village except for the usual bird calls and the monkeys still hooting. Alonso, waiting for Anton to take the lead, examines the Nigua women. He notices one in particular, shorter even than the others and wearing a kind of scarcely tailored tunic and soft shoes of leather. She is looking at him—and only at him, he realizes, her gaze as steady and focused as a bird's—while the other women's eyes move nervously to take in the Africans as they position themselves around this half of the plaza.

Alonso can even read the expression in the small woman's gaze. It is saying, *So here you are at last.* He has an unaccountable feeling of having been expected. He has time to notice that her hair is cut shorter than the others, then her eyes go to Anton.

The leader of the Africans says, "Who here speaks Spanish?"

The odd little woman takes a step forward, her gaze still on Alonso, and answers quietly, "I speak."

The voice is low-pitched, almost a croak.

Anton says, "Where are the men?"

She looks at the big man. "Gone."

"Gone where?"

"Where the Spaniards took them. To carry . . ." She looks for a word, can't find it, makes a hand gesture with a roll of a slender wrist. "Things."

Anton is giving her a hard look, but she does not wilt under it. Instead she returns her gaze to Alonso, appears to be studying him.

Anton details two of the men with pikes to scale the ladders and investigate the nearby huts, backed up on the ground by two men with matchlocks pointed at the open doorways. Everyone waits while they carry out the inspections. Anton continues to glare at the strange, diminutive Nigua, who continues to regard Alonso as if he were a new species of animal that might do something interesting at any moment.

Alonso addresses her. "What is your name?"

The question gets him a sharp turn of the head and a glare from Anton, but the Nigua answers him with a few syllables he cannot quite make out. The sounds seem to be made farther back in the throat than Spanish vowels and consonants.

She speaks again, in Spanish. "It means ... you wait something you know comes."

"Expectation," Alonso says.

She considers the sound of the name then nods agreement, still studying him.

The four men who have been looking into the huts return, signalling that they have found nothing. Anton sends them with two other pairs to check the two big houses, and again they trot away.

Alonso puts a hand to his chest and says, "I am Alonso Illescas."

He gets another sharp look from Anton and winces a little. "We have to talk to them," he tells the big man.

Anton grunts. His eyes follow the men checking the houses, then he turns to those behind him and snaps, "Watch the trail!"

They have been looking around, especially at the women, but now they resume their vigilance, pikes charged. One blows on his smouldering match until its tip glows brightly.

Alonso asks Expectation, "What are the big houses for?"

She turns and points at one then the other. "That is for men, that for women. For eating and talking and doing ... men things and women things."

"And the small huts?"

The question is a mild surprise to her. "For the night," she says, tilting her head to one side, placing a palm on her cheek, and closing her eyes. "Sometimes for the day also." Now she makes the thumb and forefinger of one hand into a ring and pushes two fingers of the other hand in and out of it.

"Ah," Alonso says. One of the Africans laughs, but whatever he is about to say is cut off by Anton's, "Quiet!"

Now there is silence as they wait for the men inspecting the big houses and other huts to return and report.

"Nothing," says the oldest of them when they come back. He is a small man, very dark, with thin cords of muscles standing out on his arms and chest. Alonso remembers his name is Paco. "No men." Then he adds, "No gold."

Expectation speaks. "No gold. Spaniards take."

"All right," Anton says. He has been thinking while the others have been doing and Alonso has been conversing. He singles out four men with matchlocks. "Go back to the town. Get the raft, load it with supplies, and bring it up the stream to where we found the canoe marks. Don't overload it. Make as many trips as necessary. Some men to pole, some to watch the banks with matchlocks ready. For the last trip, bring the women."

As the men go out the gate, he assigns duties to the rest of them: some to spread out around the perimeter of the village, some to guard the women in the little plaza. "Tell them to sit down," he says to Expectation.

She looks up at the sun. "It makes hot," she says. "The sun."

He turns to one of the hut inspectors. "Any weapons in the big houses?"

"No," says Paco. "Pots and bowls—that's all."

Anton says to Expectation, "Which was the women's place?" She points to one of the houses, and he says, "Tell them to go there."

She speaks to the women in Nigua, and they move towards the women's house, some carrying babies or leading little ones by the hand. They cast nervous glances at the men who accompany them. Expectation turns back to Anton. "Not for men, inside house."

Alonso says, "Why not?"

She turns to him. "Not good, men in women's house, women in men's house." She searches for a word. "Ghosts … No, not ghosts. Ay, yes, spirits. Spirits not like."

Anton's face grows hard and his voice is a growl. "Devil worshippers!"

Suddenly, it is not going well, Alonso realizes. He asks Expectation, "Devils? You like devils?" He makes a fierce face, fingers hooked like claws, all the while thinking, *Don't say you like them.*

Her expression is puzzled, as if she is working out a code. Then her face clears and she says, "Devils?" and points at the ground, making her face a mask of menace. "No, no devils." She pauses to think, then points at the sky. "Good spirits." She moves her arms like a bird's wings and points skyward again. "Friends."

"I think she is talking about angels," Alonso says. He does not think that at all, but it is the right thing to say to Anton at this moment. "She does not have the words."

The big man's face shows suspicion only half-faded. But after a moment he nods and says, "You stay with her. Learn their language. And teach her better Spanish."

He orders the men at the gate to close it then stalks off to inspect the sentries. Alonso and Expectation are left alone in the little plaza. She is giving him that look of evaluation again, and then her expression becomes that of someone who is satisfied, at least for the time being.

"Where do we go?" he asks her. He gestures to the plaza. "Men's house or women's?"

She wags a finger at him, smiling in a way that says she has understood the question behind the question. "My house," she says. "Spirit house."

She turns and walks across the plaza to a hut larger than the others but smaller than the big houses. She climbs the steps, and he follows. Inside there are stools to sit on and a terracotta pot near the door, sweating. She gestures for him to sit, finds two shallow bowls, takes the lid off the pot, and pours for both of them.

Alonso takes the bowl and sniffs the yellowish liquid. It has a yeasty odour.

Expectation indicates the bowl in her hand, says a Nigua word, and drinks its contents in one draught. She smacks her lips and emits a loud belch.

Alonso raises the bowl to his lips and sips. The liquid is thin, bitter, but recognizable as a kind of beer. He drinks the rest down and lets loose his own stomach-voice to echo hers.

They regard each other for a moment. She says the Nigua word again, and he repeats it, adding, "Beer."

"Beer," she says. "Good." She pours them each another bowlful and he lifts his in what he hopes is a universal gesture. She responds in the same way, and they drink together.

Then Alonso lowers the bowl and raises a finger while showing her the face of a man who is about to ask a serious question. He points the finger at her and says, "Expectation. Man or woman?"

She offers a face that says the question is not so easily answered. She puts down the bowl and raises her left-hand index finger. "Man," she says. Next she raises the finger of her right hand. "Woman." Then she brings both fingers together and curls them around each other.

"Expectation," she says.

Six

Expectation

I had sent Pablillo to Pidi with a plan: go deeper into the forest, wait a few days, then steal back and lead the women and children away; take them all to Chilianduli's *palenque* farther inland and get the war chief's advice on what to do about the dark Spaniards.

But Pidi made a plan of his own.

The Spaniards had never held themselves back when it came to our women; they were notorious for it. He thought these dark specimens would be like the others—so did I, for that matter—but he had not reckoned with their leader. Anton did not let his men choose the ones they would take into the huts. Instead, he put all of the women and children into the women's house and sent his own women as well as some of the men to guard them through the night.

Their own women came up on the balsa they had cobbled together from the wreckage down by the old town. They brought more men, too, with weapons and bundles and boxes, including the strange, curved boxes made of strakes of wood bound with metal. One of these, the small one full of black earth, they put away in the men's house, a place that was now guarded by men with spears and swords. I tried to get a closer look at it, but the older woman who had taken up residence there—Anton's wife?—saw me lurking near the bottom of the ladder and told one of the guards to shoo me away.

When I saw them down on the beach, I had counted them: three hands plus two fingers of men, and two hands less three fingers of women. I had Pablillo take this information to Pidi. The fact that their men outnumbered ours, and them with better weapons, should have been enough to make him follow my plan.

We had only two hands of men plus three boys almost of age to fight. Still, Pidi's plan had been to wait while the invaders used the women and drank corn beer. At dawn, our men would go from hut to hut and kill them one or two at a time. The women would help, striking at the dark Spaniards with whatever they had: clay pots, hardwood bowls, or the pestles they used for crushing corn into meal. Or they would hold them while our men stabbed and clubbed.

As a peace chief, Pidi had never led men into battle, but to strike while the enemy was distracted by the women seemed an opportunity too fleeting to miss. And if the dark Spaniards had behaved like the pale ones, his plan could have worked.

But when Pidi led the men and boys through the stockade at the place where they had weakened the bindings, the invaders were ready for them. Our men ran silently to the huts, but found them empty. One of them—it looked like Manga—came to the spirit house; his presence on the ladder leading up to my door brought me back to the middle world with a shock. I had been sitting upright, visible in the moonlight coming through the door, with Alonso asleep behind me in the shadow. It took me a moment to realize what was happening, and by then the man had moved on; my hissed signal did not bring him back.

It was too late. The Nigua men and boys realized the enemy were gathered in the men's house. Alonso told me later that they had seen our men, and their leader had made them issue loud snoring noises to lure our men forward. Pidi fell for the ruse. He sent two of the boys towards the sunset door to make a diversionary noise, and when they hooted and slapped their bellies with their palms, our peace chief led the other ten out into the open in a silent rush towards the sunrise door.

Disaster. Fire shot out of the barricaded doorway and there was a noise like flattened thunder. Then more noise and spouting flame came from the sunset door of the women's house. In the moonlight, I saw

Pidi and the men flung about like corn-shuck dolls, and a great gout of blood spurted from someone's head. Those who were not killed or maimed stood trembling in shock until the Africans boiled out of the men's house to stab and beat them down.

It was all over in a dozen breaths. A wail went up from the women's house, but I heard the Africans there shouting and delivering slaps and blows, and it soon quieted except for the crying of children. I was in shock myself, but I shook myself free of it and quickly climbed the spirit ladder to hide the bow weapon again. I had just time to lay the ladder against the wall before the open space was lit by torches and a man held one up to see inside the spirit house.

Alonso was sitting up then, shaking his head to clear it of the herb I had slipped into one of the bowls of beer he had consumed. I did not want to have to explain where I went or what I was doing when I left to commune with my guide. Blinking and smacking his lips, he got to his hands and knees and pushed himself halfway erect so his buttocks were resting on his heels. "What?" he said to the man in the doorway. "What's going on?"

Out in the open space, they were killing the badly wounded with swords and spears. I heard Anton issue an order and saw the two boys who had made the failed diversion dragged forward into the torchlight. One of them was Pablillo, shivering with fright, his eyes huge as he saw the bodies on the ground, the blood pooling in the dust.

I expected to see the boys killed. Instead, Anton gave orders, and someone came with rope to tie the pair's hands behind them. They were pushed and cuffed towards the men's house and made to sit at the bottom of the sunrise ladder.

Anton's eyes turned towards the spirit house, and he called to the man with the torch, who stood at the foot of my ladder. "He's all right," the man shouted back, and, with a contemptuous tone, he said something that contained the word Spanish word for *beer*.

Anton called again, and the torchbearer spoke to Alonso. "Come." He motioned with his head and said to me, "You, too."

I helped Alonso to rise and climb down the ladder. But when we got to the bottom, he took a deep breath through his nose and let it out through his open mouth. Then he shook his head and squared his shoulders. The man with the torch made to take his arm, but Alonso shook him off and walked with as much dignity as he could muster to where Anton waited. The torch man contented himself with cuffing me across the back of my head and saying, "Move."

I moved, fast enough to come level with Alonso, and we walked to where the dead lay at the feet of the men who had killed them. There was a breeze that made the torches swirl and the corpses appear to move in the flickering light. I saw that it was Pidi who had taken the terrible head wound, the first I had seen from an *arcabuz*. His skull was split like a melon, and one eye had popped out onto his cheek. It regarded me with the complacency of the dead until I looked away.

I saw now that two of our men had survived the massacre with minor wounds. They were already tied and being hustled over to where the boys sat, quivering with fright. The men who held them pushed them down to their knees.

Anton was looking around with the air of a chief whose plans have worked as he anticipated. Then he turned his attention to Alonso and me.

"Drunk?" he said.

"Tired," Alonso answered.

Anton leaned towards the young man, sniffed the air, and nodded. "Beer."

"Not much," Alonso said.

Anton sniffed again then took a hard look at me. "And what more?"

The herbs had no strong odour. I gave him back a face full of innocence. His response was to make one hand's fingers into a ring and poke two fingers of the other through it. His expression said he already knew the answer to the unspoken question.

"No," I said and meant to say no more.

But Alonso laughed, a short bark of sound. "Expectation is not a woman," he said.

Anton's face clouded. *He thinks he's being mocked,* I thought.

Alonso said, "She's a hermaphrodite." I hadn't heard the Spanish word until then. "Or he," he continued, "if you prefer." He laughed again, his breath beery. "Or both. Or neither. I have read about them in books."

I did not have much Spanish at that time, but I could guess at what he was saying. The cloud in Anton's face had darkened. "What is a hermaphrodite?" he wanted to know.

Even if I didn't know the word *hermafrodita,* I knew *hombre* and *mujer* were man and woman, and the entwined fingers gesture Alonso used was the same one I had shown him. A wave of repulsion washed over his leader's already angry countenance. Though I had been too young to see it, I had no doubt Pidi's father had looked the same when they brought my infant nakedness before him and he saw how strangely I was made.

Alonso was watching Anton closely. Whatever state of drunkenness he had achieved was fading fast. "We need her," he said.

"Her, is it now?" Anton said.

"She speaks Spanish. She's already learned a lot more from me."

Anton's head motioned towards the prisoners. "The boys will learn. You did. I did."

"She is their healer. She knows herbs. She can stitch wounds." He made the same gestures I had used when I showed him my bone needles and cotton thread.

Anton showed the first sign of wavering. I said, "Look," and knelt down to where Patya lay, his belly split open, another corpse across his legs. I pushed the impeding body aside and showed the wound I had closed on Patya's calf after we had had the fight with the Campaze raiders.

"Me, I do that," I said.

It was enough. I saw the chief in Anton overcoming whatever made him hate unnatural creatures like me. "All right," he told Alonso, showing us both an unpleasant smile. "Tomorrow, we give the savage women as wives to the men. You," he said, pointing a finger at Alonso, "get her."

The finger came to point at me. If it had been a spear-thrower, I would have been pierced through the heart.

Only I was supposed to live in the spirit house. But that thought crossed my mind and exited like a wind blowing through the open space. Alonso had been shown to me by my guide when the spirit eagle had told me of what the wind would bring. There were two interpretations to that message: first and obvious was the Africans' overthrow of everything that made up my people's lives; second, and not so obvious, was the young man who now followed me back to the hut and climbed in after me.

We sat on the stools and watched through the open doorway as the living dragged away the dead and piled them up against the sunset side of the stockade. I asked Alonso what his people did with the deceased. He mimed digging, then after a moment's thought, he indicated one of the torches and said, "Fire."

I let him know I understood then turned my thoughts inward for a while. The spirits of those slain by the Africans would be wandering now, their last breaths dissipating on the breeze. I would need to go into the underworld, find them, and show them the way. Otherwise, they might end up forever trapped between the worlds, left to grow hostile and resentful and eventually dangerous to the living. A soured spirit could bring bad luck, disease, infertility, or a bad harvest.

I would not have been able to explain this to Alonso at our present level of communication. Instead, I told him I had to sleep and indicated that he should, too. But he was understandably agitated by the events of the night and wanted to talk. After a few statements, I let him know that I was not able to follow him, although I understood more than half of what he was telling me: mostly he was cautioning me about Anton, about whom I needed no more warning than I would have about a jaguar that was snarling outside the stockade.

I used soft tones and gentle gestures to calm him, then indicated that he should take off his padded garment and lie face down on the pallet reserved for those who fell ill or were victims of haunting. Through the thin undergarment, I could feel that his upper back and neck muscles were knotted with tension. I used techniques of pressure points and stretching to dig out the worst of them. Once he was relaxed and breathing more slowly and deeply, I found the spots near the front of his neck, pressed, and put him into sleep. He stopped breathing for a little while, but I counted my heartbeats up to the correct number and gently restarted his breathing before his spirit would feel itself trapped and jerk him awake.

I let him snore, positioning myself for meditation and an entry into the other world. It did not take long to find the downward path, and once I was on it, I soon located the distraught spirits of Pidi, Manga, and the other men. I gathered them, soothed them, then called their own spirit guides to help. When they were all well set on the shining path, I let distance grow between us. Now I called my own guide.

I did not put a question to the eagle. I sensed that I was expected to work through the implications of her last message about the wind. But I studied her aspect: alert but calm, returning my spirit gaze with a clear and unruffled stare of her own. That told me I was on the right trail, which was enough. I withdrew and returned to the middle world, where Alonso still snored. I lay down on my sleeping pad and was soon asleep. I did not dream.

I found a different Anton in the morning, as cool-headed as my guide had been in the spirit world. He sent a man to collect Alonso and me, although I had been awake since before dawn, thinking about where things might go from here. Alonso was still asleep, and I had to wake him. He came down the ladder into the open space, blinking and yawning. Anton and the African men were waiting with the four prisoners.

"Tell them," Anton said to me, "that if they are good, no harm comes to them. Understand?"

"Harm means bad?" I said, and mimed cutting a throat. Behind Anton, I saw Pablillo swallow hard and turn his gaze towards the middle distance, his lower lip trembling.

"Yes," Anton said. "No bad. They live like us, all together, all good."

"The women?"

"They keep."

I told the men and boys what I thought the Africans' chief was saying. "We will live together, like one people. Your wives will not be taken from you."

One of the men, Pahta, said, "What if we take our wives and run away?"

"Where?" I said. "To one of the other Nigua villages? These people have better weapons than ours, and their chief is ambitious. I don't think he is going to be satisfied just ruling this place."

I let the implications sink in. Anton had been watching the exchange. "So?" he said.

Hupuka signalled his acceptance, as did Pahta. I told Anton, "They be good."

He ordered the prisoners to be cut loose. The four stood up, rubbing their wrists to relieve the numbness. Anton went to Hupuka, gripped his shoulder. To me, he said, "Tell him to say I am his chief."

I did as he commanded. Hupuka looked puzzled. "War chief or peace chief?"

"With these people," I said, "I think there is just one chief."

Hupuka's brow wrinkled, but when he saw the glower beginning to form on Anton's face, he quickly said, "You are my chief."

I translated, and Anton grunted. We then repeated the same process with Pahta and the two boys. Pablillo looked at Anton as if he had discovered a new father. "I will be yours and serve you," he said after parroting the Spanish.

Anton didn't need a translation. He knew when he had won a new follower.

He sent a man to tell the African women to bring the women and children from the women's house. They came, looking apprehensive at the blood still soaking the ground. Hupuka and Pahta's wives looked from their husbands, to Anton, to me.

"Speak," Anton said, and I told the two women that they could join their husbands and that there would be no more killing. I knew that Pahta's wife was not altogether happy with her husband, but this was a better outcome than she had expected. Carrying their infant son and leading an older girl by the hand, she left the crowd of women and went to stand beside him. He acknowledged her with a glance.

Hupuka's wife had only the one child, the rest having been taken when the spotted sickness came. Their reunion was more affectionate, Hupuka putting an arm around her shoulders and lifting the chin of the two-year-old boy she carried.

Now Anton turned to the African men and spoke at length. They listened with close attention. I knew only some of the words, but it was clear he was talking about the new marital arrangements. When he finished, he wanted to know if they agreed, and the way he put it to them, it would have been a strong man who declined to agree.

First, he told three of the four African women that they were to have Nigua husbands. Then he told the fourth, an older woman with streaks of grey in her hair, to come and stand beside him. The three showed some confusion at the sudden decree, and one of them looked to one of the African men. But Anton was watching, and he said something—I think it was the man's name—and the fellow met the chief's gaze for only a moment before looking down at his feet. Again, I understood only some of the words, but the gist was clear. They were staying. They had to get along with my people. This was not to be a mass rape. I heard the Spanish word for children.

Now Anton was talking to the men. They were taking it in, some of them nodding, others looking over the women with a thoughtful gaze. I heard the words for *two* and *three*. That made sense: there were far more women than there were men. So many of our men had been taken by the Spaniards or by the diseases they had brought, and we'd lost more in the ill-judged fight. There were only Hupuka and Pahta left.

Anton was winding down. I moved closer to Alonso and said, "The men must give to the women."

He had been listening closely to the chief's speech. Now he turned to me, confused. "What?"

I sought for the words. "When Nigua man and woman"—I interlocked my fingers and briefly shook the joined hands—"man gives to woman. Make good begin."

I saw him understand. He cleared his throat and said, "Anton." And when the other man turned to him, Alonso spoke rapidly. I saw Anton's brows come together. When he glanced my way, I saw the loathing was still there. But he was listening. When Alonso finished, Anton asked questions and the young man made answers accompanied by a shrug.

Alonso turned to me. "What kind of gifts?"

I struggled to find the words. I tugged at the cotton of my shirt. "Things for make eat." I formed my hands into a bowl then mimed stirring. I was trying to convey how a prospective bridegroom would give his intended cloth with which to make garments fit for a married woman, that he would carve her spoons and ladles and bowls. The more decorative and finely made the wooden objects were, the better the bride would feel, but that was beyond my reach.

Still, Alonso understood. He spoke rapidly to Anton, pointing at the men's house, where the goods they had carried from the ship were stored. Anton listened and nodded thoughtfully. He looked my way, and though I knew the dislike was never going to go away, I could see that he was reassessing my usefulness.

Anton held up a hand to stop Alonso. To me he said, "Make good begin?" I smiled to emphasize the wisdom and gestured to the women and children. "Make ..." I did not know the word for happy then, so I enlarged my smile by pulling up the corners of my mouth.

Anton made a thinking noise then turned to the Africans, issuing orders. He said Spanish words while counting off on his fingers, itemizing. A half dozen of them went into the men's house. A few moments later, they came out carrying chests and bundles of coarse cloth bound with rope. These they set down on the ground between them and the women.

Anton gave more orders. Ropes were cut and crates prised open. The bundles' coarse cloth coverings, like what hung from the tall sticks on the Spanish ship, unfolded to reveal softer materials, brightly coloured, tightly rolled up. In two of the crates were dishes and bowls of grey metal; in another, vessels and cups of what I knew to be silver, ornate and figured. It was wealth beyond imagining for our village. Even when we had been trading up and down the coast, we had not commanded riches like these.

Anton looked a question at me. I grinned and clapped my hands together, then indicated the women and said, "I tell?"

"You tell."

I turned to the women. Some of them, the widows and the ones not yet married, were eyeing the treasures. When I told them they were to be bridal gifts, the mood among them changed. The newly made widows and the mothers whose sons were lying dead by the edge of the stockade were not consoled, of course. But the others began to talk to them, and I heard the words "good for the village" and "we need men, fighting men, for when the Campazes come again."

So it was a mixed reception that the Africans received when Anton picked out one man at a time and told him to take cloth, pewter—I learned the word later—and silver from the stores and choose a bride. The young ones went first, but when Hinbu was selected by a man a few years older than she and accepted the gifts, her mother Manchis took the bolt of soft red cloth from her daughter's grasp, linked an arm in hers, and walked with her.

Anton looked at me again. "Mother," I said.

He understood and told the man—I would later learn his name was Bartolomeo—to take them both. Bartolomeo didn't like the idea at all but acquiesced. I moved my head to catch his attention and said, "Good ..." then mimed mixing and eating. Bartolomeo was partly mollified.

The choosing went on. Anton took two of the mature women for his own household, the selections made for him by Miriam, the woman who was clearly his wife. The older women followed Manchis's example and went with their daughters.

Only Alonso was left out of the process. He looked partially aggrieved, partially relieved. I wished I had the words to tell him not to worry; among our people, women married to older men were expected to take younger lovers. The practice kept the young men and the women content, although an old man might make a fuss if his wife's liaison was too flagrant and people made jokes about it. But normally, it was in everybody's interest to let the river run smooth even if there were rocks underneath, as the saying went.

My sense of it was that, under the circumstances, most people were mostly happy about the arrangements, which is about the most you could hope for. Before the Africans came, we had not been a happy village, hiding in the forest and hoping that our recent descent into poverty might be enough to keep the Campazes from coming north and finishing what disease and the Spaniards had started.

When the marrying was done, Anton allowed no time for dalliance. There were the dead to be disposed of, and the stockade needed seeing to. He divided up his men into work gangs and assigned the two Nigua men and the boys to the crew working on the village's defences. I thought that was wise of him, since it left his own people to deal with the corpses; this they did by loading them onto the half-sized balsa raft and taking them downstream to the old town, where they pulled down huts to make a pyre and burned the remains of Pidi and Manga and the others to ashes. It was not our way of doing it, but I would tell the survivors later that their spirits were not wandering lost.

Anton spoke to me. "Tell the women to make food. We will work half a day, and then the men and women can get to know each other. I understood him and passed the order along. The women went to their huts and got out the materials for making cornbread and pottages. Fires were lit in the common pits, and soon the village did not look much changed from the way things had been.

Meanwhile, Alonso was told to go down to the seashore and see if there was anything more to be salvaged. He listened to Anton's instructions then beckoned me to come with him. I delayed only long enough to go to my quarters and bring back some of yesterday's bread. We set off along the trail beside the stream, chewing as we went. Before we reached the old town, the raft with its sad cargo passed us.

The ship had been battered to pieces, and the rising tide had carried some of its wreckage over the reef and onto the beach. Not much of the cargo had come ashore, but we found some more cloth that would be usable once it was dried out, and a keg—I had learned the word—of some kind of oil used in cooking. A chair the like of which I had never seen—it had armrests and a back ornately carved into curved shapes—was resting on the tide line.

Alonso stood it upright then sat in it, striking a pose with a fist to rest his chin on. "King Alonso," he said, laughing. He looked very young at that moment.

The word was new, but I understood it. "No," I said. "It is for Anton. To make him . . ." Again I used my fingers to draw up the corners of my mouth.

The merriment in Alonso's face drained away. "Happy," he said. "We need to make Anton happy."

I repeated the word. I was not sure that Anton was capable of happiness, but I was hopeful that he could be mollified and that I would be able to deal with him once I could speak his language. He was now our chief. I was already confident that he would be a better chief than Pidi.

Alonso got up from the chair and picked up a length of wood from the tide line, using it to poke around the debris. The way his shoulders slumped reminded me for a moment of Pablillo. But Pablillo was an adolescent, suspended between childhood and manhood—and only for as long as it took him to mature into an adult, if he lived that long. Alonso was already a grown man, yet he gave the impression of being neither one thing nor another: not a Spaniard, not an African.

He was proving himself a good teacher. Under his tutelage, my vocabulary had already more than doubled. And he was a window on the wider world against which we Nigua had so far only brushed, although those slight touches had been enough to destroy our way of life. But, though I liked him, I did not think it wise to lean too much upon him. One who stands between two worlds does not enjoy the soundest footing.

Anton was solid rock. The trouble was, he despised me for my difference. Pidi had always been uncomfortable in my presence, yet he came to rely on my counsel. Now Pidi was gone, and Anton was in his place. Our old life was all done and finished, and the important thing was to deal with the situation as it stood. That meant making Anton happy.

I followed after Alonso, looking for anything useful the tide might have brought in. He was an engaging young man, if a little sad. I would be glad to learn from him. But I did not think he would last.

Still, as I went up the beach, treading in his footsteps, I wondered why the spirit eagle had shown me Alonso and not Anton. I decided to reserve judgment. What I needed to do now was learn more Spanish and study the newcomers' ways.

"How say that?" I said, pointing. Over the next few minutes, he taught me the words for beach, sea, palm tree, sky, and wind. And when we retraced our steps along the beach, he taught me the word for chair.

We carried our finds through the trees and along the stream to where the balsa had been dragged ashore. One of the Africans was washing it clean of blood. Through the gates of the old town we could see the others busily tearing down huts and assembling the wood into a pyre. The bodies of Pidi and the others were piled up just within the gates.

I was glad I had been able to guide their spirits to the path leading to the upper world. We Nigua would need all the good luck we could get in the new world we were entering.

"Anton wants me to teach you numbers," Alonso said. It had been at least two hands of days since the Africans had come, probably more, but I had been concentrating on the here and now.

"Why?" I said. His look told me that was a question that didn't need an answer. "All right, teach me numbers."

What followed was a revelation. My people had numbers for one to ten; after that, it was hands and two-hands. I had heard that the Quechua speakers had a more complicated system of counting, because they dealt in huge volumes of produce and great numbers of people and livestock. Apparently, they could do complex calculations of really large numbers using a system of strings tied in knots, though how that worked was a closely guarded secret among the empire's officials.

But what Alonso showed me, once I had mastered the basics of *uno, dos, tres,* took me far beyond anything I had ever imagined. Using a stick of charcoal on a smoothed square of balsa wood, he showed me how to add and subtract figures that I could previously have expressed only as multiple two-hands of multiple two-hands. Being able to do calculations on the board instead of on my fingers made me feel as if I had found new muscles in my mind, abilities I had never suspected were mine. Before the day was done, I was adding columns of numbers that went up into the tens of thousands.

"How high do they go?" I asked Alonso.

"There is no end," he said. "However large a number you can think of, it's always possible to add one to it. Or to double it. Or treble it."

"Treble it?" I said, and now he showed me how to multiply. My head swam.

"You'll have to learn the multiplication tables," he said. "I'll copy them out for you, and you can study them."

By the end of the day, my new mental muscles were tired, but I was immersed in a dazed happiness. It was how I had felt when Pallu first showed me the path down into the lower world and introduced me to the wonders there.

I was eager to begin again in the morning, but after a breakfast of cornbread and papaya, Alonso came back from the men's house—which was now where Anton and his wives lived—to tell me the chief wanted me. "Bring the board and charcoal," he said.

The short walk from the spirit house to what Alonso was now calling the *presidio* took me through a buzz of activity. These newcomers were much different from the Nigua men, who spent most of their days drinking beer in the men's house, occasionally going into the forest on hunting forays or being coerced by Pidi into doing some repair and maintenance work on the stockade. It had now been eleven days since the massacre, and the Africans had dug a deep ditch outside the stockade, strengthened the gate, and repaired the section through which Pidi had led the attack.

Anton had sent gangs of men to the garden plots that the women had cleared in the forest after we abandoned the old town. They had cut trees and dug up stumps—metal tools made a great difference—to expand the arable land. But the larger plots would grow far more produce than our small village could eat. When I asked Alonso what was behind the activity, he said only, "Anton has ordered it. He has something in mind."

"Can you ask him what it is?"

He gave a short laugh that contained no humour. "You don't ask Anton why. You wait until he's ready to tell you."

The unspoken 'something' in the chief's mind had also led to the building of a what Alonso called a Catalan forge. One of the Africans, Juanito, had skills as an iron worker—a *forjador,* Alonso said—and he now spent his days hammering and shaping hot metal, with Pablillo pumping a bellows made from sticks and a tapir's hide. A pile of spearheads had accumulated, and now they were being fitted to hardwood shafts by one of the Africans. Meanwhile, the smith had moved on to making long, narrow arrowheads with needle-sharp points. He had also made a heap of daggers. When I used the new word *iron* to refer to them, Alonso corrected me.

"Not iron. Steel. Better than iron."

The new weapons, like the extended garden plots, were more than we had men for. Obviously, they were elements of a plan that Anton was keeping to himself, but I got an intimation of his aims when I went up into the presidio and found the chief looking at something spread out on the table he had had built. His high-backed armchair stood to one side. I noticed that someone had sewn him a seat cushion made of cloth salvaged from the wreck.

"Look at this," he said to me when I approached. I did not bother with the courtesy gestures. The world had changed, and I had changed with it.

At first, I did not know what I was looking at: a sheet of something like cloth, except it was rigid and impossibly smooth when I reached out and touched it.

"Paper," Alonso said quietly beside me. I repeated the word to myself.

It was marked with lines and symbols that said nothing to me. I was studying it, trying to make sense of it, when Alonso pointed and said, "This is the sea. This is the river named for emeralds, and here is the old town. We are here. It is called a map."

I stared at the paper a moment longer and suddenly it all fell into place. It was a simplified rendering of the world—or at least our part of it—as it might be perceived by a bird that flew impossibly high. Another brilliant idea. No wonder the Spaniards had been able to come from lands across the sea and overthrow the Quechua speakers' empire. It wasn't just their weapons and metal armour. Their minds were capable of things we hadn't yet dreamed of.

I touched the smoothness. "Are these the mountains?" I said, and when Alonso said they were, I pointed to another mark—a ring with a roof inside it, on an island in another river—and said, "And this is Guayaquil?"

"You understand," Anton said, elbowing Alonso out of the way. "Good." I noticed that he did not stand too close to me as he indicated the unmarked space between our village and the uplands. "Now, when the old town died, where did the rest of the Nigua go?"

At that point, Anton's plan became clear. More weapons, more food from the gardens: more people, especially more men to use the weapons. He wanted an army.

The thought that I might mislead him barely occurred to me before I dismissed it. This was the world I must adapt to: Anton's world. And it could be a better world for my people. Anton was harsh, cruel. He wanted to be chief, but a chief needs a people.

We were not to be mere beasts of burden, as the Spaniards had seen us. Nor would we be suppliers of food and gold, the role the Quechua speakers had sent their soldiers to force upon us. Nor were we trophies for the Campazes to kill and collect, so they could sing songs around their fires, celebrating the ferocity of their warriors.

So when he asked me where the rest of us went, I pointed to the map and said, "Here, here, here, and there."

Anton took up a stick of charcoal and made marks where I pointed. One of the villages was on the big river. The other three were in the blank areas. "Are there streams beside these two?" he asked.

"Yes." I gestured for him to give me the charcoal. I carefully drew the watercourses as I imagined my spirit eagle might see them. The action gave me a peculiar sense of power. A shiver went up my spine.

Anton pointed to the village by the river. "How many?" he said. "How many men, and how many women?"

And that was why he had told Alonso to teach me numbers. I approved. I made calculations in my head and pointed to the place by the river. "Maybe twelve men can fight. More women—men get taken by the Spaniards." Two of the *palenques* were smaller, with maybe eight, nine men each, I told him. Then I pointed to Chiliandulі's enclave. "Big nose clan," I said. "Twenty men."

He digested the information. "Chiefs?" he said. "Good"—he tapped his head—"thinkers?" He brandished a fist. "Fighters?"

Again, I paused to consider. Unbeeruka, who was chief in the village by the river, was an intelligent man but no warrior. Mallu and Kepepahta, the other two headmen, were men of no great mental strength. Their only strategy in war was the ambush, and even then, only if they had twice the number of men as the enemy. Chiliandulі, however, had been the son of the war chief when we all lived in the old town, and he probably would have been the people's choice to continue in his father's place. But the old chief had died after we split up into small *palenques*.

I managed to convey this to Anton and learned a new word. He wrote the numbers next to the marks I had made. Then he was quiet for a while, fitting the new information into his plans. After a while he grunted and nodded. "Your Spanish is getting better," he said.

"Alonso is a good teacher."

Anton made another wordless sound that could have meant anything. "That is all. Go and learn some more words."

He turned his attention back to the map, leaning over the table and pulling at his lower lip with thumb and forefinger.

Alonso and I passed the mornings in language lessons. As Anton had said, I was getting better at Spanish. At the same time, Alonso was learning some Nigua and could now form simple phrases by attaching prefixes and suffixes to verbs. (That was a thought I could not easily have expressed before our lessons started.) My language did not have terms for nouns, verbs, articles, and so on, but Alonso told me that in Spain there were men called grammarians who spent their lives studying and thinking about nothing but words. I was impressed. I had long known that the Spaniards were a wealthy people, but to be able to support men who neither farmed nor hunted nor made useful objects argued for more wealth than I could calculate even with their numbers.

Our lessons were interrupted when I noticed that Paa, one of the women now married to Juanito, the ironsmith, had come to the spirit house. She stood at the foot of the ladder and kept her eyes on the ground, as was proper, but she was clearly agitated. I came to the doorway and asked what was wrong.

She told me that Pema, her youngest son, was ill. He had a pain in his belly, and when she'd fed him his morning gruel, he had promptly vomited it up. I said I would come and attend to him then turned to Alonso, who had been watching the exchange closely, straining to make out the sense of what we were saying.

"A child is ill," I said. "I must go and see him."

He made that gesture that I now knew was part of the Spaniards' religion, touching his head and stomach and both sides of his chest. I supposed it served to protect him from the evil that had been sent to harm Pema.

I went to the wicker basket where I kept my materials, took out some pouches of herbs, and selected the spirit antidotes that I thought were most likely to be useful. I put them in my healer's satchel and said to

Alonso, "I will need to bring the child back here for healing. Once it is dark, I will lay him down where you have been sleeping."

"Why wait for darkness?" he said.

It was an odd question. These people knew so much about so many things, but in some fields of knowledge they were like little children. "Because I will not be able to see into him until it is dark."

He looked confused, but I had no time to explain elementary healing. I turned to go down the ladder, and he said he would accompany me. I hesitated only a moment before agreeing. I would not have any use for Alonso while I was preparing Pema for the removal of whatever evil had got into him, but it would do no harm to show the young man what I could do.

We went through the alleyways that led to Paa's house. Juanito was not there, which was a relief. The Africans did not spend their idle time in the men's house but often stayed in one of their wives' huts during the rainy part of the day, working on whatever chores they had been assigned. But Juanito spent his days at the forge.

The child was lying on a pallet at the rear of the hut. Paa was waiting at the door and stepped aside to let me enter. She was flustered when Alonso followed me in without ceremony, but I told her, "We have to get used to doing things differently now," and she was glad to ignore the impropriety and concentrate on her son.

I squatted next to the little boy and studied him. He was lying naked on his back, his eyes gazing up into the reeds and rafters. I saw the pulse beating in his neck faster than it should, and his breathing was also rapid—both signs that he was inwardly struggling against an invader, as I had suspected.

I put my hand on his abdomen and pressed gently. He cried out and looked at me. I told him not to be afraid. I would find the spirit dart that had entered him and would remove it. He smiled briefly then turned to stare upwards again.

I asked Paa to bring me some hot water. She poured water from a gourd into a clay cup and went out to get hot pebbles from the cooking fire. By the time she brought me the cup, the water was boiling. I set it on the ground, took some dried river-grass leaves from a pouch in my bag, and measured out the right quantity for a child Pema's size. I could hear Pallu's voice coming out of my memory, instructing me in the correct procedure.

I used a pair of small sticks to lift out the hot stones, then blew on the liquid to cool it. The thought crossed my mind that some of my spirit might be infused into the potion; I resolved to meditate about the possible effects of that sometime when my days were not quite so busy. When a dip of my finger told me the liquid had cooled enough, I lifted Pema's head and held the cup to his lips. He drank it down in several gulps—a good sign—and held it down: an even better indicator of eventual success.

I then told Alonso and Paa to turn away. I reached into my bag and took out the several objects I had selected in the spirit house. I placed them on the child's belly and studied them while they rose and fell with his breathing, which I noticed was becoming slower. After a long moment, one of them, a red pebble I had collected from the stream bed years before, spoke to me in the way such objects do—that is to say, it became more *present* than the others were.

That was the result I had expected. I scooped the objects up and returned them to my bag. Rising to my feet, I told the child's mother that he would sleep away the afternoon. She was to bring him to the spirit house just before sunset. He was to have nothing to eat or drink.

She was worried and said the kinds of things mothers say at these times. I did not blame her. She had lost two children to the spotted sickness, against which my powers—and even Pallu's—had not prevailed. But I assured her that this was a different matter and that I believed I could suck the evil out of him.

Alonso was listening to our conversation, but we were speaking too fast for him. "What is wrong with the child?" he asked me as we went back to the spirit house.

Normally, I would not discuss such matters with a layman, and I was about to fob him off with the usual patter. But into my mind came the memory of the moment when I had looked down from the spirit eagle's eyes and met Alonso's gaze. It was not just a matter of new days and new ways; I knew that it was appropriate to discuss the issue with this young man, out of all the other newcomers. I did not question whence came that knowledge. It was in me, and I accepted it.

I told him that Pema's belly had been pierced by a spirit dart. Mixing Spanish with sign language and a few Nigua words, I managed to convey the information that the invader had probably come from his father's spirit while it was wandering lost after the killings and before I could lead it and the others onto the right path. "Ghosts do not mean to do evil," I said, "but they cannot help it. In their sadness, they reach out to the living, especially their loved ones, but their touch is poisonous."

Spaniards, it appeared, knew at least something about ghosts, because Alonso took in this information and showed that he understood. "What will you do?" he said.

I did not try to give him the full explanation. "I will look for the spirit dart, find it, and suck it out of him. I will take away its power and spit it out."

By now we were back at the spirit house. We climbed in, and I put away my materials and took out the dried herbs I would need to prepare for the operation. I poured water into my shaman's cup, powdered the medicine between my fingers, and mixed it in, stirring in the proper direction while softly chanting the appropriate song.

Then I turned to Alonso, who was sitting in his accustomed place on a stool. "I must take this medicine and then"—I did not have the Spanish word for *meditate*—"breathe and think until it is time to heal the child. You must not talk to me or touch me."

"I wanted to talk about healing," he said. "Our doctors have discovered that the body contains four humours: red, yellow, black, and green—"

The drug I had taken was beginning to have its effects. Alonso was now limned in a bright light, something I would need to think about later. I positioned myself on my meditation mat and said, "I cannot stay. You may stay, but please do not disturb me. There are dangers."

He looked troubled, but then the Old Deceivers began trying to change my perception of his features. I smiled at their temerity, closed my eyes, and concentrated on my breathing. They became black dust blowing on the wind of my power. I went down into the lower world and sought out my helpers, especially the red bird that was represented by the pebble.

When I returned, the sun was nearing the horizon. Alonso was still sitting on his stool, regarding me with an odd expression, as if I had an extra leg he had never noticed before. But he already knew I was not like others: at his request, I had shown him how I was made, the tiny stump of my penis with nothing behind it but grooved skin.

I blinked and reached for the gourd of corn beer and rinsed from my mouth the taste of the lower world. As my spirit came fully back into my body, I glanced around and saw that the precise arrangements of my materials were not as I had left them. Alonso had been snooping.

I was angered for a moment, but I remembered how, as a curious adolescent, I had done the same with Pallu's things. The old shaman might have beaten me, but instead he told me that I should leave alone that which I did not yet understand. I resolved to have a similar talk with my African.

But now Paa was arriving with Pema, the little boy limp in her arms. Juanito had come, too, which surprised me, and one of his other wives. I went down the ladder, took the boy from her, and turned to climb back up.

Juanito said, "What are you going to do with him?"

I did not speak until I had reached the top. Then I said, "Heal him."

"I will not let you do the Devil's work," he said, putting his foot on the first rung of the ladder.

I gave the child to Alonso, with a nod towards the healing pallet. I turned towards the man and put some power into my voice as Pallu had taught me. "You cannot come in."

Juanito must have developed some affection for the boy, because his eyes widened and his nostrils flared. But before he could speak, I said, "You may wait and watch from there. Not inside."

Alonso came to stand beside me. "It is not the Devil's work," he said. "It is herbs and potions. But if you are worried, I will watch for you."

Paa made a concerned sound and touched Juanito's arm. Between Alonso's assurance and his new wife's plea, the ironsmith's truculence dissolved. "I will watch from here," he said.

I brought out the thin slab of stone and kindled a small fire on it, then went to my materials and selected the red pebble and a little flake of white quartz that contained a tiny fleck of gold. With my back turned to the others, I placed the quartz between my back teeth and my cheek and put the red pebble under my tongue. Then I went and knelt beside the patient.

His breathing was easier, but his abdomen was still hard and hot. The spirit dart was where I had felt it before. I turned to the fire and said to Alonso. "Do not speak until I have finished. I must think of nothing but what I do."

He nodded, and I shook a handful of herbs onto the fire, breathing in the smoke. I held it deep inside me, where it mingled with my breath and enlarged me. I blew out the thin residue then took another fullness of the smoke, and finally a third.

By now I was immense, far stronger than any spirit dart a ghost might send into a child. I extinguished the fire to restore complete darkness. I knelt beside Pema and stared at his belly without blinking, my chest and abdomen slowly filling and emptying as I stoked my power. As I watched, the child's skin began to glow from within. The glow brightened, and the body became translucent. I continued to breathe and to concentrate until the flesh became as transparent as stream water. I saw a red flash: motion and colour that resolved itself into the shape of a scarlet worm.

I made a noise of satisfaction deep in my chest then fixed the worm in place with my unblinking gaze. It struggled, but my power was far more than the worm's already fading strength. When it lay still, I tipped myself over onto hands and knees, pausing only long enough to reposition the pebble and quartz on my tongue. Then I applied my open mouth to the child's belly, just over the spot where the worm lay.

I called upon the spirit in the red pebble to make ready, then I sucked hard against the child's skin. I felt his flesh enter my mouth and touch the pebble, which instantly became a red bird, fluttering against my front teeth. The worm was drawn up from the child's body. It struggled briefly, but the red bird opened its beak and swallowed it. The white spirit bird in the back of my mouth, which would have prevented the worm from entering my own body if it had somehow got past the red, relaxed and became a flake of quartz again. I pushed it back between my teeth and cheek.

I turned to Juanito and Paa and spat the red pebble into my hand. "There it is," I said. "It cannot harm him now."

She put a hand to her mouth as women do when they are beset by strong emotion. Juanito looked from the thing in my hand, to the darkness where the child lay, and then to his wife. She put a hand on his arm and said in Spanish, "Good. Make good."

I carried the boy out to Juanito and said to Paa, "Rub his belly gently with warm grease. The spirit blocked his bowels, and he will need to empty them. The rubbing will help."

I did not say the river-grass tea he had drunk earlier would also help move his bowels. It was not something they needed to know.

Alonso was watching me from his stool. "May I see?" he said, pointing to the stone in my hand.

"For you, it is only a stone," I said. "And in this world, it is. But in the other world, it isn't. Everything has spirit in it. It takes study and practice to learn how to see it."

The look he gave me was somewhere between sceptical and accepting. I put the pebble and the quartz back where they belonged. "I am tired now and must sleep."

He said he would go and eat with one of the families. I suspected he would see how Pema was. That was all right with me. It would show him that I was to be trusted.

As he went out the door, I said, "If you want to learn healing, I can teach you."

"When things are quiet," he said.

"Yes, when they are quiet."

Seven

Alonso Illescas

"How much of their jabber have you learned?" Anton asks.

"Some," Alonso says. "Expectation has learned far more Spanish, if you need a translator."

"What I need is someone I can trust." The big man's face contorts in a grimace of disgust. "I don't trust that thing."

"You think you can trust me?"

Anton smiles. "If I keep you close enough. Now, can you understand enough of what they say to work with one of them as a guide?"

"I think so. There are different tribes, and they don't speak each other's dialects, though they all live close by, so they use a lot of sign language. It is not hard to learn."

"Good. Be here at first light."

"Where are we going that we'll need a guide?"

"You'll see. And bring a blanket. The nights are cold."

Alonso leaves the presidio. It is time for the evening meal, and he will eat with Expectation at the spirit house. The women of the village take turns feeding the healer, as they always have; now they make an extra portion for him. It will be a vegetable stew as usual, though there might be some monkey meat stirred in, or a fish wrapped in leaves and roasted in the ashes under the cooking fire.

The food has already been delivered when he gets home. Expectation is waiting for him and begins to serve out portions from the pot into the wooden bowls. They will eat with their fingers because Alonso has not yet whittled spoons for them, although he keeps reminding himself to do so.

"What did he want?" she asks when he is seated, the bowl in his left hand. Before he answers, he says a few words of thanks for the meal and almost crosses himself. The Illescas never broke bread without saying grace, but Alonso is gradually letting Christian habits slip, rather than having to explain them to the shaman and listen to her criticisms.

"We are going somewhere," Alonso says. "Tomorrow."

"I thought as much," she says, pausing to take a mouthful, chew, and swallow. "He has had the canoes brought downstream from where Pidi hid them, and Juanito and Pablillo have been tying up bundles of spears and those long things with axes on the ends."

"Alabardas," Alonso says. Halberds.

She repeats the word then says, "And daggers."

"We're going to war?"

Expectation shrugs. "Or he means to trade them with the other villages. But that does not seem likely."

The answer comes in the morning when Anton leads eight of the Africans, plus Alonso and the Nigua man named Pahta, to where four of the canoes are drawn up on the river bank, loaded with weapons and enough food for several days. Each of the Africans has a matchlock and a bandolier of powder and shot. Anton has his heavy cutlass in a scabbard slung from a strap over his neck and shoulder.

Anton gives Pahta a dagger from the heap in the bottom of the canoe. The man's eyes widen, and he takes the weapon as if it were a holy relic. It is surely the most precious thing he has ever owned, Alonso thinks as he watches Pahta test the point against the end of a thumb. The Nigua speaks a rapid spate of syllables, wrapping both hands around the dagger.

"He thanks you," Alonso tells Anton.

"I got that," says the chief. "Now, can you tell him we want to go upstream to the river then up the river into the mountains?"

Alonso has the words and gestures. Pahta signals that he understands and says, "We are going to fight the Quechua speakers?"

Anton says, "No. We are going to attack the Campazes."

Alonso does not have to translate. Pahta's eyes go wide.

Anton says, "I sent Poquito to find the nearest village. He watched them for a few days. There is a trail that goes up into the mountains. It's not used much, and the savages don't seem to watch it the way they do trails that lead north to us or south to the Spanish lands. Tell him that."

Alonso translates. Pahta says, "I do not know that trail." He thinks for a moment. "The Campazes do not trade with the Quechua speakers, not even before the Spaniards came. And the Quechua speakers gave up trying to conquer them a long time ago. If we could find where that trail begins, we could come down where they are not expecting us."

"Tell him," Anton says, "that Poquito followed the trail to where it meets a road that runs north and south. He made a mark on a tree." The chief sketches four lines in the air, a cross-hatching. "He will be waiting for us back down the trail, near the Campaze village."

"We should bring Hupuka," Pahta says. "He has walked that road, carrying burdens for the Spaniards."

Anton thinks for only a moment then says to Alonso, "Go get him."

The canoes are dugouts, hollowed from lightweight trunks by fire and stone tools, and broad-beamed enough that two can sit abreast on the centre thwarts. No one but Pahta and Hupuka is a practised paddler, but Anton shouts at the Africans to watch the Niguas and copy them. Soon, the four boats are making good headway against the slow current of the stream.

Anton has put Alonso in the front of Pahta's canoe, with himself on the middle thwart. Even with a load of spears and three men aboard, the boat rides lightly on the surface. Alonso kneels on the boat's smooth bottom and does his best to master the art of paddling. After his muscles warm to the exercise, he comes to enjoy the rhythmic motions.

They paddle upstream, the forest closing over them and making the stream the floor of a green tunnel. Occasionally, smaller creeks join theirs. The sun is hidden, and Alonso loses track of time. But Anton is more attuned to their surroundings, or perhaps just to the clock of his stomach. At some point he tells Alonso to tell Pahta to find them somewhere to land.

Soon after, they come to a place where a narrower stream enters theirs, and Pahta steers them into it. Not far up the new watercourse, they find a spot where the vegetation has been stripped away, leaving a shelf of mud. Pahta turns the bow of the canoe towards it and jumps out at precisely the right moment, with both hands on the gunwales, and runs the boat halfway up the bank. Alonso and Anton climb out more carefully and pull the craft the rest of the way out of the water. With varying degrees of skill, the men in the other boats follow them.

Anton squints at a trail that weaves into the undergrowth at the landward end of the mud bank. "Light your matches," he tells the men and uncaps a small pot that has sat near him in the bottom of the canoe. Its contents of smouldering rope-stuff glow as he breathes upon them, and the men come and dip their rope ends into it, blowing on them to fire them up.

When all are armed, Anton has them fan out and face in all directions. Then he calls to one of the Africans, "Take a look. Leave the *arcabuz* with me."

The man hands Anton his matchlock and takes a spear from the canoe before disappearing silently into the forest. They wait, hearing only the constant noise of birds, insects, and animals. After a while, the scout returns. "Nothing, nobody," he says. "Old village, cold fires."

Pahta speaks to Alonso, who turns to Anton. "This is where their chief and the men hid out before they attacked us."

Anton grunts. "All right," he says, "but we take no chances. Half eat while the other half stand watch. Then switch."

They have brought cornbread and dried fruit, and strips of monkey meat that the women smoked on a wooden frame. It has a strong taste and at first is as hard as dried leather, but Alonso finds it gradually yields to chewing. They drink water from the stream.

When the second half of the party has eaten and drunk, Anton stands to address them. He does the trick Alonso has seen him do before, looking around the circle, meeting each man's gaze, and holding it for a moment. "The Spaniards are going to come for us. We do not have enough men. There are more Niguas hiding in places like the one over there"—he gestures with his thumb to the trail—"but if we approach them, they're likely to run and hide somewhere else. They think we're just another bunch of Spaniards."

He waits for the laughter to finish. "But they fear the Campazes more than they fear Spaniards. So we are going to take some Campaze heads."

There was silence now. Anton continued. "Those people who live north of us, on the big river ..." He looks to Alonso.

"The Cayapas," Alonso says.

"They're the ones. They trade with us and with the Niguas still hiding in the forest. They will carry word of what we've done. Then the people we want to attract will ask themselves where they want to be when the Campazes come—with us and our weapons or on their own?"

Alonso translates this for Pahta and Hupuka. Pahta is young, and his eyes shine at the pictures he is seeing in his mind. Hupuka's face is twisted in doubt. Anton sees it and stalks over to where the two Niguas are squatting. He gestures for Hupuka to rise, and the man stands up, fearful but not wanting to show it.

Anton steps close, looks the Nigua in the eye. Then without breaking the contact, he slips the strap that supports the cutlass over his head and drapes it over Hupuka's torso. He takes the man's right hand and places it onto the hilt, covers it with his own hand, and holds it there. "Translate this," he tells Alonso. Still looking into the Nigua's eyes, he says, "With this you will kill Campazes. Later, you will kill Spaniards."

"I don't need to," Alonso says. "He knows enough Spanish." And he sees Hupuka's back and shoulders straighten.

"Kill Spaniards," Hupuka says. "Many Spaniards."

Anton lets go of the man's hand and slaps him on the shoulder. "Many Spaniards," he says. "But first, the Campazes." He turns to the others. "Now, let's get the canoes back in the water. We want to make good time while we can."

They go back to the stream they were following and continue to paddle against its flow through the rest of the day. They find no convenient landing, but they pull in at a bend where the bank is low on one side and cut themselves space to pull the canoes out of the water and make beds of the cleared ferns and bracken. Before they have finished another cold meal, it starts to rain: thick, heavy drops that agglomerate in the high canopy before splattering down onto their heads and shoulders. Anton orders the canoes emptied and overturned, and they curl up under them to sleep.

The rain ends in the night, and they push on. Sometime after the midday meal, the stream divides into two smaller creeks, neither large enough for the canoes. Pahta splashes through the shallow water to the bank, pushes aside a spreading fern, and shows them a trail of beaten earth. He speaks a few Nigua words and mimes what they must do. Anton nods and orders the cargo to be distributed among some of the men while the others pick up the canoes. With the Nigua man leading the way, the portage begins.

Alonso is one of the canoe carriers, with Juanito taking up the other half of the burden. The boat is lightweight, although after a while Alonso's arms and shoulders ache from being set in the same position. All he can see is the path beneath his feet. It is a strange way to travel, and he finds his mind wandering through a series of unconnected thoughts and random images.

He thinks about Expectation and the relationship that is growing between them. They are both odd men out—if he can call the hermaphrodite a man—each existing on the fringe of the community's life, each playing a part that none of the others is equipped to play. The women do not include the healer in their gossip, nor do the Nigua men and boys admit her to their company. When she passes, they do not meet her eyes or greet her. She is not real to them unless one of them is troubled by an illness or a bad dream.

Alonso receives the same guarded looks from the Africans. With each other, the men make jokes, or trade observations on their work or each other's women, but the young man is not included. If he speaks to one of them, any reply he receives is minimally phrased and noncommittal. The African women do not speak to him at all—except for Miriam; although their conversations are brief, she is the only one willing to look at him directly and offer a smile.

He is not one of them, yet he would like to feel embraced in some way. He misses the life he used to have when he was a part—although only a minor part—of the Illescas family. Granted, his role was to do as he was told, and he was not consulted about the business's affairs; still, he had his small spheres of activity and could expect a word of praise if he performed well. Often, he was invited to eat with the junior members of the household, and Don Alvaro treated him, if not as a son, then at least as a nephew.

It is more than two months since the shipwreck. By now, Don Alvaro, up in Panama, would know that something has gone wrong. Ships sailing north from Lima would have been asked to keep a lookout for wreckage along the shore or even for signs of survivors. Any vessel that puts in to the bay at San Mateo for water will see the remains of *La Virgen* washed up on the beach. In time, the news will reach Lima. Will Don Alvaro send a pinnace to investigate? Will he be concerned for his missing almost-member of the family?

The thought brings a moistness to Alonso's eyes. The idea of Don Alvaro's worry raises a tide of sadness in the young man. And then a new thought occurs: *What have I been doing to deserve it?*

In the beginning, he had an amorphous plan—or perhaps it was no more than a vague intention—to find a way to Lima someday and report the fate of the Illescas's ship and cargo. He even envisioned himself leading an expedition back to San Mateo, of rounding up the Africans and loading them back onto a galleon.

But he has done nothing of the sort. He has sat in the healer's hut with the hermaphrodite, drinking beer and teaching Spanish, learning what it was like before the Spaniards and the diseases came. He has explained to Expectation that the illnesses that so devastated her people are less virulent among his; he speculated that the balance of humours must be more precarious among the Nigua and other tribes.

She has heard him out with interest but has countered his speculations with her own practical experiences. The evil spirit darts that poisoned her people must have come from Spanish ghosts. The Spaniards did not have the same spirits as the Nigua, so their darts were difficult for her to see. Because she could not make out the darts or the spirits that cast them, it was impossible for her to identify which beneficent spirit would be able to seize and absorb each malevolent entity. Perhaps the

Spaniards didn't even need to be ghosts to spread evil; perhaps their bad darts were encapsulated in their malice towards the peoples of her land, and the counteracting spirits had been left behind in Spain.

His thoughts have been wandering again, although they take his mind off his aches and stiffness. Behind him, holding up the rear of the canoe, Juanito marches stolidly on, his rock-hard arms and shoulders apparently as unaffected as Expectation's imagined spirit darts. Alonso is sure that her views on illness are illusory. Spain's doctors are the inheritors not only of the wisdom of the ancient world, but of the subtle insights of Moorish and Jewish physicians, who are of such stature that His Most Christian Majesty himself consults them.

And yet the odd little healer of the Niguas is not without her own clear-sightedness. As he was preparing to leave this morning, she touched him on the arm and said, "Anton will be watching you. Be careful."

"He ignores me unless he needs me for something," Alonso said. His life is simpler now. There are the routines of the day, the orders to follow, the long sessions with Expectation, each learning the other's language. He rarely finds himself letting his thoughts wander as they had on the ship, as they used to when he had idle moments in the Illescas house in far-off Seville.

The Nigua's touch on his arm became a grip. "No," she said, "he will be watching to see what you do—if you try to run away. And when he is not watching you, he will have someone else do it."

It occurs to Alonso now that he has never discussed even the thought of escape with Expectation. Yet somehow she has seen that thought, even though it has fallen to the back of his mind. So perhaps she is right. A chill goes through him as he follows the line of reasoning that leads from there: Anton said he wanted Alonso along to translate, but so far Pahta has been able to communicate directly with the chief through gestures and a few words. Alonso's intermediation has not been needed.

So if not to translate, why has he been included? Not to fight, surely. In the expedition, he alone is unarmed. So Expectation is right. Anton has brought him along as a test. The first time Alonso gives any indication that he might try to run, Anton will act. Alonso's mind, with nothing to look at but the prow of the dugout, shows him a memory: the chief standing over the wounded sailor on the beach, and the absence of emotion in the big man's face when he pressed the sword into the Spaniard's open mouth.

He may offer me the appearance of a chance to escape, he realizes. *He may turn his back at a certain moment, leaving the way clear.* But there would be someone watching, someone told to expect Alonso to flee, someone like Juanito, waiting down the trail with a dagger in his strong black hand.

Alonso shivers again. From behind him, Juanito says, "The load is too much for you?"

"No," the young man says. "I am fine."

He fixes his eyes on the worn path in front of him and tries to think of nothing but what he is doing now.

Before the afternoon turns to night—there is no evening here—the trail ends at another stream. They have been climbing as they have carried the canoes, and the new watercourse runs faster than the stream beside the village. Pahta signs that they should keep moving, and they load the boats, put them back in the water, and start paddling. Just before the sudden nightfall, they come to a place where the bank has been cleared.

Here they make a fire in a circle of stones ringed with cut logs that have all seen much use. They sit around it, chewing their rations. The Africans shift their shoulders to loosen stiffening muscles, making jokes and passing comments about their paddling skills in ways that make it clear they all have histories with one another. Pahta and Hupuka sit together, and occasionally Hupuka understands enough of what is being said to smile and nod. Anton says little, maintaining his reserve but occasionally offering a well-chosen remark or judgment that reinforces his rank as leader. He doles out praise or encouragement in judicious amounts, Alonso notices; not one word is idle, and he never becomes just one of the group.

Neither does Alonso. No one teases him or comments on his boat handling. When someone says 'we' or 'us', he knows he is not included. No one gives him more than a passing glance, and when they roll themselves up in blankets and cloaks to sleep, no one wishes him a good night. He lies on his side, watching the fire's embers slowly dim, doing his best to ignore the cacophony of night sounds from the forest.

He wonders if he will ever find his way back to the life he used to live. Somewhere along today's journey, he realizes that he has effectively given up the idea of escape. Even if he did run away, Anton would only send Poquito and Pahta after him, and they would surely catch him; he does not know how to disguise his trail. He would get lost in the forest, tumble over a cliff, or be eaten by whatever it is that makes the coughing, snarling noise he has heard some nights while lying awake in the healer's hut back in the village.

I must make myself a place among them, he thinks. In the early days of the new order, he found ways to be useful. Since they have settled down into a routine, his only role is to teach Spanish to the healer. She has learned quickly and is now able to carry on conversations without much resorting to sign language. And he has learned some Nigua, adding prefixes and suffixes to verbs to make simple phrases.

But so has everyone else. The Africans' wives are picking up Spanish, as are the Nigua men married to the three African women. He has noticed how the Africans have begun to mix some Nigua words into their talk, even with each other. *What happens when they can all talk together?* Alonso asks himself. He remembers Miriam telling Anton that he knows the ways of the Spaniards, how they think, what they might do. He wonders if that is so—or was she just being kind, trying to save him?

He thinks about what he knows. Yes, he knows the essentials of how a business is run, knows ledgers and accounts and tallying goods in a warehouse. He knows how to eat at a table without disgracing himself, how to "make a leg" upon introduction to a person of standing. He can even dance a little, though he was hardly ever invited.

And he knows how to look after pigs.

A good enough list of accomplishments to make him suitable for a household of merchants with liberal views, but not much recommendation to the leader of a band of escaped slaves who is trying to build himself... what? What is Anton's goal? To be chief of a band of reivers hiding in a forest? To steal a Spanish ship and sail it back to Africa? To die taking revenge on those who misused him?

He discounts the second and third possibilities, one for being arrant folly, the other for being pointless: Anton is neither a fool nor suicidal. And he does not merely react to events as he finds them. He creates a plan and carries it out.

"We need more men we can count on," he told this little band of raiders. And when Alonso asked what for, Anton said, "You'll see." Alonso thinks back to the rising on Santo Domingo. Don Alvaro and the other men of substance saw it as only a mindless acting-out of the maroons against their slavery, believed that they thought no farther than striking off their chains and indulging themselves in the pleasures of revenge and brigandage for as long as they could evade recapture.

And there was evidence for this view, such as the several bands of escapees who got drunk on rum and fired the houses of their owners. When the soldiers came, most of the slaves were easily disarmed and clapped back into fetters; those who rushed at the Spaniards in a blood frenzy were cut down.

But Anton was not one of those. He and the dozens who followed him stole horses and supplies and made their way into the hills, raiding only as necessary to arm and provision themselves further. They had discipline, and they were in the process of building themselves a redoubt in a mountainous area when a hard-galloping troop of dragoons cornered them in a defile and held them there with matchlock fire until the mules could drag up cannon and end the rebellion with the threat of slaughter, combined with a promise of no reprisals.

Don Alvaro and the sugar men may have been wrong, Alonso is thinking. And Expectation may well be right. If this raid yields the chief admiration among the other Nigua villages, Anton might become the leader of two hundred souls. The Cayapas, who came south to trade but otherwise kept their distance, might accept closer ties, and that would double Anton's strength. Francisco Pizarro had only a fraction as many under his command when he went up against all the forces of Atahualpa, the king of the Quechua speakers, whose armies numbered in the tens of thousands.

Alonso has never seen Pizarro, who died in the civil strife that followed the conquest. But he thinks now that if he were to stand the conquistador side by side with Anton, the only real difference between them would be colour—and the fact that Pizarro's goal was to gain great wealth and retire with it to live the life of a grandee in Spain. Anton can never do that. But he can be a king in the forest of Esmeraldas.

What do kings need? Alonso asks himself, and answers, *not just men who are useful, but men they can trust.* Poquito is one Anton trusts, and Juanito. They have found places for themselves in the hierarchy Anton is building, performing their necessary functions and making no attempts to reach beyond their stations. Miriam is also trusted; of all of them, she is probably the only one to whom Anton opens his mind.

But will Anton ever trust Alonso enough to take him into his confidence? Or will it always be, *You'll see*? Still, perhaps it is not necessary for the chief to trust the young man completely, just to trust him enough: enough to keep him alive. And now Alonso realizes that he has worked his way down to the reason he is on this expedition: not just to see if he will run if the opportunity presents itself, but to see if he will commit himself to the kingdom of Anton—a commitment complete and irrevocable.

The fire's embers are a dull orange now. Alonso pulls the edge of his blanket up over his eyes. Although the ground is hard, the day has been long and arduous. In moments he is asleep.

Two days later, after more portages and a long paddle along the river named for emeralds, they come to a waterfall. Pahta says they can take the boats no farther. They pull them onto the bank, drag them deep into the trees, hide them in the deep undergrowth. Then Anton orders the distribution of the weapons and food, leaving Pahta to carry nothing but his prized dagger. He orders the Nigua to lead the way with Hupuka, now the proud owner of an iron-tipped spear, to accompany him.

Pahta puts them on a well-worn path that angles towards the cliff, over which the river tumbles, but leads away from the waterfall. They come to a place where the rock leans inward as it rises and splits into a deep fissure that becomes a blind canyon. Into the sides of the ravine, someone long ago cut steps barely wide enough for a man to climb. Up the men go, Alonso in the middle of the file, his blanket rolled and tied over his back, a double sack of bread and dried meat hanging from his neck.

It is a long climb, but when they emerge onto the top of the escarpment, it is as if they have passed from one land to another. The forest here is thinner, the broad-leafed trees fewer and the conifers more plentiful. And the air is different: cooler and somehow less nourishing. Alonso has heard of the phenomenon, but this is his first encounter. After the strain of the ascent, he has to bend over, hands on knees, to restore his equilibrium. Short bars of coloured light dance behind his eyelids and fade only slightly when he opens his eyes.

Anton orders a rest, and they sprawl for a while on the ground, which is covered here by accumulations of dried pine needles rather than the moist black earth down in the coastal lands. When they are recovered, they eat and drink then take up their loads to follow Pahta and Hupuka along the path. Through the rest of the afternoon, the land climbs steadily, ridge leading to ridge, with only an occasional descent into a valley and a harder climb back to the heights. At the end of the day, they come to a bridge of ropes and planks strung across a deep gorge.

"We will cross in the morning," Anton says. Because a fire could be seen from far off, it will be a cold camp. Indeed, as the last of the light swiftly climbs the higher ground to the east, plunging the men into darkness, Alonso sees his own breath fogging the air before him.

In the morning, they cross the bridge one at a time. Alonso, shivering from more than just the chill air, takes his turn after the two Niguas and several of the Africans have made the crossing. The short, thick planks of the bridge's footing are solid enough, but everything else is in motion: the whole construction bounces up and down at the same time as it sways with each shift of his weight from one foot to the other. Worse, a wind stirs up when he is one-third the way across, and the bridge actually tilts slightly to the lee side.

He freezes, suspended between the two sides of the gorge, and now he makes the mistake of looking down. The drop beneath him is awe-inspiring, the river below is a grey-green ribbon. The realization of where he is, with nothing beneath him but empty air, strikes him like a shower of cold water. His skin seeks to crawl up his back, and his shoulders rise almost to his ears. His hands grip the thick ropes so tightly that the muscles in his forearms cramp.

"Keep moving!" Anton shouts from the far side. He was one of the first across. When Alonso does not budge, the chief calls him by name and says, "Look up! Look at me!"

He has to repeat himself until finally the young man raises his eyes. "Left foot forward! Don't think about it, just do it! Keep looking at me!"

Alonso takes a step. The bridge sways, but when Anton shouts again, Alonso does not look anywhere but at the face of the big man at the end of the span. He sees no encouragement there, only the expectation that he will do as he is told. Somehow, it is a settling thought. The world has become a terrifying place, yet there is order to it, and it consists of letting Anton's will be his motivating force. He has but to surrender to the newly revealed reality.

"Right foot forward!"

Alonso abdicates all responsibility for himself, for his predicament. He keeps his gaze fixed on the leader, lifts his foot, and puts it down. The order to move comes once more, and he lifts his left foot and brings it down onto the hard wood. The wind gusts again, but he ignores it. The wind is no match for Anton's will. Step by step, Alonso crosses the bridge until it is his last pace, and Anton puts a hand around the back of the young man's neck and pulls him, meal bags and all, off the end of the bridge.

Alonso stumbles forward, an involuntary yelp coming up and out of him. He is breathing heavily, struggling to fill his lungs with life. Yet never has he felt so free, so delivered, as he does at this moment. He straightens and says to Anton, "Thank you."

The chief shows no reaction. Anton is already shouting at the next man to get himself across the bridge. Alonso moves a little way along the path beyond the gorge and sits down. The lightness of spirit that came with the surrender still fills him. The world seems a brighter place.

The feeling stays with him throughout the day as they make their way higher into the mountains. But their progress is slower now. The thinness of the air affects different members of the party to different degrees, but all are feeling tired, and they have to stop frequently to sit and rest. Finally, in the mid-afternoon, they come to the end of a ridge that runs north and south and find another set of steps cut into the rock. But these steps lead downwards and bring them to a trail that snakes into a valley whose sides are thick with conifers.

By the time they reach the narrow river that cuts through the valley floor, they have come down far enough to breathe more easily. Anton consults with Pahta, bringing Alonso in to translate. The Nigua tells them that if they press on, they can reach the road that runs south from Quito before nightfall.

Anton tells them that they will trot a hundred steps then walk a hundred more, alternating the two paces. "When I led soldiers in my homeland, we could trot and walk more than twelve leagues a day," he says. "We surprised our enemies by arriving when we were unexpected."

They go in single file, Alonso clopping along in his Spanish shoes while the others' feet strike the dust of the well-travelled trail with almost silent impacts. His burdens make him clumsy, swinging with each step until he clutches them to his chest. But it feels good to feel strong again after the strange weakness of the heights. And the sense of having been delivered into a new life continues to lift him up.

He does not think now. He gazes at the back of the man in front of him and lets his feet find their way. Anton counts out the steps in a guttural chant, replacing each tenth number with a "huh!" The other men catch the rhythm, voicing the single syllable along with their leader. Alonso joins them in the echoing. It is the first time that he can remember feeling entirely absorbed into a group, unnoticed—not standing off to one side, at an angle to the rest.

The trot-and-march technique is effective. Before Alonso realizes how much time has passed, the valley bottom is darkening while the heights above are still brightly lit. In the midst of one of their hundred-pace walks, Pahta, out in front with Hupuka, holds up a hand. Anton stops counting and raises his own hand to halt the file. Pahta gestures towards the wide-spaced conifers that fill the valley bottom, then weaves his way between the trees. The others follow.

Deep into the sparsely spaced pines, Anton calls Alonso, and between the two of them, they work out the meaning of Pahta and Hupuka's words and gestures. The land has begun to rise again. If they turn due east now and climb, they will come out onto the old Inca road at a spot between two villages. There will be places where they can hole up for the night.

There is no trail, but there is no undergrowth beneath the widely spaced trees. The thick pad of needles covering the ground gives easy footing, and they ascend steadily, using spear shafts and *arcabuzes* as staffs when the way becomes steeper. But then the slope begins to level off, and in a little while, as the last light is showing on the mountain peaks to the east, they come out of the trees and find themselves at the foot of a gentle rise that flattens at its top. It continues to north and south and has the look of something man-made.

Hupuka points with his chin. "Road there."

Anton looks to left and right. "Travellers?"

Hupuka tries to frame his answer in Spanish then gives up and says several words in Nigua. Alonso translates. "People don't travel at night. Some Spaniards who didn't get rich have turned to banditry."

"Maybe we should push on," Anton says. "I wouldn't mind meeting some Spaniards."

Alonso says, "Do you want them to know we are operating in their territory?"

After a moment, Anton nods. "No, not yet." He turns to the others. "Wait. I will go see." He takes a spear from the bundle that one of the Africans carries then gestures to Alonso to follow, and together they climb the slope and reach the level ground on top. Alonso does not know what to expect from a road built by the Quechua speakers but finds it is not much different than a mountain track in Spain: a wide strip of dust and hard-packed earth.

Anton is looking south. No more than a mile away there is a cluster of lights. "Village," the chief says.

Alonso nods. "Yes." Then he realizes that Anton is watching him. The chief is holding the spear point-down. He could raise it and throw it in two heartbeats. A shock goes through the younger man; his hands tremble. *He's waiting to see if I run. It's another test.* Alonso rubs his hands together as if to warm them against the sudden chill that comes with the onset of darkness up here. He does not have to suppress the shiver that moves his shoulders. "Cold," he says.

"Come," Anton says, turning towards where the others wait down the slope. But he does not move until Alonso does. They rejoin the men and Anton says, "We will go back down into the trees. No fires."

Hupuka says something, and Alonso translates. "We will have to huddle together to keep warm."

"That's all right," the chief says.

There is mist in the early morning, and they trot and march south, staying below the road—except for Hupuka, who walks the road so that he can signal the group to go back down to the tree line if he sees any traffic. When they near the village, Hupuka comes down to join them, and they go deeper into the conifers and continue south. A mile or so past, they come back into the open, and the trot-and-march continues. At long intervals, they see trails descending through the trees. At each one, Pahta examines the nearest trunks for marks. But he finds nothing.

Every couple of leagues, they encounter another village. This high up, they do not see crops, but there are sheep as well as curious animals like the small camels that the Quechua speakers raise for their wool and use as pack-beasts. They skirt these and go far down into the trees after Hupuka warns that the llamas are as watchful as guard dogs.

It is mid-afternoon, and they are wending their way through the thinly spaced trees below a settlement, when their route cuts across a narrow track. Anton sends Pahta up the trail, and they wait. In a little while, he comes trotting back. He holds up both hands, the index and middle fingers of each crossing at right angles, and says, "I see."

"Then this is the trail," Anton says. He turns west, and the rest follow him. After a few paces, Pahta trots past to scout ahead.

The track descends steadily, trending diagonally as the slope steepens. They come across no bridged gorges or places where steps have been cut into the rock. This is not, Alonso sees, a well-travelled route; the

Quechua speakers wanted no contact with the Campazes, whose lands begin where the deep forest covers the rolling hills, and the Campazes confined their raiding to the kind of country where they wouldn't have to come out into the open and face the Inca king's armies or the Spaniards' steel, firearms, and horses.

By nightfall, they are down into the broad-leafed forest again, and the spaces between the trees are smaller and filled with undergrowth. They push through the bracken and clear room for a camp. Anton again rules out a fire, but the air here is warmer and more humid, and they sleep comfortably with their blankets pulled up to keep the biting insects off their faces. Alonso lies down, his belly full of corn bread and dried meat. It is only after he has settled that Anton and Juanito place themselves on either side of him.

He almost laughs at the thought of his blundering through the moonless dark, trying to find the trail, then climbing it towards the road and the native village, where he might be summarily hit over the head as a vagabond and bandit. *I am not,* he thinks, *the kind of man who takes a leap into the dark.* Besides, the life he lived as Alonso Illescas is steadily fading. It seems less real to him with every passing day. *The here and the now—that is what concerns me. The was-then and the someday-maybe, neither of them exists. They're phantoms, whereas Anton and Juanito are all too real.*

In the morning, they continue down into the coastal forest. The heat closes in and it rains, the fat drops collecting in the canopy and dropping like lead balls upon their heads and shoulders. Soon the rolled-up blankets they carry are sodden, and Anton warns the men twice to keep their matches dry.

Sometime after midday, Pahta comes back from scouting the twisting trail ahead. With him is Poquito, glistening, rain-wet, but with a wide smile on his normally impassive face. Anton leads them off the trail, deep into the forest, and they squat on their heels while the small brown hunter makes his report.

"It is a small village, maybe fifty men, and more than that number of women and children. There is a stockade, but it is not strong. You could cut the vines that tie the logs together and make a hole in no time at all."

"Guards?" Anton says.

"Boys only, and they spend a lot of time talking with each other."

"Dogs?"

Poquito laughs. "Some. But when they bark, the boys throw sticks at them to make them shut up."

"Have you seen the best place to cut through the stockade?"

"Yes, it is on this side. They do not expect to be attacked."

Anton makes his thinking noise and nods. He claps a hand on Poquito's shoulder and says, "Good work," then turns to the others and says, "We will eat and rest. We will wait until they are well asleep and the boys get drowsy. Then we will go.

"See this in your minds: we will listen to know where the guards are. Then Pahta and Poquito will climb over the wall and kill the ones on this side. We will cut a piece of the stockade away and go in with hot coals in the fire pot. We will set fire to two of the huts, three or four if we can. That will give us light and bring out the savages.

"I will give the signal, and those who have matchlocks will all shoot at once. Aim only at men who look like they could fight. Then drop the *arcabuzes* and go at them with spears—again, only at the men. Stay together in a line. Push the women and children and the old out of the way. Nothing fancy, just spear your man in the belly and go for the next one. When they turn and flee, throw your spears into their backs and draw your daggers. Keep killing the men.

"Is that clear?"

The men nod and say they understand, but Anton takes them through it all again until he is sure they are seeing in their heads what he is seeing in his.

They break out their rations and eat, sitting in a circle, talking in low voices about what they expect to do. Alonso is not invited into the conversation, but Pahta and Hupuka make simple contributions in their rudimentary Spanish. The Niguas' eyes are bright with anticipation. They both have spears and daggers now. Hupuka keeps running his hand up and down the shaft of his weapon, rocking slightly as he squats, singing a song to himself softly in his own language.

Alonso sees in his mind's eye the images Anton has put there. Killing the boys bothers him. He thinks of Pablillo, halfway between boydom and manhood, gangling and comically stumble-prone. Then he sees a man's hand seize his head and yank it back to plunge a dagger into his throat—Anton has demonstrated how to do it, and he made Pahta and Poquito go through the motions. Alonso's nape stiffens, and he reaches up to massage the hard-spasming muscles.

Now he sees himself entering the Campaze village. He sees the firelight, the faces contorted in fear and rage, himself advancing with levelled spear. In his mind, it all happens in silence. He knows it won't be that way when it comes. He wonders: will he be able to plunge sharp iron into another man's belly? If it were a rapier, he thinks he would be all right; he spent enough hours in practice for the motions to become automatic. He has never fought a duel, of course—slaves are expected to brawl, not stand against each other like gentlemen—but one cannot become a swordsman, even if only in the practice hall, without seeing himself doing what swordsmen do.

I will not think of it now, he tells himself. *I will let the moment come, and then I will do as I must.*

He stretches his neck forward, closes his eyes, and tries to clear his mind as Expectation has shown him, letting the other men's voices wash over him as if they were no more than the cries of birds and monkeys he can hear in the forest: sound without meaning.

Well after dark, Anton inspects each matchlock man's match and finds them all dry. "Good," he says. "Let's go, Pahta and Poquito first."

He carries the pot of coals from the small fire he made with flint and steel in the afternoon. He has given Alonso the bundle of spears to carry, tightly bound so that the shafts and iron points will not rattle together. They work their way back to the trail, which Alonso finds almost impossible to see, but Poquito seems to know the way by some extra sense. They follow in single file, one man's hand on the shoulder of the man in front. In less than half an hour, they reach the village's cleared land. The sky is overcast, but the moon is somewhere above the clouds, casting a diffuse light that shows the stockade as a dark mass across the clearing.

They pause at the edge of the trees. There are neat rows of dark, bushy plants, knee-high—probably *papas,* Alonso thinks—stretching from their position almost to the enclosure. Pahta and Poquito drop onto their bellies and crawl towards the stockade. It is only a little while before Alonso sees them rise up and press themselves against the vertical logs, listening for the sounds of the watch boys. A moment later, they move to the right and stop again, listening.

Poquito has described the obstacle. The biggest logs are no thicker than a man's thigh, and most are smaller. They are set into the earth and tied together with ropes of twisted vines that offer purchase for hands and feet. Now he and Pahta, several feet apart, silently climb up, ease over the top without showing a silhouette against the overcast, and drop down into the village.

Alonso hears a faint cry, an audible intake of breath that is never to be released. A moment later, the shape of Poquito appears above the stockade, making an unmistakable motion.

"Come on," says Anton, "and keep it quiet."

They go forward through the planted field, and when they reach the stockade, Anton calls the matchlock men together. He removes the top of the ember pot, holds it by its three cords, and blows into it. The coals brighten, illuminating the chief's face and making it look like a carved mask of some ancestral totem. He holds the pot out and tells the men to light their matches and blow them into life.

Meanwhile, Pahta and Poquito have been sawing at the vines that connect the stockade's logs. Anton says to Hupuka, "Help them. Use the sword."

The Nigua draws the cutlass, whose strap he has not taken off since the chief awarded it to him, and goes to work. Anton turns to Alonso and tells him to unbundle the spears and give one to every matchlock man. The younger man distributes them silently.

A dog barks inside the village, a startled sound. Everyone freezes, but then comes a yelp and a whimper. Pahta or Poquito have thrown a stick at the source of the noise. Hupuka whispers, "Ready for wall down," and Anton says, "Put down your weapons and lower it quietly."

The men move up to the wall and, as the last bonds are cut, they catch its weight in their upstretched hands and gently lower it to the ground. There is now a gap in the stockade, ten feet wide. The men pick up their matchlocks and spears and form a line. They move silently forward until the chief hisses for them to stop. Pahta and Poquito join them, and Alonso hands each a spear.

The village is a collection of huts grouped more or less randomly around a central open space. Unlike the Nigua houses, they are not raised on shoulder-high stilts but on solid posts that are only knee-high. The walls are made of cross-hatched sticks, the gaps filled in with bundles of grass woven through the uprights. Anton goes to the hut nearest the right side of the breach in the stockade, uncaps the ember pot, and places it against the base of a wall. He blows into the coals, and again Alonso sees a demonic mask.

The dried grass catches fire, and in a moment, flames shoot up the wall. Anton trots to the house to the left of the gap and repeats the process. By the time the wall of that house ignites, the roof of the first is ablaze. A dog barks, and another howls.

"Form up here!" Anton instructs the eight Africans with matchlocks, marshalling them into a line in the gap between the walls of the stockade. "Ground your spears! Now kneel and present your weapons! But wait until I tell you to give fire. You men with spears, kneel on either side."

The second house is now engaged. Shouts and a scream come from inside them. The blaze lights up the night. A woman carrying a small child tumbles out of the first burning hut, followed by an older girl and a man. They are both shouting a single word that Alonso assumes is Campaze for *fire*.

A man and woman come out of the second house, driving children before them, shouting the same word. Now other Campazes pour from the houses into the central space.

"Wait!" says Anton, kneeling at the left end of the firing line, just loud enough to be heard above the roar of the flames.

A mature man with a wide midriff comes out of a larger house on the other side of the compound, issuing orders. Anton says quietly to the two men nearest him, "Target the one with the belly. He's the chief." Then he raises his voice. "Aim for the men only! Give fire!"

Eight matchlocks crash and shoot fire. Several of the Campaze men drop, dead or wounded, the big-bellied man among them. The others freeze. Alonso sees darting eyes and open mouths, hears a child's wail.

Anton speaks calmly. "Drop your guns, pick up your spears, stand up, and advance! Spear the men, push aside the women!"

To the Campazes, it must seem as if devils are coming out of the fire itself. The ten Africans and two Niguas compress themselves into a group to squeeze through the gap between the burning huts, then form a line and trot towards the crowd. Poquito's count is accurate. There must be close to a hundred of them in the central space, men and women, children and old people. They are still in shock as the spears reach them.

Here it is, thinks Alonso, moving forward with the rest. *Now what?*

He is surprised to find that his mind is clear and he feels no fear. Then he realizes that somehow he has stepped outside of himself. It is as if he is a disembodied observer standing just to one side of his right shoulder. He is aware that his heart is racing and that the hands that grip the spear shaft are damp with sweat. But in this state, he is cool and focused on what is before him and what he has to do. He has a vague sense that he has felt this way before but has no memory of it. It was somewhere back in the greyness, before he was Enrique, the boy who did not speak yet was useful.

The here and the now, says a quiet, unperturbed voice in his head. *That's what we've got to deal with.* And now it says, *Stick that one.*

A Campaze man has thrust a woman and child behind him. He is unarmed, but Alonso can see that he intends to seize the spear when it comes at him. He must know some trick to disarm an attacker and use his own weapon on him. *On me,* he corrects himself.

Everyday Alonso would be dismayed, fearful. Here-and-now Alonso feints a stab at the man's knee, another at his foot. The man ignores the first but tilts forward on the second, reaching for the spear shaft.

That's a mistake, says the calm voice in Alonso's head. He steps back, does not raise the spear but circles it as if it were a rapier he is sending in under his fencing tutor's guard. The Campaze desperately flicks his other hand to catch the weapon, but his fingers meet only the steel blade. It slices through them and continues on into his belly. The abdominal muscles make no resistance, and there is only yielding softness until his thrust strikes bone.

The man is screaming, his mouth open, shock and pain widening his eyes. Alonso notes all of this as he twists and wrenches the spear point free. The man topples forward, still reaching for the spear shaft. Alonso steps backwards and sees the light go out of the Campaze's eyes. Then he steps over the corpse, seeking the next target.

It is a stocky man, just turning to flee. Alonso stabs him in the calf and sees the leg buckle. Scarcely has the man's chest struck the earth, when Alonso thrusts the iron point into the back of his neck and up into the base of the skull. The man goes instantly inert.

Next, says the imperturbable voice in his head. The Campazes are fleeing now, streaming towards a gate on the far side of the village, the Africans and Niguas in pursuit. But the gate is too narrow to let them all out at once, and they bunch up. Alonso spears a man's back just under the shoulder blade, twists the weapon free, and looks for another. But there are no more to kill. They have all run off into the darkness, except for an old man crippled by some problem with his leg joints.

He is limping through the gate. The Africans stand back and watch him. A couple of them jeer, making the kinds of sounds Alonso imagines are often heard on battlefields when the fighting is done. Then Hupuka steps forward, his cutlass raised, and with one swing of the heavy blade, he cleaves the old man's head down to the neck.

He yanks the sword free and watches the dead man fall to the muddy, foot-churned ground. In Nigua, he says, "He might have been the one who broke my father's head."

They drag the bodies into the centre of the village and make a bonfire to see by. They have killed thirty-three men plus the ancient and the two watch boys. Two women who tried to impede the slaughter are also dead. Anton comes to Alonso and says, "Ask the Niguas if the Campazes have any fears about their dead being mutilated."

Alonso is still in his disembodied state, but as he turns to find Hupuka, he feels himself abruptly fall back into his body. His hands tremble, and exhaustion suddenly takes the strength from his legs and arms. He can barely carry the weight of the blood-stained spear.

"By the way," Anton says to his back, "you did well here. How many was it you killed?"

Alonso speaks over his shoulder and hears his voice, hoarse from the dryness in his throat. "Three, but only the first one was hard."

"That's often the way," says the chief.

Alonso finds Hupuka poking about in the chief's house, lighting his investigations with a burning brand from one of the house fires. When questioned, Hupuka says, "They think a man has his full strength in the other world. When they would kill us, they would cut off our hands and slice the tendons in the backs of our knees."

Alonso returns to tell Anton. The chief orders Pahta and Poquito and two of the Africans to mutilate the dead. "Especially the big belly."

Hupuka says, "I will help." He smiles as he draws his cutlass.

Anton orders the others to gather up the matchlocks, reload them, and stack them in the open space. "I don't think they'll come back." He smiles. "But maybe one of them is smart enough to think that I'd think that."

They search the village. "Find weapons, gold, some food for the trip back, anything useful or valuable.

Hupuka comes out of the chief's house wearing a rusted crescent-moon Spanish morion and carrying a two-piece cuirass. He has sheathed his cutlass, and his other hand holds a leather scabbard from which protrudes a swept hilt. Alonso goes to him and says, "May I?"

The Nigua laughs. "It is sharp, but I don't think you could cut a head off with it," he says and hands it over.

Alonso drops his spear and draws the sword. It is a serviceable rapier, not of the best steel, and the handle is only wood wrapped in steel wire, but the balance is true. He assumes a fencer's stance and executes a series of lunges and parries, ending with an extended thrust.

He hears someone laugh, but it is not a mocking sound. Some of the Africans are looking at him, commenting to each other. And Anton is giving him a considering look. The chief comes over to him. Alonso sheathes the rapier.

"You know how to use that?" the chief says.

"I do."

"Then keep it."

"If you say so."

"But," Anton says, fixing him with a hard and steady gaze, "you use it only when I tell you."

"Of course. You are the chief."

"And you don't forget that."

They go back the way they came, bundles and baskets of booty from the Campaze village slung from their spear shafts or carried in backpacks they found in the huts before they fired them. Crossing the suspension bridge is more of a challenge, burdened as they are, but they don't mind; the men are thinking of the welcome they will receive from their wives when they bring back all the decorated combs and strings of tiny white seashells that were the Campaze women's prized possessions.

"Some of this they stole from us," Hupuka tells Alonso. He carries an extra burden: a foot-long length of polished grey stone he is convinced is the war club that felled his father. He means to have Expectation perform some ceremony over it that will empower his father in the afterlife. The thought gives him pleasure, and when they stop to rest or eat, he sits holding the trophy, singing a monotonous song too softly for Alonso to hear the words.

When they arrive back at the village, a crowd awaits them. The reception is joyous when the women see that none of the men has been hurt or killed, and even more so when the spoils of the raid are displayed in the space before the presidio. The women perform a dance, moving in a line that curves and bisects itself, their hands making precise movements. The song they sing must be very old, Alonso thinks, because some of the words are pronounced differently from the speech he has learned from Expectation.

Alonso wears his sword. Anton says that he is to wear it now on any official occasion, and this certainly qualifies. He has not asked why. As he stands watching the women's snaking dance in the light of two great bonfires, his moving gaze sometimes falls upon Anton, who sits in his great chair with the raid's loot spread on blankets at his feet. And twice he finds the chief studying him with an expression the younger man cannot name.

A few days later, a Nigua family arrives, a man with a wife and children and his elderly mother. They have been living on their own up an inland creek that feeds into the river named for emeralds. The man is brought before Anton in the presidio. With Alonso translating, the Nigua says that he was fishing in the big river a few days ago and saw boats come downstream bearing a dozen Spanish soldiers and some Quechua speakers who might have been Yumbo, the people who live high up in the foothills. The man says he has been thinking about asking to join the African-Nigua settlement, and the arrival of soldiers has tipped the balance.

"Tell him he is welcome to stay," says Anton. "He can have one of the empty houses. And give him pots and such like the others have."

When the man is gone, Anton summons Pahta and Poquito. He tells them to go to the big river, find the Spaniards, and report on what they're up to. The scouts are back in four days. The Spaniards and their servants are felling trees beside the river, just upstream from the mangrove swamps.

"They are building a fort on our side of the river," Poquito says, "and clearing the ground around it."

"Did you see cannon?" Anton asks.

"No, but they have matchlocks, halberds, swords, and armour."

Anton makes his thinking noise and then he is silent, looking down at his hands clasped in his lap. Alonso watches him and knows that the chief is weighing and discarding strategies. Finally, he lifts his head. "We will go and kill them," he says. "All of the men will go, and the healer to help any of us who are wounded." Then he looks at Alonso. "But not you. You will stay and be in charge."

Is it another test? Alonso says, "I have shown I can fight."

"Yes," says Anton, "you have. Now you will show if you can obey orders."

The expedition returns, carrying more loot from the raid: weapons, armour, pewter plates and utensils, and a cask of rum that Anton reserves for himself. The Spaniards were fools, he says. Their fort was being built of squared logs laid horizontally, and its walls were only chest-high when the Africans and Niguas attacked after breakfast. Most of the Spaniards were out in the open, cutting and shaping timber or supervising their servants. A pair were fishing. A few stood as sentries, but they were scattered. There were only four men inside the half-built fort—the commander, the commissariat, and two servants—when the twenty men burst from the trees, cut down the one sentry in their path, leaped over the walls into the small enclosure, and speared the Spaniards. Then they levelled their matchlocks and fired at the soldiers.

Six Spaniards went down, dead or wounded. Leaderless, out in the open, and under fire from their own fortification, the remainder fled for their boats drawn up on the shore before the *arcabuceros* could reload. Their Quechua-speaking servants went with them. The entire engagement had lasted less than three minutes. The attackers came out to spear the wounded and strip the dead.

"Another seven matchlocks," Anton says, "with powder and shot. Armour and steel weapons—halberds, even better than spears—and no casualties on our side." Alonso sees the chief smile, his face full of pleasure. "And all the rest of it. It couldn't have gone better."

'All the rest of it' includes the two men who were with the Spaniards in the fort. They are Africans, though neither of them has ever seen Africa, and their names are Esteban and Haraldo. They still seem dazed at their change of circumstances, but Esteban is looking about him: at the presidio, at the mixed crowd of Africans and Nigua, at Anton and the decorated chair in which he sits.

"No," says the chief, "it could not have gone better."

Eight

Alejandro de Espinosa

Fray Alejandro de Espinosa, monk of the Trinitarian Order, stood in the bows of the brigantine *La Ciudad de los Reyes* as it made its way up the long inlet that led to the estuary of the Guayas River and the port of Guayaquil. The southerly wind that had been so troublesome as they beat their way down from Panama City was now gently bearing them against the current, and once they had looped around the southern extremity of Puna Island, the pilot had little to do except watch for small boats as they headed for the second of the four channels, the one that opened between Green and Mondragon Islands.

As they entered the narrow waterway, the forest closed in and the air became thicker. To Alejandro, it lay heavy in the bottom of his lungs, and he had to summon a greater effort than usual to expel a breath. At the same time, the heat seemed to wrap him in a wet embrace. Sweat trickled down his chest and spine beneath the white robe of the Trinitarians with its red and blue cross on his breast, which clung to him as damply as if he had been caught in a sudden downpour. He pulled it free from his torso and loosened the cord that bound it at his waist, but the action brought no relief.

The town was coming into sight on the left bank, a strew of wooden structures—houses, huts, and sheds, most with reed-thatched roofs—straggled along the shore. The remains of a stockade that had once enclosed a native town leaned here and there. *La Ciudad* passed a boatyard, where black carpenters were hammering the strakes of a carrack into place, then another slipway, where a three-masted galleon careened so that a gang of native men could scrape her bottom clear of weed and barnacles.

The pilot shouted to the brig's crew up on the yards to reef the sails before giving the helmsman precise instructions as to where to set his rudder. The ship lost speed as it eased in towards a wooden jetty, where idlers had got to their feet, ready to catch the mooring cables the sailors were preparing to throw.

"Brother, if you please," said one of the sun-browned men, gesturing politely for Fray Alejandro to move to the starboard side of the bow. The monk stepped back, caught his heel on the small bundle of his possessions that he had left at his feet, and almost stumbled. The sailor, as if he had expected less than gracefulness from a religious, put a hand to the white sleeve and steadied the Trinitarian.

"Bless you, my son," Fray Alejandro said, though the seaman was close to twice his age.

La Ciudad met the dock gently, with not enough of a bump to offer Fray Alejandro even a slight risk of toppling over. He lifted his bundle, voiced another blessing on the ship and all that sailed in her, then headed for the gangplank. Moments later, the young monk walked carefully down its cleated length and, for the first time in weeks, put a foot on a surface that did not threaten to move.

The wharf was developing into a bustle of activity as passengers descended from the ship and porters arrived, shouting up their rates. Fray Alejandro wove his way through the sweating, half-clad men—a pair of knee-length cotton breeches was apparently the sole garment required on the docks—looking for the sign he had been told would identify the muleteer he was supposed to find. It was not in sight, but there were other wharves, and he headed along the jetty towards the actual shore.

A portly, red-faced man in a stained doublet, a sweat-soaked ruff limp at his neck, brushed past the monk, his gaze intent on *La Ciudad*'s captain high up on the stern castle. Fray Alejandro stepped aside but found his path blocked by a thin-faced man of mature years wearing the black cassock of a Jesuit. The monk excused himself and made to step around the priest, but the other man also stepped sideways and continued to impede his progress.

"Fray Alejandro?" The Jesuit's pure Castilian accent, along with his bearing, said that he had not risen from the lower classes. "You are he?"

"I am."

"You will come with me." The man laid a slim hand upon Fray Alejandro's sleeve, the gesture reminding the monk of the sailor's instinct to save him from a fall. But the Jesuit's intent was otherwise. When Alejandro drew back, the elegant fingers showed a surprising strength.

"Do not resist," said the priest.

"Who are you? What do you want with me?"

The Jesuit's eyes were darkly luminous in the bright equatorial sun. They neither blinked nor shifted their gaze. Alejandro was put in mind of a great snake he had once seen in the house of a Seville merchant who traded on the Guinea coast; it had regarded him with the same cold intensity.

"I am Father Luis de Acosta, and I am an advisor to the *corregidor* of Guayaquil, Don Jerónimo Ramírez Rico, and what I want with you are the answers to some questions."

Alejandro tried to pull free, but the Jesuit merely transferred his weight from one foot to another and easily retained his grip.

"I have to meet a man and arrange to travel on," Alejandro said. "I must make sure that he knows I have landed."

The cold, dark stare did not alter. "Who is this man?"

"Juan Hernandez."

"The mulatto muleteer?" said the Jesuit. "He will not depart Guayaquil for another day at least. He is waiting for cargo that is supposed to arrive on the ship that brought you."

"How do you know that?"

"It is my business to know such things: who comes to Guayaquil; who goes from Guayaquil; who stays; and, especially, why they come and go and stay."

"Let me make sure of Juan Hernandez," Alejandro said, "and then I will come with you freely."

Acosta maintained his grip. The younger man's forearm was beginning to tingle with an incipient numbness. "You will come with me now, freely or not. Must I call soldiers?" He gestured over his shoulder with his other hand. Alejandro saw two men, dressed in cuirasses and morions and holding seven-foot long halberds at the landward end of the dock. They were regarding, with mild interest, the two religious.

There seemed little choice but to submit. "You promise me I will not miss the departure of the mule train?"

"No," said the Jesuit, "I do not."

The *corregidor*'s offices were in a two-story building made of heavy squared timbers on one side of an unpaved plaza not far from the docks. Acosta steered Alejandro through a side door and down a short corridor to a small office with a table and two stools: one tall and one short. The monk was told to sit on the short one. The Jesuit went to the other side of the table and took the more elevated seat. Alejandro surmised that the difference in heights was not accidental.

There were documents and what appeared to be ledgers on the table. The priest sorted through them and came up with a square piece of vellum. It showed creases where it had been folded and half the wax blob that had sealed it. He read silently through it then fixed the monk once again with the same intense stare.

The younger man had used the time spent walking to the *corregidor*'s offices to think. He pre-empted the Jesuit by asking the first question. "How did you know my name? And what ship I was arriving on?"

The priest answered his questions with one of his own. "How many Trinitarians do you think are in Peru?"

"I have no idea. Now—"

"I can tell you," said Acosta. "One. And you are that one."

Alejandro again pulled his sodden robe clear of his chest. It was no cooler here, despite the thick wooden walls. "I go where my vocation leads me."

"Your Order does not have a house here. Nor even in Panama."

Alejandro said, "The Mercedarians will assist me if I need assistance. Now how did you know—"

"I have already answered the question," said the priest. "But if you must have it spelled out for you ..."

"I would appreciate it."

"The *corregidor* not only takes an interest in who arrives in Guayaquil but in those who intend to arrive. When a Trinitarian is heard to be wandering around Panama City asking about ships coming to this port, it is a sufficient novelty for my agents,"—he shook the piece of paper meaningfully—"to send me a report."

"I see," said Alejandro. "I am not accustomed to thinking of myself as a person of interest."

"Be thankful that I have not yet decided that you are. Our *juzgado* is intended for drunken stevedores and maddened *Indios*. You would not find it comfortable."

"What do you want of me?"

"To know why you are here."

The monk wiped sweat from his brow. He wondered why the priest did not seem to be fazed by the clammy heat, though black was hotter to wear than white. Was it a matter of seasoning? Would Alejandro eventually reach a condition where he did not feel as if he were being steamed alive?

"I am here," he said, "to minister to the captive. It is the vocation of my Order."

Acosta's thin lips permitted themselves the smallest of smiles. "That would be a general answer from any Trinitarian. I am asking why"—he glanced again at the paper—"Fray Alejandro de Espinosa in particular has washed up on the shores of the Kingdom of Quito." He paused to employ the serpent-like stare for several heartbeats—Alejandro could hear his own pulse thudding in his ears—then shot a quick question: "Are you a *converso*?"

The monk pulled the cloth free of his chest again and used a sleeve to wipe his forehead, the motion allowing him to hide his face from the priest while a rapid series of questions passed through his mind. Inclining his head also allowed him to overcome the impulse to let his eyes go to the paper in Acosta's hand. He asked himself, *Is it possible that word of the Inquisition's interest in me preceded my arrival in this backwater? If so, why am I being questioned by a Jesuit and not a Dominican? When I was told the Holy Office had no presence in the Kingdom of Quito, was I misinformed?*

He looked up, his face heat-reddened but, he hoped, guileless. "I was born and baptized into a Christian family, Father."

"But your family was not always such, was it?"

The temptation came upon Alejandro to answer that such was the case with all of Christendom if one looked far enough into the past. But he put down the wild notion with a firm mental hand; paring slivers of meaning with a Jesuit was rarely a recommended course of action. Especially a Jesuit who was well ensconced within the civil power.

"My grandfather, Isaac, accepted Christ's grace after the royal order of 1492," Alejandro said. "My father, Tomas, was born a Christian, like me."

"Yet you have come to the attention of the Holy Office?"

This required a careful answer. "I have not been summoned to appear."

Again a small smile briefly visited Acosta's mouth. "That is not what I asked."

Alejandro lifted his shoulders and let them fall. "How would I know, otherwise?"

"A very good question. Many people of your . . . heritage have sources of information within the Holy Office, especially information that might be purchased in one way or another."

"I have no such sources." It was the bare truth. Word that the Inquisition had turned its attention Alejandro's way had come from a lay clerk paid by his uncle Pedro to give early warning if the name of any member of the extended Espinoso family appeared on one of the continually expanding lists.

Acosta applied the stare for a while longer then shifted his line of attack. "Whom do you know here?"

"In Guayaquil? No one."

"You mentioned Hernandez, the muleteer."

"I was given his name in Panama City."

"By whom?"

"Several people. I was told he is rough around the edges but trustworthy."

The Jesuit regarded him with an impassive face. Alejandro waited, wondering where the next line of attack would come from.

"Hernandez is taking twenty mules up to Quito," Acosta said. It was not a question, but the monk answered anyway.

"Quito is where I wish to go."

"Why?"

"I have been told that the *encomendero* system imposes hardship on the native people."

"It does. They die by the score. What has that to do with you?"

Alejandro put some force into his voice. "They are Christians in bondage. I am a Trinitarian."

Another minimal smile from the priest. "Your Order was established to deliver from bondage pilgrims seized by infidels on the way to the Holy Land, not savages who do not want to serve their lawful masters. And many of them are no more true followers of the cross than are many *conversos* back in Spain."

"I am come to help, not to make distinctions."

The priest seemed inclined to reply, but instead glanced at his document again. "And whom do you know in the City of Quito?"

"I have a letter of introduction to Don Rodrigo de Ribadeneira."

Acosta nodded as if the statement confirmed what he already knew. "The merchant? A useful man to know, I am told. The town elders dance to whatever tune he decides to play."

"I would not know," said the monk. "I have an uncle who is known to the Ribadeneira family. He provided the letter." He smiled, a broader specimen than he had had from the Jesuit, and leaned towards where his bundle rested on the floor beside the low stool. "Would you like to see it?"

Acosta let him fiddle with the string that bound the bundle of cloth—Alejandro's cloak, unneeded since he had entered this torrid climate—before he said, "That will not be necessary. I have already been told as much."

Alejandro straightened. "Then why did you ask me?"

"To see how you would answer, of course." The priest set down the letter and folded his arms, regarding Alejandro with a disinterest that was yet penetrating. The room was silent, though the hubbub from the docks made a continuous background murmur.

Finally, the younger man said, "Is there anything more?"

The Jesuit's silence and stillness continued. Then Acosta blinked—Alejandro was sure it was the first time he'd seen it—and said, "No."

"Then I may go?"

"Yes."

The monk took up his bundle and stood. He waited a moment to see if the other man would speak then said, "Good day."

Acosta still said nothing. Alejandro turned and went towards the door. As his hand touched the latch, the voice from behind him said, "Be careful up there, Trinitarian. This is not Spain. There are no courts, no *alcaldes,* no rules except from the powerful."

"Surely the Viceroy exerts control."

For the first time, Alejandro saw real amusement on the other man's face. "He exerts. Whether he controls . . ." He raised a hand in a gesture of indeterminacy.

Juan Hernandez was not hard to find. His stable on the inland edge of the town was a ramshackle structure of mostly thatched roof supported by crooked posts. It stood beside a large corral in which two dozen mules rested in the shade of the lone remaining tree. A long, low building of heavy logs stood on the other side of the enclosure, its roof of solid planks covered by hides, and its door an imposing barrier of beams and black iron. A haymow under canvas was pegged to the ground with hemp rope, completing the establishment.

The muleteer, a man of perhaps thirty years clad in a sleeveless leather vest and trousers of coarse cloth, sat on a stool in the stable's inner shade. He was repairing a piece of harness, using strong black thread and a steel needle. He looked up as Alejandro came out of the alley, and the seams of his cream-coloured face set themselves into a deeper frown than usual. He spat into the dust at his feet and did not rise as the Trinitarian came to stand before him at the edge of the shadow.

"Good day," said the monk. "I am— "

In Guayaquil, it seemed, interrupting was a common pastime. "I know who you are," said the muleteer. "I've had the *corregidor's* pet crow out here this morning, wanting to know how you and I fit together. Wasting my time and threatening me with soldiers when I've got to get twenty mules ready to go up to the mountains."

He spat again and went back to work on the harness, grumbling something Alejandro could not make out. "May I come in out of the sun?" the monk said.

"Suit yourself."

Alejandro stepped into the shade and found that the relief was only marginal. He spoke to the top of Hernandez's head. "I am sorry Father Acosta troubled you. It was only because I asked in Panama for the name of a trustworthy man going up to Quito."

The muleteer looked up at him again, the frown as deeply embedded as before. "What are you? I have not seen that habit before."

Alejandro explained the name and nature of his Order. "We are not common in the New World yet. I am the first to arrive here."

"And immediately, Acosta calls you in and twists your balls."

"It was not so grim as that."

"But the Jesuits don't like you?" Hernandez spat again. "That, at least, could be a recommendation."

"They are prone to strong opinions," the monk said.

The mulatto went back to work on the harness, pulling thread through a hole to mend a tear in the leather. He finished the stitching, knotted the thread, then snipped off the remainder with his teeth. "What do you want?" he said.

"To accompany you to Quito." He told the muleteer about his connection to Rodrigo de Ribadeneira.

Hernandez shook his head. "My mules have enough to carry. Do you know the merchants down here are trying to make me put two hundred and fifty pounds on each animal? And for the same haulage fee. Bastards."

"I will walk."

The muleteer set down the harness and gave Alejandro a more perspicacious examination. "Can you handle mules?"

"I have done so. Pilgrims sometimes ride them."

Hernandez's tongue explored his right cheek and the space in front of his lower teeth. He found something and spat it out. "What about your rations?"

"We are a mendicant order."

"What does that mean?"

"We rely on the kindness of the faithful for our daily bread."

"You're a beggar," Hernandez translated. "You won't find many 'faithful' between here and the City of Quito. If you meet any of the Campazes, you'll be begging for more than bread."

"I see."

"You'll be begging for your life!"

"I understand."

The muleteer sighed. "Do you?" he said. He was silent for a moment, apparently studying the place where sun met shadow. Then he said, without looking at the monk, "I will give you bread and beans if you help with the mules."

"I accept."

"Providing that the help is truly helpful."

"I will do my best."

Hernandez rose and flexed his shoulders. "You can start now. Put your bundle up in the rafters. The goats here will eat anything."

Alejandro did as he was bid.

The muleteer looked him over again. "Have you nothing cooler to wear?"

"This is what I wear, in all seasons. In winter"—he gestured to the bundle—"I put on a cloak."

"You will suffer. God created this place to make the Devil suffer. Then he felt sorry for him and made Hell instead."

Alejandro shrugged. "Then I will suffer and offer my suffering to God."

Hernandez also shrugged, the gesture of a man who has done all he can in the face of madness. "Let us get to work," he said. "The goods I have been waiting for will be taxed and in the warehouse by evening. I want the mules to be in the best shape for us to load and depart tomorrow. Some of them, their hooves need attending to."

They crossed the river in two barges and followed a wide trail into the forest. Hernandez had given Alejandro a stout staff of some hard, dark wood, saying, "You will need that. But do not strike my mules with it."

The trees closed in on them soon after they left the river bank. From then on, it was like walking through a high-roofed tunnel of wood and foliage, with bare, root-raddled earth underfoot and the sky invisible beyond the canopy. Alejandro could hear the wind in the topmost branches, but down here, the air was heavy and still and so thick with moisture that it could not absorb the sweat that sprang from every pore of his body. He was soaked within minutes of starting out and had to stop to tuck the hem of his sodden robe into the cord at his waist. Hernandez had also given him a leather water bottle, but it was soon empty as he sought to replenish the liquid he was losing.

Alejandro was walking at the rear of the mule train. A couple of hours into the journey, the muleteer left the lead mule in the charge of one of the three men he had hired for the trip and came back to see how the monk was doing. He brought another water bottle and handed it over without comment.

"It is hard, this walking," Alejandro said after he had taken a drink. "Not like what I'm used to."

"Here the land is flat but hot," Hernandez said. "Fifteen leagues and we begin to climb. That's when you will need the staff. I don't want you hanging your weight off my mules. But it will be cooler."

"Good," said the monk, and took another drink.

"Of course, then it gets steeper and the air is not so good. Some people get sick."

"I have crossed mountains before. I will be all right."

"Mountains?" Hernandez made a sound that might have been laughter except that it contained no mirth. "You mean the Sierra de Estrela? The Pyrenees? You think those are mountains?"

"I thought so when I walked them."

"Wait and see." The muleteer made the same harsh bark again and went forward to the head of the column.

Despite the heat, they made good time—better than a league an hour in the morning. They stopped at a small clearing for lunch: bread and boiled beans crushed to a paste and stored in terracotta jars, washed down with a thin, sour wine from a leather skin. The three hirelings sat in a circle, their knees so close to each other that they admitted no interlopers. Hernandez brought another skin to Alejandro, who sat sweating and hoping for a breeze from the open space above. The mulatto hunkered down beside him, tearing off a piece of the coarse loaf and squirting wine into his full mouth to soften the stuff before chewing. From the way he regarded the monk, Alejandro could see that he interested the muleteer.

"You say your work is helping pilgrims," he said as he passed the wine over. "We have no pilgrims here. No saints, either."

Alejandro took a long pull from the skin. His second bottle of water had long since gone dry. "All who seek God are pilgrims," he said.

Hernandez let one eyelid droop. "Did you give answers like that when the Jesuit was asking you your business? It's a wonder you are not locked up in the *corregidor*'s jail."

Alejandro shrugged. "I say what I believe."

"So say what brings you here to this boil on the Devil's backside."

The monk told him the truth—not the whole truth, of course. He did not mention the Inquisition. And he stretched it only slightly when he said, "I had a vision. I saw *Indios* holding out their hands as if asking for alms."

In truth, it had been a dream, not a true revelation. There had been more to it, mostly a jumble of shifting images as in all dreams. But when he had awakened in his cell at the Mercedarian monastery at Huete, the only part that stayed with him was the scene of the natives holding out their empty palms—holding them out to him.

He went down to Seville to consult with his cousins, only to find that they were being watched by hired informers. His presence was soon reported to Father Alberto Ruiz, the Dominican in charge of the investigation into the Espinosas. Uncle Pedro then warned him that he was vulnerable to arrest and interrogation; the Trinitarians aroused no fear among the black-robed monks of the Holy Office, and once they had Fray Alejandro locked in a cell, they would have no compunction about using torture to get what they wanted.

What they wanted, of course, were the family's accumulated riches, which had grown at a good pace since Isaac the *converso* had served as a legal adviser in the court of Queen Isabella. The Inquisition financed its activities through the wealth confiscated from those it judged to be heretics. After more than fifty years of continuous operation, the Holy Office had amassed a vast treasury, but it was always interested in further improving its ledgers.

"God sent you to help the savages?" Hernandez said, and shrugged. "I suppose God must have a high regard for them. He not only made them by the millions, but every year He calls them to join Him in Heaven by the tens of thousands."

"And now He has called me to help them."

"By way of Ribadeneira's enterprises. You won't find much of God in his business."

Alejandro squeezed some wine from the skin onto a crust of bread and let it soak through. While he waited for it to soften, he said, "I find God in the oddest places. The trick is to know how to look for Him."

Hernandez laughed. "I like you, Brother," he said. "You entertain." He shot another jet of wine from the skin then plugged the mouth with its wooden stopper. "I hope you live longer than I think you will."

"Tell me about Quito," the monk said. "What will I find there?"

Hernandez answered without hesitation. "A rough and tricky place. It is a long way from the Viceroy's palace down in Lima. There is no government save for what the big men of the town decide amongst themselves."

"De Ribadeneira," Alejandro said. "Is he one of the big men?"

"One of the biggest. And like the rest of them, his only concern is to enrich himself so he can return to Spain and live like a grandee. In fact, better than many a grandee."

"He is only a merchant," Alejandro said.

"Ah, but such a merchant," said the muleteer. "He brings up fine goods—silk and taffeta from China, kid-skin gloves from France, lace from Flanders—and sells it to the mine owners in Potosi, who have more gold and silver than brains."

He gestured at the mules standing unburdened in the shade at the edge of the clearing. "Half of what I'm carrying is going to de Ribadeneira's warehouse. Two weeks from now, I'll be back home, loading up another shipment for him."

"Is he a godly man?"

"Not so you'd notice. He goes to mass at the great Church of San Francisco, but I think mostly to rub shoulders with the other big men. It is where they make their arrangements."

Alejandro would have asked more, but the muleteer got to his feet, took one more pull from the wineskin, and dropped it in the monk's lap. "Finish up," he said, "then get the mules reloaded. We won't stop again until nightfall."

On the second day, they began to climb, and by nightfall they had risen above the tropical forest and into a different kind of woodland that was more like the uplands of Spain. Widely spaced conifers took over from the densely packed, broad-leafed trees of the lowlands, and the air grew drier and cooler. As Hernandez had predicted, Alejandro's staff became useful as they ascended the ancient trail onto a ridge top and turned to follow it.

As the land rose higher, the trees eventually fell away, and they were walking along the tops of slopes covered in grass and small-leafed, ground-hugging plants. Tiny, precise flowers of many kinds, all new to Alejandro, decorated the landscape. The air was pure and bracing, though the monk had to work to pull enough of it into his chest as they worked their way up the steepest inclines.

He had walked mountains between Spain and France, and between Spain and Portugal, but he realized that the muleteer had again been right: he had never been this high in the world before. He knew that Heaven was not really somewhere beyond the clear, blue dome above him, yet he felt that he had never been as close to it as he was now, and he was sure he had never seen as far as he could see from up here.

A Castilian priest in Panama City had warned him that these lands were still sunk in the Devil's pit. The natives professed Christianity but clung to their old demon-haunted ways, "like the false *conversos* of Spain who go to mass but will not eat pork, and who secretly circumcise their sons." Alejandro did not argue. He was not circumcised, but his father had been, and had that fact ever become known to the Holy Office, the result would have been, at best, imprisonment for life and, at worst, the fiery 'act of faith' in the plaza before the cathedral.

For Alejandro, looking up now into the rich blue of the upland sky, it was hard to believe that any abyss-dwelling fiend could operate in this high and somehow holy place. Surely the pure light would scour the darkness at the heart of unholy beings, making them turn and flee to the sweaty, closed-in dimness of the coastal forest. His ancestors had known that God was present in these high places; that is why Moses climbed Mount Sinai to receive the law.

He was thinking such thoughts when they stopped to eat and rest the mules. Again Hernandez sought him out, bringing bread and wine and asking him, "So, Brother, what do you think of our Kingdom of Quito now?"

When Alejandro told him the thoughts that had been occupying his mind, the muleteer laughed. "Again, Brother, you entertain. Most who come up here take a look around and ask, 'Where is the gold? Where is the silver? How do I get rich?' I think maybe you are one of those men who sees God everywhere because you are looking only for Him. Meanwhile, the Devil struts all around you, beating his drum and blowing his horn, and you never notice."

"I am not an innocent," said the monk. "Trinitarians do not hide behind cloister walls. We go out into the world and do what we can to aid those who struggle not to join the Devil's parade."

Hernandez laughed again. "You won't find too many of that sort in Quito. Most are elbowing each other to get into the front rank and trampling those who can't get out of their way."

"Then I will help the trampled upon."

"If they are trodden down, it is only because they are not so good at the treading," the mulatto said.

"Even the natives?"

"Their women come every day to the market. At first, it was to sell things they had grown or made. But the Viceroy has said they did not have to collect the sales tax that every other merchant pays, so the women started to sell anything they could get their hands on." Hernandez gestured towards where the unladen mules were eating hay three of them had carried up from the coast. "I am bringing some of them cloth and hats and gloves made in China and the Philippines. Some of them are becoming rich. A couple of them are now becoming moneylenders."

The monk chewed his bread thoughtfully. After a while, he swallowed and said, "It is more complicated than I thought it would be."

"Everything is," said the muleteer. "You just have to look closely enough."

"A teacher I knew said that when there are several possible answers to a question, the simplest answer is likely to be the right one."

Another laugh from Hernandez. "Only," he said, "if the question is simple. And usually, if you think the question is simple, it means you haven't thought about it enough."

"I am starting to think you are a wise man for a muleteer," Alejandro said.

"You can learn a lot from mules," the other man said, "if you will let them teach you."

The third day in the highlands was like the first two, the weather clear and the air cool, but the sun warmed wherever it touched. To Alejandro it felt like a perfect spring day; when he said as much to Hernandez, the muleteer told him to get used to it.

"Up here, it is always like this."

"In winter and in summer?"

"Here there is no winter or summer. Every day is the same."

The monk thought it must have been like this in the Garden of Eden, but he did not share the thought with the muleteer. So far, everything he had surmised about the Kingdom of Quito had sailed out of his mind only to crash upon the rocks of Hernandez's worldly experience. He would keep the idea of a primordial paradise to himself.

But another idea was welling up inside him, prompted by the clarity of the air and the breadth of vision offered by the heights to which they continued to climb. Since the moment word had come to his family that the Holy Office had turned its hard, cold gaze his way, Alejandro had been in flight. He had been moving away from something he had good cause to fear. His escape had plunged him first into the stinking bowels of a worn-out caravel, the first ship leaving Seville on which he could buy passage. The leaking tub had pitched and shook as it thrashed its way through the waves of the Atlantic. The crossing had been too rough to allow the passengers on deck—or so the captain said—and the roster of artisans, servants, and penniless adventurers who lay in the swinging hammocks had not the rank to argue.

Then, after scarcely a few hours in the port town of Nombre de Dios, the monk had joined a caravan making its way across the isthmus, mostly through forest, where the only view was of the man in front. Then he was scurrying around Panama City, seeking passage to Guayaquil and a trustworthy name there. That was followed by two more weeks in the barquentine, where the view from the deck was a barren sea to the west, north, and south and a low, unpromising line of wilderness to the east.

And all the time he had been reckoning the distance between him and the interrogators of the Holy Office—and wondering if it was far enough. He realized now, as he ascended higher into the clear blue of this place, that for the first time in three months he was not conscious of a nagging fear. Indeed, the anxiety that had been constantly muttering in the background of his mind—when it wasn't gibbering right out in front—had, unnoticed, drained away.

He felt free, unconstrained. And as he dwelt upon the change, he discovered another: he was no longer walking away from trouble; he was walking *towards* something—something good that awaited him. What it might be, he did not know and had no need to know. It was enough to feel its beckoning, beneficial presence ahead of him.

He had long felt a vocation to help those who needed it. But it had always been a diffuse calling, a general inclination to kindness and compassion. Now he sensed that, up ahead, waited a mechanism that would act like the spectacles worn by the head of the scriptorium in a monastery he had visited in southern France. Once, when the elderly monk was away from his lectern, Alejandro had slipped the lenses over his eyes and seen the room become disconcertingly vague and unfocused; when he took them away, everything sprang back into sharp focus. For the old monk, the effect had apparently been just the opposite.

Somewhere along the path he was now treading, he would meet the person, the circumstances, or the combination of both that would perform a similar transformation for his life as the spectacles had done for the old monk's eyesight. Every step he took, every placement of the butt of his staff, brought him closer to that moment of sudden clarity. And now, between one step and another, he went from a teasing intimation to a rock-steady certainty that the moment would come.

He found himself short of breath at the strength of the revelation, although, he thought, the elevation also had something to do with it. He said a prayer to Saint John of Matha, founder of the Trinitarian Order, then steadied his breathing and took another step forward, thinking, *There, that's another one, and another, and another.*

He smiled and sang a hymn that he remembered hearing among the pilgrims on the route to Santiago de Compostela. The men shepherding the mules looked back at him, but none joined in.

That night, wrapped in his cloak, Alejandro slept well beside the charcoal fire that Hernandez allowed them. He awoke before dawn and lay looking up at the stars. They were many, and some of them formed constellations he had never seen before. He watched them for a while until suddenly his perspective shifted and, instead of looking up into space, it was as if he were staring down into a great well of darkness splashed with brilliant points of light.

After that, he could not return to sleep and spent the time before the others began to stir in prayer. When he offered a prayer to Saint John of Matha, he felt a peace descend upon him. *At last,* he thought, *I am on the path that was laid for me. I need not fear, because God and my patrón will be with me.*

For days, they had been walking north, with the coastal plain to their left and a chain of even higher mountains to their right, beyond a vast intermontane valley. Down there, Alejandro saw villages and fields, rivers and trackways. But what kept drawing his gaze was the sharp-peaked mountain ahead of them.

Pinchincha, it was called. Alejandro had been told about it by a well-travelled Mercedarian in Seville. It was a fire mountain. Five years ago, it had shaken the city of Quito on its eastern slopes, sending a column of hot ash high into the clear sky. The fine, dry stuff had fallen on the city and the fields around it, and it had to be swept up and carried out of the public squares by squads of servants and native workers. Everyone had been coughing for weeks.

It seemed an odd thing for God to have placed in such a tranquil setting, he thought. But it was probably one of those seemingly simple situations that would turn out to be more complex if he looked at it more closely. And, as the mountain rose higher above the horizon with every day's march northward, the monk turned his thoughts to what he might say to Don Rodrigo de Ribadeneira when he finally met him and handed him the letter of introduction.

The city was a little disappointing. In Spain, Alejandro had heard of the monumental architecture of the peoples of this strange realm: without iron or steel, they had so closely fitted together massive blocks of stone that Spanish masons said it must have been the work of devils. But when the mule train passed through the southern gate, all the monk could see were modern Spanish buildings of squared stone, whitewashed and with roof tiles of fired red clay. Were it not for Pinchincha looming over the town, the streets the mule train followed to Hernandez's rented warehouse could have been in any of a dozen cities Alejandro had passed through in Spain and Portugal.

"'The great buildings of the savages'?" Hernandez said. "They were all torn down and the stones reshaped for proper houses and churches. Not that there was much to begin with. Their king, the one Pizarro strangled, he had a palace here, but the common people built in adobe."

At a small square where four roads met, the muleteer pointed the way to the grand plaza of San Francisco and the Franciscan monastery with its great church beside. This was an imposing edifice, said to be the first great church built in the new world. It stood at the top of a wide flight of stairs of grey stone, the central part of its facade made of the same stuff. Around and above it rose whitewashed walls that climbed to two great bell towers.

To reach it, the monk had to cross a vast paved expanse that, for all its size, seemed crowded with Quitenos of all kinds—men and women, white, black, mulatto, or the paler brown of the natives—walking, standing and talking, carrying burdens, or drawing water from the public fountains. But he noticed that none of the black, mulatto, or native people were standing still. They were all in motion, none of it carefree.

Out in the open, a shabbily dressed man was playing a five-stringed vihuela, his fingers plucking busily at the catgut. Now he burst into song, a wailing lament, and a better-dressed man who had been about to throw a coin into the cap at the singer's feet changed his mind and walked on. All around the plaza, there was a constant hubbub of conversation and argument, especially along one side of the square, where native women had set up thatch-roofed booths of poles and woven grass. They were calling to passersby to come and try their wares, their voices thin and high-pitched, and the tone rose even higher among those who were haggling with customers of all races.

The closer Alejandro came to the church's entrance the more impressed he was by its splendour: carved pillars, the great arched doorway, the statue of the saint himself centred high above. The Franciscans had come a long way since their founder had wandered barefoot along the roads of Italy.

He mounted the steps and found a bent-backed elderly man sweeping the entrance. The man identified himself as one of the monastery's lay servants. He directed Alejandro to a small doorway down the wall with a chain that caused a bell to sound on the other side of the door. After a little while, the door opened, and a plump-faced monk in a grey habit of finer wool than Alejandro's asked him what he wanted.

"Food and shelter, please," said the Trinitarian. "I have walked all the way from Guayaquil."

"Who hasn't?" said the guardian of the door, but he bid Alejandro follow him through a well-tended garden to the office of the hospitaller. This was Fray Geronimo, an elderly brother whose wrinkled face rearranged itself into a broad smile.

"A Trinitarian!" he declared. "The first I've seen this side of the ocean!" Then the smile faded, and he said, "You are truly of that Order? We have no pilgrims to speak of." He spread his hands. "No holy places for them to seek. At least not yet."

Alejandro assured the monk he was the real item and was shown to a cell that contained a raised bed with a straw-tick mattress, a stool, and a table on which stood a jug of water and a washing bowl. The hospitaller waited until Alejandro had washed the dust from his face and hands then led him to the refectory, where the Franciscans were taking the noon meal. He was given a cob of good white bread and a wooden bowl that contained a thick and savoury stew.

"Goat," said the hospitaller, sitting across from Alejandro at one of the long tables. "Not enough sheep yet, but there will be someday." There was a pitcher from which Geronimo poured the visitor a wooden cupful of wine that, when the Trinitarian tasted it, was as good as any he had tasted since Seville.

The old man sat in silence and watched Alejandro eat. The silence could not be a rule of the house, since other grey-clad monks were quietly conversing in other parts of the long, well-lit room. No one stood at a lectern to read from scripture as they would have if this had been a Dominican monastery.

"So, Brother," the hospitaller said when the guest had laid down his spoon. "What brings you to us?"

Again Alejandro simplified his tale. "A vocation. God has called me to aid the native people." But after his epiphany on the way here, he was able to say it with more fervour than when he had been examined by Father Acosta.

"Always worthy," said Geronimo, pouring another measure of wine and pressing it upon the younger monk. "Have you a plan?"

"I have a letter of introduction to Don Rodrigo de Ribadeneira. I thought I would begin with him."

After voicing his question, the older monk formed his seamed face into an expression of warm interest. Upon hearing the answer, he lifted his tangled white brows to their utmost elevation, and his mouth opened in surprise.

"De Ribadeneira?" Geronimo said. He considered the matter for only a moment before shaking his head. "If your aim is to aid the natives, he may not be your ideal starting point."

Alejandro put down his cup. "How so?" he said.

The older monk paused as if to compose a thoughtful answer. Then he shook his head again and said, "No, better you find out for yourself."

More than that he would not say, and Alejandro thought it unmannerly to press the Franciscan. He thanked him for the meal and asked for directions to de Ribadeneira's establishment.

"I will send a servant to guide you," Geronimo said, adding, "There and back again."

It was not far. De Ribadeneira's house and place of business were a few steps down a broad street that led out from the grand plaza. Alejandro gave his name to the servant who answered the door, and was admitted and brought to an anteroom on the second floor, where he sat on one of four chairs set against the wall.

Some time later, the man returned and led him down a panelled hallway to a solid door of some black, fine-grained wood. The servant knocked, and a gruff voice answered from within. The servant opened the door and stepped aside for Alejandro to enter.

The room was large and well appointed, with tall windows looking out onto a walled courtyard in which a fountain spilled into a basin from a stone jug held in the hands of a stone child. More than that Alejandro did not see because his attention was immediately claimed by the man who sat at an ornately carved table, his back to the windows and his attention fixed on a cloth-bound ledger open before him. An ink-stained quill rested in his hand, and as Alejandro drew up before him, the pen made a quick notation beside one of a long column of numbers.

All the monk could see of the man was the top of his head, the hair shorn close to the scalp in the modern style. Two scars were visible through the dark bristles, one white and the other purple. The sight reminded him that before Rodrigo de Ribadeneira had become a successful merchant, he had been just as successful as a soldier.

Now the pen was laid down and the man looked up, his face a collection of hard planes offset by a nose that was long and straight, a beard shaped like the tip of a spear, waxed mustachios that stood out to either side, and a pair of eyes that had seen little to please the mind that regarded the world through them, and saw even less now.

"Who are you, and what do you want?"

Alejandro had brought the letter of introduction, wrapped in oiled cloth and tucked into the breast of his habit. Now he drew it forth and handed it over, saying, "Your help, sir."

De Ribadeneira took it without a word, broke the seal, and opened the folded paper. He scanned it quickly then tossed it onto the table. The gaze he turned on Alejandro had grown no warmer.

"Your uncle and I were at the Jesuits' school together. I used to protect him from bullies, and he used to pass me answers to keep the crows from whipping me.

"Then I went to be a soldier and he to be a lawyer. We have not spoken in near twenty years."

He paused and regarded Alejandro the way a farmer sizes up a cow he may or may not decide to buy. "He wants me to do something for you. What I want to know is: what can you do for me?"

"I can read and write," said the monk. "I believe literacy is in short supply hereabouts."

"I have clerks," de Ribadeneira said. He smoothed his mustachios with a knuckle. "Can you figure?"

"Yes."

The merchant turned the ledger so it faced Alejandro. He pointed to a column of figures and put his finger sideways over the one at the bottom. "Add that."

The monk put both palms on the table and leaned over the page. He resisted letting his lips move as they sometimes still did when he was confronted by more than the most basic arithmetic. After several seconds, he looked at de Ribadeneira and said, "Four hundred and seventy-two pesos."

The merchant's brows drew down. He rotated the ledger back to face him, ran his fingers down the column of numbers—Alejandro chided himself when he realized that the merchant was softly voicing his calculations—then de Ribadeneira took up his pen, inked it from the well, and corrected the total, which was out by a single peso.

He looked up at the monk again and said, "I can use you."

"My vocation is to serve the native people by bringing them to salvation," the Trinitarian said. "I would not be comfortable in a counting house."

For the first time, he saw interest on the merchant's face: a fleeting smile that showed more cynicism than honest mirth. Then he saw that de Ribadeneira had come to a decision.

"Our interests coincide," the merchant said. "I am organizing a chain of workshops where the *Indios* will weave cloth for me. Up until now, the accounts have been kept by men who used to be officials of the pagan kings. They keep their records by tying knots in pieces of string."

"Are they not honest in their accounts?" Alejandro said.

"I don't know," said the merchant. "And I do not intend to learn their methods. You will teach them our system of numbers, then check their figures to make sure they are correct."

The monk's face must have shown his hesitancy, because de Ribadeneira continued, "When you are not serving me, you may preach and teach to your heart's delight."

"I will do my best," Alejandro said.

"I will pay you—"

"I do not require a salary, only food and shelter. You may give the money to the poor."

"I may," said the merchant, "but I won't." His attention returned to the ledger. "Come back tomorrow morning, and you will meet the people you will be overseeing."

Clearly, Alejandro had ceased to hold the man's attention. He thought a silent blessing was appropriate, if perhaps not guaranteed to be effective. When he left the office, he found the servant ready to lead him out.

Later, after prayers, as he lay on the pallet in his cell at the Franciscan house, he sought again for that sense of right purpose that had come over him on the high road to Quito. Immediately it came to him, if not with the same fervour, then with a quiet strength that he found comforting.

Nine

Expectation

I became increasingly concerned about Alonso after he came back from the raid on the Campazes. He was not the same. He went about his duties with an air of complete concentration, teaching the women and children to speak Spanish. He was often called to kneel beside Anton's seat in what had been the men's house, because the chief had decided that he needed to keep written accounts of some matters: lists of supplies and weapons, assignments of specific responsibilities to the men—and one woman, Miriam—whom he had promoted to positions of subordinate authority, as well as other aspects of running the enlarged village.

Often Alonso was told to work on the map and would have me accompany him. Anton did not like to have me near, but the chief was very interested to sketch the boundaries that divided our Nigua territory from the Campazes to the south and the Cayapas to the north, more so than in regard to the territory of the Yumbo. He was most concerned with places where the Spaniards had landed in the past, before they went up-country and killed the emperor of the Quechua speakers, and where they were settled today.

My information was not as detailed as it might have been if I could have consulted Pidi and the senior men of the old village. But Pahta was knowledgeable, so I brought him in, too, and translated back and forth between him and Anton while Alonso made marks on the map.

One day, the issue was the location of the other Nigua *palenques.* I looked at Pahta, who looked at me, both of us conscious that Anton was watching us closely. I said, "Better if we tell him than if he sends out scouts to find them himself."

Pahta acquiesced. I think he was quite taken with the idea of serving a war chief who clearly had a plan and was determined to make it work. It was a big change from life under Pidi, or even under Pidi's father when we had all lived in the old town. Then, at least until the Spaniards came, life had been a largely settled affair, with few opportunities for an ordinary man like Pahta to rise in the world.

We calculated walking and paddling times and applied them to the map—I still thought it was a wonderful invention—and Alonso marked the paths and streams and the hidden villages they led to. Next to each point of interest he put down figures as I gave him the estimated numbers of fighting men, women of childbearing age, and children and old people there.

When Alonso wasn't actively working, he became very still and his gaze became unfocused, as if he were seeing inwardly into memory or imagination. I was sure it was the former that so occupied him. I had seen similar states come over Nigua men after we fled the old town and its many dead. The long stare meant that a man had been abandoned by his power animal, the spirit that enlivened him and protected him against the range of evils that could stealthily seep into his undefended orifices—especially the nose, which carried breath into the core of one's being—and steal his strength.

Alonso had almost certainly lost his guiding spirit, but it would be difficult to raise the subject with him because he was ignorant of such realities and had actively resisted my attempts to explain them to him.

"Hush," he had said, pitching his voice low and glancing around, when last I had raised the subject of spirit guides. All Nigua knew about these, even the children. He had leaned towards me, as we sat on our stools in the spirit house, and whispered, "Anton believes in devils. Deeply. If he thinks you are consorting with evil spirits, he will kill you without a second thought."

"I am combating evil spirits, not—" I had stumbled over the word *consorting*, as it was new to me, and that was when Alonso put his fingers to my lips, closing off my voice and my breath.

"No," he said. "I need you to live."

I let the subject drop. It had been of only theoretical interest then. But that was before he came back from the raid so obviously bereft. Now it was a matter of much greater concern. I kept a close watch on Alonso; sometimes a strong spirit guide can force its way back into its place, often during a deep sleep.

But my housemate did not show any signs of improvement. The enjoyable conversations we conducted before had now ceased. It was like sharing a hut with a shadow.

Alonso had lost a part of himself during the raid on the Campazes, but he had come back with something else: a long, narrow-bladed, two-edged knife, much different from the heavier, wide-bladed weapons that he and the others had taken from the Spaniards on the beach. It was called a rapier, he told me when I asked, and it was made out of something called Toledo steel, which was like iron but better in some way that had to do with fire, though I did not understand the details.

He wore the rapier wherever he went now. It came with a close-fitting sheath of leather, over wood attached to a belt of metal links fastened together with a buckle of yellow metal that was not gold but something called brass. I was surprised that Anton made no fuss about Alonso going armed about the village. The chief had issued weapons to the two dark men who had come back with him from the fight with the Spaniards. He had strict rules about handling the weapons inside the village: only those who were on sentry duty could carry them; otherwise they were to be stored in their individual huts.

"We will have no fights to the death," the chief told us all. "We are too few to sustain unnecessary losses. If you have disagreements, you may settle them with your fists until the loser has had enough or cannot get up from the ground. As long as no one is killed or crippled, I will not interfere."

The new law was accepted by all except Esteban, one of the two who had been rescued from the Spanish soldiers. I suspected he was accustomed to taking orders from Spaniards but not from other Africans. He was heavily muscled, and his face was marked with a scar that ran from the corner of his right eye down to his upper lip. The first time he was put on sentry duty—sent down the trail with another, to watch the landing by the stream—he came back after his watch and went to sit in the circle formed by some of the other men who had finished their tasks for the day. He sat cross-legged on the ground, drinking from a gourd of corn beer they were passing around. His halberd lay beside him. From time to time, he touched the shaft as he laughed and joked with the others.

All this was within sight of the presidio. After a while, the chief appeared in the sunrise doorway, as he did from time to time, and looked about. His gaze fell upon the halberd and passed on. Then he stretched and flexed his big shoulders and called to the man with the weapon, telling him to put it in his hut.

Esteban did not obey. He lifted the gourd and said, "When I have finished drinking," then took a good long swallow of the beer. He set it down and said something to the other men, something about a man who could not satisfy his women. A few of the others laughed—but now the laughter was tinged with nervousness. Esteban did not look at Anton again.

The chief's face became calm, and he turned and went back into the big house. The man with the halberd patted its shaft again and made some other low-voiced remark. Two of the men in the circle got up and moved away. The others stayed where they were, but I could see the tension in them; when one of them took a swig from the gourd, it trembled in his grasp, and some of the liquid spilled down his chin and bare chest.

Anton came out of the presidio and down the ladder. His face was still without emotion. He had the look of a man who is concentrating on his work. From his hand hung a length of tapered hardwood, as thick as my forearm and swelling to a knobbed burl at one end; a loop of leather at the other fitted loosely over his wrist. It had belonged to the dead Nigua chief and Anton claimed it from his corpse.

He walked with a methodical pace towards the circle of sitting men, all of whom leapt to their feet and scattered like birds chased from a garden by the watch boys. The man with the halberd rose with them but did not flee. He did not show the same studied calmness as Anton, but he looked confident. He took a step forward, the weapon angled towards the ground, its axe blade pointing up. As Anton neared, he dug the halberd's point into the dirt, flicked a clod towards the chief's face, then brought the weapon level and made a quick thrust towards Anton's belly.

Anton's expression did not change. As the point came at him, his free hand moved with the speed of a striking snake to seize the shaft just behind the head. He yanked it towards him, pulling the other man off balance, and pivoted so that the weapon's point went past him, spitting nothing but air. At the same time, he brought the club straight up, catching the other man under the chin and snapping his head back.

It had all happened in one smooth manoeuvre. Esteban let go of the halberd, and his knees buckled. He spat blood and, I think, a piece of his tongue, then sank down until he was sitting on the ground. He shook his head, drops of blood flying, and put one hand onto the ground to begin levering himself up. But Anton stepped in and struck the straightened arm at the elbow. I heard the *crack* as the bone snapped. The man screamed as the arm gave way under him, and he collapsed on one side.

Still wearing the look of a craftsman plying his skills, Anton bent towards him and swung the club to break one of the man's knees. This brought a howl like a child's and a clumsy attempt to roll away, but the chief followed and targeted the other knee, then the other elbow.

By now Esteban was crying, begging Anton to stop, blubbering and promising he would do something—it was hard to understand what he was saying at this point. But the club kept rising and falling, and the bones kept breaking: feet, ankles, ribs, collarbones, shins, upper arms, and more. At some point, the man lost consciousness. I thought, in fact, that his spirit had fled the pain and terror once and for all, but when Anton finally ceased, I could hear the rasp of the broken man's breath and see bubbles of blood swelling and diminishing at the base of his mashed nose.

Anton straightened up, nodded once as if to himself, then raised his gaze to see the entire village ranged about the scene of punishment. He looked from one set of eyes to another, all around the circle, and again I was struck by his air of detached observation. When his gaze fell on me, it lingered for a moment. I felt a shiver go through me, and when his attention moved on, I wondered—not for the first time—what kind of spirit moved inside our war chief.

Alonso was nearby, wearing his rapier. I was vaguely conscious of his having come running just as the fight started, his hand on its hilt of straight metal bars above a brass cup. Now Anton's eyes met Alonso's before dropping to where the younger man's hand still rested on his weapon. The chief's gaze came up to meet Alonso's and he nodded again and said, "Finish him."

Alonso did not hesitate. His face took on a stillness. His brows drew together a little, like those of a man who is concentrating on a precise task. He drew the rapier with a smooth motion and came to stand above the broken thing at the centre of the circle. Esteban was lying on his side, one leg at an unnatural angle. Alonso pressed the point of the rapier to the back of the man's neck and pushed it through the centre as easily as I might put my finger into a piece of cornbread.

The man on the ground did not even shudder. He simply stopped breathing; his body showed that curious slumping that only the dead can achieve. I thought I had better get back to the spirit house to help guide Esteban's ghost away from this world: the manner of his death made it clear that his would not be a good spirit to let linger.

But before I left, I regarded Alonso as he wiped the tip of his blade on the man's shirt, first one side then the other. He did it with the same methodical economy of motion with which Anton had delivered his harsh judgment. I saw the young man raise his eyes again to the chief. Something passed between them. They were connected now as they had not been before. Anton picked up the fallen halberd and carried it back to the presidio.

I went back to the spirit house with a puzzle to consider. Could Anton, to whom the very notion of spirit guides was a death-worthy evil, have possibly drawn Alonso's spirit from him and now be holding it in thrall? I wished I could guide Alonso down into the underworld to see where his guardian spirit had ended up—and, of course, restore it to him.

But that was impossible when I could not even raise the subject. I resolved, once I had the dead man's business settled, to consult my monkey-eagle spirit. I needed some good advice.

What, I asked myself, *has the wind brought us? And what more will it bring?*

"Alonso says you are not Spaniards but Africans," I said to Miriam.

"He is right," she said.

"What kind of place is Africa?"

She looked at me for a moment and laughed. "An unhappy one." She lifted the hem of her cotton shirt to wipe the sweat from her face. "I cannot talk about this now. We are busy."

That was true. It was a beer-making day, and most of the women in the village were gathered in the women's house for the communal work. The drink was made from sprouted yellow corn that had been heated to generate malt. It was brewed in big clay pots made in the highlands, which the Quechua speakers had traded to us in return for the little white seashells that they used to prize before the Spaniards brought coins of copper, gold, and silver. Today, the beer was stirred and heated; it would sit for several days, the mouths of the pots sealed by tight wooden plugs. In five days, it would be drinkable but weak. In ten, it would be stronger.

It was not unusual for me to be in the women's house on beer-making days; it was well known that if a woman harboured a malevolent spirit—even though she might not know it—it could cause the beer to turn out bitter or fusty. If I was on the scene, the putative trouble-making spirit would be afraid to come out, knowing that I would see it and later punish it harshly.

Miriam did not make Anton's beer. One of his Nigua wives did that. But she oversaw the process and, more important, listened to what the women said as they chaffed each other. Traditionally, the women's house was where our women could speak most freely, and the tradition had endured since the change. Miriam had by now learned a great deal of our language from her fellow wives—I had come to recognize her intelligence—and she used these collective working times as opportunities to keep in touch with the deeper currents in our village's life.

"Could we speak after?" I said. "I am interested."

She gave me another look then, and I felt myself being weighed and examined. But I had long ago developed the ability to return a bland and innocent aspect on such occasions, and after a while she wiped her face again and said, "Come to the presidio after this."

"I will," I said, and let her go back to her work as chief wife of the chief.

I had chosen this day because Anton was not in the former men's house. The growth in the village's population meant that more land needed to be cleared for corn and other crops. Under Pidi, there had been four clearings. Now Anton was directing the men and boys in making a larger space. The work was going much faster than in the old times because they were using steel axes salvaged from the ship, but it was the kind of effort that required the presence of a chief to prevent the men from resting too frequently.

Before I went up the sunrise-side ladder into the presidio, I made my courtesy out of habit. Miriam was sitting just inside the doorway, out of the sun, and her sharp eye noticed.

"What did you do with your hand, just then?" she said after telling me to sit. She unstoppered the terracotta jug beside her, poured two measures of beer into wooden bowls, and handed one over to me. I recognized the bowls as ritual vessels from the old days, when I would not have been allowed to touch them—nor would Miriam or any woman.

I took the offered drink and swallowed. It was old beer, left to grow strong and dark in the pot. The jug had kept it cool in that wondrous way that terracotta can perform.

I answered her question. "An old gesture of politeness." I explained about how this used to be a place only for men and how I was admitted only on the chief's word. I had to show respect.

"Now that has gone by," she said.

"Yes."

"And your position is more … secure."

She was watching me closely. I judged this was not a time for blandness. "Is it?" I said.

She put a corner of her lower lip between her teeth and said, "Anton finds you useful. So did the women at the beer-making today."

"Though they made jokes about me when I was gone."

"Not too many," she said, "and not too cruel."

"They are polite enough when they are sick, or their children are."

She shrugged. "Each of us has to find our place in the world. Where I come from, you would have been killed at birth as a witch child."

"Do Christians do such things, too?"

"I was not a Christian." She paused to think for a moment. "Nor am I now."

I took this in. "You are not a Spaniard, but an African. You are not a Christian, but a … ?"

"It is complicated," she said. She gathered her thoughts for a moment. "Africa is not a country, but a land of many countries, many peoples. Nobody knows how many."

"What was your country?"

"It is called Kaabu, and my people are the Mandinka."

I sat silently and sipped a little more, my face showing that I wanted to hear more. She obliged, as people usually do, her eyes looking at me but seeing images in her mind.

"Once we were a great empire called Mali," she said.

"Like the empire of the Quechua speakers?"

"Bigger, I think. We had so much gold, all the world came to us. But they could not rob us because we had armies: soldiers on horses, spearmen by the thousands, and most of all, we had the bows and arrows." She took a sip of beer. "And the arrows were poisoned."

"Ah," I said. "Like ours."

She came back from the past, and now she was definitely seeing me. "You know how to make poisons?" she said.

I had long ago learned that the best way to give a false answer to a question was to give a true answer to a different query. "I know how to cure some kinds of poisonings."

I took another sip and asked her to tell me more about her old land of gold. She shrugged and continued, but I knew she had filed away my mention of poison arrows and that she would tell Anton.

"After hundreds of years, there arose different factions. You understand 'factions'?"

I assured her I did.

"The factions fought, and that weakened the empire, and when we were weak, the outsiders came. First, they raided. Then they came in force. Finally, a hundred years ago or more, the Tuaregs took Timbuktu, our great city."

We paused to drink more beer, and she refilled our bowls. We sat in silence for a moment, hearing the background sounds of the village. Then I said, "That was Mali. You said you were of . . ." I made as if to search my memory for the name, although I remember everything. "Kaabu."

"Kaabu, yes," she said. "We were a province of the empire, but when it fell, we held out against the invaders. We were a land of soldiers, and they could not crush us."

A land of soldiers, I thought. *That makes sense.*

"Kaabu still exists," she said, and again I saw her look inward. "Kaabu is still strong."

I let her dream for a few moments and said, gently, "How do you come to be here?"

She blinked and shook herself free of the reverie. "Factions again," she said. "Anton was a *fariya,* a commander of many soldiers, though he was young. My husband was one of his officers." She paused, remembering, and I saw the corners of her mouth turn down.

"There was a dispute between the *nyanko* Anton and my husband served and another *nyanko*—the word means 'lord'—and it came to a fight."

She paused again, and I could see long-suppressed pain climbing up inside of her. But I needed to know and so I said, "You did not win."

"The other *nyanko* had been preparing. He had built up a large slave army, and they struck when Anton's lord was not yet ready. We were overwhelmed. My husband was killed. Anton was wounded and captured. Those who did not die were sold to the Portuguese, along with their families."

"How was he wounded? I see no scars."

"You also see no children, no pregnancies. I am too old, but his Nigua wives are not."

It was time to change the subject. I had heard Alonso speak of the Portuguese. They were another sort of Spaniard, though apparently they spoke a different language—like us and the Campazes. I asked, and Miriam said they lived next to the Spaniards' country and supplied them with slaves from Africa. I made noises of polite interest to encourage her to speak more, but she had gone inside of herself again. She cast her gaze around the huts ringing the plaza and said, "I used to live in a palace. Now . . ."

She fell silent again. After a while, I said, "Is Alonso African or Spaniard?"

The question apparently amused her, though only faintly. "A good question. I don't think even he knows the answer." Her brow wrinkled a little then cleared. "I think he might be Mandinka. When Anton and I speak in our old tongue, Alonso listens as if the sounds of the language call to him. He might even have been one of the children of our *nyanko*. But something terrible happened to him when he was a little boy, and all of who he used to be just"—she lifted the backs of her fingers to her lips and blew a puff of air across them—"disappeared."

I covered my excitement by raising the bowl to my lips and drinking. She had just given me an important piece of information, if I could fit it into what I already knew and suspected.

I would have to think about it. And when I could frame the question properly, I would visit my spirit guide and seek wisdom. One thing I knew all on my own, however, was that I needed to know what had happened to the young man when he was a child and how that fit with what was happening to him now.

Because my fate was entwined with his. That was why the monkey-eagle had shown him to me.

I asked a few more questions about Kaabu, its people, and their ways, so that Miriam would not think that I had come only to learn about Alonso. That was from force of habit: a shaman always disguises his interests. We finished the second bowl of beer, and I said I had duties to perform. She let me go, but from the way she studied me, I did not think I had fooled her at all.

Back at the spirit house, I composed myself to meditate. Alonso was with Anton in the new fields, keeping notes and probably doing calculations. That thought put me in mind of the things that could be done with the Spaniards' numbers. I had developed a fascination for multiplying and dividing—Alonso had shown me the methods—and I was doing more and more complicated calculations in my head, without resorting to the smoothed wood and charcoal.

I had carefully counted out a hundred pebbles and used them to prove the figures: setting out nine groups of nine, for example, and finding them to make eighty-one, just as the marks on the board or the figures I spoke in my mind said they must. The reliability of it all was still a revelation to me. The world in which I had grown up was a fluid place, where one thing shaded into another. But Spanish numbers were solid, absolute, as sharply defined as the edges of Spanish steel and iron weapons. No wonder they had conquered the Quechua speakers, though the emperor's armies outnumbered them by hundreds to one—a calculation I could now make on my board.

But now I put aside my interest in numbers and concentrated on regulating my breathing and stilling my mind. When the sounds of the village retreated from my awareness and all was still within me, I called up the image of Alonso, and when I had it steady in my mind's view, I studied it. I saw him as he was now, a young man just about to enter into his mature years. Then I saw him as an old man, his face seamed and his beard gone white. Then I threw him back across the years and saw him as a child.

I found I could not get a clear view of him. His features faded into generalities. His eyes were blank and without expression. The child was not a person, but only the shell of one. I sought to push the image farther back into the past and was a little surprised to discover that it did not change. I could not see Alonso as a toddler or an infant, nor as a child of seven or eight, even though those images should have been immanent in his present appearance and my abilities should have recovered them.

He was a mystery. I had known that from the moment I saw him through the eagle's eyes. More than that, he was *my* mystery, mine to solve. The wind had brought him to me and brought much change to the people, for whom I was responsible in a way that Pidi and his father had never been. For their sake, and for the sake of the long lines of Nigua who would extend into the future, far beyond my sight, I had to make Alonso the business of my life.

He did not come back to the spirit house for the evening meal. Instead, he ate with Anton and Miriam because the chief wanted to talk to him about some plan. Alonso was becoming Anton's shadow: always near, always ready to undertake some task.

The Nigua woman whose turn it was to feed us brought bowls of a meaty stew—the men had been out hunting and had speared a tapir trapped in a pit—and a gourd full of new beer. I told her to take Alonso's to the presidio and was interested to see that the prospect of entering what had been the men's house did not trouble her. She was adapting to the new ways, as were most of us. It probably helped that the Africans, for the most part, made good husbands.

The old tradition of men and women eating separately in their respective houses had also sunk without a ripple. Men and their wives now ate outside their houses, usually with a smudgy fire to keep off the biting insects. After the meal, men would gather around somebody's fire to talk, and sometimes they would sing. The women would form two or three groups. There were cliques just as there had always been, but the African and Nigua women mixed together equably.

Anton did not eat with anyone but Miriam. His other wives ate together but in a separate part of the big house. After the meal, he did not join any of the others, but he would walk about the village and accept the greetings of the people, sometimes singling out one person or another for a brief conversation.

It was not the way Pidi or his father used to exercise their authority, but I believed that Anton was acting a role that was familiar to him and to many of the Africans. And it seemed to be working: after the beating with the club, there were no more incidents of incipient insurrection. Fortunately, I had been able to find the dead man's spirit and send it on its way, so there were no disturbing influences among the people.

When Alonso came up the ladder, he looked tired. I offered him some of the beer, but he took only a polite sip before going to lie on his pallet. He often did that now instead of sitting on the stool and talking with me by the light of the clay lamp that burned Spanish oil. He would lie on his back, staring unblinkingly up into the reeds and rafters but not seeing them. He reminded me of a child's corn husk doll, abandoned after its owner had finished playing for the day.

After a while, I said, "You have not been sleeping well. You make sounds and movements."

He turned his head my way. "Do I?"

"Yes." I waited to see if he would say anything more, but he went back to staring at nothing. "If you do not sleep well, you are tired in the day."

"I am tired a lot," he said.

"I have a medicine that will give you a better sleep."

He said nothing. Sometimes I was not sure he heard me; his ears were listening to sounds only he could hear, sounds that came from the hollow place inside him where his guiding spirit should have been.

I said, "Would you like to take some?"

He turned to look at me again. "Does it work?"

I nodded. "I use it myself when my mind is too busy." That was not quite true. When I wanted to go deep into my own passages, I used the medicine, though in less of a dose than I intended to give to Alonso.

"I will try it," he said, though without enthusiasm. "I am tired in the mornings . . ." He trailed off.

I had already ground the dried materials and measured a dose in a bowl. Now I poured the new beer into it and stirred. The powder did not dissolve but floated in the yellow liquid. He sat up, and I handed him the bowl. He drank it all in one draught, belched, and lay down again.

"Sleep well," I said. I watched, sipping beer, until I saw his eyes close and his breathing change rhythm. I waited a little longer then mixed my own dose of the herb, wet it, and drank it down.

Then I composed myself, paid attention to my breathing, and waited for the descent into the underworld.

"He has lost his guiding spirit," I told the monkey eagle. "A long time ago, I think. When he was a child."

The spirit did not respond in words, but I received an answer. She agreed with me. Then she seemed to enlarge herself, and I knew that I was being drawn into her. Moments later, I was seeing the world from the eagle's perspective. We were flying in the upper air, very high, the world nothing but a faint suggestion far below us. Then we swooped low and I saw a land and a sea coast, but it was not our land, nor our sea.

There was forest, but it was not like our forest: the trees were not so tall nor so closely packed, and the ground beneath them was dry and dusty. I saw villages and towns, but the houses were built of bricks made of dried mud, and their roofs were as flat as floors, and some of them were two and three stories high.

We passed over a city bigger than any I had ever seen, and at its centre was a sprawling palace of mud brick, with courtyards and shaded walks. There were many people, dark of skin, dressed in robes of white cotton and with their heads swathed in cloth. I saw markets and squares shaded by great trees whose branches spread wide, and beyond the city's wooden walls was a river of brown water. I saw canoes large enough to hold fifty men, their paddles rising and falling in rhythmic unison like the legs of some great insect as they breasted the current.

And now my vision swept out over the plain beyond the city, past the gardens and fields, to where a vast cloud of dust marked the advance of an army. They came in their thousands, some of them riding on long-legged beasts that wore armour of quilted cloth, the riders carrying long lances and short javelins, curved swords at their waists. And for every rider there were five men who ran on foot, bare-chested, carrying tall bows and quivers of arrows.

In the middle of the army rode a man in fine clothes, with gold around his neck and his wrists and on the hilt and scabbard of his sword. A *nyanko*, I thought. He drew his weapon and pointed at the city, and the masses of soldiers rushed forward with ladders to scale the wooden walls, the riders leaving their horses and lances, flinging their javelins at the men who came running to defend the parapets. The invaders were too many, their arrows and javelins were tipped with poison, and soon they were swarming through the streets, killing those who resisted and binding those who did not. I saw women slash their children's throats and throw themselves down wells to escape servitude.

And now we were back to the palace. A man like the one who led the invading army stood in a courtyard, surrounded by ranks of spearmen who faced a gate of strong wooden beams. Above them on the balconies of the palace were men with bows and arrows and javelins. Behind them, in the building's inner rooms, women wept and drew their children to them.

Then the gate splintered and burst inward, huge men with axes breaking through to be shot down immediately by arrows and flung javelins. But over their bodies came men with wooden shields and weapons of their own to throw into the mass of spearmen who rushed to engage them. The fight went on without mercy and without quarter: bellies pierced, limbs and heads chopped off, blood turning the dust of the ground into scarlet mud.

The spearmen fought desperately to protect their chief. The men on the balconies shot all their arrows and threw all their javelins, drawing their curved swords and leaping down to join the fight. But the invaders were too many. Though their bodies piled up and made a breastwork of the dead and dying for the defenders, new attackers came pushing through the gateway. Others set ladders against the wall in the street outside and climbed atop the wall and ran along it to hurl javelins down on the defenders from three sides.

Soon there were only twenty defenders left, now ten, now five, now none. The lord of the city stood amidst his heaped dead, sword in hand. None had touched him. The invaders drew back, made a space around him and a lane to the gate. Some dragged bodies aside to make a clear path for their chief, who now came riding his tall beast. He ducked his head to ride through the gate. The animal shied at the scent of blood, but he quietened it with a gentle pat on its neck and a soft word. Behind him came ten tall men armed with long spears that had iron hooks behind their points.

The lord of the town raised his sword; he was offering a challenge. The man on the horse smiled and shook his head. He issued an order, and the ten bodyguards surged forward over the barrier of the fallen.

The man with the sword sought to fight them, but he was up against skilled adversaries who used their long hooked spears to pierce his sword arm and sever the tendons above his heels. He fell, weaponless and crippled, and the tall men seized him and dragged him before the man on the horse. One of them put his foot on the defeated chief's neck and pushed his face into the bloody dust.

Now other men rushed into the palace and soon came out, herding women and children ahead of them. One of the invaders held a small boy dressed in a white robe with gold stitched into its collar and hem. The child's face was a blank mask of shock. Now the man who held him called out to the man on the horse, and what the conqueror heard brought another cruel smile to his face.

He beckoned for the boy to be brought to him, slid one leg over the animal's long-haired neck, and dropped lightly to the ground. The child was dragged before him, his body stiff with fright. He now saw the lord, whose face was pressed into the dirt, and cried out something. The chief of the invaders spoke, and the bodyguard who had his foot on the man's neck released the pressure. Two others seized the man's arms and pulled him upright so that he was kneeling on his torn ankles.

The triumphant lord spoke. The man holding the boy tore the child's robes away, leaving him naked. The child looked around, bewildered, and saw only the misery of the man on his knees and the heartless mockery of the victors.

The cruel lord paused for a long moment to let his defeated enemy contemplate what was about to happen. The man struggled in the grasp of those who held him. He spoke to the victor, his face showing an agony that had nothing to do with the pain of his wounds.

But that was just what the enemy chief had been waiting for. When I saw what he intended, I looked away. When I looked back, the child had been discarded. He lay trembling at the conqueror's feet.

The lord of the victorious army nodded to one of his bodyguards. The men holding the crippled lord stepped away, leaving him swaying. He reached his unwounded arm out to the child. At that moment, a guard swung his axe in a sideways arc, striking the kneeling man in the back of the neck and severing his head from his body.

Blood from the decapitated man's neck spurted onto the child. The boy made a fitful attempt to brush the gore away. Then his face became blank. I knew his spirit had fled from him.

The scene dwindled as my spirit guide spiralled up into the air. Soon the city was lost beneath us and we passed over the sea, still rising into the thin blue of the upper sky. A timeless time passed, and then I was back in my body with the sleeping Alonso in the spirit hut—the place where Pallu, when he had drunk old beer, had sometimes used me like the cruel lord used Alonso.

I watched Alonso's chest rise and fall as he slept, otherwise motionless, on the pallet where I had restored the alienated spirits of several of my people, curing them and bringing them back into the life of the village.

But whether I could bring back to Alonso what had been taken from him in the carnage of that courtyard was a problem I could only ponder. I feared the solution would be beyond my powers.

*T*EN

ALONSO ILLESCAS

Alonso is feeling better rested today than he has in weeks — indeed in all the time since *La Virgen* broke up on the reef. Some of the stiffness has gone out of his back, and his neck does not make cracking noises when he turns his head from one side to another. He is sure Expectation's medicine has had something to do with it. He will ask her to administer another dose tonight.

He has spent the morning in the new garden plots with Anton, dogging the chief's heels as the big man directs the crews that are clearing the land. The steel axes have been effective at felling the trees, though the work of digging up the roots is hard and slow. Still, the men say they do not mind the work. It is not easy to labour in the damp heat of the coastal forest, but it is better than the stoop labour of cutting cane in the sugar plantations of Hispaniola. And it is their own food they are growing: theirs and their wives' and their children's.

Alonso's job is to carry the smoothed board of pale wood and a stick of dry charcoal, and to make a note of anything Anton wants recorded. Usually, he is told to put down the names of any crew who are showing exceptional diligence so that the members may be rewarded that night with a jug of the strong beer that Anton keeps in the presidio. The men like it better than the weak new beer that is the daily drink.

A substantial area has now been cleared, the trees cut down and hauled away, the slash and ground cover burned off, and the ashes turned into the soil with hoes. Men are now shaping the earth into ridges and furrows for the *papa* tubers that the Niguas long ago acquired from the Quechua speakers, by way of the Yumbo and the Cayapas.

When work stops for the midday meal, Anton beckons Alonso to him. "Take five men and the raft, and go down to the fields behind the old town. Dig up as many *papas* as you can and bring them here. Tomorrow we will plant them."

"Yes," Alonso says. He picks out a crew of five, three who were on *La Virgen* and two Niguas who had fought the Campazes. Anton has organized all the groups, mixing them together, breaking up any tight partnerships, encouraging competition between crews, and rewarding the winners with strong beer and sometimes even a half-day of leisure.

The men are careful around Alonso. He does not browbeat them the way Anton sometimes does; he does not even frown or make disparaging remarks. He gives orders in a quiet voice that the men strain to hear. But he wears the sword belt and its scabbarded blade, as Anton has ordered. He does not put a hand to its hilt in a threatening manner like some bravo on the Seville waterfront. The only time he touches the sword is when it impedes his movement.

He knows that the men tread warily about him. The knowledge neither pleases nor disturbs. Alonso has reached a new plateau in his existence, though he was not aware of climbing towards it until he suddenly recognized that he was there. It happened during the fight against the Campazes, when he acquired the sword he now wears.

He sometimes thinks back on that night. As he advanced against the Campaze warrior, a curious coolness descended upon him. He remembers it quite clearly; it was as if he had stepped to one side of himself, into a zone of calmness and tranquillity. Time slowed. The sounds of the fighting diminished to a distant murmur. He was not a disinterested spectator, however; he closely directed his body's motions. But he did so without fear or anger or even excitement. He could tell what his opponent intended to do, and he saw what to do in response. When the moment came, he acted without hesitation, sliding the spear point into the enemy's belly as easily as he would slice an apple.

Alonso has reflected on his new outlook. He is aware that in the past it would have troubled him. But it does not trouble him now. He cannot say that he is happy now, but he is not unhappy. He has a place in the new order of things. He has work that he finds he is suited for.

If only he were not so tired, so often. If only he did not lie down with his back muscles stiff and aching and wake up with them no different. But now the healer has given him a potion that has eased the discomfort. Two or three more nights like the last one, he thinks, and he will be fit and fine again.

He leads the five men back to the village, where they collect baskets and take the trail to the landing where the raft lies. Along the way, they pass the man watching the path, leaning against a tree with his spear butt resting on the ground and its shaft loosely held in the crook of his elbow. The man's name is Fernando, and Alonso once wrote his name on the board then summoned him in the evening for a dressing-down from Anton.

Fernando hears them coming from behind him and turns his head. When he sees it is Alonso, he straightens and gets a proper grip on the spear. "All fine here," he says.

"Good," says Alonso, not bothering to stop. He pushes through the bushes and onto the landing. The crew sidle past him to load the baskets onto the raft and push it into the water. When they take up their poles, he steps aboard and they make their way down the stream. No one speaks.

It is the first time Alonso has been back to the old town's overgrown gardens since the castaways came up to the hidden village. He sets the five men to work, loosening the earth around the *papa* roots so that they can be pulled up. The tubers come with them, curious brown-skinned lumps of starch that Alonso has come to enjoy boiled in a copper pot or sliced and fried on a greased flat stone beside the fire.

Out in the open, the midday sun is hot. There is not a breath of wind from the stillness of the sea, and the humid air wraps itself around Alonso like warm flesh. But he does not sweat as much as he used to. His body has accustomed itself to the steamy heat, and some of the women have made him a long, sleeveless shirt of light cotton decorated at neck and hem with colourful stitching. They have also woven him a pair of sandals to replace his brass-buckled Spanish shoes. Without his doublet and hose, the air can reach his flesh and cool him. But no matter how hot it gets, he remains cool inside.

With the men working well, he drifts away across the field. He finds a digging stick someone has left—perhaps it was dropped by one of the sailors when they rushed back to the ship. He pokes idly at the abandoned food plants, lifts away creepers that are beginning to cover them, his thoughts on nothing more than what he is doing here and now.

He looks up into an unbroken expanse of blue. A bird, too far away to recognize as anything other than a moving dot, is flying above the trees that stretch inland. Alonso remembers a time before in this field—close to this very spot—when he looked up and saw the circling eagle, its pale wings spread and the individual feathers at their tips plainly visible against the sky. He had the impression then that it was staring at him, that he could actually see its golden eyes, though surely that is a false memory, the creature having been so far away. He remembers, too, the shock of energy that passed through him, so different from how he is today.

He feels a tickling sensation on one cheek and uses a finger to brush away the fly before it can bite. But there is no fly. His finger comes away wet. He realizes that tears are running down both cheeks, and suddenly he hunches forward as a deep-throated sob erupts from him. He hears a moan followed by another sob.

Alonso has stepped outside himself again. But time has not slowed down. He is not aware of tiny details in his field of vision as he was during the fight at the mine. Indeed, he cannot see at all now, his eyes are so flooded with tears. The forest is a blur of green and darkness, all shapes diffuse, all perspective lost.

In his mind's eye, he watches himself crying, hears the sounds that come up his throat from deep inside him, feels the convulsions that clutch at his diaphragm and bend him over. He has no explanation for the paroxysm of … what? He cannot put a name to it. Is it grief? Is it sadness? Is it a profound sense of loss and loneliness? Of being far from home, so far he cannot even think where home might be?

And then, as sudden as the onset, the spasm is over. He is back in himself once more. He wipes his eyes with the backs of his hands and tries to pull up the hem of his long shirt to clean his face. The sword belt hampers him, so he unbuckles it and lets it drop, wiping his face properly with the cotton and snuffling up the wet mucus clogging his nose.

He turns and ducks under a leafy branch. He steps out of green dimness into the bright open space of the fields, under the clear blue sky and the fierce white heat of the midday sun. The men are still digging up *papa* plants and filling the baskets with tubers. Expectation has told him that each fat, hard root can be cut into pieces, and each piece, once planted, will grow into a whole new plant. And each new plant will produce new tubers, the way a stalk of wheat will contain several grains.

Alonso reminds himself: he has a place. He has a purpose. What he is doing today will feed the people and help make them secure. To be useful is all he has ever sought in life, from as far back as he can remember. He will call being useful a victory and think no more of it.

Time has passed. The new fields are cleared and planted. Anton has a plan to bring cuttings from the fruit trees in the old orchards and graft them onto new plantings beside the village. The stockade has been strengthened, as have the two gates, and the forest has been cut back to offer clear fields of fire. A killing ground, the chief calls it. "What the Spaniards were laying out around their fort."

Alonso and Expectation are called to the presidio. It is after the noon-time meal, and, with the major projects completed, Anton has instituted a break during the worst heat of the day. As they cross the plaza to the big house, they see people sitting where there is shade, talking, drinking new beer, a couple of them playing a game with a wooden board and dried beans for counters. Others are sleeping in the huts, although while passing one house Alonso hears sounds of pleasure.

Expectation says, "A few months, and we will have more babies."

Alonso says nothing. None of the newborns will be his. He has been approached by some of the older women and even two of the younger wives, but always he has put them off with one excuse or another. He has had women before—he used to go with the apprentices from the Illescas house in Seville to a brothel they favoured—but found the experience unsettling, even when he was able to complete the act.

He knows that the healer is watching him and is sure that she knows about him and the wives; Expectation listens closely to the women when they chaff each other over the beer making and when they're working in the fields. "We need more people," Alonso says.

They are at the foot of the ladder leading into the former men's house. Alonso sees the hermaphrodite make the usual odd motion of the right hand before ascending the steps. Inside the presidio, Anton is standing behind the table he has had made, the map spread on it. He calls them to him and points to one of the places Expectation has identified as a Nigua village.

"Has anything changed here?" he says.

The healer looks at the chief. "Are you asking me if I have been in contact with other Nigua people?"

Anton meets her gaze, his expression blank. "And if I am asking?"

"The answer is no."

The chief continues to regard her in silence. Expectation does not look away. After a long moment, Anton says, "Has anyone else been in contact?"

"Not that I know of. But you know that Cayapas traders have come, as they always have."

"Do we need to worry about them spying on us?"

"They do not talk to the Spaniards," she says. "At the first sight of them, they flee deep into the forest." The healer cocks her head to one side, thinks about it. "But they trade with other Niguas in the *palenques*, so those others will know what has happened here. And they will know about how you killed the Spaniards and the Campazes."

Anton digests the information. "But they have not come to us."

It is not a question, but the healer responds. "I believe they will wait to see what you do. And how you do it."

Again, Anton is thinking, his gaze wandering on the map. Alonso and Expectation wait. After a while, the chief looks up. "I am sending you, both of you, to talk to them. You will take Pahta and one of the crews."

"All right," says Expectation. Alonso nods.

Anton continues. "You will invite them to come live with us. Tell them they will be well treated."

Alonso speaks for the first time. "Will you give them gifts?"

Anton considers the suggestion and asks Expectation, "Would it help?"

She thinks about it for only a moment. "Steel knives and copper pots. It would show them that you are not like the Spaniards, who offered only curses and blows."

Anton nods. "Agreed. But take only a few gifts, enough to make them want more. And make it clear they will be safe here. Or at least safer."

"Yes. The Campazes will come north. If they find the scattered *palenques* before they find our village, there will be little the small bands of our people can do to fight them."

"We need more fighting men," Anton says. He looks at Expectation. "Not men who will run and hide in the forest."

Now it is her turn to shrug. "The forest is a good place to fight from if you know it well enough. We have fought the Campazes since the beginning of the world, and though they are fierce, we are still here."

"Tell your people in the forest that we will give them metal weapons. The Campazes will learn to think twice about attacking us."

The Nigua smiles. "Thinking Campazes," she says. "That would be something new. Mostly, they just feel."

"You will go tomorrow," Anton says. "You may leave now. Alonso, stay."

Alonso sees the dislike in Anton's face as he watches the healer depart. "She is being useful," he says.

Anton makes a noise that says he is not convinced. "You trust her?" he says.

Alonso thinks about it. "The women trust her. One of the reasons things have gone so well is because she tells them it is best that they accept the new ways."

"But do you trust her?"

Alonso doesn't have to think about it. "Yes, I trust her. She has helped me, and she works hard to make things good."

The chief shakes his head. "No, I don't want you to trust her. I want you to watch her, think about what you see, and tell me if she does anything that can make trouble."

"I do watch her," Alonso says. "She ... interests me. She has a different way of looking at things."

"She has learned a lot of Spanish, and fast," Anton says, as if Expectation's success at the task the chief has set her is a cause for suspicion.

"She is intelligent."

"I know that. She is also a power among her people. As you say, the women trust her. What about the men? And the boys?"

"They trust her, too—but as a healer." Alonso shrugs. "But they are few."

"Not for much longer. If your mission succeeds, we will have a lot of savages living with us. Men, with weapons."

"I don't think you should call them savages," Alonso says. "They are not cannibals. They have good manners, after their own fashion."

Anton regards him blankly for a moment, and Alonso feels himself being weighed and sorted again. Then the chief says, "While you have been teaching her Spanish, have you learned their tongue?"

"Yes. It has simple roots, although there are many different suffixes and prefixes."

Anton makes a dismissive gesture. "But you can understand them when they talk?"

"Yes, most of the time."

The chief nods. "Good. Then when your little friend talks to the people in the other village, you listen. If she says anything suspicious, you let me know."

"She won't. She means well."

Anton lets his exasperation show. "You don't know what she means," he says. "She was a power under the old chief. She is a power now. If anything goes wrong, she will have had a hand in it."

"And if everything goes right?" Alonso says. "Will it not be because she has helped make it so?"

He can see that he is making the chief angry, but he does not see Expectation as a problem for the new way of life. Instead, she is one of its strongest underpinnings.

Anton's eyes have narrowed and his voice is pitched low. "Whose side are you on?" he says.

"I did not know there were sides to choose between," Alonso says.

"There are always sides, always choices. You would know that if you'd inherited—" He breaks off and looks back at the map again, but Alonso is sure that he is not looking at what is before him.

"Inherited?" the young man says. "What? From whom?"

Anton looks up. "From your people."

"I don't know who my people are. I mean *were*."

"Miriam thinks you are Mandinka, like us," Anton says. "Have you never wondered, never tried to find out?"

Alonso did used to wonder but has long since got over his desire to probe the mystery. The time before he was ten years old is nothing but a grey blankness. If he tries to push through it, he feels a chill fear and his neck and back muscles stiffen. He tells Anton, "Until recently, I was an Illescas. I had duties and a place in the family. That was enough for me."

He sees the chief's face grow purposely still. "Are you," the big man asks, neutrally, "still an Illescas?"

"No," says Alonso. "That is behind me now."

"And what is before you?"

"A new life."

Anton regards him silently for a moment. "What does *naa* mean?"

Alonso does not know. And yet, he realizes, the word has some meaning for him. It stirs some emotion in him—no, it calls up a roiling mixture of emotions, feelings that swirl around each other, clash against each other. His stomach moves inside him, and he feels as if the breath has been sucked from his lungs.

Anton is watching him closely. Now he says, "What does *baabaa* mean?"

Alonso has to look away. A sudden wave of shame flashes through him, and he can't bear to see the chief's face at this moment, though he does not know why. "I don't know," he says. "What is it?"

But Anton is finished with the matter. "Go get some rest," he says. "You start early in the morning."

Alonso finds he is looking down at his feet now. He does not raise his gaze to the chief but turns and makes his way out of the presidio.

His steps are uncertain as he goes down the ladder. He stops at the bottom. He feels short of breath again, and there is a kind of silent pressure in the back of his head. When he reaches a hand to the nape of his neck, he finds the muscles stiff as wood.

Anton's voice comes to him from inside the big house. "… may be right," he is saying to someone. "I asked him …"

The chief is moving deeper into the building. Alonso hears the sound now but not the meaning. And he is sure it is Miriam's voice that responds, though it comes as only a murmur. He stands where he is for a long moment, his hand reflexively rubbing the back of his neck. Then he realizes that he has stopped breathing. He takes a long, wavering inhalation, fills his lungs with the warm, wet air, and crosses the open space to the healer's hut.

He will ask her to make more of the potion that lets him sleep.

Expectation has explained to Alonso that her people have always been divided into families and clans. Then the death sickness came with the Spaniards' arrival, and Nigua men were impressed to carry goods up-country. Many of them never returned. The survivors who left the old town by the sea to establish hidden villages in the forest grouped themselves by lineages. The people they were going to contact were part of a clan known as the eaters, a name that went back into the mists beyond memory.

"When they left, they were seven men and boys, and fifteen women and girls," she says as they walk the trail Pahta has shown them, "plus small children too young to have received their names yet."

They are following a game trail, a narrow tunnel through the forest that winds its way gradually upward on one of the tree-covered slopes that make the coastal forest resemble a rumpled carpet. They have been walking since dawn, with one stop beside a small stream that trickled down the hill. Alonso has not seen the sun since they left the village and plunged into the green twilight.

"Will they be there when we arrive?" he asks the healer, looking back over his shoulder to where she walks just behind him.

"The men may run and hide."

"They won't try to fight?" He does not like the idea of poisoned arrows and darts coming from the dimness between the trees. He has developed a healthy respect for the Niguas' knowledge of the secret powers of plants.

"I have thought about this," Expectation says. "When we get near, Pahta will go ahead and tell them we are coming. We will give them time to talk about it and prepare themselves." She steps over a protruding root that makes a hollow filled with water from the night's rain. "They will probably have been expecting us for some time and will have made plans for what to do, depending on what we want from them."

"Will they want to join us?"

"If we are not cruel to them. They know they are helpless if the Campazes come north on a raid and find them. They would all be dead."

Alonso sees an image of blood and bodies: men, women, and children, their flesh hacked, their skulls split open. He pushes it out of his mind, and only when he has done so does he realize that the dead he imagined were not New World savages but people his own colour.

"Why do the Campazes kill you?" he says.

"Why do snakes kill hatchling birds?" the Nigua says. "Because it is their nature."

In the afternoon, Pahta calls a halt beside another streamlet. "It is not far now," he tells Alonso in Spanish that has improved considerably. "I will go and talk to them."

"Wait," says Alonso. He turns to one of the African men carrying the bundles of gifts. "Diego, unpack your load."

When the canvas-wrapped package is opened, Alonso selects from its contents a good knife, an ivory comb, a brass goblet, and a length of Chinese taffeta. He wraps his choices in the cloth, ties a knot, and hands the bundle to Pahta.

"Show them the gifts we bring," he says. "Tell them every man will have steel weapons and every woman will have a copper cooking pot. And when the Campazes come, we will kill them with guns."

As he speaks, another image rises in his mind: the open space in the new village at dawn. A mob of savages, bedecked in feathers and armed with spears and bows, creeps through the open gate. They spread out, aiming for the sleeping huts. Suddenly, fire and smoke erupts from all sides. The warriors fall, twisting in agony, and a tide of Africans comes racing, spears levelled, swords raised. And Alonso sees himself in the front of the charge, rapier in hand.

The fantasy surprises him. It is not his kind of thought, yet there it is, rising up from somewhere within him. As Pahta moves off up the trail, Alonso sits by the stream, scoops up a handful of water. His mouth has gone dry.

The meeting in the eaters' village begins well. The Africans have come in breastplates and morions, matchlocks over their shoulders and swords at their belts. But Alonso has told them to smile and rest the butts of the firearms on the ground.

They have brought three bundles of gifts, and Expectation supervises their distribution. Each of the men gets a knife, the two eldest are given spears with iron points. Each of the women receives a painted cup and some cloth, softer and more colourful than the cotton shifts they wear. There are only three copper kettles, and two of the women argue over who should have one of them, until a toothless grandmother awards the pot to one of the disputants along with a stream of vituperative Nigua Alonso only half understands, though he does grasp that arguing in front of strangers is bad manners.

Expectation weighs in, reminding them that every woman will receive her own kettle, as well as metal utensils and an iron hatchet for splitting kindling. And a husband, she says, along with sister wives to help with the work.

She has explained to Alonso that the widows and unwed young women of the eaters clan cannot marry any of the men of their own lineage. With so many Nigua men dead of disease and Spanish abuse, the women here have been fearing a life without children or a home of their own. It has been a strain on them, she tells him.

The Africans have been received in the open space at the centre of the village. This village is smaller than the one they took over, with fewer huts and no stockade. The men's house has no walls except for the partitions that shield the ceremonial dishes from women's view. The people look poorer, their clothes more worn, the children pot-bellied but thin-limbed.

But the men are wary. They handle their new knives but keep looking from the corners of their eyes at the strangers in armour, at their swords and *arcabuzes*. The women, it seems to Alonso, are more receptive, but none of them has yet spoken up. There has been no discussion of how to respond to the offer of inclusion in the new society. Perhaps there cannot be while the strangers are among them.

Expectation is repeating herself now. Alonso touches her arm and, when she turns, draws her away.

"I'm thinking," he says, "that we may have to leave and come back for an answer another day."

"If we do," she says, "we may find them gone. They may decide to take the gifts and find another place to hide."

"The men are the problem. They think we will make them slaves as the Spaniards did."

She shrugs. "Let me try again."

But Alonso says, "No, let me."

He goes to stand before the men, addresses them, though he knows the women are listening. He speaks in Nigua and has to repeat his opening words because they are drowned out by exclamations and murmurs from the eaters.

He starts again. "You think we are like the other men. We are not. We will not make you work for us. You will work for yourselves, for your families. You know we have fought the Campazes—Nigua and African together. And we fought them with iron spears and the weapons that spit fire. We brought back many good things they had stolen from the Nigua."

They are all looking at him now, and he sees new thoughts working in some of the men. He spreads his arms and says, "We will be your brothers." He pauses to gauge the reception. "We will go now back up the trail so that you may talk about it. We ..." He has to struggle for a moment to find the right Nigua word and hopes the one he finally chooses means what he wants it to mean. "We hope you will join us."

With that, he makes a leg, as he used to bow in the Illescas house, long ago and far away in Seville. Then he turns and collects Expectation, who is looking at him with a quizzical expression.

"I didn't know you had learned so much Nigua," she whispers.

"Neither did I." He speaks to the Africans, telling them they will move back along the trail a ways and wait. But to Pahta, he says, "Stay with them. Tell the men how it has been for you."

"I will," says the Nigua, "but I hope you don't mind if I tell them you meant 'we hope' when you said 'we fart.'"

They go back along the trail, far enough that they cannot hear what is going on in the village. They cut some space in the undergrowth and squat or sit, passing around a gourd of corn beer Expectation had acquired from one of the women. Alonso rests his back against a tree, and Expectation sits beside him. The stiffness has come back into his neck, and he massages the muscles, slowly bobbing his head forward to loosen them.

"I think that went well," Expectation says. "No Spaniard has ever spoken to them in Nigua. Even the Quechua speakers never bothered to learn more than a few words."

"I hope so," he says in her language, this time carefully pronouncing the difficult word. In Spanish he says, "We will need more people."

She laughs, and there is a silence until she says, "You are sleeping more quietly lately."

"It is the herbs you give me."

"Do you still not remember your dreams?"

"No, I never have." The answer is not quite true. Sometimes Alonso wakes with a sense of having just been involved in some situation, some conversation. But if he tries to grasp the meaning of it, it evaporates from his grasp. He has long since stopped trying.

Again Expectation is silent. After a while, she says, "My people say that a man who cannot remember his dreams has lost … a part of himself."

"Obviously," Alonso says, smiling. "The part that remembers dreams."

"We also know that there is a way to recover that lost part."

The day is hot, as ever, but Alonso feels a chill creep between his shoulder blades, as if he is beset by a sudden fear. Yet he feels nothing. The Nigua's words—*a way to recover that lost part*—hang in his mind like a cold fog. He would like them to disperse, but they do not. He keeps hearing them repeated, and he answers Expectation not because he wants to discuss his dreams but because he wants to get her voice out of his head.

"What good would it do me to remember my dreams?"

Again, she seems to choose her words carefully. "Dreams are the way you speak to yourself with honesty. A man may pretend to himself that things are this way or that way. He may even believe it, even though he also knows he is only pretending. But dreams speak truth."

Alonso makes a sound of mild scepticism. "I have heard people talk about their dreams. Giants and flying, falling from great heights, running but not getting anywhere. That is not truth."

"Dreams speak truth, but you have to know the language." She laughs. "Otherwise hopes turn into farts."

"Do you know the language?"

"I have to," she says. "It is part of healing. Not all wounds can be seen. But they are still wounds."

Alonso feels the chill again. He cranes his neck to see along the trail to the village. "How long do you think it will take them to make up their minds?" he says.

"As long as it takes," she says, picking up a twig and rolling it between her palms. "Pahta has cousins among them, women who have lost their husbands. They will support him. And you made an impression."

They fall silent. After a while, Alonso says, "Perhaps our men shouldn't have worn armour."

"No, they should. You can make a kind offer, but you have to make it from strength."

And so they wait while the afternoon draws on. Alonso half dozes, sitting up. He knows he should remain alert, perhaps even set sentries at both ends of the trail. But Expectation knows the people they are dealing with, and she shows no sign of being worried. He is convinced she means well.

He rouses himself, looks at her. "I trust you," he says in Nigua.

She answers him in the same language. "I know."

Pahta comes back along the trail. The Africans watch him closely. They have not been dozing and have kept their armour on and their weapons close to hand. But Expectation says, "Good."

The Nigua man comes and squats in front of Alonso. "They will come," he says. "It is too late to start tonight, and they want to have a feast. They have killed a tapir."

Expectation smiles. "They are not called the eaters for nothing."

Alonso looks from one to the other. "It will be safe?"

She says, "If you want them to trust you, you have to trust them."

Traditionally, Nigua men eat in the men's house, the food brought to the door by the women, who eat with the children in their own big house. But when the meal is almost ready, Alonso speaks to Expectation.

"Tell them that we would like to eat all together, men, women, and children, out in the open. In a circle, all mixed together." He sees the Nigua healer thinking about it and says, "New life, new ways."

"We can try," she says.

"Do you agree?"

"Yes."

The men, Nigua and African, have been drinking beer in the men's house while the women spit-roast the tapir over an open fire and cook its offal on flat stones greased with the animal's fat. Expectation steps out into the middle of the dusty central space, now lit only by the cooking fires, and claps her hands for attention. She addresses herself primarily to the women, and Alonso watches closely to see their reaction. He sees some frowns, some confusion, hears some murmurs as the women talk to each other.

Expectation speaks again, too fast for him to follow. He hears Nigua words he recognizes—*friend, good, happy*—and then for a moment he thinks she is talking about breathing, until her gestures towards the sky and the way she places her small fist against her chest tell him that she is talking about spirit. The women are listening, and the frowns are softening. One of the younger women calls something to another young one, and there is laughter. The healer has stopped speaking, and the women are looking at one another.

Then the old matriarch who settled the dispute over the kettle pushes her way between two of the matrons. Leaning on a stick, she makes her slow way to a spot near the roasting tapir and laboriously lowers herself to the ground. She tells one of the young women, "Bring me," followed by a word Alonso does not know. The woman fills a shallow wooden bowl with the sliced organ meats cooking on the flat stones and produces a small stick sharpened at one end.

The old woman uses the stick to pick out a piece of pale cooked meat and puts it in her mouth, chewing it noisily with her few teeth. She swallows and grunts in satisfaction, then looks up at where the men are watching from their house without walls. "If you want to eat," she says, "come down and sit."

The women fill bowls with meat sliced from the roast, portions of offal, and tubers and greens that have been boiled in the new copper kettles. But they do not take them to the foot of the ladder to the men's house. Instead, they stand, waiting.

Pahta descends from the men's house and goes to sit near the old woman. She ignores him, intent on her next morsel of fried meat. He accepts a bowl and eating-stick from one of the women and begins to eat. The Africans follow him down, unbuckling their breastplates; they have already left their helmets in the big house. Some of the women bring them bowls and return with their own food and sit with them.

If there are any hold-outs among the men, they do not stand on traditional principles for long. Soon the entire complement of Niguas and Africans are sitting together, eating together. The newcomers have a few words of the local language, and the Niguas know a little Spanish. But most of the communication is by signs and smiles and belches.

A woman brings food to Alonso and Expectation, and they sit together where people move aside to give them a place in the circle. Alonso tastes the roast tapir and finds it like wild boar, a favourite dish of his namesake and godfather in Seville.

For a moment, he is carried back to those days. It is only two years since he left Spain for Hispaniola, but it seems a lifetime ago. Someone passes him a gourd of beer. He drinks. When he is finished, the past has left him. He is where he is and when he is, and the faces he sees in the firelight are content, the men smiling, the younger women talking to each other behind their hands.

"It is going well," he says to Expectation.

"Yes," she says, "it is."

ELEVEN

ALEJANDRO DE ESPINOSA

Fray Alejandro had now been a year in the employ, so to speak, of Rodrigo de Ribadeneira, and the passage of time had not greatly warmed either man to the other. The original plan, whereby the monk would teach Spanish numbers—actually, they were Arabic numerals, he reminded himself—to the native overseers of the merchant's cloth-weaving *Indios* had not succeeded. The Quechua-speaking *Indios* were simply unable to grasp the principles of simple arithmetic—or so it appeared from the errors they systematically made when he took them carefully through the lessons he planned for them. Yet they could perform complex calculations using their pieces of knotted string, calculations whose accuracy was confirmed when Alejandro converted the terms to the numbers he understood.

"They can't learn, because they don't want to," de Ribadeneira concluded when the monk finally had to report that the project had failed. "If they do the accounting in terms we can understand, they give up the ability to cloud the returns. They probably practised the same tricks on Atahualpa's inspectors."

The merchant had come up with a new approach. Quito was filling up with new arrivals from Europe and from the Spanish possessions in North America. The original influx into the conquered Inca Empire had brought mostly soldiers and adventurers, sailors and vagabonds. But now the land was settled and trade was expanding, the newcomers climbing up from the coast were more likely to be notaries and accountants, merchants, and skilled artisans like the expert silversmiths who were turning out fine work to grace the tables of *hidalgos* and newly rich commoners like the man sitting across the table from Alejandro, here in the counting room where they had first met.

"I'm going to remove the native overseers," said de Ribadeneira, "and replace them with Spaniards. At the same time, I'm reorganizing the business completely. Having them weave cloth the way they did in the old days, with each weaver working on a small loom in his cottage and taking time off to scratch in his garden, is just not producing enough cloth.

"I bought a skilled carpenter, a black. He cost me six hundred and fifty pesos, but he's worth it. He's making me new looms, wider and stronger. I'm putting up buildings in the villages, where I'll have six, seven, eight looms all together. The *Indios* will work them in shifts, with Spanish station men to keep them at it and my carpenter to maintain the machines."

The merchant's gaze locked onto Alejandro's, and he pointed an inquisitory finger at the Trinitarian. "Do you know how much wool cloth I can sell to the miners at Potosi?"

"No," said Alejandro, "I don't."

"Of course you don't. Nobody does. But I can tell you it will be a lot more this year than last, though not as much as next year."

Alejandro knew about Potosi, the 'mountain of silver' discovered to the south-east. From a rough camp, it had sprung up into a city of thousands, and thousands more were flocking to it. Fortunes could be made, though not by the *Indios* and blacks who did the digging down in the chill, dank passages underground. But the weather above ground was equally cold and damp. Warm woollens sold well in Potosi, and Quito merchants who could send mule trains of good cloth down to the mines would receive a steady flow of silver pesos. De Ribadeneira intended his portion of that flow to become a flood.

Once he had the looms built and the sweatshops operating, the merchant would have a perfect system for becoming rich. Under the regime established by the Spanish Crown after the fall of the native empire, the *Indios* were required to pay tribute to the new overlords in the same way they had paid tribute to their old masters, the Inca.

The coin in which they paid was their labour. Under the old regime, villages had been required to meet set quotas for farming, herding, carrying burdens, weaving, or any other work Atahualpa's officers had determined was necessary to the welfare of the state and its hierarchy. The Spaniards had simply transferred the native form of taxation-in-kind to their own purposes—while ramping up the quotas beyond anything the royal court down in Cuzco had ever imagined.

The Spanish Crown, in the person of the Viceroy, then divided up the vast pool of labour owed by the conquered into licenses, and granted them to the conquerors. The soldiers, adventurers, sailors, and vagabonds who had slaughtered the native armies and strangled their emperor could now call upon the unpaid labour of thousands, and even tens of thousands, of *Indio* peasants and craftsmen for months at a time.

The system was called the *encomienda*—the trust—and those who held the grants were *encomenderos*. Rodrigo de Ribadeneira had been a soldier, but he had not been in the right battles to have won a grant from the Viceroy. But his wife's father—Lopez de Zuniga—had been awarded the right to make thousands of natives work for him in the *encomienda* of Chambo, near the town of Riobamba, about fifty leagues south of Quito. Dona Ana de Ribadeneira had inherited her father's grant, and her husband was using it to make the family even richer.

Now, with the project to teach Spanish accounting methods to the native overseers abandoned, Alejandro foresaw his usefulness to the *encomendero* coming to an end. "So," he said, "you will not need me any longer."

"Not so," said de Ribadeneira. "I have a new assignment for you."

"What would that be?"

His employer leaned back in his padded chair and steepled his fingers. "You have heard about the blacks who survived the sinking of the Illescas ship?"

"I have heard rumours," the monk said.

"The rumours are true. There were perhaps two dozen of them who came ashore. They have conquered the local savages and have set themselves up as a petty kingdom in the jungles of Esmeraldas."

"I see," Alejandro said, though he did not.

De Ribadeneira's brows drew down into a dark vee. "My wife's father financed an expedition to recapture them. It did not go well. They lost most of their weapons, including powder and shot. Meanwhile, the blacks are drawing in savages who do not wish to work for us.

"They now have maybe fifty fighting men with firearms and armour, swords and pikes. Nobody knows how many *Indio* warriors they may have equipped with iron and steel weapons."

The Trinitarian nodded. "Are the natives Christians?" he asked.

De Ribadeneira's expression made it plain that the monk had focused on the least important aspect of the situation. "No," he said. "Some have tried to bring the savages of the coast to Christ. The lucky ones have returned in very poor condition. Most missionaries are never heard from again."

Alejandro crossed himself and said, "Bless their souls. They have received a martyr's reward and sit at the right hand of God."

"I'm sure," said the merchant. "But here's what's important. You remember I said my carpenter cost me six hundred and fifty pesos?" At the monk's nod, he went on, "Those slaves are worth three hundred to five hundred a head at least, even allowing for the fact that their new owners would have to fetter them to keep them from running away again."

He paused as if he expected a response from the Trinitarian. When none was forthcoming, he said, "That is fifteen thousand pesos, Brother."

"Ah," said Alejandro.

"But there is more than money involved."

"Really? What else?"

"Quito needs a port of its own."

Alejandro had some experience in that matter. "Guayaquil is only some forty leagues away. I know because I have walked it."

De Ribadeneira had a sound he made whenever he heard foolishness. He made it now. "Guayaquil means carrying everything by pack mule. Do you know how much that costs? And the muleteers start to cry if you ask them to load much more than two hundred pounds onto their animals."

"That is a lot of weight," the monk said. "The creatures— "

"Never mind. The Esmeraldas is navigable far upstream. If we had a port at the mouth of the river, shipping costs would plummet. Both ways."

"Both ways?" Alejandro wondered what could be shipped from Quito and turn a profit. His experience was that goods came up from the coast on loaded mules, and the mules went back down unburdened.

De Ribadeneira was shaking his head. "You are truly an unworldly man, are you not, Brother?"

"I would hope so," said the monk. "There seem to be more than enough of the other kind."

The merchant sighed as a man sighs when he wants to draw attention to his forbearance. "With the new looms and the new overseers, I can make good cloth cheaper than the Flemish wool unloaded on the docks at Lima. And good cloth in many colours—fly's-wing, king's-cape, argentine, and raisin—not just indigo."

"Ah," Alejandro said again.

"But there is more to it than that," de Ribadeneira said.

"Really? More than that?"

"Here is the more," said the merchant, "and you will not speak of this to anyone, will you?"

Alejandro had very few conversations that did not centre on religious questions. "No," he said.

"I have made representations to the Viceroy in Lima," the other man said. He leaned forward now, his forearms solidly planted on the table, his hands forming fists. "If I recapture the escaped slaves and bring the savages to the Church, I will be made the governor of the province of Esmeraldas. Then I will build a port at the mouth of the river."

He looked at Alejandro to see if he was being fully understood. After a moment he said, "And I will collect the revenues that flow through the port."

"Ah," said the monk. He now thought he understood. "You will become rich. Or, really, richer."

De Ribadeneira's face told him he had indeed grasped what the man was getting at. "I am glad you understand, Brother."

The merchant's approval prompted Alejandro to say plainly what he would normally have left unsaid in an encounter with his employer. "What I do not understand is why you are telling me this."

"Because," said de Ribadeneira, "I am fitting out an *entrada*—a military expedition—to bring the blacks back and reduce the savages to obedience to the Crown and to God."

"Ah," said Alejandro, even though his question had not been answered.

"And I am sending you along as part of it."

The monk blinked in surprise. He was all the way back to not understanding any of it. "Me?" he said. "On a military expedition?"

"You."

"But why?"

"You don't know?"

"No idea."

De Ribadeneira leaned back again, his chair creaking as it accepted the readjustment of his weight. "How many people," he said, "do you think I can trust?"

Alejandro thought about it. After the silence lengthened, he said, "I don't know."

The merchant held up a hand and ticked off the fingers. "My wife," he said. "Some of my family. My major-domo, but only because his success depends entirely on mine. Some of the men I fought with in the civil wars, including the one who will lead this *entrada*."

"I see," said Alejandro.

The merchant touched a final finger. "And you."

"Me?"

"You are the only man I know who is without guile, who tells me nothing but the truth—at least the truth as you know it. You are without … an agenda."

"Not so," said the monk. "I have a vocation. God has called me to—"

"To serve the savages."

"Natives," said Alejandro.

"Call them what you will. How better could you answer your vocation than by bringing a new flock into the Church?"

It was true, although missionary work with people who had not yet heard the Gospel was really better performed by an ordained priest. "Will there be a priest on the expedition?" he asked.

De Ribadeneira hesitated. "Probably not. But there will be you." He gave the smallest of shrugs. "And the Holy Spirit. That ought to be enough, don't you think?"

"I suppose," the monk said, "it will have to be."

The man who was leading the *entrada* into Esmeraldas was Martin de Carranza, a hard-bitten old soldier—'tough as my boots' was how he was described to the monk by his new travelling companion. The companion, Gonzalo de Avila, was a Portuguese mercenary. He was a tall, thin specimen with a long nose on a small round head—'a combination that would have looked incongruous on a grown man if his shoulders had not been as narrow as the rest of him. At dawn three days later, when Alejandro came down the narrow street carrying his few possessions tied into a bundle slung over his shoulder, Avila was waiting by the south gate with a file of ten men in clothes of leather and rough wool.

"They told me you were a Trinitarian," the man said when he saw the plain brown robe Alejandro was wearing. "I didn't think so. There are no Trinitarians in the New World."

De Ribadeneira had sent his major-domo to catch the monk as he was about to depart and tell him he must wear the habit of a Mercedarian friar. Besides the brown woollen robe he was now wearing—his protests had been overridden—there was wrapped in his bundle another habit of thin cotton to wear once he was down in the soupy air of the coast. "The master does not want," the servant had said, "to give the Viceroy's advisers any excuse to disavow the *entrada* if anything goes wrong."

The major-domo had also reinforced de Ribadeneira's strict order that the monk was not to discuss with the soldiers any of the matters they had talked about, especially the prospect of a governorship of Esmeraldas. Thus Alejandro's response to Avila's observation was, "It's complicated."

"Most things are, especially to a simple man like me. That is why I take my pay and do my job and let the bosses deal with the 'complications,'" the Portuguese said.

He had a small mouth to match his small head, though heredity had given him oversized teeth that crowded together along his gums as if they were considering leaping out as soon as one of them got up the courage. He abruptly reached out and seized the tied end of Alejandro's bundle, saying, "Give me that. It can go on one of the mules."

There were four of the beasts to carry their supplies and equipment, but no muleteers to manage them. Avila waved away the monk's protests as he took the tied-up blanket from him and hung it from one of the forks of a mule's pack saddle. He prodded the bundle and said, "What is that in there, a book?"

"Yes," said the monk. His friend at the monastery had lent him a copy of Saint Isidore's book on the Jews.

The soldier shrugged. "Might come in handy."

"What for?"

The soldier tapped the bandolier of powder flasks he wore over his leather jerkin. "A piece of paper keeps the powder and bullet from falling out the end of the *arcabuz,*" he said. "Holy paper's best for that. Makes the shot fly true."

Before Alejandro could express his opposition to such usage of a saint's life, the tall man had turned and seized the mule's reins. He gave them a sharp tug. The animal braced itself and refused to budge, so Avila kicked it once in the belly. The mule squealed in protest but moved forward. He led it through the gate, gave a half-mocking salute to the sleepy guards leaning on their halberds, and set off down the old road that had been beaten into the earth by long-dead *Indios.* The other ten soldiers put the pack beasts into motion and followed.

Alejandro brought up the rear of the little column. It was only as he settled into the business of walking that he realized he had left his staff behind at his *patrón*'s house. In the confusion—he hadto change his old habit for the new one, untie his bundle, and retie it around the cotton robe—and propelled by his desire to escape the major-domo's hectoring tone, he had left his staff leaning beside the front door.

He was castigating himself for this lapse of concentration when he suddenly found that he was not alone at the rear of the column. Avila had stepped aside from his place in the lead, waited for the monk to catch up, and now fell in beside him.

"So," he said, "are you just accompanying us down to Guayaquil, or are you part of this ill-judged foray into the jungle?"

"Ill-judged?" Alejandro said. "How so?"

The Portuguese took time to dig some remnant of his breakfast out of his side teeth before answering. "How long since we first came down to the coast from New Spain?" he said.

Alejandro had to think. "Twenty years?"

"More," said Avila. He paused to suck at his teeth, his tongue working in his cheek. "In that time, up here we've conquered more *Indios* than we can count and put down a serious rebellion after the conquest."

"Yes?"

"Yes. But how many of them are down there in those forests?"

The monk did not know and said so.

"A few thousand," the soldier said. "There were more when the Pizarro brothers first came down, but they died from the pox and the sweating sickness. They left their big towns on the coast and went into the forest, and nobody's seen them since—unless they wanted to be seen."

The way he said it told Alejandro that there was more to come. He waited.

"When they want to be seen," Avila said, "they appear on the trail up ahead of you, and you go running to catch them. But when you get there, they are nowhere to be found."

"Ah," said the monk.

"And that," the Portuguese went on, "is when the darts and arrows come silently out of the green." He turned his head to look at Alejandro and said, "Do you know what they do with those darts and arrows?"

"I don't."

Avila leaned towards him as they walked, and lowered his voice. "They make the heads out of sharp bone splinters, but they bore little holes into the bone. And do you know why they do that?"

Alejandro had heard something about this. He spoke as softly as Avila. "Poison."

"That's right. Poison in the little holes, poison that gets into your blood." He nodded vigorously then showed his crooked yellow teeth in a smile. "Does that frighten you, Brother?"

"It does," Alejandro said.

"It should. I hear they have a poison that makes your muscles cramp and seize so hard that your spine bends backwards like a bow. You can hear the ribs popping out of their sockets."

"How awful."

"And then it snaps, and you die, foaming at the mouth and twitching."

"God save us," said the monk.

"And they say there is another one," the Portuguese said, "that makes you bleed from the gums, the eyes, the ears, from your ass and from your cock. Blood and sludge pour out of you, then your throat swells so you can't breathe, and you choke to death." He shook his small, round head. "A lonely, solitary death," he finished.

"Why lonely?" Alejandro said. "Where are your companions?"

"Running down the trail the moment the first arrow strikes," Avila said. "There's no other way to survive." He made a thoughtful noise. "Unless, of course, you run right into where the rest of the bastards are waiting."

"I came through the forest when I first came up to Quito," Alejandro said. "By mule train from Guayaquil. The muleteer was Juan Hernandez. He mentioned nothing of this."

"Did he not?" said Avila. "Probably he did not want to frighten you." He looked thoughtful for a moment, then said, "Or perhaps Hernandez leaves the *Indios* little presents to keep them sweet."

Alejandro was considering turning back now. But his bundle was on the lead mule with Fray Geronimo's book inside it. He would not want its beautifully lettered pages to be torn into patches for matchlock men to shoot fruitlessly into the undergrowth while envenomed darts and arrows came to pluck their lives.

But now he realized that Avila was laughing at him. "Don't worry, Brother," the Portuguese said. "This *entrada* is being led by Captain Martin de Carranza, an old campaigner who's as tough as my boots and as crafty as a serpent. He'll do it right. He always does."

"You were just enjoying yourself," the monk said. "Taking advantage of my innocence."

"It's a long walk to Guayaquil," Avila said, smiling his wayward smile. "You've got to find something to pass the time."

Guayaquil was even busier than Alejandro remembered it, the streets and taverns full of soldiers down from Panama and Nicaragua to enlist in Captain Carranza's expedition. There was talk of gold in the rivers, and emeralds to be plucked from the earth, of legions of savages to be reduced so that their labour could be allocated to brave men who brought new lands under the rule of the King. The days had passed when soldiers could get rich by soldiering; now it was the merchants who were making the fortunes, importing and even exporting the goods that filled the port's warehouses and burdened the backs of mules and asses.

Avila led them out of the forest, through the fields, and into the town. They asked at the gate where Carranza's headquarters were located and were directed to a two-storey timber house beside a walled compound. In the arch of the doorway, a bearded young man with extravagant mustachios leaned against a heavy door, arms folded, as they came up the street. He wore a brown doublet, neatly buttoned, and boots of cordovan leather; from a wide belt slung about his hips hung a scabbarded rapier with a well-worn hilt—a soldier, the monk thought, but clearly one who reckoned himself above the rank and file.

When Avila identified himself, the man told them the captain was closeted with his senior officers and not to be disturbed. They could leave the mules and their packs in the compound.

"There is a tavern that way," the man said, his accent hinting at an Andalusian origin. With the point of his neatly trimmed beard, he indicated the direction. "A blue door. You'll find plenty of new recruits there, spending the pesos they hope to earn."

"The animals are not ours," said Avila. "We are paying by the day."

"Then leave the packs and take the mules away. Whose are they?"

Avila gave Alejandro a mischievous sideways look and said, "They belong to Juan Hernandez."

"He is not far from the docks. Take them to him. Then wait in the tavern until you are sent for. Your goods will be safe here."

The Portuguese shrugged and called to the men to do as the fellow said. As one of the soldiers tugged at the lead mule's reins, Avila lifted the monk's blanket bundle from the saddle and passed it to him.

"Coming to the tavern, Brother?" he said.

"No," Alejandro said. He then addressed himself to the man in the doorway. "I have a letter of introduction from Don Rodrigo de Ribadeneira."

The soldier seemed to notice him for the first time. He spat into the dust of the street and said, "You could have a message from Santiago himself, and you'd still have to wait."

Alejandro thought for a moment and said, "Who are you?"

"Miguel Cabello de Balboa," was the answer. "Father Miguel, if you want the full title."

"I was told there was no priest on this expedition," Alejandro said.

"Yesterday that was true. Today it is not."

Avila had carried his armour and baggage into the compound and arrived back in the street in time to hear Cabello. "A priest?" he said, looking the man up and down. "I took you for a soldier. An officer."

The priest gave him a cool look. He unfolded his arms and hooked his thumbs in the sword belt. "I was a soldier before I took my vows."

"And you will be going with us on the *entrada*?" Avila said.

"With you, if you are accepted," said Cabello. He glanced at Avila's worn boots and indifferent hose and added, "A lot of riff-raff have accumulated lately."

"The forest has a way of winnowing out the 'riff-raff'," Avila said. "And the unprepared."

The priest studied the Portuguese now. "You have been out there?" he said.

"Oh, yes," said Avila. "More important, I have come back."

Alejandro recognized that he was witnessing a duel. But it turned out to be one of those contests where the duellists make the first few preliminary passes then stand back to size each other up.

"The tavern, as I say, is that way," Cabello said.

"A blue door, as you say," said Avila. He touched a finger to his hairline and turned to the monk. "Are you coming?"

"I will go with you to Juan Hernandez," Alejandro said. "I think he will give me a bed, if only on straw in his stable." He faced Cabello and inclined his head, saying, "Father."

"Brother," said the man in the doorway, with the slightest of nods.

Hernandez was sitting on the same stump and might even have been repairing, again, the same piece of harness. He set it aside and stood up as Avila and Alejandro led the four mules into the stable yard. He gave the two men a sharp look and immediately inspected the animals, running his hands up and down their legs, inspecting their mouths for lesions, and pulling off the pack saddles to search for sores.

Only when he was satisfied did he turn to Avila. "You are here a day early," he said. "Did you overwork my mules?"

"We left a day early," said the Portuguese, "as soon as the brother was ready to travel."

Hernandez gave the Trinitarian a less searching inspection than he had given the mules. "You have changed your habit," he said. "Are you a Mercedarian now?"

Avila answered before the monk could. "It's complicated," he said. "Too much so for simple souls like us."

"May I sleep in your stable tonight?" Alejandro said. "I have to see Captain Carranza, but he is too busy right now."

Hernandez's brows climbed. "You're not going on that fool's quest?"

"My *patrón* has sent me. And there are souls to be won for Christ."

The muleteer made a noise of derision. "It has not been established that the Campazes have souls. Poison arrows—those they have in abundance. And the women have knives of obsidian to peel the hide from your body, inch by inch, if the poison doesn't work fast enough."

The monk looked from Hernandez to Avila and said, "Do I wear a sign that says *frighten me?*"

"He's a brave little missionary," Avila said. "I've done my best, but he won't be told."

Hernandez almost smiled. "You can sleep in the straw, Brother," he said, "and I'll feed you on beans if you help get these four rubbed down and fed."

Avila was already on his way out of the yard. His hand went up in a backwards wave. Hernandez watched him go and turned to the monk. "He's going with Carranza?"

"I think so."

"Then stay close to him. When he runs, you run, too. Don't think, just run." He took hold of the reins of two of the mules. "Get those two," he said.

Captain Martin de Carranza tossed de Ribadeneira's letter onto the scarred table, leaned back in his chair, and said, "I have no need of a monk. I asked your *patrón* for twenty soldiers. He sends me ten." He gave Alejandro a dismissive look from under heavy black brows. "And you."

"I do not seek pay," said Alejandro, "nor any share in whatever treasures you may find. Nor, of course, to be awarded an *encomienda*."

"What do you seek?" Carranza laughed, a soldier's harsh bark. "Martyrdom? You hope someday to be Santo . . ."—he glanced at the paper again—"Alejandro?"

"I am called to bring the *Indios* to Holy Mother Church. It is my only goal."

The captain was still amusing himself. "San Alejandro," he said, "patron of long journeys through insect-infested forests. Patron of bad water and even worse air." He gestured vaguely towards the window. "Out there you will sicken and die, Brother."

"That is in God's hands, Captain."

"I already have a priest," Carranza said.

"Your priest wears a sword."

"Not such a bad idea where we are going. A cleric's robe will not stop a poisoned arrow."

"The arrows will stop when those now in darkness have come to know the light of truth."

Carranza leaned forward and stared straight into Alejandro's eyes. "Or are you simply a spy?"

The monk returned the challenging look with one of bland innocence. "Do you really think I have what it takes to be a spy?"

The other man regarded him for a long moment. "You are either what you say you are, or you are a master of deception."

"Exactly," said Alejandro.

Carranza grunted and looked away. "If you come along, you must be useful."

"People are always saying that to me. I try to live up to their expectations."

"You will do chores, gather firewood, help the cooks. No wandering off to pray for an hour."

"My work will be an offering to God. My lips will pray while my hands are busy at worldly tasks."

Another grunt, then, "What about that Portuguese you came down from Quito with?"

"What about him?"

"Is he a friend of yours?"

Alejandro shrugged. "Better to say he finds me amusing."

"I don't trust Portugueses," Carranza said. "They are loose where a Spaniard is taut."

The monk could think of nothing to say to this other than, "I lack your wide experience."

The captain gave him another considering look, a long examination that apparently did nothing to warm him to Alejandro. So he turned towards the door that led from his office into an anteroom and shouted, "Father Miguel!"

A chair creaked in the other room, and the priest appeared in the doorway. He still wore his soldier's garb and sword. "Captain?"

Carranza extended a finger more or less in Alejandro's direction. "He will be coming with us."

Cabello's eyebrows went up and his mouth quirked. "I see," he said.

"One of our backers has sent him. Make sure he is useful."

The priest looked at Alejandro. "You can read and write?"

"Yes, Father."

"How are your numbers?"

"Adequate."

Cabello looked to Carranza. "I can use him as a quartermaster's assistant." He thought for a moment. "And we could do with someone to copy letters."

Carranza made a small noise of assent and added, "Within reason."

Cabello's face showed that he had understood the inference. "All right." He crooked a beckoning finger. "Come with me, Brother."

Alejandro bade farewell to Carranza, but the captain was already absorbed in one of the papers on his desk.

The room was stifling, even though the shutters were back and the unglazed window open to the sultry air of Guayaquil. Cabello had given Alejandro a stool and a desk no larger than a lectern and set him to totalling up supplies and gear for the *entrada*. He hunched over the accounts, trying to remember to wipe sweat from his forehead before droplets could run down his nose and take the plunge onto the paper.

After an hour of this, the soldier-priest came back and examined the single sheet of paper on which the monk was summarizing the tallies of the various materials and the pesos each cost. After a thorough inspection, Cabello said, "Good enough. Finish what you have before you and come find me."

It took another hour before Alejandro was satisfied that he had included everything and that his figures were right. He ordered the sheets into a stack with the comprehensive accounting on top and rotated his neck to ease the stiffness. He pulled the cotton habit clear of his chest, but he found it soaked in perspiration. He went out into the compound.

The priest was at the well in a corner of the enclosed yard, drawing up half a bucketful of water from the depths. He raised the wooden bucket and tilted the container until the water ran over his head. He shook the drops from his close-cropped black hair as he noticed Alejandro's approach. He threw the bucket down into the well and hauled it back up again. Alejandro saw there was strength in the priest's arms and shoulders, and when Cabello handed him the bucket, the monk saw the calluses of a swordsman on the right hand.

"Douse your head," the priest said. "At least you had sense enough to change your wool habit for a cotton one. Men die of the heat in this place."

Alejandro upended the bucket and let the water stream across his head. It felt cool on his shaved tonsure, but as soon as he had shaken the drops free, the damp heat closed in again like a hot wet towel.

"It would not be so bad if it were dry," he said.

Cabello laughed. "The soldiers say this is where Satan came to learn how to build Hell."

"You were a soldier, father."

"I was."

"What made you take holy orders?"

"I had an … experience."

"A vocation?"

Cabello smiled. "Nothing so grand. No great epiphany, no angelic visitation." He drew his hand from crown to forehead, squeezing out the last of the water. "Let us say I saw a door open, a door I had not known was there. I stepped through it, and here I am."

"But you still wear a sword, Father."

"Yes," said Cabello, "I do."

Alejandro worked in the mornings. Supplies and men were still coming in. Rodrigo de Ribadeneira sent another ten with funds to keep them on half pay until the expedition left. The monk kept the accounts and copied routine letters, both those coming in and those going out. More sensitive correspondence, such as any letters between Carranza and the Viceroy in Lima, never crossed his desk. Cabello took care of those.

The whole town stopped for the siesta, when the heat of the day lay upon Guayaquil like invisible lava, the sun directly overhead and the sky turned almost white. Alejandro would douse himself with water from the well and lie on his cot, naked except for a cloth about his hips, in the small room he had been allocated near the top of Carranza's house. The air was stifling and so heavy with moisture he thought he could feel it flowing in and out of his lungs like a liquid. He hung his cotton robe on a peg beside the door, but when he rose to put it on again, it was no drier than when he'd taken it off.

In the afternoons, he would go out into the town. The taverns were full of soldiers and sailors, the streets alive with a dozen different dialects and languages. Unlike the highlands, there were relatively few natives, and they seemed a crushed and cowed people. From the few and brief conversations he had with them, mostly men carrying goods to and from ships in the harbour, he discovered that the Puna were all Christians, even the women who worked in the brothels.

"They were tough bastards," Juan Hernandez told him. "They used to fight the Inca's soldiers when they would come up from Tumbe. They'd get whipped, then they'd store up their anger for a few years and rebel. I think they used to eat the ones the Inca left behind.

"Then Pizarro came and built a camp by the sea. His guides told him the Puna people were going to attack him. Maybe they were, maybe they weren't, maybe they'd eaten some of the guides' relatives and they wanted to make trouble. So Pizarro captured some of the chiefs and burned their feet until they admitted they were planning something.

"Torturing the chiefs made the people angry. They came out to fight, but the Spaniards had long pikes and *arcabuzes*, and men on horseback with sabres and lances. They cut and stabbed and shot until the bodies lay in heaps, and they went into the villages where the women and children were hiding and finished the job.

"That's why you don't see too many Puna around, and no old ones at all."

He saw Avila sitting under a tree in the yard of a tavern. Avila saw him through the arch that led to the street and called to him, "Come, Brother. Drink some wine."

Alejandro entered and sat in the shade. He accepted a wooden cup of something that tasted more like vinegar. When he made a face, Avila said, "On half pay, one learns to make accommodations. So, Brother, have you saved any souls yet?"

"No."

"That's what I like about you, Brother," the soldier said. "Ask me if I have won any battles, and I will tell you tales of my great deeds, some of them almost true. You just tell the truth."

Alejandro drank more of the wine. He had been walking in the heat and sweating out his moisture. "I am hoping to serve God once we leave this place and go up the river."

"You would be better to stay here. I have now heard the plan. We are to reduce the Campazes, by kindness or otherwise, then proceed north to the Esmeraldas River, where our newfound *Indio* friends will lead us to the *cimmarones*. We will capture them and take them up the river to Quito."

"Is that a good plan?"

"One never knows whether a plan is good or not until after it has been worked."

Alejandro said, "You should have been a scholar, Gonzalo. You argue like a seminarian. He drank some more of the wine and said, "Tell me this: is our Captain Carranza the kind of man who can carry a plan through to its conclusion?"

Avila looked out through the arch to where a yellow dog was urinating on the corner of a shack. He waited until the dog had finished and said, "Captain Carranza is known to be more interested in gold than in God. They say there is much gold in these rivers but those who go looking for it end up being eaten by the Campazes."

"You are teasing me again," Alejandro said.

"Only about the eating," said Avila, "and even that might be true. You hear things, Brother."

"You can't help hearing things, but you can help whether you listen."

"Well, listen to me now, Brother. I like you. Your innocence is ... refreshing. When I am stumbling through the jungle after our brave captain, it would comfort me to think of you safe and innocent up in Quito, teaching little brown children to say their paternosters."

"I would wish to comfort you," said the monk, "but God does not seem to have called me to that task."

"I cannot persuade you?"

"No."

The Portuguese drank more of his sour wine and put a little in the monk's cup. "Drink up, then," he said. "And when we are in the jungle, stay close to me."

"Yes, and when you run, I must run, too."

"But not as fast as me," said Avila. "When the time for running comes, all thoughts of comfort will vanish from my mind."

After a month of clerking for Carranza, Alejandro came down to breakfast at daybreak to find the house in a chaos of activity. Soldiers were bustling in and out of the yard, collecting the weapons and armour that had been stored in the sheds. A string of mules was being loaded with food stores and all the impedimenta of a military expedition. The air was filled with curses and shouted orders. The monk ran back upstairs, packed his few possessions in his blanket, and came down to find the first mules already being led east towards the river, escorted by soldiers in squads of ten.

In the yard, he found Avila putting on his armour. "Help me with the buckles," the Portuguese said, lifting an arm to show where the breast and back plates were connected by leather straps.

Alejandro slipped the leather through the metal clasps and snugged them tight. "So we're going," he said.

"We were waiting for the boats to be brought up from the boatyards."

There had been no mention of boats in the accounts he had worked on. He had thought that when the time came, they would just walk into the forest as Hernandez had done with his mules. "Up the river?" he said.

"You should have been here for the captain's little talk," Avila said, yanking on the neckline of his breastplate to seat the armour properly.

"I pray before dawn. My room is on the far side of the house." He handed the soldier the sword and scabbard that had been leaning against a crate and watched while Avila belted the weapon on. "What did he say?"

"What we expected. We will take the boats up the Babahoyo River and look for a town. Then we will offer the savages some presents and ask them if they want to become Christians and serve the King."

"It sounds rather easy. Why, then, do we need eighty soldiers?"

"Because," the Portuguese said, "it won't work." He picked up his helmet with its crescent-shaped rim pointed at front and back and looked to see how the ten soldiers he had brought down from Quito were doing. They were older men, veterans who didn't need to be told how to do their jobs.

Avila watched them in silence until they were all squared away. "Right, column of twos, fall in. Vasquez, Quemada, those two mules. March."

There were seven flat-bottomed boats, each big enough to take a dozen soldiers with their supplies heaped in the middle. They floated in the shallows, tethered to stakes on the shore while the brown river tried to carry them down to the sea. There was an eighth craft, smaller and meant to carry men without cargo. Carranza and Cabello were already seated in it, the captain at the prow and the soldier-priest at the transom, with four soldiers bent over two pairs of oars amidships.

The operation went smoothly. The boats were loaded and the men clambered aboard. A dugout canoe carrying several *Indio* men came up the river from the port downstream. When they were abreast of Carranza's boat, they paddled against the current just enough to hold themselves level with the commander.

When all the boats were manned, their oars out and dipping into the water, Carranza called, "Let's go."

Alejandro was surprised to see that after they slipped their tethers, the boats turned towards the sea, running with the river's current. But after a few minutes, the land on their left ended and they were rounding the point of a long peninsula. They turned north against the flow of a wider stream that looked to be a mile across. Each boat had three pairs of oars, and now six of the soldiers, their backs to the direction of travel, began to pull against the sluggish current.

There were fields on both sides of the rivers, flat land that supported stands of corn and rows of other crops. Alejandro could see natives working in them, men and women who straightened from their stoop labour to watch with impassive faces as the boats went upstream. But soon the crop lands gave way to forest, and after they had passed a few low-lying wooded islands, the channel narrowed. From then on, Alejandro found it a monotonous business: the men rowed, and the forested shores swept by, trees and more trees with never a break.

"Is there a town upstream?" he asked Avila after an hour or so.

The Portuguese shrugged. "There was supposed to be one, but not close. The Puna Island people didn't get along with the Campazes. If they met, they fought, so the land between them was empty except for hunters and the scouts they would send out to keep an eye on each other."

The heat grew as they moved upstream, the water having no effect on the temperature of the air. Alejandro trailed a hand over the side of the boat, letting the river's coolness flow over his wrist—until Avila made sinuous motions with his own hand, mimicking a fish swimming, then forming his fingers into a semblance of teeth closing on the fingers of his other hand. The monk pulled his hand back into the boat.

After two hours, word passed down from the commander at the front of the flotilla: the six rowers in each boat would be relieved by the other six men. They all pulled in to an indentation in the shoreline where the current became a self-defeating eddy and the soldiers, conscious that their armour would carry them swiftly down to the bottom of the murk, carried out the manoeuvre with care, grasping at overhead tree branches to steady themselves as they traded places.

The day wore on. At midday, they landed on a flat little island and made fires. Alejandro helped to gather fuel from dried driftwood that littered the island's shore. "No shortage of wood, at least," he said to Avila when he brought an armful to where one of the men was kindling a cooking fire.

"No," said the soldier, looking out at the forest beyond the river, "no shortage of that."

They ate and rested, put the boats back into the stream, and rowed on. The land remained flat, a thickly forested plain, and the river meandered lazily in broad, sweeping curves. Their course was now as much east as north, and the banks were slowly closing in; the river that had seemed a mile wide at Guayaquil was now no more than two hundred yards across.

They saw no sign of human habitation, not so much as a plume of smoke from beyond the trees at the water's edge and certainly nothing like a landing. Besides the rowers' shifts changing every two hours, the only break in the routine of their passage was the occasional island, devoid of life except for the flocks of birds that rose, in shrieking waves of colour, if the flotilla came too close.

At the end of the daylight, they were in a stream that had narrowed farther. Carranza conferred with the *Indios* in the canoe, who pointed back the way they had come. His orders were passed back: turn and go downstream to the last island they had passed. There the men pulled the bows of the boats ashore and tethered them to stakes driven into the ground. They built fires and cooked their rations, swatting at the insects that swarmed out of the darkness, biting and drinking blood.

Avila threw damp leaves on their fire after the salted fish and beans had been heated in an iron pot. The smoke billowed up, sour and hot, but it reduced the myriad of flies to a few dozen hardy specimens. Alejandro would have liked to sit and look into the fire, an innocent pleasure he had enjoyed since childhood. But there were no flames to watch, so he wrapped his head and shoulders in his cloak to foil the worst of the biters and lay down to sleep.

They continued upstream, the river growing gradually narrower, though the current did not become much stronger. The land they were traversing remained flat and thickly forested, and nowhere did they come upon an *Indio* settlement. Here and there, they saw traces of villages: places along the shore where the land had been cleared for crops and where there had been huts surrounded by a stockade. But as they drew in to the bank to investigate, they saw only charred remains and overgrown fields, the fruit orchards chopped down.

"Has there been a war?" Alejandro asked Avila when the Portuguese came back to the boat. Carranza had detailed him and a few of his men to investigate one of the destroyed villages.

"From what I've been told," the soldier said, "the Campazes take war to other people's territory. This they have done themselves. They have gone deep into the forest to hide."

"They are afraid?"

Avila chewed at a corner of his mouth and shook his head. "I don't think so. They must know what we did to the Puna people. They want to meet us where the advantage is all theirs."

They continued upriver for the rest of the day. Except for a few more burned-out settlements, they encountered no sign of human existence. Before the sun could make the sudden disappearance that characterized nightfall in this latitude, Carranza had them put in at another island and make camp. The little plot of land was barely above the level of the water, and previous floods had littered it with deadwood, from tangles of branches to huge stumps. The captain ordered the men to drag the larger pieces into lines to make a ragged breastwork facing the northern bank of the river—which here ran mostly east to west. They dragged the boats right out of the water to make another barrier on the south side, with their supplies unloaded and inside the barricade. Then they built fires to prepare the evening meal.

With the darkness came more flying legions of biting insects. The men made the fires smoke and sat, huddled and coughing, swatting the more desperate biters that braved the fumes. Carranza summoned the under officers to his fire. Alejandro was not invited, but Avila came back, swatting his neck and cheeks as he passed between plumes of smoke, and told his men what the captain had decided.

"We have passed many places where streams issue into the river. Tomorrow, we will work our way downstream to the first we encounter. A single boat will go up the tributary and see what there is to be seen. The rest of the *entrada* will wait for the scout boat to come back." He paused and spat into the fire. "We drew lots. Our boat goes in first."

In the morning, they reloaded the boats except for Avila's craft. Its supplies were distributed among the others. Less than a league downstream they came to a spot where a stream flowed in from the north. Avila told the men to row for the confluence while Carranza ordered the other six boats to tie up on the south bank of the Babahoyo.

Avila's craft had to cross an underwater sandbar at the mouth of the smaller river, but once they were beyond it, there was room enough to row. They set off against its gentle flow and worked their way upstream. The forest to either side looked no different from that which flanked the big waterway, and there were no signs of human habitation, past or present. After they had travelled almost an hour, Avila remarked on the strangeness of that fact.

"It's a decent little stream," he said. "Why did no one put a village beside it?"

"Perhaps the water is bad?" Alejandro suggested.

Avila dipped up a handful, sniffed at it. "No," he said, "it's fine."

The width of the stream varied. For long stretches, there was only just enough room to accommodate the oars, but then they would come to places where the banks fell back and the current eased; here they were crossing a long, narrow lake.

At the third of these, also the widest and longest, they saw an island. It had been cleared of vegetation, and there were odd-looking structures dotted around the open space.

Alejandro peered at them. "They are too small to be huts," he said.

Avila's expression sharpened. "So they are," he said. He looked around at his men and said, "Run us up onto the downstream end, where it comes to a point. Diego and Mateo, stay with the boat. The rest of you, blow on your matches and follow me."

They beached the boat on a sloping patch of mud, and the men swarmed out. Avila told the ten matchlock men to form two lines and to face the banks of the river-lake. "We are just within arrow shot," he said. "But if anyone comes at us, it will have to be in canoes. If that happens, we shoot, volley fire, then back to the boat and downstream fast. Nobody stops for souvenirs."

"Souvenirs?" Alejandro said.

"You'll see, Brother." The Portuguese led them towards the nearest of the peculiar structures. They were a little more than waist-high, made of sticks stooked together and tied near the top. Avila approached the first one with his sword drawn and used the tip to prod between the lengths of wood and pry them apart. There was a hollow space within filled with what looked to be a length of woven grass or reeds.

Avila prodded again and once more, then put away his sword, saying, "No snakes." He took hold of the top of the conical heap of canes and pulled it upward. The bottom ends of the sticks came out of the ground, and he tossed the whole thing aside. Revealed was a length of coarse material made of woven reeds, also conical in shape, wrapped around something and tied with cords of plaited grass.

The Portuguese spoke to his men. "Anything?" When they reported that there was nothing to see, he said, "Don't look at what I'm doing. Watch the trees on the shore."

Now he took a knife out of his boot and sliced through the grass bonds. They fell away, and his fingers found the edge of the woven material and began to unwrap what it covered. The reed cloth had been passed several times around the hidden object, and Avila unwound it carefully and methodically.

Alejandro stooped to follow what the soldier was doing. As another round of the coarse fabric came away, he saw dried mud on top of something dark, its texture of rotted leather. Another turn of Avila's hand and more of the object was revealed. At first it was a jumble of shapes, and then suddenly he realized what he was looking at.

"It's a corpse," he said, reflexively crossing himself.

"Indeed it is," said Avila, loosening another wind of the reed cloth and showing the bent legs of a body that had been left sitting upright, knees pressed beneath its chin and arms clasped around its legs, the hands tied by leather thongs that were now rotted away. A cap of clay had been pressed down onto the hair and moulded into a kind of helmet.

The Portuguese pulled away the last of the covering and smiled. "Not only a corpse," he said. "A rich corpse."

Alejandro saw them now: three pieces of worked gold, including a pair of heavy earrings whose weight had torn them from the rotted ears and a crescent whose pointed ends curved around until they almost touched. Avila picked the last one from where it hand fallen in the little gap between knees and chest. He put it to his nose so that the ends entered his nostrils. "Like that," he said to the monk, holding his head back so the nose piece remained in place.

"I think," Avila said, "that the captain's strategy is about to change—seriously change."

He made a quick search of the tomb's other contents and found an ornate bone comb and a bracelet of small white shells. "Right," he said. "Let's see what's in the others."

He straightened and spoke sharply to one of the soldiers, who had craned his neck to see what his officer had found. The man snapped his head around and went back to watching the trees across the lake. Avila was already moving to the next pile of sticks, his sword out to probe for snakes. He was humming a tune Alejandro had heard through the windows of a tavern.

*T*WELVE

ALONSO ILLESCAS

"Who does Anton think I am?" Alonso asks Miriam when he sees that the chief has left the presidio.

He is standing at the foot of the entrance steps. She has been sitting in the wide doorway, eyes closed and face in repose, either thinking or remembering. Now her face takes on the practised expression that slaves learn to show when a master asks a question whose answer it is unwise to know.

"I don't know what you're talking about," she says. She closes her eyes, shutting out both him and his question.

But Alonso persists. "Some time back, he talked about my inheriting something. And he asked me if I knew the meanings of some African words: *naa* and *baabaa*."

She kept her eyes closed. "Did you know them?"

"No."

"Let it lie," she says. "Let it be Anton's problem, not yours."

He is almost willing to take her advice but for an itch in the back of his mind, the kind of itch an old wound can make long after it is healed. He has to ask her. "What do those words mean?"

She sighs, opens her eyes, and studies him for a moment. He sees her make up her mind. "They mean *mother* and *father* in the Mandinka language. Anton thinks you are Mandinka, like us, from a kingdom called Kaabu. Also like us." She studies him again. "Does any of that call up a memory?"

"No," says Alonso, feeling the itchy place. "Not a memory. But I think … No, I don't know what I think."

"Then let it go," she says. "Kaabu is only a dream, a place out of a story now. We will never see it again." She laughs softly. "And if we ever did, the same people who sold us to the Portuguese would just sell us to them again."

"What people? Who were they?"

"The ones who won the war." She laughs again just a little, and there is no mirth in the sound, only a familiar melancholy. "You can tell the difference between them and us; they are living in the palace, while we are scraping out a peasant's life in a faraway forest."

Alonso is probing his mind again: war, a palace, slaves. The exercise conjures up nothing but a vague sense that it ought to yield some result. Yet it doesn't except for an unsettling feeling that there is indeed something to be conjured. But it's like one of the fleeting moments when he awakes in the morning, when he senses that he has been involved in some business that has just that moment fled deeper into the recesses of his mind.

He knows Miriam is watching him. After a few moments, he gives up. "It feels as if I ought to know something, but when I try to think about it, it runs away like water into sand."

Her face sharpens and her hand makes a dismissive gesture. "Then let it. It can do you no good."

"I suppose," he says. "Whatever the past, it means nothing now. We are here and have to make ourselves useful."

She gives him a small smile. "A better way to look at it."

He nods. But he does not depart. He stands there, looking at nothing. "And yet …"

"Listen," she says, her tone sharp. When he looks up at her, a little startled, she sighs again and says softly, patting the floor of the doorway beside her, "Come up here."

When he is settled at her side, she leans her head towards him, though her gaze remains on the plaza and the place beyond it where Juanito the ironsmith has set up his forge. Anton is in there, under the roof, talking with the smith about something that has seized his attention.

"I am going to tell you something," Miriam says, "and I want you to listen and understand. Then I want you to act like an intelligent young man. Understood?"

"Not really," Alonso says. "Why all the mystery? What does it have to do with me?"

"There was a war between two *nyankos*—do you know that word?"

"No." But again it stirs a faint echo.

"It means lord, or better to say, a general who rules for himself."

"I understand," says Alonso. He has read history in Don Alonso's library. He thinks of Julius Caesar's book about the war against the Gauls.

Miriam says, "We were on the losing side. Our lord was killed, and his family were sold as slaves."

"Yes," says Alonso. He waits to see if anything comes to him, but again there is only the vague feeling of discomfort.

She has been watching him. Now she says, "Our lord had a son, eight or nine years old." She waits for a reaction. "Today he would be your age, if he lived."

"Yes," says Alonso again, and then the implication sinks in. He smiles and shakes his head. "You don't mean that Anton thinks—"

"You look," she says, "very much like our *nyanko*."

He does not know what to say to that. After a moment he says, "I can't see how it matters. As you say, they won, we lost, here we are."

"It matters. The boy's name was Tirmakhan Traore. He claimed descent from the great general who founded Kaabu."

The name calls up nothing in Alonso. "So?"

"So if you are Tirmakhan, Anton owes you his loyal obedience."

That makes Alonso laugh. "It's a debt I do not expect to collect," he says, but he is pulled up sharp when he sees the expression on the woman's face.

"There is nothing humorous about it. If you are descended from the great Tirmakhan Traore, you may have inherited the qualities that can make you a leader of men."

She has turned to him now, and her face is drawn. "If Anton believes you are a potential leader, that makes you a potential rival. He will not abide anyone who poses a threat to his position."

"But I am clearly not an Anton," Alonso says.

"No, you are not. But you brought in the eaters. Then you went out and brought in the red shirt clan. You came, you spoke to them, they followed you. Then a few more families came in on their own, because they'd heard of you. You have the respect of the Niguas, and many of our own people were impressed that you did it without getting anybody hurt or killed."

"I just talked to them."

"Yes, in their own language," Miriam says, "and you talked to them well."

"I did what Anton asked me to do."

"Yes. And now Anton is thinking about that, and what it means."

"It means I am useful to him."

"Yes, but what else are you?"

"Nothing."

She shakes her head. "No, not nothing. You are a potential power. The strange little creature you consort with is also a power—especially among the women."

"They don't like her," Alonso protests. "They make jokes."

"They don't have to like her to listen to her. She influences the Nigua women—and some of our own—and the women influence the men. Put you and . . . her together, and who knows what you are?" She glances towards the forge. "Most important, what does Anton think the two of you are?"

Alonso opens his mouth to deny what she is implying, but before he can speak she says, "Don't argue. I am trying to help you."

"I believe that," Alonso says. "What should I do?"

"Move out of the little witch's hut and stay away from her. Get a wife and get her pregnant." Miriam looks up and across the open space. "Go down now. I see him through the doorway over there."

He climbs down and turns away, but he hears her parting words. "Think about what I've said. And don't say anything to the witch."

Alonso walks back across the plaza, his mind on what he has just learned. He has understood what Miriam said, but he is having trouble fitting the information into all else that he knows. For as long as he can remember he has striven to be useful, because being useful will make him safe. It is a bargain he made with the world long ago, far back in the mist from which he emerged to become first Enrique, the voiceless boy who ran and fetched and carried and held whenever he was bid, and then Alonso, the servant who embraced more and more complex tasks and more and more responsibility.

The other side of the need to be useful is fear. During his years with the Illescas, the years of becoming almost one of the family, the fear had receded, stage by stage, until it was barely noticeable—a memory of a memory. Then it had all come rushing back in the moments on the beach, when Anton and the others had swarmed up from the sand and killed the sailors. Like the waves that lifted *La Virgen* onto the reef and smashed her timbers, the fear came welling up, swelling over him again when he found himself in this new place with these new people.

But he dealt with it. He has called up his old skills, his old ease with deference, to build a dyke between his safety and the fear that Anton instils in him. Now Miriam has told him it is not enough to be useful. It is not enough to be Alonso the biddable, the one who thinks of his master's interests and proposes strategies and solutions. It is not enough even to be Alonso the killer, who does what must be done to keep the fear quiescent on the other side of the dyke.

Now, she has told Alonso, it is Anton who fears *him*, fears who he might be, fears what he might do. And Anton is not a man who makes himself useful to those he fears. Alonso remembers the man who kept his spear, the way Anton came down from his presidio, the calm determination of his walk, the way his club rose and fell with the mechanical regularity of a shuttle passing back and forth across a loom.

Alonso has no strategy for being feared. For him, fear is a river that can flow shallow or deep, but it flows in only one direction.

He looks up and finds that he has crossed the open space, without seeing any of it. Now he realizes that Anton is before him, coming out of the building that houses Juanito's forge. Unlike the Nigua's huts, this is a structure that Juanito designed for his purposes, taking the posts and woven walls of two empty huts and refashioning them into a building that sits on the ground instead of stilts. It has a wide open frontage under a sloping lean-to roof where the ironsmith has built his furnace and assembled his ingots and tools. Behind is a single room where Juanito lives with his two wives, one African and one Nigua.

His conference with the ironsmith finished, Anton has emerged from the inner room through the single doorway and is now just stepping out from under the lean-to roof into the plaza, on his way back to the presidio. He blinks after being so long in the shade, and his gaze goes to Alonso.

Alonso looks away and realizes at once that it is the wrong thing to do. He immediately looks back at the chief and sees the expression that flickers across the big man's face. It lasts less than a heartbeat, but the impression is permanent. Now Anton looks past him to the big house.

Is Miriam still sitting in the doorway? Has she gone inside? Alonso does not know and certainly cannot turn to look. He nods a greeting to Anton and makes to pass by, but the chief puts out a hand to stop him. It is the lightest of touches, just fingertips against Alonso's chest, but it sends a white flash of deep cold through the younger man's torso. His legs begin to tremble.

Anton is looking at him, his face impassive now, just the way he looked when he came down with the club. "What?" he says.

Alonso's stomach churns, and he finds inspiration. "I think I am ill," he says. "Perhaps those shellfish the children brought up from the shore." He puts a hand to his stomach. "I need the latrine."

He feels sweat cold on his forehead even in the midday heat. Anton regards him for a long moment. Alonso does not meet his eyes, fixing his gaze on the chief's lower teeth instead, which are visible through his half-open mouth. He has never noticed that the middle front teeth lean towards each other.

Then Anton says, "Go see the healer. When she has tended to you, tell her to warn the other women to throw any of the shellfish that are left in the river."

"I will," Alonso says. Anton has lowered his restraining hand. The younger man walks on, his head lowered. He does not have to feign the trembling in his legs. He goes beyond the stockade to where the latrines have been dug. He does not have to feign the looseness of his bowels either.

"Miriam told me something today," Alonso says to Expectation after the evening meal. She is powdering some dried plants in her stone mortar, grinding steadily with her rough stone pestle. He is lying on his sleeping pallet. The dose of bitter herbs she gave him when he reported the stomach upset is making his limbs feel heavy, his mind drowsy. But he has thought about what the African woman said and has decided he needs to tell Expectation about it.

He relays the information succinctly. He lowers his voice, even though they cannot be heard over the singing and conversation going on in the light of the communal fires outside. As he hears himself speak, he is conscious of the unreality of what he is saying, even as the fear it calls up in him tells him that his situation is all too real.

Expectation keeps grinding as she listens, pausing once to add a few more dried leaves to the mortar. When he finishes, her small face compresses into a pattern of wrinkles but clears as she nods. "That makes sense," she says, her voice soft.

"Not to me," Alonso says. "I mean, I understand what she was saying, but somehow I cannot make sense of it to myself."

"That is because you do not look at the world the way Anton does."

"How could I?"

She goes back to grinding. "I think you had better develop the ability."

"It is not enough to be useful, is it?" Alonso says. "That is what I have been thinking."

"No, not enough. When you are dealing with a man like Anton, it is good to be useful, but it is better to be no threat."

"But I am no threat."

She pauses in her work now and looks at him sideways on. Her eyes are very dark in the dim light from the grease lamp. He can see only the crescents of the whites. "Are you not?" she says.

He starts to answer, but she raises the hand that holds the pestle to forestall him. "Look at it from Anton's point of view," she says. "He looks around at the people under him and he says, 'Juanito is very useful. Pahta is useful as a scout. This one or that one is less useful but still plays some part.'

"That is how he looks with one eye. When he looks with the other, he says, 'Juanito is possibly a threat because he is strong and people like the iron tools he makes. But he has no ambition, so I need watch him only a little. And Pahta is not a threat because no one will follow him.'"

She rests down the pestle in the mortar and her voice drops even lower. "He looks at me and says, 'Expectation is useful. She makes medicine and helps keep the Nigua people calm, especially the women. The Nigua women influence their husbands, so if they are content, the men are content.

"'But she is also a threat, because she knows poisons and she has influence. If there was a …'"

It is one of the those rare occasions when she lacks the Spanish word. Alonso supplies it. "A conspiracy?"

She nods. "He thinks, 'If there is a conspiracy and she is part of it, who knows? A woman brings me a cup of beer, and by the time I notice the odd taste, it is too late.'"

"I don't think you would do that," Alonso says.

"It is not a question of whether or not I would do it," she says. "It is a question of whether or not Anton thinks I could." She looks down into the mortar and stirs its contents with a fingertip. "He has only to go from thinking 'could' to thinking 'just might'. At that point the eye that sees me as useful closes and there is only the eye that sees me as a threat.

"And then I am dead."

"I do not want you dead," says Alonso.

"Nor do I," says the healer. "But now we come to you." She wets a finger, takes up some of the crushed herbs, touches the tip of her tongue. Her already compressed face tightens even more from the bitterness.

Alonso says, "I am no threat to Anton."

"Remember what Miriam said. You are respected among both our peoples. You lead when you need to. You do not threaten, but you can kill when necessary. And now it is possible you are descended from a famous *hidalgo*."

"I don't think—"

She cuts him off. "How many of these Africans are of this Mandinka tribe?"

He isn't sure. "Six or seven of the men, I think. Miriam and one of the women."

"That's maybe enough. It's enough to make the core of a ... conspiracy." She thinks for a moment. "Is Juanito one of them?"

"I think so."

"Well, there you are. What was the name of your great ancestor?"

"He is not my ancestor. I do not know if I am even Mandinka."

"The name?"

Alonso remembers, though he wishes he did not. "Tirmakhan Traore."

She nods. "Let that be the last time that name ever crosses your lips." She adds a few more shredded leaves to the mortar and continues grinding. "Now go to sleep."

Alonso has been holding one thing back. "Miriam says I should stay away from you."

Expectation pauses again. "She may be right. No, she *is* right." She grinds again. "We'd better find you a wife."

Stay away from the little witch. Several days have passed, and the main activity in the village has been building new houses and moving the stockade to accommodate the enlarged population. Two more Nigua families have come in, and a Cayapas trader has brought another African, a man named Ercolo who has scars on his back and ankles. Anton awarded the Cayapa an iron spearhead and told him that he would pay a bounty for any escapees delivered safely.

The men have been cutting timber and digging post holes, the women weaving the mats that make the walls and the reed thatch for the roofs. Some of the Africans wanted to build their houses flat on the ground, the way they did where they came from, but Anton ruled against them. "Snakes," was all he said.

Alonso has chosen one of the smaller huts and moved his few possessions into it. The women continue to bring him meals, just as they did when he lived with Expectation. Now whoever has their turn simply delivers to two locations instead of one.

On Alonso's first night in the new place, Anton and Miriam come by. It is his practice to tour the village after people have finished eating, to look things over and to let anyone who has something to say speak to him. It is a Nigua custom, but it has gone down well with the Africans too.

The chief climbs up uninvited into the hut and looks around in the light of the grease lamp, pushing on the posts to see they are well seated and poking at the thatch. "Good," he says, to no one in particular. Then he turns to where Alonso is sitting on his stool. "Why?"

The younger man has rehearsed his answer. "She has learned Spanish. I have learned Nigua. And when she has sick people, they use my bed."

Anton makes his neutral throat sound and nods. He goes back down the entrance steps and walks away. Miriam follows him, but turns her head briefly before she disappears into the darkness to give Alonso her own little nod, as if to say, *That went well.*

But Alonso is only a little comforted by her approval. Since their conversation, he has been beset by doubts. He understands that he must not let Anton know that he is aware of the chief's suspicions, especially not the possibility—Alonso considers it a fantasy—that he might be a lost aristocrat of the Mandinka people. He has thought about that further and knows it cannot be true. He has known *hidalgos* in Seville and in the New World, and all of them, even the children, have a sense of security, of unquestioned entitlement, that is foreign to Alonso. Aristocrats do not live in fear; they create it in others, effortlessly and even without meaning to. One has only to see a *caballero* stop in a village square and ask directions of some peasant artisan. Their postures tell the complete story, one with head and nose held high, the other with rounded shoulders and straw hat clasped in both hands.

Alonso knows he is no lordling. He wishes he could simply go to Anton and say, "Well, now, it is a ridiculous suggestion, is it not? Let us put it out of our minds and get on with the things that matter."

But if he did that, Anton would know that he knew what was in the chief's mind. And Anton does not like anyone to know what he is thinking until he is ready to tell them.

So Alonso sits in his new hut and drinks corn beer and misses the conversations he used to have with Expectation, although some of her ideas are strange. They have talked about her interest in breathing, and she has shown him some of the techniques she uses to control hers. He has tried them himself, especially lying on his back and breathing in slowly, filling the belly until it can hold no more, then doing the same with the chest, now holding while his heart beats loud in his ears, then slowly releasing the air belly first until it is flat and still and the chest slowly sinks to emptiness. The heart beats its count again, and the cycle recommences.

The exercise has a calming effect. Alonso has made it his regular habit now before sleep. It clarifies his mind somehow. When he is breathing and counting heartbeats, he is conscious of nothing else, not even the fear that has always been with him, sleeping during his latter years with the Illescas but now up on all fours, its ruff bristling, its ineffectual fangs gleaming in the darkness.

He hears footsteps in the darkness, approaching. When the walker steps into the faint light thrown by his lamp, he sees it is Expectation. She does not look up as she passes but speaks softly. "When you are asked, say yes."

And then she is gone. Alonso wants to call after her, though he does not know whether it is to ask her what she meant or just to blurt out a panicky plea not to involve him in any conspiracy. But she is gone, disappeared down the dark passageway between the huts. He remembers that he meant to tell her that *conspiracy* is a word related to breath: that it means, literally, 'to breathe together'. It would interest her.

Then he is back to worrying. He sits in his doorway, feet resting on the ladder, the cup of corn beer loose in his hand. He sips it, not tasting its thin bitterness. He sees a flare of light from the direction of the plaza. Someone is building a bonfire. Moments later he hears the clang of iron on iron. Juanito is beating on a hanging bar of metal with an iron rod. All around him, Alonso hears the sounds of people leaving their huts, voices, footsteps, somebody laughing at someone else's remark. They are moving towards the central space. It is one of Anton's innovations, though it is really a custom borrowed from the Nigua: a communal gathering that everyone must attend.

Alonso is one of the last to arrive at the plaza. Two fires have been lit to illuminate the common space. Anton sits between them on the armchair he has had brought down from the presidio. Miriam stands beside him, her hand on his shoulder. The rest of the village is seated in a crescent facing the chief, the last few arrivals finding places at the back of the crowd. Alonso sits behind some of the women. He has a good view of the proceedings.

The process is simple. If someone has a complaint against someone else, they can stand up and state their case. Anyone who has something to offer about the situation can do so, but all must wait until Anton gives permission to speak. It is a good system, Alonso thinks, because it involves everyone in the dispute. In a Nigua village, he has learned, everything is everyone's business.

The crowd has been murmuring, people craning their necks to see who will rise to start the proceedings. Then the wizened matriarch of the red shirt clan rises to her feet, aided by one of her daughters. Another daughter hands her a staff, and the old woman takes a step forward. Her face is seamed and her hair has grown thin, but her voice is firm when she speaks in her own language.

"Xinbu, the daughter of my daughter Kucha, is not happy with the man who chose her," she says, gesturing with her free hand towards a young woman who can be of no more than eighteen years. She has her face lowered, but the matron beside her lifts the girl's chin so that the firelight falls upon her. She is moon-faced like many of her people, but the moon is defaced by a bruise on her cheekbone and a discoloration of the eye above it.

"He is not kind to her. He is her first man, and she did not know what to expect. She wants to leave him and find another man."

As the old woman states the case, Miriam has been speaking quietly in Anton's ear. Alonso knows that she has learned more of the local tongue than the chief has; he spends most of his time with the other Africans, and they converse in Spanish, although sometimes he speaks Mandinka with those who come from the same background.

When the grandmother is finished, she is helped to sit down by her daughters. Anton gestures to the young woman, beckoning her to stand. She does so, blushing, eyes lowered, but when the old woman says something to her, she raises her gaze to the chief.

Anton says, "Is it so, what we have heard?"

He has spoken in Spanish, and the girl answers in the same language. "Yes. He is not good." As she speaks, she points to one of the African men who came from the Cayapas. He sits, scowling, with his friends some distance away.

"Mateo," Anton says to him, "what do you say?"

The man starts to say something while still seated. Anton interrupts him. "Stand when you speak to me."

Mateo's scowl deepens, and Alonso thinks, *He's not doing himself any favours.*

"I work hard," the man says. "I come home and she is gossiping with her sisters and cousins. I tell her I am hungry, but it is always one of my other wives who cooks and brings me dinner. And at night when I want to lie with her, she hides behind one of the others and says she does not want the ugly baby that I will put in her."

The last remark raises general laughter. Mateo is not a good-looking man. He glares around at the mockery and sees that even his friends cannot keep straight faces. "I will beat her again so that she learns—"

He is cut off by a rising tide of disapproving voices. Nigua men do not beat their wives, Alonso knows. Any one of them who tried it would find himself without cooked food or fresh corn beer and with a cold bed. Mateo has made a profound error. He sits down, muttering to his friends, but they give him no encouragement.

Anton has been paying more attention to the crowd than to Mateo. He turns and asks Miriam something, and she answers quietly. Then the chief addresses the young woman. "Xinbu," he says, "do you want to live with another man?"

She gives Mateo one withering glance then looks straight at the man in the chair. "Yes, Chief."

Anton looks over at the grandmother. "And the family?"

The old woman and her daughters, four of them, stand up. "My daughter should have a new man," says Kucha, the woman who held up the girl's chin. She also gives Mateo a hard stare. "A better man."

Mateo begins to shout abuse at the matron and tries to rise, but his friends hold him back, with worried glances towards the man in the chair. He finally subsides but is clearly unhappy.

Anton has been taking all of it in. "What does the village say?"

He looks inquiringly about the half-circle, his gaze falling on this man and that woman. Xinbu and her family do not speak now, but many of the villagers do, especially the Nigua women. The mood is clearly for the young woman and against Mateo.

"Very well," says the chief. "Mateo and Xinbu are no longer married." He speaks to the girl. "Have you chosen a new man?"

Again she holds her head up. "Yes."

"Who is it?"

She looks around the firelit faces, as do many of the other people amid the general murmur. She finds Alonso at the rear of the crowd. She points. "Alonso," she says.

The murmur becomes a general chattering. There is some laughter, and many people are looking about to see where the nominated bridegroom is sitting.

Anton has not had to search for Alonso. He knows where every person of interest is in the crowd. Now he gestures with one finger for the young man to rise. Alonso does so, confused at his sudden transition from mildly interested spectator of the domestic drama to a key participant. He looks about him, sees all the expectant faces turned his way—all, that is, except Expectation, who is looking into the flames of one of the bonfires.

He remembers her whisper: *When you are asked, say yes.*

Anton is speaking. "Alonso Illescas"—Alonso is almost startled to hear his full name—"this woman, Xinbu, daughter of Kucha"—Miriam has been speaking into the chief's ear again—"this woman wants you to be her man. Do you accept her?"

Alonso looks over at the young woman, still standing, though with her mother's plump arm around her shoulders. Xinbu looks at him, and he does not know how to read her expression. Then she blushes and looks away.

Say yes. It is as if the healer is speaking in his ear. He turns to Anton. "Yes," he says. "I should have a wife."

The sound that comes from the seated villagers reminds Alonso of the time he went with the Illescas apprentices to attend a comedic play at the theatre in Seville. When, after many comic contretemps, the star-crossed lovers at last won through to their mutual destiny, he heard relief, amusement, and a tone that said anticipation had been satisfactorily rewarded.

The business finished, people begin to rise. Many of them come to congratulate Alonso on his new status. They pat his arms and smile, and there are even a few suggestive remarks and hand gestures. Embarrassed, nonplussed, Alonso accepts the compliments awkwardly until he can press through the well-wishers to where Xinbu and her female relatives stand in a group, watching his approach.

He has no idea what he is about to say to them. When he arrives, it turns out to be, "I hardly know you."

The matriarch laughs, showing her few remaining teeth. She takes Alonso's hand and puts it in Xinbu's. "Don't worry," she says. "You will."

The girl's hand is warm and firm. Alonso can feel the calluses that come from grinding corn and hoeing weeds. She is looking up at him now, and again he cannot quite define her expression, but he is fairly sure that, among the mixture of feelings showing in her face, he does not see submissiveness.

Now she takes a good grip on his hand and says in Spanish, "Let us go to our house."

She leads and he follows, her relatives coming after them. She releases his hand only when it is time to climb the steps. She picks up the cup he left by the door, sniffs the dregs of the corn beer he was drinking, and flings them out and into the dust. "My mother's is better," she says.

She looks around the single room, sees Alonso's few possessions hanging from pegs driven into the wall posts. His old Spanish clothes are in a lidded basket on the far side of the room. She lifts the lid and inspects the contents, sniffs again, then comes back to where his rapier in its scabbard hangs from a peg beside the door.

"Don't touch that," he says, coming up the steps. "It is sharp."

She runs a finger down the leather sheath but does not try to draw the sword. Alonso knows that, among the Nigua, there are men's things and women's things, and weapons are for men. He has no experience of how to live with a woman, but he believes his best course is to let the rules of her people be his guide.

"Well," he says, "Xinbu. How shall we begin?"

She smiles, and he sees that it has been better to start with a question than with an order. She turns to her female relatives standing at the bottom of the ladder and speaks a rapid flow of Nigua. They scatter.

She turns back to Alonso. "They will bring all the things we need," she says. She nudges his narrow sleeping mat with one bare toe. "Including a bigger bed."

Then she smiles again.

The days pass as Alonso adjusts and adapts to his new circumstances. He—or at least his household—has acquired pots, utensils, implements, a small table with legs no longer than his hand, stools, and a woven backrest that he can lean against when he sits in the doorway. There is also a wide, thin mattress stuffed with grass that crackles when anyone moves on it. Xinbu has made it clear that she expects regular movement on the pallet.

"Expectation has told us that you are ... shy about being a man with a woman," she says, the first night when they are finally alone together. Before that, it was necessary for her male and female relatives to gather at their house to sing traditional songs to the beat of a little drum. If the songs were not sung, she explained, the ancestors would not know that their two spirits had come to reside in the same place and the ancestors would not be able to tell the spirits that they must now get along with each other.

"I am not sure I have a spirit," Alonso told her.

"Everyone has a spirit," the young woman replied, placing a palm against his chest, "though, in the case of some people, their spirits leave them and wander in the underworld. But Expectation can bring them back."

They have settled into a routine. During the days, Alonso continues to be Anton's factotum, overseeing specific projects according to the chief's priorities. Xinbu does her own work, preparing food, working in the fields, fastidiously sweeping out the hut. She is also spending time on the family's shared loom, weaving him cloth that she will make into a new shirt with stitching on the collar appropriate to a married man.

In the evenings, they eat together, often with some of her relatives, of which there are many. Most of these meals are eaten communally, Xinbu's family forming a distinct group among the now large crowd that sits down in the plaza for the last meal. Now that he is part of a family and a clan, Alonso becomes more aware of the other such groupings among the Nigua and notes that the Africans have been quietly fitted into the existing divisions of the people they supposedly dominate.

His perspective has widened in other ways. After the killings on the beach, his guiding principle was to be safe through being useful. He was therefore glad when Anton made him responsible for overseeing the work of the growing village. He was even glad when the chief allotted to him the task of killing when it needed to be done. At every step he thought, *This is good because it shows Anton that I am of use to him.*

But now he realizes that he was seeing his situation only from his own perspective. After his conversation with Miriam, he can look at things from Anton's point of view. And now he sees that the leader might not only be encouraging Alonso to be useful; Anton might also be deliberately putting Alonso into roles in which his supposed heritage as the descendant of warlords might reveal itself.

He knew already that he was being tested. Now he understands that the testing is not of his abilities. He is being tested for his potential danger to Anton. And Anton has a brutally direct way of responding to any challenge to his authority. It is a quandary: the more useful Alonso makes himself, the more he walks a razor-edged bridge that exists in the mind of the chief.

It also occurs to him that Anton is consciously creating Alonso as a potential rival for the chair from which the chief delivers his judgments. If a tide of resentment and rebellion begins to run through the village, Anton will have already created a channel through which it will flow—a channel that leads straight to Alonso, the apparent pretender to the chiefdom. The opposition, should it develop, will have a natural point around which it can coalesce.

By keeping that natural point under his gaze, Anton will know if opposition begins to build against his rule. And he will know where to aim the methodical blows of the gore-stained club to end the revolt before it starts.

But I do not want to be either a pretender or a ruler, Alonso thinks. *I want only to be safe.*

He thought himself safe. Now he must think again.

Thirteen

Expectation

The people were happy about the marriage of Alonso and Xinbu. I listened closely when the women were making the beer, and the main feeling was that they liked Alonso and wanted to see him happy. Also, it was plain that no one liked Mateo, and people were glad to see him taught a lesson. He still had two wives: a pair of sisters who had been widowed, one losing her husband to the spotted sickness, and the other husband's death coming when he was somewhere up in the highlands, forced to carry for the Spaniards.

The sisters were mature women and knew how to handle a bad husband. Their mother said she wished that Mateo had defied Anton over the dissolution of the marriage so that he could have ended up under the club. At that, one of the sisters said, "He is not so bad. It is only when he has been drinking strong beer with his friends. Then you have to know how to handle him."

I steered the conversation back to Alonso, because I wanted to know if his new status had made them look at him differently. It had. They had thought him strange before; the fact that he lived with me had made some wonder if he was some kind of shaman, too. He had respect, and some fear—especially among those who had seen him kill—but no one had warmed to him much. Now when Xinbu talked about his shy and gentle ways, the women greeted her observations with approving sounds.

So that had worked as I had hoped. The mixing of the peoples was also going well. Although the Africans—I had started using Alonso's term instead of "dark Spaniards"—had stepped in as our new rulers, they were adopting our ways. I had talked with Alonso about that and had come to understand that they came from many different countries, with many different languages and customs. The Spaniards had stripped them of that, made them all speak the same language and live under one system—and it was a system that held them at the bottom.

When they came into Nigua land, they found a better way to live, one that was all ready to receive them. I gathered that most of them had come from places where women were subordinate to their fathers, brothers, and husbands, so our ways were a surprise. But with some exceptions, like Mateo, the Africans adjusted themselves to the Nigua way. That gave them happy wives, and there was no better path to a happy life than a happy wife. That was an old saying among the Nigua. The African women had no trouble adjusting to Nigua husbands, although some of them found being deferred to a novel experience.

But later that afternoon, after the cloth tops had been stretched and tightened over the brewing pots and the women went out of their big house to find other chores, Xinbu came and said she wanted to speak with me. I told her to come to the spirit house in a little while then hurried home to make preparations.

Thus I had a package of ground herbs ready for her when she came up the ladder. "These will help him sleep," I told her, "and I will show you how to ease the stiffness in his neck."

She took the little packet of powder and thanked me, saying she would bring me a honey cake in payment. I showed her the way to press hard on places in the neck and shoulders that would make knotted muscles unwind, and she proved to be a quick learner. But there turned out to be more on her mind.

"He says he thinks he does not have"—she touched the space between her breasts—"a spirit."

"Ah," I said and waited.

"But I think he may have a bad spirit within him," she continued, "a spirit he does not know is there, though it tortures him when he sleeps."

"Has he told you of any dreams?" I asked.

"He says he does not dream. But he twists and calls out in the night. Is that not dreaming?"

I did not want to discuss Alonso too much with her, but she needed to be reassured. A bad spirit in the house is a danger to everybody. "He does not have a bad spirit in him," I said. "I have studied him, and I am sure of that." I saw her brows relax and the tension go out of her body. "But I think Alonso is right about having lost his spirit. It happened long ago when he was a child and there was no one around who knew how to find it and bring it back to him. Somehow he has learned to live without it."

"Is that possible?" she said.

"It must be, because there he is, walking and talking."

"They are very different, these new people," she said, shaking her head.

I made a gesture of agreement. "They are, but we will show them the right way to be. It will take time, but it is already happening."

She smiled at that and said, "What can I do about Alonso? Can he put a baby in me if he does not have a spirit to help the baby find the way?"

"You would like to have a baby?"

Her face lit up with a soft and wistful glow. "Oh, yes."

"And does Alonso also wish it?"

"I think so," she said. "The other day I said something about how it would be when we have a little one, and he did not reprove me. He even smiled a little."

That was a good sign, I thought. I told her, "Do not talk about babies with him yet. Help him to sleep and relax, using the herbs and the finger pressing." I lowered my voice and said, "Does he do with you all that a husband should do?"

Now she smiled a proper smile. "Oh, yes. He is not rough like Mateo was, but he … manages. And when I showed him what things I like, he did them." She thought for a moment and said, "If he slept well afterwards, I think he could do even better."

"All right," I said. "If he talks again about his spirit, try to get him to tell you more. Then you come and tell me."

"Do you think you could find his spirit?"

I decided to give her an honest answer. "If I am right about him, it is more than twenty years since he lost his guide. It will have spent a long time away from him, moving ever deeper into the underworld. That could make it hard to find and hard to convince to return."

She made a sad face, and I was moved. They had known each other only a little while, yet she was genuinely concerned for him.

"But maybe not," I said. "Maybe his spirit has been yearning for someone to come and rescue it. I will think about it." I gestured towards the door. "In the meantime, help him to sleep better."

I was composing myself for meditation when I heard a discreet cough and opened my eyes to see Pablillo standing at the bottom of my ladder. His Spanish had become good enough that Anton had begun using him as a messenger.

"He wants to see you," he said.

"Is it sickness?" I said.

"No."

I followed him across the open space. At the base of the big house's ladder, I made the appropriate gesture and saw that he noticed me do it. I smiled up at him—he was coming into his full growth now—and said, "It can't do any harm."

The plaited walls had been rolled up to let a breeze flow through. Otherwise the heat in the place would have been insufferable. I found Anton leaning over his big map spread over the table, the corners held down by bowls that used to be sacred. He looked up at me as I approached, and I saw that he had put on his most impassive face. He said nothing, just watched me.

I stood there for a while. "You sent for me."

He continued his silence, staring at me. I wondered if he thought that, under his steady gaze, I would do something interesting. Instead, I fixed my own stare on the bridge of his nose and paid attention to my breathing.

A moment passed, and then it was as if he wakened suddenly from sleep. His finger stabbed at a spot on the map, north of where we were, near the territory of the Cayapas. "These are your people," he said.

I approached and looked where he pointed. "The big nose clan," I said. "Their headman is called Chilianduli."

"They have not come to us," he said. "Will they fight if we go to them?"

It was a good question. The big noses had more of a reputation for belligerence than the eaters or the red shirts or Pidi's beer people clan. Chilianduli was a man in his prime and had been the war chief in fights against Campazes when they came raiding. He had killed his first man when he was not much older than Pablillo.

I said, "They might."

"Depending on what?"

"On how you approach them."

He rolled his hand through the air. "More."

"If you send men with iron swords and armour," I said, "they could take it as a challenge—join us or else. Chilianduli is a proud man. He could not show weakness in front of his clan."

"So I should send you?" He made no effort to disguise his scepticism.

"He does not like me. My … condition offends him."

He made his thinking sound down in his throat. "I should send Alonso?"

I kept my face neutral. We were playing a game and we both knew it, but only he was allowed to acknowledge that this was a contest. "That would also be offensive," I said.

"Then what?" he said. And thus it became my turn, but I had to play it right.

"When we all lived together in the old town," I said, "there would sometimes be—I think *tensions* is the Spanish word—between families or clans. If things had not gone too far and both sides wanted to avoid making things worse, one side would invite the other to a feast."

"A feast?" The scepticism was still there, but it had weakened.

"Yes. Lots of food, lots of beer, weak and strong. Singing and dancing. Maybe some individual contests, men wrestling, throwing spears at targets, a canoe race."

"Sounds like a party," Anton said. He was looking at me again, but I could read the expression this time.

"I am being serious," I said. "It was how we got along when there were thousands of us, all living in one town."

He made his thinking noise again, and I saw that he was considering my suggestion. "What else?" he said.

I made my last move. "You might have to wrestle him."

"Chilian . . . ?"

"Duli," I said. "Chilianduli. He likes to wrestle."

"You mean he is good at it." And he showed me again his game-playing face, to which I made no response. "He might beat me."

"He also likes to drink," I said.

"And the wrestling comes after the drinking?"

"Usually."

Another grunt. It told me I was playing well, but I already knew that. Anton looked down at the map, but I knew he was seeing images in his mind and calculating moves and outcomes. Then he looked up and said, "How is such a feast arranged?"

"When we were all in one village, the matriarch of the inviting clan went to the matriarch of the other and brought a bowl of food and a jug of beer. The second old woman fed it to the headman of the clan. If he ate and drank it all, the invitation was accepted."

"Whom would we send?"

I thought for a moment. "This is not clan to clan, so it should be from the most senior of the old women. That is Mandas of the red shirts."

"It is a long way for an old woman to go."

"True. Someone will have to carry her."

"Is there more?"

"Oh, yes," I said. "The food and beer must be carried in sacred vessels. Women are not—or were not—allowed to see them, so the men have to take the food the women prepare and transfer it to the bowls. Then they have to be carried in baskets with the lids held down tightly."

He was looking at me in that doubt-laden way again, as if I might be trying to perpetrate some elaborate prank on him. "What sacred vessels?" he said.

"Well," I said, pointing, "that one on the corner of the map, and this one over here."

I think it was the first time I had ever seen Anton really laugh. "Take them," he said.

"I cannot," I said. "I am not allowed to see them, either. If you agree, I will ask Pahta to handle them."

"All right, but go and see Mandas, tell her I want her to go. We will make a litter to carry her."

I did not want to try his patience but I thought I needed to say, "I will ask her. She cannot be compelled."

"She can if I am doing the compelling."

I was on a very slim branch, but I had to take another step. "I do not wish to offend, but if you try to impose your will on one of the grandmothers, especially Mandas, you will undo all the good you have done."

His face drew in. For a moment he was as ugly as Mateo. "Will she rise up against me?"

"No."

He shrugged. "Then what?"

"All the women would be against you."

"The Nigua women," he corrected me.

"Yes. They would be unhappy. That means the men would be unhappy. You would be ruling an unhappy people." I thought I had pushed it as far as I dared. But it was Anton who spoke the final conclusion.

"You mean a people unhappy under my rule."

"Yes." I waited, needing to know how Anton would receive such counsel. He looked down at the map again, then he ran his hand over his face, wiping away the sheen of sweat that had sprouted while we spoke.

When he looked up I knew that he was himself unhappy, but he was convinced. "Will you ask her?"

"Better if Miriam does, but I can accompany her to translate."

He nodded. I saw he was getting a better understanding of how things worked among our people. I could not say he liked what he was learning or that he would agree to continue this way once he had consolidated his power. But for now he was willing to bend a little.

Then he gave me that searching look again and said, "Should Alonso go, too? To deliver the invitation?"

I did not have to think about that. "No," I said.

"Why not? Too busy being a husband?"

"He is not well," I said.

He let his concern show. "I had not heard. What is wrong with him?"

"He has lost . . . some part of himself," I said. "He does not sleep well."

He was suddenly angry. "I know what you are talking about. Miriam has explained it to me. You traffic with demons."

I spoke gently, reasonably. "That is a Christian concept. We are not Christians."

"Nor am I," Anton said. "I am a servant of Allah. Not a good servant, I know. I do not pray five times a day, and I drink rum."

I did not know what to say to this. I spread my hands and bowed my head, waiting.

"We will not discuss Alonso," he said after a while. "And you will not talk about your demons in my presence. Understood?"

"Understood," I said.

"All right, go and speak with Miriam. Tell her what needs to be done."

I said I would and left. After I descended the ladder, I had to stand for a moment at the side of the big house, just breathing and counting my heartbeats until they slowed.

The grandmothers said Chilianduli's clan got its name from something that happened shortly after the beginning of the world, when the first Nigua man and woman came up out of a hole in one of the hills far inland—no one remembered where—and began to plant the forest and call all the animals out of the soil. The first children of the first man and woman were the beginnings of all the clans. One day, the mother of all told one of her sons to go to the river and bring her a fish, but he argued with her. She hit him on the nose with a piece of firewood, and it swelled up. The story was probably true because, although not all members of Chilianduli's clan had big noses, everyone knew they liked to argue.

They came, all fifty-seven of them—men, women and children—down the Esmeraldas River from their hidden village. They travelled on rafts towing canoes to the stream beside the old town, where they left the rafts and, guided by Pahta, came up in canoes in the late afternoon. At the landing, Anton and Miriam waited for them with the elders of our three clans. Anton had let me instruct him in the traditional greetings that a Nigua chief should offer, then he stood back and let the grandmothers play their parts.

It all went well. Chilianduli had come out of his canoe wearing a suspicious look, but after the matriarchs had greeted their big nose counterparts, he threw back his feathered cape of many colours, baring his heavy chest and thick arms to show how he bore no weapons. Then he stepped forward to clasp Anton's forearms just below the elbows, while the chief clasped his. They held onto each other a little longer than custom required, and I could see that each was quietly testing the other's strength.

It ought to be an interesting match, I thought, though I knew I would not be there to see it.

Besides his interest in Chilianduli's strength, Anton could not help noticing the gold hanging from the clan leader's nostrils and earlobes. I saw his eyes flick over the baubles, though his face showed only the smile of welcome. Then they let go of each other, and our people struck up the welcome song and—a good sign—the big noses still in the canoes sang the responses loudly and without lowering their eyes from ours.

Then they came out onto the landing, and we all went together along the hidden trail and through the gate into the village. I watched Chilianduli as he entered the compound and saw he was impressed by the size of the place and the good order of the houses and the stockade. His step faltered, but only a little, when he saw the Africans and their Nigua wives drawn up in a semicircle on the far side of the plaza. But then the women sang their welcome song, and their husbands' dark faces smiled as Anton had drilled them.

The women went to their cooking fires and kettles. I watched as the big nose women followed them, their eyes on the gleaming copper, polished all the day before by boys and girls using handfuls of sand. The grandmothers gathered in their own place and sat but kept watch over the cooks, occasionally calling out advice.

The men sat down in a circle, ours spreading out so that there were plenty of gaps in which the big nose men could sit. Our Nigua men made the traditional gestures and offers, and the Africans copied them, again as Anton had drilled them. And again it worked. The children and young women brought cups and bowls of weak beer, and as the guests drank, the last vestiges of tension dissolved. Stomachs were rubbed and fingers pointed at the cooking fires and big kettles, the smell of roasting tapir and stewing monkey filling the air.

Anton led Chilianduli to a place of honour where two stools had been set side by side on a Spanish blanket. They sat together, and Miriam and the clan leader's wife brought them bowls of new beer. They drank together, each emptying half his bowl and exchanging bowls before finishing the rest. Chilianduli belched appropriately. Anton did the same.

Then Anton stood up and made a brief speech in Spanish while Miriam translated. Chilianduli followed, and Miriam rendered his remarks from the Nigua—she had become quite fluent. The grandmothers of the three clans were impressed by her and, though she was not really old enough, had accepted her as the matriarch of the Africans. Now the grandmothers of the big noses smiled on her, too.

That will help, I thought.

More beer made the rounds, and now Anton ordered the gifts to be brought out. Several of our men, African and Nigua, went up into the presidio and returned bearing bundles and chests. They rattled with sounds of metal implements jostling against each other. All the big nose, men and women alike, took notice. Then the bearers went back to the big house and came back with even more. I heard sounds of excitement from the plaza, big noses of both sexes and all ages talking to each other.

The goods were put down before the two men on stools. Anton leaned forward, threw back the edges of the blankets that wrapped the bundles, and opened the lids of the chests. Then he stood up and spoke in Nigua, his accent strange but the simple words understandable to the guests.

"We give gifts. Spear points and knives for men, kettles and spoons for women."

He reached down and lifted out samples of each, clashing a couple of spear points together so the guests could hear the ring of the metal. A murmur of approval went around the circle of seated men and from the women at the cooking fires. The mood loosened even further, and I heard calls for more beer as the children hurried to meet the demand.

Anton told the gift bearers to rewrap the bundles, close the chests, and take them over to where the matriarchs sat. Since weapons were being given at a time when men were drinking, the grandmothers would take charge of the presents until the morning.

And now the feasting began.

By nightfall, the bulk of the food had been eaten. The women were giving their men old beer, and voices were loud around the firelit circle. But the people remained happy. I imagined the big noses, despite the proper form of the invitation, must have been uncertain about sitting down to eat and drink with a strange people. They had been reassured by the equally proper form of the welcome and by discovering that the Africans were not like the Spaniards. The Africans, for their part, would have been at least a little nervous about receiving so many strangers. Now the built-up tension was being discharged in loud merriment.

I had eaten little and taken no beer, knowing what I had to do. I waited until the first of the big noses, a squat and powerful man of mature years named Palapcha, rose and stepped out into the firelight to invite someone to wrestle with him. This was always a feature of feasts involving big noses, and I had talked to Peg, one of Juanito's wives, to nudge her into preparing for the moment. She had been persuasive, and now the ironsmith put down his wooden cup and stood up to face Palapcha.

A sound of anticipation went up from the crowd as the two men approached each other, sizing each other up. Juanito shook his shoulders and rotated his neck to loosen himself while Palapcha bent and scooped up a handful of dust that he rubbed between his palms. Each dropped into a crouch and moved closer, circling, wary.

"Wait!" cried a voice. It was Chilianduli. He stood up and removed the half-crescent of gold that hung from his nose to lie upon his upper lip. He held the gleaming thing up for all to see and said, "For the winner!"

There were shouts from the men and softer tones of appreciation from the women. Now it was Anton's turn. He looked to where Miriam was coming out of the darkness, carrying something that she handed to him. He stood up and shook out a shimmering length of the blue fabric the Spaniards called silk. "For the winner!" he said in Nigua.

This time, the louder cries came from the women. If Palapcha's wife could make herself a dress of the blue stuff, there was not a woman in the big nose clan who would not envy her. Now she leaned forward, her eyes bright from more than just the fire and the beer, and told her husband to win or sleep alone tonight. Everyone laughed, including Palapcha, but then he set himself and made a little beckoning motion to Juanito, and the circling began in earnest.

With all eyes on the two men, I rose from my place far from Anton and Chilianduli and slipped into the darkness at the back of the seated crowd where Alonso sat with Xinbu. I touched him on the shoulder. He rose without a word and came with me. I saw Xinbu's face turn towards us and hoped that I would be able to repay the hope that I saw there.

It was only a few steps to where the spirit house stood. The firelight did not illuminate it much, and even if someone looked our way, after watching the wrestlers in the brightly lit open space, their eyes would see only darkness. Alonso went up the steps, and I followed. Pablillo was already there, seated on one of the stools. He had lit the grease lamp as I had asked him to.

"Good boy," I said and rolled down the woven mat that covered the doorway. I twisted a second wick of cotton for the lamp, which was fashioned from a jaguar's skull and filled with the oil that had come from the Spaniards' ship. The second flame gave us plenty of light to see by.

"Sit here," I said to Alonso, gesturing to the pallet where he used to sleep. He did, and I brought him the cup in which I had prepared the potion earlier in the day. He looked at it for a moment, then at me.

"You must," I said.

For a moment I saw in his face the sadness at the heart of him, but then he showed me the expression he must have adopted as a boy, the first time he realized life required him to square up and push on. He drowned the liquid in one draught, grimaced at the bitter aftertaste, and handed me the cup.

"Now," I said, "lie on your back and think about your breathing."

I watched for a while as his belly and chest rose and fell in the usual cycle. Gradually it slowed. Then I turned to Pablillo and said, "Take up your drum and the stick."

They were waiting for him beside his stool. He picked them up and said, "Now?"

"Wait until I am ready." I sat on the second sleeping mat next to Alonso's and spent a few moments centring myself. Then I lay back and said, "Begin."

I listened to the first few dozen beats. They were the rhythm I had practised with Pablillo—he might have a talent for the art, I thought—but still I reminded him, "Do not stop. I will need to hear you when I am on the return journey."

"I will not stop," he said.

I closed my eyes and called up in my mind the image of the canoe I had been fashioning in my mind in recent days. I had imagined myself cutting down the tree, using a stone axe instead of one of the Spaniards' steel ones. Then I had seen myself using fire and sharp stone to hollow out the interior and to sear it so that water would not seep through the delicate wood. I had carved struts of hard wood to strengthen the boat, and I had painted eagle eyes on its prow to guide me through the lower world.

When I could see the canoe clearly as a glowing shape in darkness, I held the image in my mind and softly began singing my power song:

Spirits come to me,
To me come spirits.
Friends they are to me,
My friends are they.

As I sang this song over and over, I felt the powers of my spirit guides fill me: my eagle, the jaguar, the red cat, the tapir, the green turtle who swims in the sea, three kinds of hummingbird, the tree mouse, the white-shouldered squirrel, and the white-faced bear that only Pallu had seen in the flesh but whose spirit he had taught me to call.

They came to me, each in its own way, and filled my chest until it felt hollow and light, full of breath even though I was hardly breathing at all, so slow was my respiration. Around the image of my spirit canoe, the darkness fell back and was replaced by a glow of warm gold. When I saw that, I knew it was time.

I changed my song:

My canoe is light and strong.
Into the underworld it travels.
My spirits guide its course.
I float upon the waters.

This I sang many times and, as I did so, I was no longer looking at the canoe—I was sitting in it, facing forward, while it floated on a narrow river of pale golden light. I followed its flow into a valley with steep sides shrouded in darkness. The current strengthened, but I continued to sing even as the canoe and I rushed towards a gap that glowed as red as the coals of a dying fire.

I knew my way here and did not hesitate when the canoe shot through the narrow opening into a place of cold and loneliness. Dark creatures, huge and shaped like fantastical insects, loomed up on either side of me, their creaking voices telling me that I was lost, all was lost, that only despair and fruitless longing awaited me, that I should stop and accept their cold solace.

But I sang my song. I knew them, the Old Deceivers, and because I knew them they had no power over me. Soon I had left them behind, and now the river slowed to a meandering stream passing grass-covered banks with scattered trees tall against a blue sky. I could not see the sun, but the scene was filled with light.

I began to look for Alonso's lost spirit. I doubted I would find it so soon. I didn't even know what kind of animal it was. I had learned that Africa had many different creatures, though I could not quite believe the stories about an animal as big as a hut with teeth as long as a man's leg. If it did exist, I hoped it was not Alonso's spirit; I had made a small canoe.

There was no horizon here. The plain stretched away into a mistiness like the border of a dream. I could see vague motion in the far distance, and sometimes from the sense of movement emerged the shape of an animal. As I moved along with the river, I saw several different kinds of creature, many of them strange. Some took an interest in me, others ignored me completely. What I was looking for was a beast that showed itself to me more than once.

A face came into view, a cat's face made along the same lines as a jaguarundi. But its fur was pale yellow instead of red, and there were dark spots on it like little paw prints. Its eyes were large, clearly a predator's forward-looking gaze, but it lacked the heavy jaw of a jaguar. I saw it first from a distance, and then it moved towards me, becoming clearer. When it knew that I was aware of it, it turned and ran off very swiftly, and its backbone flexed with a limberness I had seen in no other creature.

My canoe continued down the smoothly flowing river. In the distance I could hear Pablillo's tapping of the drum like soft thunder, far off. It reassured me. I looked about again and saw other animals, vague and distant shapes. Then the spotted cat appeared, pacing along the bank farther downstream. It stopped, sat, and licked a forepaw. Then it glanced at me, turned, and sprang away. Again I was struck by its great speed as it disappeared into the vagueness.

I see, I thought. I sang my spirits song again to alert the helpers within me to the moment that was not far off. I watched for the spotted cat. Soon after, I saw it again, peering at me from behind a strange-looking tree whose branches flattened at the top so that it looked as if it had been trimmed with one of the glass-edged sickles the Quechua speakers use to cut their quinoa. When it saw that I had seen it, the cat drew back into the shade and was lost to view.

That makes three times, I said to myself. A lost animal spirit that wants to be reunited with its former host will show itself four times. The shaman must act on the fourth appearance, for there will be no fifth. I readied myself for the fourth, because I knew it would be sudden and close.

The canoe glided around a long shallow curve, and in the bight of the river I saw the dark-spotted yellow cat, stretched languidly just along the shore's edge, its eyes on me and its small pink tongue lolling loosely. I directed the canoe to move so that it glided towards the bank. Closer and closer I came to the recumbent animal, its eyes never leaving mine. I softly sang my gathering song and felt the crowd of spirits within me rising up to help.

Slowly, drawing nearer and nearer, two arm's lengths, then one, then there it was beside me. The beast rose to its feet and turned its head away, its haunches dropping to propel a great spring. But I shot out my hand and caught the ruff of its neck, pulling it into the canoe and close to my chest where my own spirit friends were gathered. The cat stiffened under my grip, its claws scraped against the bottom of the canoe, and it was all I could do to hold it tight to me.

Come, spirit, I said. *Alonso waits for you. He will make you a home.*

The tension went out of its body then, and it lay against my chest like a sleeping child. Still, I kept a strong grip on it while I turned my mind towards the far-off tapping of the drum and willed the canoe to take me back. It turned into the current and began to gather speed, and I thought to myself, *It is well.*

The canoe flew up the river. The landscape darkened and, as if awakening from a dream, I found myself lying on the mat beside Alonso. I sat up and motioned for Pablillo to cease drumming, giving him a brief smile to show that all was well. Then I reached into the basket where I had left it on the floor at Alonso's head and brought out the hollowed tube of bone taken from the leg of a wading bird.

I knelt beside my sleeping patient and softly sang the song that tells a spirit it is time for it to go home. I repeated this several times until I felt that the message had been received. Then I put the tube to my lips, bent over so that its other end touched Alonso's chest just above the heart, and softly blew through the bone. In a moment, I felt the cat spirit leave me and enter Alonso. His chest rose and fell in one deep, slow exchange of breath—a good sign. Still, I moved until I was kneeling above his head so I could put the end of the tube at the place where, as an infant, he would have had a soft spot, and I blew softly again. Two insertions were always better than one, Pallu had taught me.

The treatment was concluded. I had found Alonso's lost spirit guide and restored it to him. Now only time would tell how he would change, though the change would turn him back into the person he used to be before the spirit was driven out of him.

I sat on my stool, drained as I always was after one of these operations. I became aware again of the noise of the feast. I did not know how much time had lapsed while I was in the lower world—time is different there—but the celebrations were still going on. I extinguished the grease lamp's wicks and told Pablillo to roll up the mat and uncover the doorway. That gave me a good view of the plaza and the activity there.

The fires had been built up for light. The wrestling match between Juanito and Palapcha was over. The two of them were sitting together and drinking beer, so that had ended well, whoever had won. Now they were watching along with everyone else as two new contestants circled each other.

Anton and Chiliandulí were in the first stages of the bout, circling and feeling each other out with little shoves and slaps on the arms. I could see that Anton had taken my advice to heart: he had plied the head of the big nose clan with the strong liquor rescued from the shipwreck. It had seemed amazing to me when Alonso told me that one cup of the stuff was as strong as an entire gourd of old beer. But the way Chiliandulí blinked and wavered on his feet as he tried to maintain a wrestler's crouching stance told me that this drink called rum was all Alonso had said it was.

Anton had kept his head out of the keg of liquor, that was clear. But just as clearly, he meant to defeat Chiliandulí without humiliating him. He allowed the Nigua to put a hold on him and struggled convincingly before he managed to break the man's grip, to the cheers of all the spectators. Now he threw the clan chief over his hip but followed up so slowly that Chiliandulí was able to stagger to his feet and face him.

But this was only going to end one way, and after a few more throws and grips, Anton swept Chiliandulí's unsteady legs out from under him and threw himself down on his prostrate opponent. The victory was complete, but the huge belch emitted by the Nigua when the African landed on him made it a lighter moment for the watchers.

Good, I thought. I said to Pablillo, "Some of those big nose girls were eying you, and some of their married older sisters as well. Go and enjoy yourself."

He slid down the ladder and went towards the merriment. Anton had helped Chiliandulí to rise and they had their arms around each other's shoulders, heading back to their stools while the combined peoples laughed and called out to them. Then somebody began to sing a bawdy old song, and the rest joined in. I noticed that many of the Africans knew the Nigua words and were singing along.

Very good, indeed, I thought. Then I turned to take another look at my patient and found him sleeping quietly. I watched the rise and fall of his chest and wondered, *when he wakes up, who will he be?*

Fourteen

Alejandro de Espinosa

The Carranza expedition had changed its tactics. All thoughts of recapturing escaped slaves fled the captain's mind. No longer would they go up and down the Babahoyo's tributaries looking for native settlements. Instead, they went looking for islands, especially islands with cemeteries. Some of these occurred on rivers wide enough for the boats to row, but early in the search they had discovered that more of them were to be found on narrow lakes—Carranza was convinced they were artificially created—in streams that fed into the smaller rivers.

His rationale was plausible, Alejandro thought, though insincere. The captain said, "We will despoil their cemeteries. That will make them angry, and they will come against us. But we will choose the killing ground: we will fortify an island, and when they come across the water, our *arcabuzes* and crossbows will shoot them down and our steel will open their bellies."

The men cheered at that, and they cheered louder when Carranza said they would all go back to Quito rich in gold.

To begin with, they had explored the little waterways by taking a boat as far as it would go before getting out and wading upstream. This had proved to be a poor approach: one of the soldiers had broken an ankle when he stepped into a pothole on the stream bed, and the man-made lakes had been dug too deep for wading. The soldiers who could swim could make it there, but it meant giving up their armour, which they were loath to do. And then, if they found appreciable amounts of golden grave goods, it made for a heavy swim back to the shallow stream.

So Carranza sent one of the boats and ten soldiers back downstream to find canoes and bring them upriver. He sent the crippled soldier back as well, after reassuring the man that he was entitled to his full share of the spoils—that had all been worked out before the recruits signed the articles of the *entrada,* which Father Miguel dictated and Fray Alejandro drew up.

Avila, as the first discoverer of treasure, was entitled to an extra share above what was warranted by his rank. When they had first rowed their boat back to the rest of the flotilla and had drawn up gunwale to gunwale with Carranza and Cabello in the lead craft, Alejandro had seen the captain's eyes gleam as the Portuguese passed over his helmet, half-filled with gold.

And then the monk had glanced over and seen the same expression on the face of the soldier-turned-priest. It was only for a moment, before Cabello swiftly reassumed his normal haughty impassivity, but for that instant the priest had definitely given in to the sin of avarice. Then the moment passed, and the captain was giving orders. They would return to the large island on which they had been camping and turn it into a fortified base. From now on, the *entrada* was to be a hunt for gold.

"Is that what the Viceroy wanted when he approved the mission?" Alejandro said. "I thought the goal was to punch through the Campazes and recapture the Africans."

He was dragging a heavy branch from the water's edge to the breastwork they were making a few yards up the gentle slope of the island; Avila had explained that they were making a killing ground between the barrier and the water. The enemy would have to get out of their canoes and charge up to the barricade, where they would clump together and make better targets for the matchlocks and the pikemen.

"The Viceroy," said Avila, after telling Alejandro where to place the branch and turn it so that its projecting twigs pointed outward, "approves of gold, especially gold that comes to him while he sits in Lima and shuffles papers."

"But the aim was to reduce the *Indios,*" Alejandro said.

"And reduce them we will." Avila was whittling the outward-facing ends of the twigs into sharp points. "But first we have to find them."

He adjusted the branch's placement to his satisfaction. "Or, to be candid, we will let them find us. We were not having any success coming to them. But relieving their dead of their gold and other items"—he had kept the fine-toothed comb for himself—"will induce them to come to us."

"Not peacefully," Alejandro said, moving down to the water's edge for another piece of flotsam.

"No, not peacefully. But they will be peaceful after enough of them are dead."

The hunt for gold continued once the boat sent downstream came back with three canoes in tow. The Campazes may have retreated inland, but it was clear that they had occupied this territory for many generations. Avila theorized that the island cemeteries were only for the great men of the nation and a few revered matriarchs.

"The important question is: where do they get the gold?" They were seated on a log beside one of the smoking campfires as the night fell with the suddenness of a curtain.

The monk coughed as a particularly acrid gust came his way. "I have heard there are two sources," he said, enduring another spasm before he could continue. "They use flat wooden bowls to sift gold dust from the silt at the bottom of streams, occasionally finding a nugget. Or they trade—that is they used to trade—the little white seashells to the Quechua speakers in the highlands."

"Well," said Avila, wafting away a particularly determined insect, "there will be no more of that." He stretched out his legs and contemplated the state of his boots, which were suffering from the perpetual damp. "Let us hope that there is still plenty of dust and nuggets in the streams. If an enterprising man had a *encomienda* of five thousand savages—"

"Christian subjects of the King," Alejandro corrected him.

"Fine. Five thousand Christian subjects swirling silt in pans for three months of the year, the yield in gold would be considerable. Five years here, then it's back to Spain, buy a big house, take a seat on the *cabildo*, and marry the daughter of an *hidalgo*."

"I did not think they let Portuguese become town councillors," said Alejandro. "Far less marry a *dona*."

"I was speaking of the general ambition," said Avila. "My own goals are different."

It occurred to the monk that he had never heard his companion—for they seemed to have become more than simply associates on an *entrada*—speak of his aims. He felt comfortable asking, "And what would those goals be?"

The soldier poked at the fire with a long stick, making the smoke billow more thickly. He quirked his mouth and sucked on one end of his moustache. "In a word: freedom."

"You are free now," said Alejandro.

Avila gave a dismissive grunt. "Free to find someone to give me orders and apportion my reward," he said. "That is a limited liberty, you must admit."

"It is more than most obtain."

The soldier poked the fire again. "I am not of the most. I am of the few."

"You have said what you don't desire, not what you do."

"That is because I have not yet found what I am looking for," Avila said. "To tell the complete truth, I do not know what it is, only that I *will* know it when I see it."

"Utopia?" said the monk.

"What is that?"

"A place in a book written by an English martyr. A land where everything was perfect."

"Heaven on earth?" said Avila. "I don't expect to see that."

"No," said Alejandro, "not Heaven. A land made up for the sake of argument."

The monk would have moved on, but the digression had started Avila thinking. "There is something in it, though: the idea of a made-up land. We come from an old world, where everything has been decided—who's a peasant, who's a king—and every man knows his place.

"Then we come here, and there are still categories and divisions, but the walls between them are not so thick and not so high."

"True," said Alejandro. "Take my friend Juan Hernandez— "

"Your friend?"

The monk shrugged. "I consider him so."

"Does he consider you so?"

"Never mind. My point is, in Seville, a mulatto might own a mule or two and hire out to haul goods from the docks to a merchant's warehouse. But he wouldn't own thirty or forty mules. Here, he can build a business as big as he can make it."

"They still won't let him marry an *hidalgo*'s daughter," Avila said.

"I doubt he wants to. But he can build a good house and have servants and leave his sons an inheritance and his daughters dowries."

"True," said Avila, "and maybe that is the life I will make for myself, if I live to spend the gold we've found." His teeth tugged at his moustache again, and he said, "But I think I want something wider than a house and an inheritance and dowries for daughters."

"Then what?"

"I don't know. Not yet. Maybe the land I want to live in doesn't exist yet. Maybe I will have to make it up."

They had been three weeks collecting gold, and the men had become adept at finding streams and following them to where the island cemeteries lay. The heap of gold now filled three sizable coffers, whose lids contained complicated, built-in locks. They were kept in Captain Carranza's tent. Alejandro thought it instructive that their leader had brought empty chests with him: the hunt for gold had always been one of the *entrada*'s ambitions; he had just been too naive to see what everyone else had.

On the second day of the fourth week, they had their first case of fever. One of the soldiers on daytime guard duty in the encampment swayed and sat down on a log. His face was pale, and sweat streamed from under his helmet to run in rivulets down his cheeks and into his beard. His name was Gregorio, and he was one of Avila's troop that had been taken off search duty for the day and set to guard the camp.

Avila came and said, "It looks like the shaking fever. Brother, help me get him some shade."

They laid the man down—he was indeed shivering violently now, his teeth clicking against each other like castanets—and rigged an awning out of some sticks and a blanket. Alejandro brought him some sour wine, but Gregorio was shaking too hard to hold the cup or even drink from it while the spasm had him in its grip. The monk finally got some into him and laid him down to rest—as well as he could manage with steel covering his front and back.

By nightfall they had a second case. They laid him beside the first, and the captain came from his tent to look at them. "In the morning," he said, "we'll send them on the boat back to Guayaquil. It's time we replenished our supplies anyway."

The boat set off shortly after dawn, six soldiers rowing and the two invalids sitting slumped together on a vacant thwart. The decision as to who the rowers would be had been left to the men and decided by the casting of lots; the winners would have a day and a night to enjoy in Guayaquil's taverns and brothels.

After the men had seen the boat off with bawdy remarks shouted back and forth across the widening water, Carranza called them together. He declared a day without foraging. "Every man will see to the condition of his weapons," he said, "and I want the breastworks strengthened and more shelters built against the sun and the rain."

As he spoke, the first few drops of water fell. Men ran to put out pannikins and buckets, because what fell from the sky was purer than what they drew from the silty river. Soon the containers were full and overflowing as the drops became sheets of heavy, blinding rain. It fell throughout the morning and abruptly stopped by midday. The men relit the fires that had been doused by the downpour and stripped off some of their clothes and hung them to dry. They were cooking beans and salt pork when they heard a shout from the lookout at the downstream point of the island.

The boat was coming back, rowed by three soldiers. It ran up onto the grey sand and men came down to pull it ashore. By then a crowd had gathered, and Carranza and the priest pushed their way through it. The captain took in the situation at a glance. He pointed at the four soldiers nearest the boat and said, "You four, get the bodies out. The rest of you, stand to! Do you think this is a day at the fair? Stop gawking and get to your posts!"

Alejandro went to help the four soldiers pull the dead from the boat: the two who had had the shaking sickness and three of the soldiers. Their necks and arms were pierced by slim arrows and little feathered darts. More missiles were stuck into the thwarts and sides of the boat, and still more lay loose in the bottom. The monk presumed these had glanced off the men's chest and back armour and their sharp-pointed helmets.

The three who had survived were getting out of the boat, their limbs trembling from the exertion of rowing fast against the river's rain-swollen current. One had a little dart sticking from the padded shoulder of his doublet. When Alejandro saw it, he plucked it free. The man turned, saw what he held in his hand, and went pale.

"Report," Carranza said.

The sergeant in charge said, "About two hours downstream, the river is split by an island. We thought about camping there, but the channels on either side were too narrow."

The captain nodded. "I remember the place."

"They had made thick ropes and stretched them across both channels. The barriers were just above the water and it was raining hard, so we didn't see them until we were almost on them. We started to back water as fast as we could, and then the arrows and darts came."

"How many of them were there?"

"I don't know. We never saw even one. Just the arrows and darts coming out of the trees. Some of them must have climbed up, because they came raining down on us." He made a high-pitched sound that might have been a laugh.

Carranza slapped him across the face. "Stand to attention and speak like a man!"

The soldier drew himself up, the mark of his captain's hand red on his livid face. "Yes, Captain. The darts and arrows that came from above were the worst. You can see the dead were struck in their legs where they had no armour or padding.

"We rowed until we were out of range. They did not pursue us." He thought for a moment. "From the number of missiles, I would estimate there were no more than twenty of them."

The captain took this in and told the three survivors to get themselves fed then stand to with the rest. The dead would remain where they were, laid side by side on the shore, until a burial party could be organized. He told one of the men to bring him some of the darts and arrows and then to go back to their posts.

He examined the weapons. Alejandro picked up an arrow and did the same. Its head was a sliver of bone that had had a needle-fine point before it snapped off after striking armour. Thin grooves were etched in the bone and pressed into them was a grey substance. Alejandro raised the arrowhead to his nose and sniffed gently. It smelled like damp ground.

He threw the thing from him and saw that Carranza and Cabello were looking at him. "You have an opinion, Brother?" the priest said.

"My opinion, Father, is we are in trouble."

"No," said Carranza. "The savages are in trouble. Now begins the fighting and, as we all know, when the fighting comes, the savages lose."

It was not a time for argument, so Alejandro did not ask whether 'we all' included the Campazes.

Still, he saw that Carranza had learned something from the skirmish downriver. He put twenty men to work building roofs on poles behind the breastworks to shelter the soldiers from plunging missiles. They used the cloth that would have been given as gifts to the Campazes if they had met on peaceful terms.

It was a good tactic, except that when the next downpour came, the fabric became soaked and tore free from where it had been tied to the upper ends of the poles. Where it didn't tear loose, it so overburdened the narrow supports that the shelters tipped and toppled over. Then the cloth had to be wrung out, two men pulling and twisting lengths of it between them.

Alejandro and Avila were doing this work. The monk said, quietly, "I am concerned about what is happening."

"You should be," said the Portuguese. "People are dying. Even people with armour, which you lack."

"I am concerned," he said, "because I think our captain thinks he knows what the *Indios* are thinking. But I don't think he does."

"I try to avoid too much thinking," said Avila, grunting as he gave his end of the twisted roll of cloth another turn.

But Alejandro pushed on, regardless of his companion's grim levity. "He thinks the Campazes will come at him in a body, the way the Puna Island *Indios* came against Pizarro."

"But you don't think so?"

"I think the Campazes have had a lot of time to think about what happened to the Puna, who were just as fierce as they are." Alejandro let his end of the cloth untwist so that Avila could shake it. "And I think they've decided not to get themselves all killed the same way."

"Help me get this back up on the poles," the Portuguese said. As he was retying the thongs that held one of the corners, he said, just for the monk's ear, "I'll tell you what I think. I think you're right."

The soldiers stood to all day, half the force on watch and half resting, changing every two hours. No one came against them. In shifts they ate their evening meal: cold rations because no one wanted fires that would backlight the sentries at the barricades. Then the night came, but the Campazes didn't. In the moments before dawn, Carranza went around the camp, stirring the men because this was the time to expect a sudden rush from a flotilla of canoes.

But no canoes came, just the sudden dawn and another sudden downpour that soaked the overhead shelters. Water streamed from the soldiers' morions, got between their armour and the cloth or leather they wore underneath, and soaked their hose and small clothes.

"Miserable," said Avila, hunched with Alejandro under their shelter, whose roof sagged ominously in the middle. He was sucking the water from a sodden crust before chewing its pulpy mass.

"At least we're in no danger of dying of thirst," said the monk.

"A small blessing, indeed."

The day wore on, the rain stopped, and still the Campazes did not come.

"I thought they were supposed to be fierce," said a man named Pedro as night came crashing down. He was crouching behind the breastwork and peering through one of its chinks at the river's shore.

"I am sure they are," said Avila. "But it turns out they're not stupid." He watched the shore for a while as it disappeared into the night. "You know, I'm thinking that the Inca king had some pretty tough soldiers, down the river and down the coast in the town of Tumbe. They must have come up here on rafts and in canoes to see if they could conquer these savages.

"Now Tumbe is ours and we're here, and I don't think we're going to have any more luck than the Inca's boys did."

"We've got steel and *arcabuzes*," said Pedro. "That's got to make a difference."

Avila's shrug half conceded the point. "If we can convince the Campazes to stay visible long enough to use them, then maybe. But so far ..."

He let the rest of the sentence hang unspoken in the night air. Then he said, "Let's keep our eyes and ears open."

They stood two-hour watches again through the night after another cold dinner of bread and dried meat, though the midday meal had been hot beans and boiled pork. Again, their captain went around in the moments before sunrise, readying them for a mass attack. And again it did not come.

The day was like the ones that preceded it, watch on and watch off, rain in the morning and lasting past midday so that the cooking fires had to be lit under shelters. But the shelters collapsed from the weight of the water, and the men had to eat cold rations, sitting in their soaked clothes.

The night came, and nothing had changed. "Do you think they have gone away and left us to stew in our own misery?" Alejandro asked Avila.

"I wouldn't mind some stew," the Portuguese said. "Venison." They were crouched behind the breastworks on the side of the island where the channel to the shore was narrower than on the other side. When the attack came, it would likely be here. If it ever came.

Avila shifted his armour to try to ease the discomfort of its weight over his soaked clothing. "I don't think so," he said after some thought.

"They killed five men, and they've kept us bottled up here for a few days. That's not much of a victory to go home and tell the missus about."

"But you don't think they'll come halloing and whooping onto the pikes and into the gunfire?"

"I do not."

It was a dark night. There was a moon somewhere, but it was not directly over the gap the river made in the forest canopy, and thick clouds blocked most of its light. As always, there was constant noise from beyond the trees: hoots and growls and chirrupings and grunts. Something slapped the surface of the river downstream, and Alejandro jumped.

"Fish," said Avila. "I don't think the things you hear are the things to worry about."

He was right. Deep into the night but still long before dawn, Alejandro was woken by a scream. He had been sleeping under one of the shelters in the middle of the island, his and Avila's section having been relieved of watch duty when their two-hour shift was up. He heard a rush of footsteps and shouts in the darkness, all of them in Spanish.

The commotion was coming from the downstream end of the island, on the side that faced the wider channel of the river. Now everyone was awake, and the order came, "Stand to! Stand to! Everybody up!"

Men were coming out of the shelters, reaching for their weapons and their helmets—they had slept in their cuirasses—stumbling and cursing in the darkness. It was then that the arrows came, falling almost vertically from the sky. Most struck earth or the shelter roofs. Some bounced off armour or helmets. But a few hit skulls or legs or arms.

Those who were hit screamed and tore the missiles loose, but it was already too late. They felt the chill and the nausea, their muscles lost strength, and their bowels loosened. They lay on the damp ground and twitched and foamed, and in a very little time they were dead.

Carranza gave orders and the soldiers lined up, their precious matches kept under cover, glowing. They poured fresh, dry gunpowder into the pans, aimed across the water, and when the order to fire came, they touched match to powder. The flames shot out, illuminating the great puffs of smoke, and thirty lead balls flew through the forest, striking branches and leaves until each found a solid trunk to bury itself in.

No screams or cries of wounded men followed the volley. Instead, there was a silence as the forest's usual nocturnal noisemakers were shocked by the crash of musketry. Then the normal cacophony struck up again. The men waited for another shower of missiles or a rush of canoes across the water. But nothing came.

"Here's what happened," Avila told Alejandro and his men over breakfast after he came back from the briefing of under officers in the captain's tent. "One of them swam across the wide side of the river and crept up the shore to the breastwork. He made a little noise, just enough to cause the nearest man—it was that Gonzalez, the one with the wart on his lip—to look through the loophole. The savage saw the gleam of his eye, or maybe he just heard the man breathing, and he stuck a poison arrow through the gap."

"Into his eye?" said one of the soldiers.

"Into his eye. Gonzalez screams, we all rush out, a bunch of them high in the trees shoot arrows up into the air, and they fall on us while we're milling around." He tore off some bread, dipped it into what was left of the olive oil, and chewed. "Three more dead." He counted on his fingers, "That makes eight. Or one-tenth of our force."

"The man who stabbed Gonzalez?" Alejandro said.

"Eased back into the water and swam away."

This was not the way things were supposed to go when Spaniards fought *Indios*, the monk knew. Battles were decisive affairs. The *Indios* charged and were impaled on pikes and torn to pieces by flying lead and iron. Then the cavalry charged and cut them down.

But always that had happened on cleared ground where the *Indios* had conveniently massed themselves and given the Spaniards clear targets. This hiding in the trees or sneaking through the night was new. And it was highly effective.

"Maybe," he said, more to himself than to the others, "we should give back the gold."

Avila swallowed the bread he was chewing and reached for the wine skin. "I don't think that would satisfy them," he said. "And neither will killing a few of us."

Just before nightfall, twenty soldiers armed with spears and swords were silently ferried across the river in canoes that then returned to the island. They found a trail, walked inland for twenty minutes or so, and hid themselves in bushes on either side of the track. They lay on their bellies, listening to the sounds of the night forest without slapping at the insects that came to prey on them. Their sergeant had strung a length of twine across the trail from which he hung two iron spoons that would clink together if disturbed.

The spoons were not disturbed. When dawn came, the men rose stiffly. One who had fallen asleep was kicked awake by his superior. Another who lay a few yards farther along the trail could not be awakened—someone had quietly put a knotted leather cord around his neck and garrotted him. When they fell in along the trail, they found that a Basque soldier named Juan Carrera was missing. They searched the bushes. He was not found.

They started back to the shore to signal for the canoes to come pick them up. Along the way, one of them stepped on something sharp that pierced the worn sole of his boot. He leaned against a tree to pull the thing out and saw it was a sharpened sliver of bone set in a base of wood. The bone was grooved like the arrow heads. Within moments, the man was twitching and foaming on the ground.

Now, with two dead to carry, they made their way back to the river slowly and carefully, eyes on the trail. They found several more of the poisoned spikes buried in the leaf mould. By the time they arrived on the shore, they were sweating and cursing, their eyes darting from ground to forest and up into the trees as they waved frantically at their comrades on the island.

"I don't think the captain will try that again," said Avila when he came back from the command briefing.

"What will he do?" one of the men asked. They were hunkered down under a row of shelters just inside the breastwork, facing the narrower channel.

"He said he was open to suggestions."

"If we could find their village ..." suggested a man named Baltasar.

"If we managed to survive the search," said Pedro. His voice sounded odd to Alejandro. When he turned to look at the man, he saw that he was pale and shivering, his eyes bright with fever.

Two more men came down with the shaking sickness before nightfall. They were put into a shelter in the middle of the island. The camp had stood to all day in alternating watches of four hours length. There was only bread and some hard cheese for dinner, and the portions were carefully measured by the cooks.

No attacks came that night but, above the forest's nocturnal cacophony, they could hear a man screaming. The sound came in a rhythm, starting off as short, sharp yelps then escalating to a full-throated shriek of agony. It would stop abruptly, to be followed by a silence that would last just long enough for the Spaniards to begin to breathe easily. Then it would start again.

"Now we know what happened to Juan Carrera," said Avila.

"I will pray for him," said Alejandro.

"Not as hard as he is praying to die."

The morning found them haggard, red-eyed, their nerves stretched thin and raw. The captain addressed them. "We need food. We brought nets to fish in the river. I want volunteers to catch fish. You will be guarded by *arcabuzes*."

He waited. No one spoke.

Carranza wiped the perspiration from his face. The day was barely begun, but the heat sat upon them like hot dough, the air so full of water that it could not absorb their sweat. "Double shares to any man who volunteers."

After a moment, four men raised their hands. They collected the nets and went over the breastwork that faced the wider channel. Behind them, thirty men with *arcabuzes*, matches smoking, and ten more with crossbows stood behind the barrier, their eyes constantly searching the trees across the water.

The fishermen did not go far from the shore but stood in the shallows, casting the circular, lead-weighted nets into the brown flow then pulling the cord that closed the mesh and drawing it back to them. There were fish in the river, and they caught a few. They were of several types, and no one could name them, but Alejandro thought he had seen one of them, a red-scaled fish as long as his forearm with a spiky fin along its spine, being sold in the fish market at Guayaquil.

Familiar or not, the fish were gutted and grilled on the cook fires for the midday meal. The cooks left the heads on, and most of the men crunched their way through these parts as well as the flesh. Alejandro was given half a small fish and some hard bread. The wine ration was also reduced.

"Soon, we will be drinking the river," said Avila.

The day passed and then the night, with no sign of the Campazes. But when dawn came, a lookout shouted and the camp sprang to life. But no arrows or darts flew, and no brown forms showed themselves among the trees. Instead, they saw a raw, red, man-sized thing in the shape of an X on the far shore. It was lashed to a wooden frame.

"Juan Carrera has come back to us," Avila said, his face grim.

While matchlock men lined the breastwork, their weapons aimed and their matches smoking, two men in a canoe went across the channel, cut the corpse from its lashings, and carried it back to the island.

"I correct myself," the Portuguese said, when he saw the body. "Not all of him has come back."

They brought the ruined carcass inside the fortifications. Father Miguel came and kneeled beside the body to deliver the last rites. Carrera was missing his eyes, his tongue, his genitals, his fingers and toes, and much of his skin. Some of the latter had been selectively burned away, the rest cut from him in strips.

They did not bury him on the island. Like the others who had died of wounds or fever, he was placed in the river and pushed out into the current. The brown water carried him away.

The days passed. The soldiers stood watch, but the Campazes did not come against them. The volunteers—there were more of them now—fished to earn their double shares, and more men came down with fevers. In addition to the shivering fever, the camp developed cases of what Avila called 'siege fever'—aching joints and muscles, vomiting, and a cough that would not ease. Within a week, three men died of it and several more lay in the shelters that had become the infirmary, groaning and calling out to persons only they could see.

"We can't do much more of this," Avila confided to Alejandro one evening. "We're out of flour and wine, and the latrine pits are overflowing."

"What will the captain do?"

"If he has any sense, he'll stop waiting for the savages to cooperate. We'll load up the boats and go down the river."

"But they blocked the river."

"We have axes."

"They will shoot at us from the trees."

"And we will shoot back," Avila said. "Plus, we could rig screens on the sides of the boats." He lowered his voice even further. "The thing is, if we do not all go soon, some of the men will go on their own."

"They might end up like Carrera," the monk said.

"If we stay too long, we all will."

It happened the next night. When the camp awoke to the dawn, one of the canoes and two of the soldiers were gone. That day, the island was full of quiet conversations that were quickly cut off when the captain came by on his twice-daily rounds. More men fell ill.

They listened through the night for screams, but none came. "They must have made it," men were saying.

"Or they didn't," Avila told his few remaining soldiers, "but the enemy wants us to think they did, so more of us will take our chances."

Between the sick and the dead, Carranza's force had been reduced to half its original complement. And more men were coughing and shivering. He called his officers together for a brief conference, and the word was passed: during the night, they would load the boats and make thick screens out of the cloth and poles from the shelters. Two hours before dawn, they would set off with the boats roped together, stern to bow, so they could not be separated. The canoes would be towed behind the last boat.

The sick would lie in the bottoms. The current would be in their favour, so only two men would row each craft while the rest sat ready with matchlocks and crossbows to suppress any attacks from the shores.

When they came to the rope barrier that had foiled the resupply mission, men with axes would cut through the blockade.

They carried the vessels down to the water, set them afloat, and loaded them with sick men and their few dwindling supplies. The treasure coffers went in the last boat along with Captain Carranza and his soldier-priest. The night was moonless, the strip of sky visible above the river only by its splash of stars. They steered out into the middle, and the rowers bent to their work.

The sky lightened as abruptly as ever. They had come well down the river and nothing had happened. "Perhaps," said Alejandro, from his place in the lead boat, "they have gone home."

"They were always 'home'," said Avila, his gaze constantly shifting from place to place as he faced the shore to their left. "And I have come to think of them as quite persistent."

An hour after sunrise, they reached the place where a narrow island divided the stream and the *Indios'* thick rope had blocked both channels. But it was plain to see that floating debris had torn the barrier loose from its moorings and the way was clear on either side of the island. The man with the axe, sitting in the bow of the boat near Alejandro and Avila, heaved an audible sigh of relief.

"Steer for the right," the captain called out, and the little flotilla headed for the wider of the two channels. But here they were very close to the thickly wooded shore and the soldiers poked their matchlocks between the screens and blew on their smouldering matches. The monk could hear one of them muttering a prayer.

Then they were through the gap, and nothing had happened. Alejandro looked at Avila, his brows raised in a silent question. The Portuguese showed him one callused palm and a face that said, *Not yet.*

The land had been gently dropping towards the sea so that the current ran swiftly. But by the afternoon they came down into a flat, forested plain. The river widened and slowed, ambling in fat, lazy curves with weakly rotating eddies along the banks, where the water looked darker in the shade of overhanging branches. In places, dense stands of reeds stood between the forest and the water.

Mid-afternoon, they came around a curve to see a structure on the left bank, a platform of rough logs built on stilts that rose to three times the height of a man. From it, on rawhide thongs that cut into their wrists, dangled the two men who had absconded with the canoe. They had not been quite as badly treated as Juan Carrera and were still alive, but they were in great distress.

Captain Carranza did not order the boats to approach the structure. He would not send men into the reeds and the muddy bottom from which they sprouted. Instead, he ordered the soldiers on the left sides of the boats to aim and fire. The weapons spat fire and smoke, and the hanging men's bodies jerked as the lead balls struck them.

"Reload!" Carranza called. "Row on!"

Alejandro said a prayer for the dead that their time in purgatory be shortened by the agonies they had endured in their last moments. As the boats rounded the next bend in the river and took the bodies from sight, he said a prayer for the living as well.

They rowed until they came upon one of the islands where they had camped on the way upriver. The breastworks were still in place, as were the mounds of earth confined by logs and rocks on which the cooks had built their fires. The river was wide here, and Carranza kept the boats in the middle of the channel's sluggish flow while he sent men in canoes to reconnoitre the old campsite for the kinds of surprises he had learned to expect from the Campazes. But there were no slivers of poisoned bone sticking up from the ground, no evidence that the *Indios* had been there at all except for the gift of human excrement deposited on one of the stove mounds.

The boats came ashore, and the soldiers set about making the old fortifications stronger and stringing alarm cords with their dangling bits of metal along the shoreline. Cooking fires were lit, and some volunteers cast nets into the river while men with matchlocks and crossbows stood guard. The last of the flour was cooked into pan breads and distributed hot with the grilled flesh of the few fish that the net-throwers had managed to catch.

"Tomorrow," Avila confided quietly to Alejandro, "we will breakfast on the last of the beans. After that, nothing."

"How far are we from Guayaquil?" the monk asked.

Avila shrugged. "I am thinking forty leagues, maybe more. In fact, definitely more because the river does not often run straight."

The monk was working it out in his head. A league was how far a man could walk in an hour—a healthy, well-fed man on a flat road. If they were marching, they could easily cover the distance in four days. But they were not marching. They were rowing boats downstream, which should have been quicker except that the river meandered and almost doubled back on itself in places. And they were not healthy; fever had killed more of them since the first attempt to send boats downstream, and those who had not died were weakened. And none of them were well fed.

He gave up trying to calculate. "How long?" he said.

"Three days, I think." Avila licked the last bits of fish from his fingers. "Unless we are stopped."

They were stopped late in the morning of the second day. The little flotilla came around a bend and saw ahead of them a stretch of river that held two islands, low-rise humps of sand that divided the water into three channels. The Campazes had lashed together logs and strung them across the channels. But before they tied the logs end to end, they had driven sharpened poles into the wood at all angles, so that as the current caused the logs to rotate slowly, the sharp points rose and fell. Carranza called a halt midstream, the rowers backing their oars against the current.

"On land," said Avila, "a thing like that is called a *cheval de frise*. The Dutch use them to stop cavalry charges. I have never seen one on water, but I am thinking that it will stop a boat."

"The axe men will cut through them," the monk said.

"If they last long enough."

Alejandro was peering at the shores downstream. "I don't see any *Indios*."

"The only ones of us who have seen *Indios* are Juan Carrera and those two poor bastards we put out of their misery." He spat over the side of the boat. "I, myself, could happily endure never seeing a Campaze."

The forest on either side was dense, trees of many different species growing close together, competing with each other for sunlight and soil. Between them, the open space created by the river had encouraged a riot of vines and bushes to sprout and claw their way towards the light.

"We won't see them until they shoot, and maybe not even then," said the Portuguese. He looked over at Carranza, who was studying the barrier downstream, shading his eyes against the glare of sun on water. Then he turned and looked at the trees, first on one side of the river and then on the other.

Now the captain was shouting orders, his voice high-pitched but carrying over the water. A soldier in the prow of Alejandro's boat was untying the knot that tethered it to the one ahead.

Avila was the senior man in their boat. He turned to the men and gave instructions. To Alejandro, he said, "You remain in the boat, Brother. You don't want to go where we are going."

All of the boats veered towards the right bank of the river except Carranza's, which remained midstream, its rowers backing water against the current.

"He's not the smartest soldier in the Kingdom of Quito," mused Avila as they neared the shore. "But he is at least capable of learning." He spoke quickly to the men. "We go in there," he said, pointing with his drawn sword. "Then we spread out a little and go through the forest that way." He pointed downstream. "They will be lined up to shoot at us on the water, but we will come at them through the trees."

They reached the bank. Two of the rowers remained in the boat with Alejandro. Everyone else followed Avila ashore, matches smoking, swords drawn, and spears at the port arms. They disappeared among the trees, and Alejandro heard the sounds of steel slashing a path through the undergrowth. The rest of the boats, save for Carranza's, unloaded their soldiers on the same bank, and the men went inland.

The rowers left in the boats took them back out into the stream and held position as before. They waited, and Alejandro suddenly realized that he was not hearing the usual soundscape of forest noises. In fact, a large flock of birds that had been chattering at each other in a couple of adjacent trees now took to the air with squawks of alarm and flew off in a whir of wings.

Moments passed with the only sound the gentle gurgle of oars stirring water and the drip of droplets from their vanes as they came up and went in again for the next stroke. Then there was a shot from downstream, followed by a shout, then many shouts, and a series of high-pitched yips, all from the right side of the river.

"Forward!" Carranza's order put the boats in motion, his taking the lead. It was still laden with armed men, matches smoking and crossbows levelled. In its bow stood a burly soldier, armour on his head and torso, his limbs swathed in layers of cloth, and a heavy axe in his hands.

The captain's boat came up to the barrier, the rowers backing water so that the bow drifted slowly against the spikes of the *cheval de frise*. The axe man knocked away one of the sharpened poles then cut through another and one more. That brought the prow of the boat up against a place where two logs were tied together by a thick cable of woven fibre. Two strokes of the axe, and the link was severed. The rowers pushed with their oars to help the current drive the logs downstream, and the boat slipped through the widening gap.

More shouts and shots were coming from the forest on the right bank now, and screams punctuated the cries of angry, excited men. Only a few arrows came from the trees on that side, but the men in the boats were well screened by their cloth barriers and just one Spaniard cried out in horror as he felt the prick of a poisoned point. There was no second flight of missiles.

Alejandro's boat and the others went through the gap. Captain Carranza was shouting orders to hold their places below the broken barrier and to be ready to move in and take the soldiers off.

The sounds of fighting had died down on the right bank, but now someone in the captain's boat cried out, "They're coming!"

Canoes had appeared as if by magic on the far side of the river beyond the leftmost of the two islands. The canoes were filled with small brown men with naked chests, strings of beads and shells around their necks and upper arms, feathers plaited in their hair, and expressions of pure rage on their faces.

In moments, the canoes were across the left channel and the Campazes were swarming onto the left-side island, screaming war cries and,

Alejandro supposed, deadly insults at the Spaniards. They ran to the near side of their island, formed a line, and drew the strings of bows longer than they were tall.

While they were coming across to the island, Carranza had used the time to order the matchlock and crossbow men in his boat to face the left bank and train their weapons on the visible targets. Now the command came. "Give fire!" Ten *arcabuzes* spat fire and lead towards the Campazes, just as the *Indios* loosed their own flight.

There was scarcely any arc to the arrows, and the missiles were not much deterred by the screens of thick cloth. But most of those that penetrated glanced off breastplates and morions, and others missed entirely. An arrow smashed into the inner face of Alejandro's boat, not more than a hand's-width from where he sat. The fragile bone point did not pierce the hardwood of the boat's strake but shattered upon impact. A sharp fragment struck his cheek a stinging blow. He touched the spot with a finger and saw it come away bloody.

For all the heat of the day, a frigid chill shot through the monk. The Campazes' poison only had to touch blood to enter the body and wreak havoc. He sat, trembling, hardly able to articulate a prayer, whispering only, "Oh, Our Lady," over and over, waiting to feel the spasms and the wracking convulsions.

But they did not come. After a few more moments of dread anticipation, he realized that he had been spared. He crossed himself, thanked the Virgin, and for the first time since the arrow had struck, looked to see what was happening.

The *Indios* on the island were falling back, dragging their wounded with them as the soldiers in the captain's boat levelled their reloaded firearms and aimed their restrung crossbows for another volley. Carranza's voice called out the order to give fire, and again the *arcabuzes* crashed and the crossbows gave their strange *clack*.

But the Campazes were stooped and crouching. The shots and bolts flew over their heads except for one, which pierced an unlucky warrior through the face. The man let go of the comrade he had been dragging free and fell face forward into the island's sand, the wooden bolt protruding from his forehead and propping up his head while the rest of him lay prone.

"To the shore!" Carranza was ordering the other boats to pull in to the right bank of the river, where the men who had gone ashore were appearing between the trees, waving and calling. Alejandro saw Avila among them, sword in hand, its point red. He followed Avila's gaze to the far side of the river, and saw the Campazes who had fled the island paddling furiously back to safety. In moments, they were out of their canoes and disappearing into the forest as a few bullets and crossbow bolts pursued them.

And now it was all quiet on the river. The soldiers who had gone ashore piled back into the boats, sweating and grinning. They had not lost a single man, and the only wounded was a man who, rushing forward, had crashed through a bush and met a low-hanging branch that had broken his nose. His comrades were making fun of him as the rowers bent to their oars and, under Carranza's orders, pulled hard to move the boats downriver.

"We killed a dozen of them, Brother," Avila said. "They must have thought we were more of their own kind coming to join them. They were crouching and peeping out at the river, and then we were on them. They barked like little dogs and ran away."

Alejandro wanted to answer him but found he could not make his lips and tongue form words. He looked up at the Portuguese soldier, distraught, his own breathing loud in his ears.

Avila moved closer, put a hand on his shoulder, and peered into his face. "Are you all right, Brother? Tell me you weren't hit."

Alejandro remembered the arrowhead shattering. He touched his cheek where the fragment had drawn blood. It had already coagulated. He shook his head.

"It's all right now," said the soldier. "That was their big try, and we've shown them what steel and gunpowder can do. They'll think twice about bracing us again."

Avila was right. There were no more barriers, no more face-to-face encounters. The Campazes shot arrows and darts from concealment as the boats went downstream. Two more soldiers died from the poisoned tips, and two more died from sickness before, exhausted and hungry, the survivors saw the walls and wharves of Guayaquil in the distance.

In all that time, Alejandro did not speak a word. He sat in the boat and trembled, and when he slept, he saw the Campazes boiling out of their canoes, screaming their war cries, and aiming their poisonous arrows straight at him.

Avila helped him out of the boat in the sweltering air of the port. It was two hours past noon, and the heat was at its worst. The monk was weak from hunger and sat on a bollard while the soldiers found scant shade against the side of a warehouse. They slumped and lay there like dolls that had lost their stuffing.

There was a tavern up a side street. Captain Carranza and Father Miguel went there and came back with two native boys laden with round, flat loaves and full skins of wine. The food and drink were passed around. Avila poured wine into a wooden bowl and dipped a cob of bread in it. He brought the sodden mass to Alejandro's lips and said, "Eat, Brother. It is over."

The monk sucked the moisture from the reddened, wet bread and chewed the pulpy mass. He nodded his gratitude to the Portuguese, but the voice inside his head contradicted its motion.

No, he thought. *It isn't.*

And with the voice came a certainty that he would accompany no more *entradas.* It was not what God had called him to do.

Fifteen

Alonso Illescas

Alonso keeps noticing the sky. Somehow it seems brighter, larger. It is as if there is more of it than he is used to seeing. It may have something to do with his back, he thinks, and with whatever Expectation did, several days ago now, to ease the chronic stiffness in the major muscles and especially in his neck. He wonders if he has been walking around for years with his head bent lower than it should have been, with his field of vision so reduced—so long that he was not even aware of it.

He has spent the past two days supervising a crew of Africans and Niguas, working on a project suggested by one of the eaters. The abandoned orchards behind the old town have gone to seed, and several new saplings have shot up where fruit fell to the ground. One of the Nigua men, Tsatsi, says that if the saplings are carefully dug up, preserving their roots, they can be transplanted to the cleared land by the new village. Cuttings from the old trees could then be grafted onto the new, and soon they would be bearing fruit. Tsatsi knows this because his father, before he died from the sickness that killed many Niguas forced by the Spaniards to go up-country, was the old town's ablest orchardist.

Alonso has little to do as supervisor. Tsatsi directs the work, showing the others where to dig around the new trees, taking up roots and soil together, and transferring them to big baskets that the women have woven especially for this task. They have been working through the morning, and now there are nine young trees standing in their containers. When they have twenty, they will be loaded onto the balsa raft and poled upstream to the site of the new orchard.

Alonso looks around. Not far away is the spot where he was standing when *La Virgen*'s captain's whistle had caused the rush back to the beach. He remembers the bird high in the sky that gave him the odd feeling, and he realizes that there is a way to test this odd sense that the sky has somehow changed. He walks over to the old crop fields and finds the exact place—at least he is fairly sure—where he stood that day. He looks up to where he remembers seeing the eagle and is surprised to feel a tinge of disappointment that the bird has not appeared again.

But he puts that thought aside and takes in a full sense of the sky, comparing what he sees now to his memory of that earlier moment. There are clouds to the east, though the sky was clear in that direction the first time he was here. He studies them then lets his gaze wander up into the unbroken blue, avoiding the blaze of the sun almost directly overhead.

Alonso's is an educated mind, trained by good tutors in the classical discipline of objective thought. He is able to apply logic and eschew sentimentality. Therefore, after a lengthy study of the sky, he has to conclude that it is neither wider nor brighter than when he saw it before. And yet, in some indefinable sense, though there is not more *of* it, there is somehow more *to* it.

He thinks about what he is experiencing. Logic says that if the observer perceives a change in the thing observed, yet it is plain that the thing has not actually changed, then the change must be in the observer. *Something has happened to me,* he concludes.

I am different, but I am aware of the difference only because I sense that things outside me have changed, though, in fact, they have not.

He observes the men working. They are all familiar to him. He knows their names, the names of their wives, even the names of their children. He knows their different characters: who is quick to anger, who is likely to intervene to cool a temper before it flares too hot, who would step back to avoid a conflict, who would egg on a pair of disputants just to see the sparks fly.

He studies them now but sees nothing different in them. They are as they were and, Alonso supposes, he is as he was, at least in regard to them. And yet he is not as he was, because when he looks inside of himself he feels a sense of lightness, as if for years he carried a burden, and now that burden has been lifted from his shoulders.

Like the sky, he thinks. Somehow, there is more to it than he used to see, and somehow there is more to himself than he used to reckon on. *But what it might be,* he thinks, *I cannot tell.*

Still, despite the mystery, he likes the way he feels, and as he watches the men dig up the little trees, he asks himself, *Is this what it means to be happy?*

The only shadow over his new buoyancy is Anton. When Alonso was called to the presidio to hear about the plan to replant the new village's orchard, something happened—though what that something was, he cannot quite grasp.

Pablillo came for him. The boy was now on more or less permanent messenger duty for the chief. Alonso was sitting in the doorway of his house, talking idly with two of the Nigua men about the idea of felling trees for new canoes—the eaters clan had not needed them in their landlocked village. Now that the new fields were cleared and planted, with the women tending the rising crops, there was time for boat building.

"I will speak to Anton about it," Alonso said when Pablillo brought the summons. As he set off across the dusty plaza to the chief's house, his gaze was drawn to the sky, as it had been lately, and he was conscious that something was making him more cheerful than he could remember being since his time crossing the isthmus with Don Alvaro Illescas.

So he had a smile on his face when he ascended the ladder into the presidio and saw Anton farther back in the building, talking with Tsatsi the orchardist. The forepart of the big house was in shadow, but Anton had rolled up two of the side panels to let breeze and light pass through.

The chief's Nigua was not perfect, nor was Tsatsi's Spanish, so they were conversing in a mixture of both languages, the orchardist adding in hand signs. Anton was intent on grasping the man's meaning, leaning forward on his stool while Tsatsi sat cross-legged before him, sketching pictures in the air.

Then Alonso stepped from the gloom into the light, and Anton turned to see him. The chief's glance was casual, and then it wasn't casual at all. He fixed his gaze on Alonso's face, and the younger man felt as if he had been struck by an invisible force.

Anton rarely showed emotion—and never surprise if he could help it. But in his chief's face Alonso saw surprise, and maybe more—maybe even shock—before the big man exerted his control and returned his features to their usual hard neutrality.

Alonso realized he was wearing a little smile, just out of the cheerfulness that had accompanied him across the plaza. He felt it fade from his lips and offered Anton a submissive inclination of his head, lowering his gaze to the floor and saying, as he would have said to the Spanish merchant who bought and renamed him, "You sent for me?"

When he looked up, Anton was his usual self, projecting strength and authority. "Tsatsi," he said, "says he can give us trees that bear fruit sooner than we expected. I'm not sure I understand it completely, so I want you to hear him."

"That would be good," Alonso said, giving the Nigua an encouraging smile. He sat down in the same position as Tsatsi and said, "Tell me."

What he heard made sense. Fruit orchards were being established at Santo Domingo's sugar plantations. Alonso had nothing to do with them, but he had heard something about cuttings and graftings. He turned to Anton and said, "I think he's right."

Again, he saw the leader's face flicker to impassivity, but Alonso caught a brief glimpse of the big man's expression. He had never seen Anton look like that, hadn't imagined that he ever would see fear take hold of the chief's face. And it was not the fear a man shows when he confronts danger—a drawn dagger or a sea wave that overtops a ship's aftcastle. It was the fear a man can't help showing when he thinks he has seen a ghost.

Thinking back on it now, Alonso decides that he will ask Miriam. She, of all of them, is the one in whom Anton confides. He will find a moment to speak with her when Anton is busy.

But it is a busy time for everyone, and Alonso is spending most of it supervising the orchard crew. And when he is in the village, Miriam is never far from the presidio, never far from Anton.

At the next beer-making, Alonso thinks. That will be three or four days from now, when the saplings are all transplanted and staked and the grafting can be left to Tsatsi and a couple of boys to help him.

The practice of an evening communal meal has modified. The new mixed society has not gone back to the old Nigua way, with men eating separately from bowls brought to them by the women. But the whole village no longer sits in a circle around the cooking fires. That institution has been made unworkable by the increase in the population that cannot be matched by an increase in the size of the common area. Instead, families sit together—men, women, and children—and the families that make up the different clans clump together.

The African men have multiple wives, sometimes drawn from different clans but, in the Nigua way, the women have worked out compromises. So tonight Juanito and his wives sit with the eaters clan, to which one of his wives is born; tomorrow they will eat with the other wife's relatives, who come from Pidi's beer clan lineage.

Anton and Miriam eat together at the foot of the presidio's ladder. It is his practice to invite others, on political grounds, to join them. Those who eat with the chief are provided with stools while all the rest of the village sit on the ground, although the women have woven mats to put between their families and the dusty earth.

And the entire system breaks down when, as frequently happens, dinner is accompanied by rain. Then every family eats in its own hut.

But tonight is dry, and Alonso is musing on the evolution of the people's eating habits as he sits on his finely woven mat, waiting for Xinbu to bring their bowls of stew. The eaters caught a tapir in a pit and have shared the meat with the rest of the village, the choicest cuts of organ meat going to Anton and his guests—which tonight include Chilianduli and his wife, Paytya.

Alonso is drinking new beer and thinking about what he sees around him. He has decided that even though the Nigua are a weaker people than the Africans who conquered them, their ways are stronger. *They have deeper roots,* he thinks, *and they are in the land where those roots are sunk, whereas we*—he includes himself as one of the conquerors—*have been torn up from our roots and have not been in any place long enough to put down new ones.* Then he finds a new way to look at it: *we are like the new branches grafted onto a standing tree. We have no roots, yet we bear good fruit.*

It is not a problem, he thinks. *It is what was needed when we came off the ship and faced a new life in this wet, hot forest. We have been lucky.*

Xinbu comes, bearing bowls. Alonso takes his and blows on the steaming surface. The smell makes water flood his mouth, but he swallows and says, "Thank you," to his wife. She smiles at him and sits cross-legged beside him and blows on her own food to cool it.

He voices the question that he has wanted to ask her since he studied the sky over the old village that morning. "Do I seem different to you?"

He knows she is perceptive, even if she is young. He sees her thinking about her reply, and it pleases him to have a wife who considers before she speaks.

"You are happier, I think," she says. "You do not make such a lot of noise when you sleep."

"Because Expectation healed my sore back?"

She gives him a different kind of smile. "That," she says, "and maybe because of what we do before you sleep."

It is true. She is an eager and willing bed mate. At first, her appetite disconcerted him, but he has adjusted to the situation. He does not know if he will ever be able to lose himself in the act of congress—a part of him will always float above their entwined bodies, observing without judgment—but most of his being is fully engaged in the sensations and rhythms.

"You are right," he says. "I am lucky you chose me." It is the proper thing to say, the Nigua thing, and now he sees a smile of satisfaction that disappears as she spoons up her first taste of the tapir stew.

"But do I seem different when I am awake?" he says.

She looks at him, spoon paused between bowl and lip, and her brows make a thoughtful vee. "Yes. That is probably because Expectation found your lost spirit animal and restored it to you. That would be sure to make a difference."

He does not reply and takes a first sip of the broth from the rim of the bowl, but she has seen the expression that touched his face before he could remove it. She says, "Everyone has talked about it. The people are pleased. They like you and want you to be …" She searches for a word. "Full, like a man should be."

"Full," he says, as neutrally as he can manage.

"Full of spirit."

"Expectation talked about me and my … problem?" Alonso is surprised and, as he takes in the implications, annoyed at the healer's lack of propriety.

But Xinbu is equally shocked at the implication. "Of course not! Never! But she had Pablillo for a drummer, and he was too young. And now he's grown enough to be giving two of the older eater wives their due—"

"What does that mean?" Alonso says.

"They futter him when their husbands are out working or hunting."

The word is new to him. But he understands its meaning from the context.

Xinbu has kept on, saying, "To impress them, he told them about what Expectation did for you, and of course they talked about it at the beer-making. Everybody said they were glad for you. And for me."

She addresses herself to the food again, but Alonso can tell that she is well pleased to have a husband 'everybody'—meaning the Nigua women—is happy for. Status among these people, he has learned, depends largely upon popular approval. Alonso had their respect. He now appears to have won affection.

"Good," he says. "I want you to be happy."

She smiles at him over the rim of her bowl and is about to say something when the sound of raised voices makes them look where Anton and Chilianduli sit on stools with their wives and Chilianduli's daughter. Her name is Kepepahta, and everyone knows that her father has proposed that she marry Anton. It is generally felt that the leader of the newly combined people should have a big nose wife to bind him more closely to those he leads.

Alonso has heard all about this from Xinbu. There has been a great deal of talk about it among the women, mostly arising from the fact that the prospective young bride has yet to state her preference in the matter. In many societies, her wishes would not be an issue. She would be given and received as a chattel. Among the Nigua, the issue is more complicated. If Kepepahta is less than willing, she would come under pressure from her family and clan elders—the women, that is—to view the match as a good one for her and the village.

Most young women would be swayed by family pressure and the objective value of being the leader's spouse, even if she were only a lesser wife. But Kepepahta, Xinbu reported to Alonso when they lay together after lovemaking, is known to have a strong character—she is not spoiled or overly wilful. The fact that she has not immediately agreed to the marriage in the several weeks since the feast and wrestling match has put all the village women, and even the men, on alert.

Now Kepepahta's voice can be heard all across the common area, accompanied but not overridden by her mother Paytya's higher-pitched tone and a few bass insertions from Chiliandulí. All other conversations have stopped, and every eye is fixed on the little group at the bottom of the presidio's ladder.

Xinbu speaks out of the side of her mouth, keeping her gaze on the scene as Kepepahta stands up and makes a gesture of finality. "It looks as though Kepepahta has made her decision."

"It does," says Alonso. "I hope this is not going to mean trouble. Things have been going well."

Now Anton is speaking, pitching his voice low, but not to the young woman with her arms folded, half turned away. Alonso can see Kepepahta's eyes moving and realizes she is measuring the response of the people, especially the elder women of the big nose clan.

When he comments on this to Xinbu, his wife says, "Yes, but it's not over yet."

He looks at her. "What do you know?"

She has a mischievous look. "There have been ... conversations."

"There are always conversations," he says. "Nigua life is one long, complicated conversation. Very complicated."

Her eyebrows rise and fall quickly, twice. "These conversations have been simple. Does she want to marry Anton or not? If not him, then whom?"

"All right," he says. "Then whom?"

For an answer, she just looks at him, and her expression is of one who is suppressing mirth. Suddenly, the warm food in his belly turns cold.

"No," he says.

Alonso's neck feels stiff again. He looks from his wife to the group before the presidio. They are looking at him. Kepepahta is pointing at him, saying something he cannot hear because the silence that has lain over the rest of the village is now drowned in a hubbub of voices. He hears a few ripples of laughter. And they are all looking at him.

He turns to Xinbu. "What have you done?"

She shrugs. "Anton frightens her," she says.

"He should. He frightens me. And I am useful to him."

Xinbu is not finished. "She does not think Miriam would be a sisterly co-wife."

Alonso has to concede that Kepepahta has probably read the situation well. "But why me?"

"Because everybody likes you. And Chiliandulі cannot complain that he is being slighted, because you are Anton's sub-chief." She smiles. "It is a perfect solution."

From a Nigua point of view, Alonso knows, she is right. But Anton is not a Nigua. He has not really adopted the conquered people's ways. He has just not interfered with their time-honoured practices because it makes village life run smoothly. But that is only part of Anton's reason for accommodating the manners of the people he has conquered. The other part—the major part—is that their customs have not challenged his authority.

Until now. Until this moment, the only opposition to Anton's rule was the African who kept his halberd. And Anton dealt with that rebel immediately and with brutal efficiency. Then he left it to Alonso to finish the business.

What will he do now?

Kepepahta has moved away from the group seated on the stools. She is crossing the open space to where the matriarchs of her clan are seated. Paytya is following after her daughter, her face bespeaking a clash of feelings. Now she sees the smiles on the grandmothers as they beckon the young woman to sit. Paytya casts one last look back at her husband and Anton and another over at Alonso. He sees her sigh, and her expression clears.

"There," Xinbu says. "It's settled. I like her. We'll get on just fine."

"You don't know what you've done," Alonso says. The coldness in his stomach has spread to his limbs. A shiver goes through his back muscles, and he feels the old tension reasserting itself.

Anton is rising to his feet. So is Miriam, and she is saying something to him, her face upturned towards his, her lips moving as she speaks hurriedly, her hands grasping his upper arm.

His face is without emotion as he turns towards the ladder leading up into the presidio. Miriam pulls on his arm, letting her weight hold him back, speaking urgently. He is not listening. His foot steps onto the first rung of the ladder.

Chilianduli is watching with growing alarm. He stands up and says something to Anton. The chief cuts him off with a dismissive wave of the hand and a few words Alonso cannot hear. The Nigua headman is confused. He looks over to where his wife and daughter sit with the old women and moves his hands in a gesture that says, *What can we poor men do in a case like this?*

Anton removes Miriam's grip from his arm, prying up her fingers and pushing them away. He climbs into the presidio, and she goes after him. Chilianduli shrugs and sits down. There is a gourd of beer near his stool, and he pours some into a bowl and drinks from it, the image of a man accepting the unavoidable. He glances over at Alonso, shrugs, and drinks again.

Alonso is trembling, still sitting on the mat Xinbu wove, the bowl of half-eaten stew in his lap. He does not know what to do. His rapier is hanging on a peg in his hut, only steps away. If Anton comes out of the presidio, marching towards him with the bloodstained club, he will have time to get it before the chief arrives. Or he could run into the forest. He knows the trails better than Anton, who rarely leaves the presidio and the plaza, and he is sure he could outrun him.

But would Anton send men to bring him back? Surely, he would. The chief is not one to leave things hanging. And Alonso could not hide from Poquito and Pahta. They would find him and bring him back.

Or would they? He is on good terms with both men. They like him and, he thinks, respect him. But they fear Anton. They would not disappoint him lest he take his anger out on them. He looks around the firelit plaza at the faces turned towards him, African and Nigua. He sees many different expressions: alarm, calculation, puzzlement, and concern as the situation begins to sink in. Some, all of them African, are putting on masks of careful neutrality. Others, all of them Nigua, are still smiling and laughing; for them, the humour of Kepepahta's stroke has not yet been buried under Anton's anger.

There is one face Alonso does not see. Expectation is not in view. He looks over his shoulder, to where her hut stands at the edge of the plaza. There is no light within, but the flickering lights of the communal fires cast a faint illumination, enough to show him the pale shape of a small face against the dark interior.

She is watching him. No, he realizes, she is watching the presidio. He turns and sees Anton at the top of the steps, Miriam beside him, still speaking into his ear. But the urgency has gone from her manner. And Anton is not holding the burl-ended club.

"What is happening?" Xinbu is saying, and Alonso realizes she is repeating herself.

"I think it will be all right," he says. The fear is still alive within him. He can feel it in his thighs as he hands her the bowl and rises to his feet, because Anton is beckoning him to come to the big house.

The villagers have fallen silent. The only sounds are the faint crackle and pop of the fires. Alonso crosses the couple of dozen paces to the foot of the steps at whose top Anton and Miriam wait. He inclines his head to the chief then looks up at the two of them. Anton has put on his chiefly face, impassive and imperturbable, though there is something in his eyes that belies the appearance of unconcern. Alonso glances at Miriam and reads a message there.

No, he thinks, *this is not all over. It may not be all right.*

Anton steps back into the interior of the big house. Miriam stays where she is, waits until Alonso has ascended the ladder. As he passes her, she whispers, "Careful," and follows him into the inner reaches of the presidio.

Alonso finds Anton seated in his chair of state, the fingers of one hand tapping silently on a carved arm. The club, which normally hangs by its wrist-strap from a peg in a post, leans against the side of the throne. The chief watches the younger man approach, and behind the assumed mask Alonso sees accusation. He stops before the seated man and says nothing, Miriam's whispered word still sounding softly in his mind.

Anton stares at him, and Alonso returns his gaze with all the neutrality he can muster. There is a silence between them, surrounded by the murmurs of the crowd outside. It lengthens as Anton's fingers continue to tap the arm of the chair. Finally, the chief speaks.

"Explain."

Alonso knows it will not help to be seen thinking about an answer. Besides, he is still coming to grips with the situation. He says, "I don't know if I can."

"Is it your doing?"

"No. I think it was Xinbu's idea. And Kepepahta's. They are of an age."

Anton is looking at him again and letting the silence extend. Alonso says, "She just said so. They'd been keeping it a secret."

"What about the little monster?"

Alonso is surprised. "Expectation? What would she have to do with it?"

He sees anger flare in the other man's face and sees it just as swiftly brought under control. Anton's tone is measured as he says, "Are you that innocent?"

Miriam speaks from behind Alonso. "I think he is."

Anton makes a noise of derision.

Alonso turns his head and looks at Miriam. She is measuring him with as hard a stare as any he has seen from the man in the chair. He turns back to Anton. "What do you think is going on here?"

"A plot," Miriam says. She steps around Alonso to stand beside Anton's chair, puts a hand on the chief's shoulder.

Alonso shakes his head in disbelief. "A plot. To what end?"

"To remove Anton as chief."

"So Expectation can take over?"

Anton can no longer maintain the pretence of calm. "No, you idiot, so *you* can!"

Alonso blinks. "Me?" He looks from one to the other of them, uncomprehending. "I don't want to be chief!"

"Oh, well," Anton says, "then there's nothing to worry about!" His hands grip the arms of his chair and he says something in another tongue. Alonso does not recognize the words, but he has no doubt the chief is cursing.

"You are being used," Miriam says. "You are being … positioned. We all are."

"No."

Anton glares at him. "Yes!"

"Why?"

The chief throws up his hands and makes a sound of frustration.

Miriam says, "It is about control. Expectation controlled the village before we came. Now—" Alonso begins to speak, but she throws out a hand and silences him with the gesture and the expression on her face. "Now she has regained a measure of that control through the old women, but she wants it all."

Again Alonso can only ask the obvious question. "But why? Things are going well."

Anton speaks as if addressing a not very intelligent child. "So she can feel safe."

"From what?"

"From what may happen if she does not have control."

Alonso puts both hands to his head then throws them up into the air. "And what may happen?"

Miriam says, "From her point of view, anything."

Alonso is having trouble taking this in. His fear has faded, but in its place is an emotion that takes him back to a state he thought to have long since left behind: he feels like an abandoned child. He pushes the feeling down inside him and reaches to restore the rational Alonso, who knows how to make sense out of the world. He says, "I just wanted to be useful."

"We know," Miriam says. "That is how *you* make yourself feel safe."

As she speaks, Alonso realizes that he has not spoken the whole truth. His life has changed. He is no longer just that simple user of logic. Now he has Xinbu. She is a point of connection to regions of himself that have lain unexplored all of his life. At first she was a strange and clumsy complication, as if he had grown a third foot and had to relearn the basics of walking. Now he has made the adaptation, and she is a part of what he does, what he thinks, how he is.

He wants that process to continue. He wants to see where it takes him.

"I don't want to be chief," he says again. "I don't want to be positioned. I like my life as it is." He pauses to think for a moment. "I'm not sure I want another wife."

Anton gives Miriam a look that puts Alonso in mind of two parents trying to deal with a backward child. To Alonso he says, "I think we've established that it's not a question of what you want. Not even what I want." He waves a hand towards the doorway and the plaza beyond, where the people still sit and eat and talk. "It's about what *they* want."

"They want," says Miriam, "to be Nigua. And they want us to be Nigua, too."

"Is that so bad?" Alonso asks.

"Maybe," she says. "Maybe not."

Anton says, "Eventually, we are going to have to fight. The Spaniards will come again." He shows a bleak smile. "We are worth a lot of money to them."

"They did not do so well against the Campazes," Alonso says. Word of Carranza's debacle has filtered from Guayaquil up to Quito and down to the forest. "It will be a while before they try that again."

"So that gives the next captain plenty of opportunity to learn from Carranza's mistakes," Anton says. "They will come. And if they are smart, they will try to divide us from the Nigua, even try to get them to betray us."

Miriam says, "We need to be united. That is why the marriage with Chiliánduli's daughter is important."

"Then I will refuse her," Alonso says.

"No," says Anton. "You will accept her."

"What about the positioning? The plot?" He still doesn't believe that Expectation is a rainforest Machiavelli, but it is Anton's and Miriam's beliefs that will determine what happens.

Miriam says, "We have a strategy: we will adopt you."

"You will what?"

"You will be our son. Kepepahta will be our daughter. The connection will be made. We will find out how the Nigua handle these things and we will use their … procedures."

"You're serious?"

Anton speaks. "Deadly serious."

"And suppose I don't want to be your son?"

Miriam and Anton look at each other, but it is Miriam who speaks. "Then you would not be useful."

Alonso finds it hard to believe that while he has been making a life, trying to be useful, he has been a piece on a chess board, positioned by the little hermaphrodite. But he has no doubt he is now being positioned by the two people in front of him.

"Do as you think best," he says. "I just want to live my life."

"Good," says Anton. "And now you can live it with two wives."

"Now," says Miriam, "go ask Chilianduli to come in. We'll need to ask him how adoptions are done here. You can stay to translate."

The news is well received by the village. An adoption is an important event, even more so when it involves the family of a chief, and there has been an undercurrent of concern that Anton has not produced a son or daughter of his own. Another feast will be required, and a date is set for ten days hence. After Anton makes the announcement to the people waiting outside, Chilianduli puts his strong arm around Alonso's shoulders, and the young man feels his bones compress against each other. Xinbu and Kepepahta walk off together, their heads bent to each other as they discuss the arrangements for the wedding and after.

Alonso has no part to play other than to do what others require of him. He goes about his daily tasks and accepts the good-natured comments that arise from his being a young man about to have two young wives. Sex is an open subject among the Nigua, and he is offered some quite specific advice on how to manage his expanding household. The most detailed suggestions come from the matrons and grandmothers, who give him gap-toothed grins and make gestures that leave little to the imagination.

In the days leading up to the wedding, he wants to have a word with Expectation but can never find her. He is told she has gone into the forest to collect medicinal plants, or that she is spending time at the seashore for some unspecified purpose, or that she is in her house but the door has been rolled down, signifying she cannot be disturbed while conducting a healing ceremony.

Finally, he pretends to go off on an expedition to the seashore. There have been rumours of two shipwrecks farther down the coast, and the currents may have carried debris up this way. Boys who are almost old enough to become men will paddle canoes out to sea to look for whatever might be carried up from the south. Alonso goes out the gate and down to the hidden landing, but when the expedition pushes off, he slips into the forest and sits beneath a tree, slapping at mosquitoes and waiting. When he thinks an hour has gone by, he goes back up the trail to the village.

It is a beer-making day, and the women are gathered in the big house, mashing the corn and stirring it into the big pots of water that have been heated on fires outside. There is the usual low buzz of conversation punctuated by the occasional raised voice, when one of the women shouts something she wants all the rest to hear, usually followed by laughter.

Men do not go into the women's house. Among the Africans, there has been no formal prohibition, but the first couple of times men tried to enter the big house to speak to their wives when the women were all together, the storm of mockery and derisive commentary, much of it relating to sexual performance, drove them back.

Now, as Alonso climbs the ladder to the open doorway, a chorus of *oohs* and *ays* rises, and the focus soon falls on Xinbu and Kepepahta. The older women's remarks are immediately ribald and graphic. The two young women blush and make shooing motions at their husband, but he ignores them, his gaze picking through the crowd until he sees Expectation slipping behind a broad-hipped matron.

He calls her name, then a second time. The mockery stops, and there is silence now. Expectation is not one of the women. She is accepted among them during the beer-making, but the acceptance goes only so far. The woman she is sheltering behind moves aside, as do others near her, until she stands alone.

"I want to speak with you," Alonso says.

She looks at him, her small face showing no emotion, but her eyes are not still. He sees that she is studying his face, his posture, reading him, and he does not need to speak with her to know that Miriam and Anton's suspicions are not unfounded.

"Come outside." He descends the ladder and waits.

She walks the length of the big house, the women watching her. Now there is no commentary, no ribaldry. She climbs down and looks up at him. "Well?"

"Let us go somewhere we can talk without being overheard."

"My house," she says and turns in that direction.

"Not quite," he says, following, and when they get to the bottom of her ladder he stops and says, "Here will do."

She turns and looks up at him. Just as he has been surprised by the size of the sky, he is now aware, as if for the first time, how very small the healer is. She has somehow drawn herself inward, contracting, like a tortoise pulling its limbs and head into shelter. Looking down at her diminutive face, like a miniature moon with its features all close together, he scarcely recognizes her.

"Anton and Miriam think you are ... manipulating me," he says.

"Do they?"

She looks across the plaza to the presidio, and Alonso follows her gaze. Through the space made by rolling up one of the wall mats, he can see Anton in the dimness within. After a moment, Miriam comes to join the chief. They are watching him and the hermaphrodite.

Expectation looks back at Alonso, and has to crane her neck because they are standing close together. "They told you that?"

"Yes."

She looks down, nods to herself. "All right," she says. "Why do they think that?"

The question takes Alonso by surprise. When he imagined how this conversation would go, that was not a response he expected. "Why? Because it's true."

Now she is looking up at him again, holding his gaze. "Do you think I am manipulating you? Why would I do that?"

"Anton thinks you want me to be chief. Then you would be safe."

"Safe?" she now shows some emotion, her face crinkling as she laughs. "None of us is safe. The Campazes could come at any moment, five of their warriors to every one of ours. The Spaniards could come with steel and *arcabuzes*. There is no 'safe' for us."

She laughs again. "Besides, if we have to fight—no, *when* we have to fight—will we be safer with you leading us or Anton?"

He wants to bring the discussion back to where he thought it would go. "You are afraid of Anton."

"Everybody is. He kills people who disobey him. That is why I don't disobey him." She glances at the presidio again. "I thought something like this might happen. That is why I have kept my distance the past few days, to let passions cool."

It sounds reasonable, but Alonso presses on. "You used to have power, control, before we came. You're trying to get it back."

"Am I? Then wouldn't I be trying to 'manipulate' Anton?"

Alonso sees the flaw in that. "He doesn't like you."

"Neither did Pidi, but we worked together."

Once more the conversation has wandered away from Alonso's expectations. He tries again to bring it back to solid ground. "Are you saying you haven't tried to manipulate me?"

"I have tried to help you. I have tried to heal you—with, I think, some success."

"But …" He remembers one of the key points he wanted to press. "The business with Kepepahta. What part did you play in that?"

The small shoulders lift and settle. "That was Xinbu's idea. They are cousins. And Anton frightens the girl. So does Miriam."

"You're saying you had nothing to do with it?"

"How could I? I'm not a member of Chilianduli's clan, certainly, and I'm not one of the grandmothers—and they were the ones who decided."

Alonso cannot seem to get a grip. When he thought about what Miriam and Anton told him, it all seemed straightforward, logical. Now it feels as though he's trying to push smoke into a box. "But you have influence among the grandmothers," he says.

"Influence?" Expectation pulls a mocking face. "I have their tolerance, and not always that. I am there for the beer-making and the clothes-washing. But when the old women sit together in the big house and decide how things will go, I receive no invitation."

"But—"

"You keep saying that. Stop. There is no *but.* Anton and Miriam have these thoughts about me because they are a chief and a chief's wife with no son to follow them. It makes them worry, and if there is nothing real to worry about, they will worry about something that isn't real." She shrugs again. "Kepepahta was how they were going to get a son, plus a connection to Chiliandulí's people. Then the girl decides she wants to marry you, so they put two and two together and come up with a conspiracy."

When she says it, it makes sense to Alonso. Anton has always been touchy, although Alonso thought Miriam more sensible. But she lives with the chief and does not mix with the other women, not even the Africans. Maybe Anton has worn her down.

"I don't know what to do," he says.

"Then do nothing. Do your work, marry the girl, live a normal life, make some babies. Let things settle down."

Now it's Alonso's turn to glance at the presidio, where the two shadows are still watching them. "You think that will happen?"

"I don't know what will happen," Expectation says. "We do what we have to and hope it will all turn out for the best. So far"—she gestures to include the village—"this has worked. Maybe it will keep on working, maybe it won't." She shrugs again. "Either way, we will do as we must."

As she climbs the ladder into her hut, Alonso does not know if he is reassured or not. This morning, the situation seemed clear to him. He would tell Expectation to leave him out of her plans. Once she knew that her schemes were discovered, she would back off. All would be well.

Instead he feels like a child who has misunderstood what adults have been doing and, after stating his views, has been told that he should not worry his immature head about it.

He crosses the plaza and goes up into the presidio. Anton and Miriam are waiting for him. He says, "I have told her."

Miriam says, "What did she say?"

"I am not quite sure. But I have told her I do not wish to be chief. I want to live a normal life, do my work, look after my wife."

"Wives," she corrects him.

"Yes."

Anton shrugs. "Maybe it's enough she knows that we know. And that Alonso knows."

"Maybe," Miriam says. "We will watch and see."

Alonso says, "I will go down to the bay and see if the boys find anything washing up from the shipwrecks."

"Good," Anton says. Whatever he is thinking does not show in his face.

The boys in the canoes find nothing, but they fish while they are out on the water and bring their catches ashore, where they build smoky fires and lay the cleaned fish on racks to dry.

They spend two days at the seashore. Alonso has little to do to supervise the Nigua. They are born fishers. He sits on a driftwood log and watches them work and play and thinks that Expectation is right: so far, it has worked.

A shout from down the beach makes him look up. Pablillo is pointing out to sea. The three canoes that have been out in the water have turned towards the shore and the boys in them are paddling as fast as they can.

Alonso stands and looks to where Pablillo is pointing. Far out to sea, in the south-west, where the big current runs up from Peru, he sees a tiny patch of white against the blue. As he watches, shading his eyes against the afternoon sun, the patch grows larger.

It is a ship. And it is coming towards them.

Sixteen

Expectation

Time had passed, and I finally had the leisure to return to my long-ago abandoned meditation on breath.

I knew what every shaman knew: that breath was life. Babies were born dead—warm and whole of body, but inanimate—until they took their first breath and began to live. And the last thing the dying did was stop breathing. So it was clear that breath, going in or coming out, was the key to the great secret. That was old wisdom.

But lately I had become interested in another quality of the mystery of breath: its relation to heat. Again, everyone knew that making heat was a necessary preliminary to making fire. The fire maker spins the shaft between his calloused palms, causing its tip to rub against the notched footboard. In a little while, the tinder in the notch grows hot or even begins to smoke.

But there is no fire until the fire maker blows on the tinder and turns the heat into flame.

Just like a baby, the flame then pursues its own life. The fire maker can put away his tools and simply feed the infant fire's hunger.

Still, it was not really that simple. If I rubbed my hands together, I would generate heat. If I kept on rubbing them, the heat would become intense, even painful, and my palms would glow like dull coals. But if I blew on them, no flame would appear.

Clearly, fire was in the wood, just as life was in the newborn, but it could only be called out by breath. Fire was not in my hands. Nor was it in the stone querns that the women used to grind meal. I had borrowed one and spun it until the touching surfaces grew quite hot, but again when I breathed upon them, I could not call forth fire.

Lately, I had acquired a new piece of knowledge. I already knew that breath, which called out fire, strangely had the power to cool hot soup and tea. But I had been told something new by Hupuka, one of the village men the Spaniards had forced to carry their burdens up the riverside trail. They had gone far up into the highlands where the air is cold and where breath becomes visible, though that seems to take away some of the life-sustaining strength it has down here in the mother forest, where people are clearly meant to live. Our men had got weak there, and some sickened and died.

Hupuka had told me that when the Spaniards' hands became chilled by the cold air, they cupped them in front of their mouths and breathed into the hollow space to warm their flesh. He had copied them—he showed me how—and discovered that the action had some temporary effect.

That news set me to wondering: did breath become different in the highlands, beyond the fact that it became a kind of short-lived mist? I asked Hupuka if, while he was working for the Spaniards, he had ever cooled his soup, or seen anyone else do it, by breathing on it. Indeed, he had.

They had been fed on corn bread and soup, though it was strange, he said, that even when the soup boiled in its cauldron, it was never as hot as it was down here. But it was hot enough to need cooling, and Spanish breath seemed no different, he said, for he had seen them do it, too.

The remark about the boiling soup distracted me. Perhaps fire was not as hot in the uplands? No, Hupuka assured me, fire burned and flames made light as well as heat.

It was puzzling, yet I sensed there was some way to unpick the mystery. But I didn't get the chance.

I heard the shouting and looked out of the spirit house to see the boys come running into the village. Pablillo was the oldest and fastest. He went straight to the presidio, took the steps two at a time, and disappeared. The other boys ran to their family huts or wherever they saw their mothers in the groups of women working here and there around the plaza.

I did not see Alonso. I waited to see if he would come after them, at an adult's pace, but he did not. *Is this it?* I wondered. *Has Anton taken preventative action?*

I went back inside and found the basket I had prepared for sudden flight. I took it with me down to the ground and left it where it would be handy, beside one of the posts that supported the hut. By then, Anton had come out of the presidio, Miriam beside him and Pablillo, too, his face flushed with excitement.

Anton called to Juanito at his forge across the open space. The smith picked up a bar of iron and went to where he had hung a large triangle of black metal at the front of his lean-to. He stuck the bar through the triangle and swung it back and forth. The sound struck my ears like the roaring voice of an angry spirit.

The village gathered in the plaza, and the men came running from the fields. In moments, we were all there except for Poquito and two of the eaters, who had gone hunting. And Alonso.

Anton spoke from the doorway of the presidio. "A ship has come into the bay by the old town. It may bring soldiers to capture us."

A buzz of voices started up and immediately died when Anton shouted over it. "Orders! All men are to take weapons and assemble at the landing. Women and children are to pack essentials and be ready to go into the forest. Every woman is to bring as much food as she can carry. Children, too.

"Here is the plan: if they land soldiers, we will kill them on the beach before they can get out of the boats and organize themselves. If that does not succeed, we will fall back here and go into the forest. Then we will kill them from ambush until they give up and go away.

"We will burn the crops and houses and leave them nothing." He looked around at the upturned faces. "Any questions?" There were none. "Then get to it."

The men gathered at the foot of the presidio, and Anton detailed ten of them to enter and distribute weapons. The women and children ran to their tasks, and even the eldest of the grandmothers hobbled to their huts. In a moment, the only person standing in the plaza was me.

Anton saw me. "Healer!" he shouted. "Get your herbs and potions and bandages. You'll come with us!"

He waited to see me nod in response then turned back to the task of arming and organizing the men. I picked up my emergency kit and took it back into the spirit hut. A short while later, I was crossing the plaza, carrying Pallu's old tapir-skin satchel with a shoulder strap. It slapped against the side of my knee with every other step.

The weapons were being distributed. Men were strapping bandoliers of wooden powder bottles over their shoulders, hanging cutlasses and daggers from their belts, choosing the daggers from a heap at the bottom of the steps. I saw Pablillo bend and pick up a dagger, look around to see if anyone meant to forbid him, and shove it under his belt. He moved off to the back edge of the crowd, where he would be visible to the boys and women, and stood with a hand on its hilt in the most manly pose he could contrive.

I sidled over to him and said, "What about Alonso?"

He looked down at me, and the man instantly became a boy again, the excitement widening his eyes and bringing a pubescent squawk back to his voice. "He stayed to watch them. He will meet us in the field by the old town."

"What did you see?"

"A big ship. Many sails. It rose up over the horizon and came towards us."

"Definitely not just sailing past?"

"Definitely not."

Anton shouted Pablillo's name. I stepped away, shielded by the taller bodies around me. The boy went running to the base of the presidio ladder. Anton asked him, "Does Alonso have his sword?"

"No, Chief."

"Go to his house and get it. You will take it to him."

Pablillo visibly swelled with pride and ran off. Anton surveyed the men. "Never mind getting the armour on, those of you who have it. More important to get to the beach before they land."

He himself was wearing a front-and-back cuirass and a half-moon helmet. He carried a cutlass, and his executioner's club hung by its cord from his belt. He came down the steps. The men parted for him, and he strode through the gap. When he reached what had been the back of the crowd, it became the front.

"Let's go!" he said. He saw me standing off to one side and said, "You, too."

The men followed him across the plaza and out of the gate. I followed the men. At the landing, it was clear there was not enough room in the canoes and the salvaged raft for all of us. Anton gave priority to the men armed with *arcabuzes*, halberds, and spears then picked out some of those who carried only swords. The rest would come down to the old town by game trails. He ordered Pablillo and me to accompany him on the raft along with a select coterie of *arcabuceros*, all of them Africans.

We set off. The Africans poled the raft downstream, the canoes with mixed crews following. The men around me talked among themselves, their voices low and full of tension, until Anton ordered quiet. I was struck by how they were able to go from being farmers and craftsmen to being warriors, with nothing to mark the transition: no ritual, no ceremony, no dance to summon the spirits. But then, when I looked back at the Nigua men in the canoes, I saw the same readiness to fight. For all that the newcomers had adopted our ways, we had accepted some of theirs.

It was not a long journey to the seashore. The narrow stream fed into the river, and soon we were at the place where the forest thinned and the old orchards began. Anton ordered us to land there, and the men ran the raft and canoes up onto the sloping mud of the bank. He sent Poquito and Pahta to work their way down the river bank to where they could see the beach and the sea, with instructions to look for Alonso and bring him back.

We waited until the men who had come by the game trails reached us, breathless from their run but with their eyes bright. Then Anton organized his force: spearmen and halberdiers in the centre in two ranks; a group of eight matchlock men on each wing. Those who had only swords and daggers he divided into two groups and placed them also on the wings, behind the *arcabuceros*.

When everyone was in place he said, "Here is what we will do. We will go forward to the screen of trees between the old town and the beach and wait. When the enemy comes ashore, we will let them get out of the boats. When there are enough of them in the killing ground, the *arcabuceros* on the left wing will give fire, and the *arcabuceros* on the right wing will do the same. You must aim at any Spaniards that have matchlocks. Then you quickly reload.

"While the *arcabuceros* are reloading, the men with spears and halberds will attack in a double rank. Your job is to pin them down, push them back towards the sea while killing any you can. At the same time, the men with swords and daggers will move around the ends of our line. Make a lot of noise and rush at them. Make the bastards worry they're going to be surrounded.

"Then our matchlock men will come down onto the beach and shoot any Spaniard who offers a clear target. That should make them run for their boats. And once they're running, we'll kill them all."

There were growls and shouts of assent, especially from the Africans, but the Nigua men were just as eager to get at the invaders. I had to respect Anton's way with the men. He had drawn them a clear picture, and they had seen it in their minds. They did not need a spirit guide. They had a war chief. And that was something I would need to remember.

We moved out, across the old overgrown fields and into the abandoned town. The formation broke up as we made our way between the mouldering old houses and over the fallen stockade, but the men reformed themselves as we approached the trees that screened us from the shore.

Alonso appeared from the cover of the trees. I could see Pahta and Poquito crouching where the three of them had been hidden. They were watching whatever was going on out on the water. Alonso held up two hands in a signal that clearly said: *Stop.* He came forward, shaking his head. In the year and more since his marriage, he had become more solid—that was how I thought of it, as if he had acquired more substance to fill out his skin.

Anton ordered a halt and came forward to meet Alonso. I had been behind the ranks of spearmen, but now I unslung my satchel and let it drop as I edged forward to hear.

"What is it?" Anton said, his voice low.

"I expected sailors or soldiers," Alonso said. "But it's just one boat. I think they are priests or monks."

Anton blinked twice, slowly, as I saw him take in the information and adjust. He turned to the men. "Stay here," he said. "I am going to take a look."

He indicated with a lift of his chin that they should go back to where Alonso had been. They moved into the trees to squat on their heels beside Poquito and Pahta. I came to stand behind them, being not much taller standing than they were crouching.

The ship was the first I'd ever seen at this close distance. It was standing still in the water, its sails rolled up. Chains led down into the sea at front and back. I could see men on the decks, but not large numbers of them. I saw no armour or helmets, no spears or matchlocks in their hands, just men in rough and sometimes ragged clothing, many of them bare chested.

They had lowered a boat into the water. It was just crossing the reef. It was not as large as those I'd been told about, the ones that brought the first Spaniards to our shore. Only four men were rowing it, none of them in armour. In the forward part, another four men crouched. One was wearing leather and a hat that sat on his head like a flat loaf of cornbread. The other three were bareheaded and dressed in robes, two in brown, the third in black. The last wore something made of shiny metal on a chain around his neck.

The tide was running with them, and the boat ran up onto the sand of the beach about fifty paces to the left of where we were hidden. The rowers stowed their oars, and two of them jumped out and grabbed the sides of the vessel, pushing it up the beach. Immediately the two left in the boat began passing them boxes and bundles that had been stored in the rear of the craft. Meanwhile, the man in leather and the three in robes climbed over the sides of the boat and walked a little way up the beach.

"That one's a soldier," Anton whispered. He was surely right. The man was tall and thin with a small, round head, wearing a garment of stiff leather that went all the way down to his mid-thighs and boots that came almost high enough to meet it. From his belt hung a long-bladed sword, like Alonso's, in a scabbard; when he turned around to survey the scene, I saw a sheathed dagger hanging from the other side of his belt.

"But the others," Alonso was whispering to Anton, "they are priests. Well, no, the one with the big cross is a priest. I think the others are monks."

"I can see that," Anton said. "But what are they doing here? That's the question."

There was silence, both men thinking. Then Anton said, "We could grab them, take them back to the village, ask them."

"The sailors would follow. We'd have to fight." He shrugged. "When we don't really have to."

Anton made the noise he made when he was thinking.

Alonso said, "We had better decide soon. They're just about finished unloading the boat. If I'd just landed on a beach, the next thing I would do is start to explore."

The men in robes were getting the sailors to move the things they had unloaded farther up the beach. The sailors were grumbling, looking up and down the beach and into the trees. They wanted to get back to the ship. But when the man in leather came over and said something in a commanding voice, they did as they were told.

"All right," Anton said. "I'll take the men back to the village. Pahta, you keep watch. I'll leave Pablillo with you to bring a message if you need to send one. And I'll send someone down to take over at sunset."

He turned to Alonso. "You come with me."

"I would like to stay and watch."

"You," Anton repeated, "come with me."

Alonso shrugged. He got into a half crouch and made his way out of the trees, giving me a look of half surprise as he found me in his way. Then he was finding Pablillo in his path, offering him the long sword. He took it but did not buckle on the belt. Anton came after him, and the look he gave me had no surprise in it, and certainly no approval.

He spoke softly to the men who were waiting where he had left them. "False alarm. It's just some priests or monks. Don't see any soldiers. We'll go back to the village quietly, and we'll keep an eye on them until we find out what they're up to. Quietly, I said." He gave a hard look at one of the Africans who'd slung his spear over his shoulder so that its steel head clashed against that of another man.

As silently as we could, we filtered back through the old town, across the fields and orchards, and put the raft and canoes back into the river. The men who were going home by land trotted off along the trail.

There was a buzz of low-voiced conversation once we were some distance upstream. Anton did not discourage it. He stood in the centre of the raft, tugging at a corner of his lip with his eye teeth and making his thinking noise. Alonso squatted nearby, his sword across his thighs, his expression equally thoughtful. He had the look of a man who has discovered he has an unexpected option. When he felt Anton's gaze on him, his face became as uncommunicative as the leader's.

Pablillo came back before sunset. He said the three men in long clothes were still on the beach. The others had rowed the boat back to the ship, where it was lifted and put upside-down on the deck. The ship then spread its sails and sailed away.

"Sailed away?" Anton said. "Which way?"

"South," said the boy.

We were in the presidio—Anton, Alonso, Miriam, Chilianduli, and Juanito the smith. I had not been invited ,but Chilianduli asked for me to translate.

"Alonso can translate," Anton said.

But when Alonso translated that to the clan chief, Chilianduli waved the idea away and Alonso translated his remarks. "Expectation is not a man and I do not like her, but she knows things," he said. "It is necessary to include her."

I heard this because I was outside in the growing darkness, close enough to hear what was being said through the hole created by rolling up the side wall. Around me, the village was busy. By the time the women had undone their hurried packing, it was long past time to get dinner on.

Miriam was coming out to look for me as I approached the entrance ladder. We exchanged looks without warmth, and I went up and inside.

Anton began to tell me about the ship leaving, and I said, "I heard. What are the men on the beach doing?"

I had directed the question to Pablillo. He looked from me to Anton, saw only impatience in the chief's face, and said, "They found the old town and began carrying wood back to where they had stored their goods."

He spoke in Spanish; he had got quite good at it. I rendered the information in Nigua for Chiliandulí.

Anton took over. "Then what?"

"It looked like they were building a hut."

"On the beach."

"Yes."

That struck Anton as strange, when there were the remains of a town a short walk from where they had landed.

"They did not like the town," Pablillo volunteered. "They frowned and spat and did this." He touched his hand to his forehead and chest then kissed his fingers. I did not know the meaning of the final gesture.

"They think the place is evil," Alonso said. "They fear demons or lingering witchcraft."

Anton made a noise with his tongue and teeth and for a moment cast his gaze towards the roof thatching above. "Christians," he said, as if it explained everything. To Pablillo he said, "Anything else?"

There was. Before the men had gone into the town, they had put two crates near each other and laid a plank on them. They had covered the plank with a length of colourful cloth with figures on it, then put dishes on the cloth.

"And something like a tree made of metal, standing up. It had a carving on it, I think of a man flying like a bird."

"Huh," said Anton.

"It looked like they were going to make a meal. Instead, they kneeled down in the sand and did that thing with the hands again. Then they talked to the little bird man." He paused as if expecting a question. When it did not come, he said, "The bird man did not talk back."

I translated all this for Chiliandulí. He thought Pablillo must have been too far away to see clearly. But Alonso weighed in. "They are holy men doing what holy men do."

Alonso and I had talked about these things, once we had enough words in common. I had been curious about how the Spaniards dealt with matters of the spirit world. What he told me did not make much sense.

The Spaniards believed there was only one powerful spirit, which was nonsense because I had met many of them down in the underworld. Their one special spirit was a kind of father and, though he had no wife, he had managed to sire a son. But the son was also the father somehow, and there was a third aspect to the two of them: the breath of the father had long ago become a separate entity. And that, too, was silly, because all spirits *were* a kind of breath, else how could I breathe them back into people who had lost them?

It got even more complicated. The father had demanded that the son be sacrificed by being hung on a tree, but of course the son could not really die because he was a spirit. Why that had to happen, I could never quite grasp. It had to do with something the first Spaniards had done. They had eaten fruit off a tree after a snake spirit told them to do so. All people everywhere were in trouble because of that meal.

Well, obviously that was wrong, I told him. The ancestors of the Nigua had come out of a gourd that grew in a garden that belonged to the jaguar spirit. The garden had been somewhere up towards the mountains, but after the first people emerged from the gourd, they cut it in half and made boats out of it to put in the Esmeraldas River and float down to the sea. They were two brothers and two sisters, and they made the first married couples, but on the way down the river, one of the boats capsized and the couple in it drowned. They lived in the water and were friendly to the Nigua, which is why we could go up and down the rivers without fear. At least, that was one version of our origins, the one most people preferred.

"Besides," I told Alonso, "you should never listen to snake spirits. They are allied to the Old Deceivers."

There was more to it. The Spaniards had feasts where they ate the flesh and drank the blood of the spirit son.

"The Campazes do that sometimes with prisoners," I said. "It is a disgusting practice."

It was not a real feast, he assured me, they only ate a little bit of bread and drank a sip of the beer they called wine.

"No," I said, "not a feast at all. And it cannot be a strong spirit if it can be contained in a sip and a morsel? I don't think it could do very much for you."

Only a few of the Africans were believers in the father and son. Most knew about the underworld, though the animal spirits in their land were different. I had asked one of the women if there was a spotted cat that could run very fast, its backbone flexing like no other beast I had ever seen. She told me there were two kinds of spotted cat, and the one I was describing was called a cheetah. She was interested to know how I had seen one, but I demurred.

A few of the Africans believed in a different father spirit. This one had no son, and he did not let people drink beer. His influence had faded since we had all begun living together.

"Why do they kneel?" Chilianduli said, when I translated Alonso's confirmation of what Pablillo had observed. "Are they afraid of falling over if a spirit enters them?"

Alonso looked at me, but I had nothing to add. "It would take too long to explain," he said, then had to explain to Anton what the exchange with Chilianduli had been about.

The chief was doing a good job of not showing his exasperation. To Poquito he said, "Go and relieve Pahta. Watch but do not be seen. Take Pablillo with you and send him back with word if they leave the beach. Or if the ship comes back."

The two left, and the rest of us waited while the chief chewed his inner lip and studied whatever he was seeing behind his eyes. After a while, he looked to Alonso and said, "What do you think?"

Alonso had been thinking, too. But he weighed his words before he spoke. "I can tell you what Don Alvaro told me. The Viceroy has long wanted to 'reduce' this region—that means to bring the people into the Church and make them subjects of the King."

He pinched his lower lip. "They have sent soldiers. Twice, if the expedition against the Campazes was meant to get through them to us. Neither of those attempts worked. Now it could be they are sending a priest, perhaps with gifts and promises that the Nigua will not be forced to offer labour as tribute."

Anton made his thinking noise again. "But they know *we* are here. And they know we are in charge."

Alonso nodded. "Yes, they do. So it may not be just a religious mission to the Nigua. It may be a diplomatic mission to … you."

"Or it may be a way to draw us down to the beach, get us kneeling and praying. Meanwhile a shipload of soldiers and sailors land down the coast and come up to catch us."

"That could be it, too," Alonso said. "So we watch them. And maybe we send some men down the coast to watch for surprises."

"Yes," said Anton. "But if it does turn out to be a diplomatic mission, how do we handle it?"

Miriam spoke for the first time. "We send Alonso." When Anton swung his head towards her, she matched his gaze. I could see that the proposition took Anton by surprise, and he did not find it a pleasant experience. He looked from her to Alonso, and the brief glances he cast Chiliandulí's way and mine told me this was a matter he did not want to discuss in front of a Nigua.

But the African woman bore in, though she did not raise her voice. "Alonso has been around Spaniards all his life—not just rough-handed overseers but the grandees who live in big houses. He knows their ways. He can listen to what they say while making note of what they don't. He can reply to them in their own kind of speech. Can you do it?"

Anton said nothing.

Miriam said, "We have to think about what's best for the people. You're a proud man, and that's good. Leaders have to be sure of themselves. But what works for the people has to come first."

Anton's eyes were large. I could see the whites. I could also see that Miriam was fighting not to let her courage falter. She took a breath and said, "Besides, it's a way to fool them."

That caught the chief's attention. His eyes narrowed a little. "How?"

Miriam said, "We know they hear about us. We trade with the Cayapas, and they trade with the Yumbo, who trade with Quechua speakers up in the high country. Alonso was in charge of us on the ship; the

Cayapas have seen him working with men in the fields, directing them. They may think he is charge here. And the Spaniards will have sought out that kind of information."

That thought did not please the chief. "I am in charge. They should know that. I am the one they will have to deal with."

Alonso looked between them as the argument went on. His face said, *Not this again,* and he clearly had something he wished to say. But Miriam saw it and held up a hand, softly pressing the air towards him. Turning back to Anton, she said, "You used to fight battles. You will probably have to fight others. Did you want your enemy to know how you were organized?"

Anton's grunt said he was not happy with her analysis but was coming around. He looked to Alonso. "What do you say?"

"I don't want to be chief."

"You're not," Anton said. "But can you fool the Spaniards?"

"Oh, I can do that," Alonso said. "I have seen the Illescases negotiating with officials in Seville and Panama. It is mostly a matter not of what you say but what you don't." He smiled a little. "The victory often goes to he who says the least."

Anton nodded, but it was the nod of one whose agreement is reluctant. Now he fixed Alonso with his hard look, his chief's look, and said, "When we were on the ship, you were their man. How do we know you are now ours?"

Alonso blinked. I was glad to see the question took him by surprise. He reached up and reflexively pinched the muscles at the back of his neck. "I suppose," he said, as if he were weighing the matter, "the Illescases would be pleased with me if I helped put all of you back in chains. You are worth a lot of pesos."

"Exactly," said Anton. "They might even give you some more cast-off clothes, maybe some shoes with silver buckles."

Alonso's face changed. I saw a starkness in his expression that I had not seen before. I thought it might be the spirit of the spotted cat rising in him, making him show the face he had shown to the men he had killed.

But his voice was soft when he said, "But I would have to go back to being their house pet, sitting at the farthest end of the table, speaking only when I was spoken to."

He looked at me, then through the gap in the wall. Out there, the women were bringing food to their men, sitting to eat with them. Somewhere, Xinbu and Kepepahta were keeping a kettle hot on the fire, waiting for their husband.

"I would have to leave my wives, and the child that Xinbu has born me and the one that is growing in Kepepahta's womb." He paused and looked straight at Anton, and his face was hard. "I would sooner die."

The council ended with Anton arranging to send men down the coast to see if the ship had turned in to land soldiers. Meanwhile, the three at the beach would be kept under constant observation, with shifts of watchers and regular reports of everything the Spaniards did.

I did not speak with Alonso after the meeting broke up. Instead, I went back to the spirit house and prepared myself. I made some tea and drank it then sat cross-legged on the mat and concentrated on my breathing. Soon a golden light dawned in the shadows at the base of the hut's wall and gradually grew and spread until it filled my vision, even with my eyes closed. I steadied myself and called out to my spirit guide.

He had been avoiding me of late. I had questions about how the affairs of the village—especially those of Anton and Alonso—might develop. When I called out, I received no answer. It was not rejection, however. I felt an awareness that the time was not right for a response. That had happened before, and I had learned to be comfortable with waiting.

But tonight, when I called, the answer came back: *I am here.* It was not in words, but there was a palpable presence, and when I slipped down into the underworld, the monkey eagle was waiting for me, its golden eyes huge, their unwinking gaze fixed on me. As always, I felt a jolt within me as the spirit touched me intimately and granted me a portion of its power.

The men on the beach, I thought. *I would know them.*

The eagle spirit's eyes grew larger, then larger still. I let myself fall into them, and in an instant I was being carried on the great grey wings up into the night sky. The moon was almost full, rising over the mountains, shedding light ahead of us as we winged towards the coast. As ever in the way of spirit flight, it was but moments before we were above the shoreline, where a campfire burned and three men sat around it.

I was interested to see these three through spirit eyes, which see deeper than our ordinary vision. Now, as we swooped down to hover not very far above them, their physical forms faded, to be replaced by three tall flames that burned without flickering—and each was different from the others.

One was a short and rounded penumbra of pale yellow surrounding a core of orange and a kernel of deep red at its heart. *A man of no great consequence,* I thought and felt my spirit guide concur. *A follower who will do as he is told and finds comfort in being led.*

The second man showed a tall, narrow flame of white mingled with pale blue—an unusual colour bespeaking an unusual man. *This one,* my spirit sense told me, *is also not a leader, but nor will he be easily swayed from any course he believes to be right.*

The third flame was fierce in its brightness, bright yellow shot through with flashes of brilliant red. *One to watch—and to be wary of. He has appetites that cause him to clash against himself. He contains a struggle that could burst out of him and set fire to the world.*

I rose higher and looked at their campsite. Above the tide line, they had built a rude hut out of materials they had found on the beach and in the old town. It surrounded the construction of crates and plank that Pablillo had reported to the council. I focused on the metal tree and the man who hung on it and saw that it was an object of power. Yet I had no sense that its power connected to the red-flame man, though there was clearly a linkage to the one who shone a pale blue in the darkness.

They had not made themselves a house. Instead, they wrapped themselves in blankets and lay down to sleep on the sand. The man of the blue flame lay on his back, his eyes open to the stars, his lips moving. For a while, the light that came from him brightened. It ebbed as he closed his eyes and ceased to speak to the sky.

As we turned away from him, I heard an echo of my inner voice saying, *What the wind brings.*

Xinbu had made Alonso a new shirt with an embroidery of tiny feathers worked into its collar and hem. The fabric was fine stuff salvaged from the wrecked ship. He had also a pair of half boots of chewed-soft leather, dyed red with stitching of bleached-white cord. Chilianduli presented him with a staff carved from black wood with inlays of white shell fragments in swirls and straight lines. From its top hung a skein of colourful feathers.

He carried no weapon, but he was accompanied by Juanito and another of the Africans, both chosen for size and strength. Each carried a halberd and a heavy sword. Two Nigua men went with the delegation, both armed with spears. One of them was Hupuka, with his cutlass slung from its strap across his chest.

"Only Alonso will speak," Anton ordered. "You others will stand aloof and alert. Understood?"

It was two days after the council meeting. The men sent south had reported no sign of the ship and no Spaniards on the shore. The three on the beach had remained where they were, eating the food they had brought with them. They had built nothing more than the crude hut that sheltered what the Africans referred to as an *altar.* They had not gone exploring, although when they went to the river for fresh water, they would stand and look upstream.

"They are waiting for us to come to them," Anton had concluded. "And so we shall."

Alonso and the four accompanying him rode the balsa raft down the stream and into the river. The whole village turned out to see them off. As the raft was being carried to the water, I took the opportunity to stand next to Alonso and say, "Be careful of the leader. He is a dangerous man."

Alonso looked down at me, a question in his face. I said, "I have looked at him. He fights with himself"—I touched my chest—"inside. He may find a reason to fight with you."

"How do you know?"

"There is looking, and then there is … looking. I have seen inside him. He … burns. Some fires like to spread."

Alonso's expression said he would like to ask me more, but now was not the time. "I will tread carefully," he said. "But thank you for the warning."

The raft was ready then, his four attendants on board. Alonso splashed barefoot through the shallow water, carrying his boots, and Juanito pulled him aboard. The four set their poles and pushed out into the middle of the stream. In a few moments, they were around a bend and gone.

In the evening they were back. Alonso came straight to the presidio. Moments later, the word went out for the same people who had been at the previous council to gather again. I waited so that I could arrive at the same time as Chilianduli. I made the same reflexive gesture before ascending into what had been the men's house. He saw, and his brows rose.

"Habit," I said.

He gave me a bemused look. "You're sure you're not worried some spirit will take against you?"

"Spirits are the least of my worries," I said. Then we went in.

The table with the map had been moved to one side. A couple of tallow candles stood on its surface, and grease lamps hung from the rafters, casting a yellow glow over the room. Anton was seated in his chair, the rest sitting on stools in a half-circle facing him. One stool was empty, and Chilianduli took it. I stood behind him and received only the smallest and coolest glance from the chief.

Alonso had a piece of paper rolled up in his hand and bound with a strip of red cloth. When all were settled, he held up the tube. "Miriam was right," he said. "They think I am in charge." He thought for a moment. "Or they want us to think they think that."

Anton moved his chin to indicate the paper. "What is it?"

"It is a letter from the Viceroy," Alonso said.

"To you?"

"To me." Alonso's face had shown a number of conflicting expressions since he had begun to speak. Now it settled into the look of a man who has reached a moment in his life when he knows everything that follows will be different.

Anton's tone was one of mild interest. "What does the Viceroy have to say to you?"

Alonso leaned forward, resting his forearms on his knees, turning the tube of paper between his two hands. "He wants us," he said, "to move down to the seashore and build a port."

"A port?" said Anton.

"Yes. The Spaniards have always wanted to have a port to connect with the Esmeraldas River. They could ship goods to and from Quito without having to go through Guayaquil."

"We are not all that close to the river," Anton said. "It is in Cayapas territory."

"I said that to the priest," Alonso said. "He is the Viceroy's emissary. To us."

"To *us*?" Anton said.

Alonso had the look of a man who has to admit to an embarrassing fact. "To me."

"Go on," said Anton. "What did the priest say about the Cayapas?"

"That we should reduce them."

"Conquer them, he means."

"Yes."

The chief looked up into the rafters where smoke from the grease lamps lay in a layer. There was no breeze. The air was heavy and still. "So we fight for them. So we bleed for them. Then what? They put us in chains again? We labour for them? Down in the mines?"

Alonso gestured with the paper. "They say not. We are to be free subjects of His Most Catholic Majesty. The Nigua and the Cayapas will not be subject to the *encomendero*. They can work for wages." He tapped the scroll pensively on his knee, then said, "They want to send us priests to convert the people."

Anton kept his gaze on the thin layer of grey smoke. "And soldiers to make sure the people do as the priests say?"

"Probably," Alonso said. "And customs inspectors and notaries and tax agents and all the other elements of the King's bureaucracy."

"And when we're thoroughly surrounded by all of that," Anton said, and now he dropped his gaze to meet Alonso's, "they'll take us, one by one, and put us back in our place. The ones they don't hang."

Juanito grunted at that prospect. Alonso turned and spoke to him. "Again, they say not."

"And why," said Anton, "would we believe that?"

Alonso looked at Miriam now. "Because this"—he held up the paper—"comes from the Viceroy." He unrolled it, and we all saw the marks on the paper and, at the bottom, a big red circle with some kind of design in it.

"That is his official seal," he said. "Take this into any royal court and the judge will say, 'Here is the King's will, expressed through his viceroy. It cannot be opposed.'"

Juanito grunted again, and Anton said, "Speak."

The ironsmith leaned forward, his pose mimicking Alonso's. "When they took me from my home, I saw no court. No judge spoke. They tied me with ropes and put a wooden yoke on my neck and the neck of the man in front of me. And off we went."

"Yes," said Alonso, his voice mild, "but you did not control what they wanted. They want the port. To get it, they have given us this." He flourished the piece of paper. "It is real. It is legal."

"Spanish law is good only for Spaniards," Anton said, "because it is enforced only by Spaniards."

"Not according to this," Alonso said.

"Convince me," said Anton, in a tone that said it could not be done. He leaned back in his throne.

Alonso sighed. *This is the moment,* I thought. He looked around at the others, his gaze lingering a little longer on Miriam. Then he straightened and faced Anton squarely.

"This is not just a list of promises," he said. "It is an official declaration that we now inhabit the Province of Esmeraldas in the Kingdom of Quito. It is law."

"Again," Anton said, moving his arm in an airy gesture, "who will enforce this law?"

"The Governor of Esmeraldas."

And now Anton became very still. "And who is the Governor of Esmeraldas?" he said.

Alonso held up the scroll again. "According to this," he said, "it is me."

Seventeen

Alejandro de Espinosa

When Fray Alejandro Espinosa boarded the galleon at Guayaquil, the sailor at the top of the gangway told him that Father Cabello was waiting for him in his cabin. The way the man said it, Alejandro understood that he would not receive a friendly welcome to this viceregal expedition to the *zambos*, as the mix of *Indios* and Africans now ruling Esmeraldas was being called. Still, he made his way to the priest's cabin without delaying to stow his small baggage, the letter from Don Rodrigo de Ribadeneira in his hand.

In the cabin, Cabello, pen in hand, sat at a table that was no more than a piece of polished wood chained by its outer corners to a bulkhead and hinged where it met the wall. The door was open to admit air, and the priest turned at the monk's softly delivered knock on the jamb. When he saw Alejandro, he made a wordless sound of impatience and turned back to the documents in front of him.

Alejandro took the grunt for an invitation to enter and went to stand at the edge of Cabello's field of vision. When the priest turned his head in the monk's direction, the Trinitarian proffered the small square of folded paper sealed by a splotch of red wax. His calloused hands tore open the letter, read it, and flicked it onto the table.

For a lengthening moment, Cabello stared at the fitted cedar planks of the bulkhead. "I did not ask for you to accompany this embassy."

Alejandro kept his tone mild. "I did not ask to be sent. Don Rodrigo is my *patrón*. I am obliged to oblige him."

Cabello turned now and looked up at him. "And to report to him?"

"Of course." When he saw the expression that sprang to life on the priest's face, he realized that further explanation was necessary. "He has not sent me to spy on you, Father," he said. "He wants to know everything there is to be learned about the *zambos*. He is weighing a large investment to build a port, and Don Rodrigo is not a man to put his money at unnecessary risk."

Cabello continued to glare at him, but after a moment, Alejandro saw him overcome his anger. "Very well," the priest said, though clearly the situation did not sit well with him. "Do I remember that you can write a clear hand?"

"Yes, Father."

"Then you can act as my secretary. Brother Iago is strong and willing, but he is more skilled with a shovel than a quill." He made a sound of unwilling surrender. "You will not have a cabin. You and Brother Iago will sleep on deck. There are awnings against the sun and the rain."

"That will be fine. It is not a long trip, I gather."

"No, the captain assures me the wind and currents are in our favour." Cabello picked up the letter from de Ribadeneira, glanced it once, then refolded it and put it on a heap of other papers at the back of his desk. He picked up his pen and returned to the document he had been preparing before Alejandro's arrival. The monk realized that he had ceased to hold the priest's attention and withdrew.

Back on deck, he further realized that the ship had only been waiting for him before casting off from the dock. The air was filled with shouts, the sound of bare feet running, and the grunts of sailors as they winched up the anchor and used long poles to push the lightweight craft away from its mooring. The sails remained reefed except for one triangular sheet of canvas strung between the foremast and the bowsprit. It caught the light breeze and carried the ship out into the stream, where the current bore them down through the widening estuary towards the sea.

Everyone in Alejandro's sight was also in motion except for a stocky, tonsured man in a brown habit standing at the rail. Alejandro went to him and said, "Fray Iago? I am Fray Alejandro."

A round face, brown and with a nose that had once been broken and badly set, turned his way, inspected him stolidly and returned no greeting. "Have you seen Father Cabello? He has been waiting for you."

"I have."

"Good," said the man and returned his gaze to the island they were passing. Alejandro suspected that the two monks would not have many long conversations. He stepped away, went forward to where the bulkhead of the forecastle rose from the deck, took hold of a stay, and watched the estuary widen before them.

He did not require the approval, or even the acceptance, of the men he would be working with, though he would try not to antagonize them unnecessarily. He intended to do his best for the merchant who had sent him on this mission, the latest of several tasks with which Don Rodrigo had trusted him. He was even looking forward to encountering the *zambos*—particularly the Nigua contingent.

The *Indios* from Guayaquil south and all through the highlands conquered by Pizarro were all well converted to the true faith—although they retained some of their habits, having attached their old practices to this or that saint. The Church maintained a watching brief on these remnants of paganism, trusting to erase them gradually as the young people grew up to replace the old.

But in Esmeraldas, Alejandro expected to meet raw paganism in all its darkness, to which he would bring the light of salvation. At last, he was being offered an opportunity to answer his vocation, to serve God by undertaking the work to which he had been called.

"Dreaming, Brother?" said a voice behind him—a voice he knew but had not heard in some time.

He turned, surprised and pleased to see a familiar long-nosed face wearing an expression of amused condescension. "*Serjente* Avila! It is good to see you again. I did not know you were coming on this expedition."

He offered his hand, and the Portuguese took it. "Neither did I," he said, "until I heard you were. That was when I decided to attach myself to the embassy."

"Does Father Cabello know?"

"He will soon enough, but I do not need his approval. The *Guadeloupe*'s captain is also Portuguese. Our families have known each other forever. More to the point, we have done some drinking and wenching together. He signed me on as a supernumerary."

Alejandro smiled. "You mean to keep an eye on me."

Avila returned the smile. "I do. Someone must."

"I am told the Nigua are of a milder disposition than the Campaze," the monk said.

"I have heard the same. But the runaways? It seems unlikely that a storm took all the crew and passengers yet spared a parcel of slaves who had cut throats and burned cane fields across half of Hispaniola."

"They will not cut our throats. We are bringing them what they most desire."

Avila shrugged. "Unless what they most desire is cutting Spanish throats."

Alejandro shook his head. "They have been free for years now. What they will want most of all is to remain free. That is what we bring them."

Avila's face suggested he was not convinced but would not argue. "I have some wine in my cabin," he said. "Would you like some?"

"I would." Then the words sank in. "You have a cabin?"

"I told you, the captain and I go back a long way. I saved him once from being . . . well, let us just say I spared him from an acute embarrassment."

"I will not ask you to speak further," Alejandro said.

"The cabin has a fold-down cot." Avila made a gesture that said it was available.

Alejandro wavered only a moment. "No," he said. "It will be but a night or two on deck, and that is where Father Cabello expects me to sleep. There is no point antagonizing him."

Another shrug from the Portuguese. "I also have some good goat's cheese from Quito. And fresh bread."

"That, I will not say no to," Alejandro said.

In the morning of the third day's sailing, the *Guadeloupe* turned towards the unseen shore. First, a distant range of wooded hills came into view. As they neared the land, the forest spread out to either side until it filled the horizon. Only when they were well into the wide bay did they see the narrow strip of beach and the thin line of surf.

Sailors began unlashing the canvas that covered several crates and casks on the amidships deck as others climbed into the rigging to reef the sails and slow their progress. The ship glided slowly towards the shore until the captain ordered the last reefs taken in and the anchors dropped at bow and stern.

A small boat was lowered and loaded with the expedition's goods, four sailors waiting with their oars resting along the gunwales. Only then did Father Cabello come up from his cabin, a leather satchel under his arm. He gestured for Alejandro and Iago to climb down the heavy netting the sailors had hung over the side. Alejandro tossed his rolled bundle to one of the men in the boat and climbed carefully down, but the sailors held the small craft against the ship's side, where it bobbed up and down in the gentle swell, and guided the monk's foot to a safe landing.

A moment later, he was seated on a thwart watching Iago and the priest make their way down the netting. The monk came with the ponderous motion of a bullock negotiating a steep path. Cabello descended with a rigid dignity, and Alejandro could not help thinking it was a good thing the sailors were not in a mood to play tricks.

The rowers were readying themselves to push off when a shout from above stopped them. Down the side of the ship Avila came nimbly, his sword belt over his shoulder to prevent the scabbard from tripping him up. He settled himself next to Alejandro and returned a bland stare to the priest's hostile look.

"If I'd wanted a military escort—" Cabello began.

"You'd have a hard time finding a better one than me," the Portuguese said. "But don't concern yourself. I just wanted to take a look around the place."

Cabello opened his mouth again, but the sailors had already pushed away from the *Guadeloupe,* and now they dug their oar blades into the sea and set off for the beach. No one spoke for the next several minutes, though Avila gave Alejandro a theatrical wink once the priest's attention was fixed on the shore. The monk kept his face neutral.

After a final stroke of the oars, two of the sailors leaped out and helped run the boat up onto the sand. "Out, and quickly!" the leading seaman said. Even before Cabello's feet touched the ground, they were lifting cargo from the boat and running it up the sand to place it just above the tide line.

Alejandro got out on the other side of the boat from the hurrying men. Avila was ahead of him, strapping on his sword belt and walking towards the trees that grew only a couple of dozen paces from the water. He drew the narrow-bladed weapon and used it to push aside some undergrowth, then stepped lightly into the space he had created. Two more steps, and he was out of view.

The priest stopped short of the trees. He turned, fists on hips, to look up and down the beach, his expression pensive. Fray Iago stood within reach in the posture of a subordinate who waits for an expected order. Alejandro helped the sailors bring up the last of the chests then stood beside the heap of goods.

Father Cabello nodded in the manner of a man who has concluded one thought and is ready for another. He turned to the leading seaman and said, "Move the cargo farther up the beach." He pointed to a place where the trees fell back and there was a wider stretch of sand between them and the sea.

The sailor balked. "My orders were to bring you ashore and unload the boat. If you want things moved—"

"I am," said Cabello, "a priest of Our Holy Mother Church and an ambassador of His Excellency the Viceroy. You will do as I say, or I will see you flogged."

Pride struggled with fear in the sailor's face. Fear won. He shouted orders at the other three men, and they began to move the cargo.

Alejandro went to help them but stopped at a peremptory call of his name. He turned to see the priest pointing at a spot near where the sailors were depositing the goods. "We will build a shrine there," Cabello said, "and I will say a mass."

"Very good, Father," the Trinitarian said. "What will we build it out of?"

The priest looked at the trees and undergrowth lining the beach. At that moment, Avila stepped back into view. "There is a derelict native town beyond the trees. Some of the houses still look serviceable."

Cabello frowned and shook his head. "We will stay on the beach," he said. "It is as God made it. Whatever the savages have made is of the Devil."

"You will have brought holy water, will you not, Father?" the soldier said. "Would that not undo the Devil's designs?"

Cabello's face went cold. "Do you mock me, Portuguese? Do you mock the Church?"

"Never, Father," said Avila. "It is a curse on me that my face appears to fleer though I speak in all innocence."

The priest gave him a hard look while Avila showed a face that was almost saintly in its inoffensiveness. Finally, Cabello inspected the thick-boled trees before them and said, "We might as well look at the town. But first we will say a mass, that we may enter the Devil's den in a state of grace."

Under the priest's direction, the two monks and a sailor created an improvised altar from two crates and a polished board. Alejandro searched in the crate for the paraphernalia of the mass and a tall, silver crucifix on which hung an ivory Christ.

Cabello called the two monks to him before the altar. He placed the stole over his shoulders, and all three faced the altar, knelt, and crossed themselves. Behind them, the sailors and Avila came to kneel as well. The priest turned to them and said, "This is not for you."

Even Iago looked shocked. Softly, Alejandro said, "Father, they are here with us on this foreign shore. Surely, they are deserving of our Lord's protection."

Cabello gave him a sideways glance that would have clabbered milk but rose and said, without turning to look at the kneeling men, "You may stay. God's blessing will be upon you."

But he leaned down towards Alejandro and whispered, "Do not presume to instruct me in my office, Brother."

Alejandro bowed his head. The mass continued at an unhurried pace, though only Cabello and the monks took the sacramental bread and wine. The priest spoke the final words: *missa est.* Then he brusquely told the sailors to get on their feet and help bring materials from the town. Cabello armed himself with a bottle of holy water and bid Avila lead the way.

They surrounded the altar shrine with three walls and roofed it with palm fronds that were easily found up and down the beach. When it was done, Cabello said they would sleep in the open, on the beach. He dismissed the sailors.

Alejandro walked with Avila to the boat. Avila said, "We are being watched, you know."

"I expected we would be."

"I will speak to the captain. We will sail out of sight, over the horizon, and tack up and down the coast. If there is trouble, make a fire that smokes. We will come." Avila looked to where Cabello stood in the door to their dwelling, a frown hardening his face as he watched the monk and the soldier.

Alejandro said, "If there is trouble, there may not be time for you to get here."

"Still—"

"I will trust to God. And I trust he will keep you well, too." He made the sign of the cross. "But I bless you in His name for your kindness."

Avila laughed. "Kindness," he said, then decided to swallow whatever else he had been about to say. He touched Alejandro's arm. "Just don't let that bastard get you killed."

"He is a priest of Holy Mother Church," the monk said. "You must not call him that."

"Brother," Avila said, climbing into the boat, where two sailors had run it down to the water and were preparing to push it out into the low surf, "have you not yet learned that some priests are bastards?"

Alejandro raised a hand in farewell. The sailors pushed the boat out then jumped in and seized the oars. Before the leading seaman called for the first stroke, he threw the monk a look that said he agreed with the soldier. Alejandro watched them pull away. Then he composed his face and turned to walk to the hut.

There was still unpacking to be done. No doubt Father Cabello would want him to take some notes. The priest had let him know that he intended to keep a diary of their experiences, the better to write his report to the Viceroy at the end of the mission.

Alejandro was at the stream that ran down to the sea near the shrine and their dwelling. He went upstream to a shady spot where the water ran cooler and dipped the leather bucket. As he brought it up and straightened, he saw a raft coming from the forest, bearing five men. The current was carrying them at a steady rate and they were not poling, but two of the men—a native and an African—used spear butts to keep the raft from drifting against the bank.

The monk waited, holding the dripping full bucket against his knee, until the lightweight platform came level. The men used their spears now to stop its progress, and Alejandro stood back as the two who had been guiding its progress stepped onto the bank. One of the spearmen on board threw them a rope of braided grass, and they efficiently tied the balsa to a tree that overhung the stream. Then they all came onto the bank, spread out until they formed a crescent facing the Trinitarian.

"Who might you be?" said the black man who carried no spear, though he wore a sword belt from which hung a rapier with a cup hilt.

Alejandro introduced himself and added, "We have been sent by the Viceroy in Lima. We are a priest and two monks, and we mean no harm." He looked at the man with the sword, saw an intelligent face, and knew that he was being inspected in turn. "May I ask whom I have the honour of addressing?"

That won him a smile. "A diplomat," said the African. "Well, well."

"No," Alejandro said, "only a simple servant of God. The diplomat is on the beach. He is Father Miguel Cabello de Balboa."

The other man nodded but showed no sense of hurry. He continued to study Alejandro for a moment. "What kind of monk are you? Mercedarian? Not a Benedictine."

"Trinitarian."

A new look now, and the man's hand went idly to his sword's hilt. "That is not a Trinitarian habit."

"I had only the one I wore in Spain. It is much too hot for this climate."

"Ah." Another nod, another searching stare. "Do you find many pilgrims to assist?"

"Only myself. I need all the help I can find." He waited while the other man continued to study him. He had noted that when the African's hand had strayed to his sword, the other four had become more alert. When the silence lengthened, Alejandro said, "If I had wanted to deceive you, I would have described myself as a Mercedarian, from whom I received this habit."

The other man took this in and, after a moment, seemed to accept the explanation. "Very well. Let us go meet your diplomat," he said, pointing with his chin towards the beach.

Alejandro did not move. "And by what name may I introduce you?"

"Alonso Illescas."

"Ah," said the monk. "This way, please." He turned and set off the way he had come, then looked back over his shoulder and added, "Your Excellency."

The day was already growing hot, and Father Cabello was seated on a stool in the shade under the shrine's roof, reading a document. Fray Iago was making pan bread on an iron skillet over a driftwood fire a few feet away, the flames almost invisible in the bright sunlight. He looked up as Alejandro came into view and his face, which had been red from the heat of the cooking fire, went pale as he saw the five armed men.

Iago spoke to the priest, and Alejandro saw Cabello turn to them, his initial surprise swiftly turning to a studied calm. The priest rose and came out into the light, rolling up in his hands the document he had been looking at. He put hands and scroll behind him and waited patiently until the Trinitarian led the Africans and Niguas to him.

"Father Miguel Cabello de Balboa," Alejandro said, "I have the honour to present Señor Alonso Illescas ..." The monk made an inclusive gesture. "And his friends."

Cabello politely inclined his head. "With great pleasure," he said, giving the customary formal greeting; he would have said more, but Alonso had turned a quizzical gaze on Alejandro. "Only 'Señor'? A moment ago it was 'Your Excellency'."

A flash of irritation crossed the priest's face and he shot a hard glance at the Trinitarian. Then he recollected himself and spoke to the African. "You have come armed. We are, as you see, men of God. We mean you no harm. On the contrary, we bring you good news."

Alonso said nothing, only raised an eyebrow.

"I speak," Cabello went on, "with the authority of Don Lope García de Castro, the interim Viceroy of Peru, who has sent me to make peace with you and your people and to offer you his protection in the name of the King."

He waited for Alonso to reply. The African rested his hand on the pommel of his sword and made a mild answer. "Up until now, the only protection we have needed has been *from* the King's soldiers. And we have provided it ourselves."

"That is true," said the priest, "but how long do you think that can continue? The land is filling up with new settlers. The savages are being reduced—"

"We have heard," Alonso interrupted, his tone still gentle, "that some of your settlers went hunting for gold in the forests east of the mountains. The gold they found was ... not to their taste."

Alejandro was impressed. The *zambos* might be confined to a coastal forest, but they were not cut off from the world. There had been a disastrous Spanish *entrada* into the Amazon forest to search for the legendary El Dorado, the city of gold. A fierce tribe of forest *Indios* had captured the captain, staked him out on the ground, and mockingly poured molten gold down his throat.

"You are well informed," said Cabello.

"We've found it necessary," said Alonso.

The priest retained his composure. "I am well informed, too. I consulted Don Alvaro Illescas before setting out from Lima. He told me you are an educated man."

"Above my station, some might say."

Cabello smiled. "Unless your station should"—he brought one hand out from behind his back and made a rolling motion—"be altered."

Alonso matched his smile. "It already has," he said.

Now the priest brought forth the other hand, the one that held the rolled-up parchment. "And now it will again, if you would care to read this letter the Viceroy has charged me to bring to you."

"To me?"

"To you."

Alonso took the document and unrolled it. Alejandro saw his face register brief bemusement at the clerkly hand and the enlarged ornate capital letter that adorned the first word. Then his brows drew down as he began to read.

The monk watched the African with interest. He had known black slaves and freedmen and was aware that their personalities differed as much as between any population. But this one was different—and not just because he could read without moving his lips, which Fray Iago could not do. Alonso Illescas showed the calm dignity that Alejandro associated with the *hidalgos* of Spain, and not even all of them. He had heard that Africa had its black kings and princes, some of them with bloodlines as long as that of Spain's grandees. Watching this man, the monk was thinking, *Perhaps there is such a thing as breeding. And I am seeing it here on this beach.*

Alonso finished reading the letter. He examined the seal affixed to the parchment beside the convoluted signature of the Viceroy. Then he looked at Cabello again. "This is real?" he said.

"Yes."

"And you are this Father Cabello mentioned here?"

"I am."

"Show me your right hand." When the priest held out his hand, Alonso took it and turned it over to examine the palm. "When I practised with a sword, I grew calluses like those."

"I was a soldier before I received my vocation."

"And what are you now?" Alonso said.

"A servant of God . . . and of the King."

Alonso said nothing for a long moment while he regarded the priest. He looked briefly at Iago, who stood sweating while his pan bread was burning, then at Alejandro. "And you," he said. "Whose servant are you?"

"God's," the monk answered, "but I am obliged to Don Rodrigo de Ribadeneira."

"The merchant prince of Quito?" Alonso said. "Does he have a letter for me, too?"

"No, but he would very much like to see a port at the mouth of the Esmeraldas River."

Father Cabello cleared his throat. "Fray Alejandro is merely my secretary. He is not commissioned to discuss anything." The look he gave the Trinitarian was freighted with warning.

Alonso took this in without comment. "And what of my people?" he said.

"They are manumitted, if you accept the offer."

"I meant *all* my people."

Cabello looked at the two Niguas. "The sav—" He caught himself. "You are the governor. The *Indios* are under your direction. Their labour cannot be assigned by anyone else."

"Which … *Indios*?" Alonso said. "There are other tribes, our neighbours."

"All those in the coastal forest, from the Esmeraldas to the Babahoyo River."

Alonso nodded. Alejandro could see him taking in the information, assessing it, correlating it with what he already knew. Most men, white or black, when told that they were being appointed governor of a province of the Kingdom of Quito, would be hard-pressed not to execute a jig on the spot. But the African read through the letter again, rolled it up, and tucked it into the bosom of his cotton shirt, a garment the same as those his companions wore in all but details.

Alejandro corrected himself. *Not companions. Retainers.*

The monk also saw that Cabello was waiting for some kind of response, but the look Alonso gave the priest was mild and pleasant. "Your breakfast," he said, "is burning."

Indeed, it was, and now Fray Iago gave a cry of dismay as he saw the smoke rising from the charred bread. He snatched up a cloth and seized the handle of the pan, but the cloth was too thin for proper insulation, and this time the sound that escaped him was a cry of pain. He dropped the pan, its contents spilling out onto the sand.

For a moment, Father Cabello showed the face of a serious man beset by idiots, but he composed himself.

Alonso said, "I will have some food brought to you." He thought for a moment. "And I will encourage my people to attend a mass, if you would be so kind as to accept them. It has been a long time since we had the comfort of religion."

"All will be welcome," the priest said. He indicated the bulge in the African's shirt where the letter now lay. "And the ... matters we have discussed?"

"I am not a king," Alonso said. He gestured to include the Africans and Niguas. "We must talk about things. But first we will see you provided for."

Alejandro saw Cabello recognize that he had got all he was going to get from this encounter. "As Your Excellency wishes," he said with just enough inclination of his head to be significant.

Alonso smiled again. Alejandro thought, *He does that a lot.* Then the African said, "I am not yet a governor, either." He raised a hand. "Good day."

With that, he turned and walked back towards the tree-shaded stream at a measured pace, the four men following him. The priest watched them until they were lost to view, standing with the fingers of his right hand tapping his thigh. Then he turned to Alejandro, his face filled with cold anger.

"You will not speak again unless you are spoken to," he said.

"Yes, Father."

"I am not finished. If you do that again, de Ribadeneira or no de Ribadeneira, I will have you marched in chains onto the first ship out of Lima with a recommendation to the royal officers in Madrid that you be prosecuted for sedition."

Alejandro knew it was no idle threat. Others had left Lima in chains. "Yes, Father."

The rising heat of the day had them both sweating. Cabello wiped his brow with his sleeve and said, only half to himself, "I may do so anyway."

Then he rounded on Iago, nursing his burned hand, and said, "Imbecile! You have ruined breakfast! Make some more."

He might not have been the brightest of his order, but Iago knew that the only correct response was silent, rapid compliance. As he scurried to mix a new batch of dough, Alejandro watched the priest reseat himself in the shrine's shade where, tapping his fingers on one knee, he turned his thoughts to what had happened over the past few minutes.

The Trinitarian looked at the place where the visitors had stepped out of sight. He had been affected by the African's bearing: *his innate dignity* were the words that came unbidden to his mind. He contrasted his impression of Alonso Illescas with his view of Father Cabello, or indeed of Don Rodrigo, and he wondered, *Has God shown me something today?*

They came back in the afternoon: a multitude of men, women, and children, some African, some Nigua, and some—carried in their mothers' arms or toddling beside them—a mixture of both races. They came down the stream in dugout canoes and on the balsa raft, which was piled high with fired-clay pots and baskets that they unloaded and carried to where the Spaniards had piled their dwindling supply of stores. Alejandro accepted a square basket with a fitted lid from a smiling African woman—he was surprised to see half a dozen such among the crowd; somehow he had assumed that all the escaped slaves were men—and when he lifted the lid he found round loaves of fragrant corn bread. His mouth watered, and he had to swallow before he could say, "Thank you."

Alonso had come not at the forefront of the crowd but in its midst, and as he neared the shrine, Alejandro noted a difference. He did not wear his sword; it was carried for him by a gangly adolescent boy who was quite clearly proud to do so. Alonso had also changed his garments. He wore a pale shirt heavily embroidered at the collar, and over it a multicoloured robe of fine cloth to which thousands of bird's feathers had been attached in geometric patterns. His lower legs were bare, but his feet were encased in buskins of soft leather, dyed red and stitched all over in swirls of white thread.

He says he is not a king, the monk thought, *but he looks every inch of one.*

The crowd came to stand before the shrine in a thick demi-lune. There were at least a hundred people, and it was obvious that they had grouped themselves as families. Those who had walked before Alonso now stepped aside, making a clear path for him to approach where Father Cabello stood, his hands folded before him.

When he reached the priest, Alonso extended his hand. In the palm was a piece of dark-dyed cloth wrapped around something substantial.

He said, "Beyond the gifts of food, we wish to make this offering to the Church, and I hope that you will allow me to place it on the altar, Father."

With his other hand he unfolded the cloth to reveal a shapeless lump of something that Alejandro, standing to one side, could not quite make out—until the African elevated his hand and the object caught the sun and glistened brightly.

Gold, Alejandro thought. *A nugget the like of which would buy a fine house in Seville.*

Father Cabello was gesturing smoothly for Alonso to approach the altar and place the precious object beside the chalice. The priest's face was composed, but Alejandro had seen the way the man's eyes had widened when the nugget was revealed, the way he instinctively leaned towards the treasure before he could recover his aplomb. The monk had seen the same expression flicker across Cabello's countenance when Avila had brought back the first gold from the island tombs of the Campaze.

He has not shed himself of earthly appetites, Alejandro thought. It was noticeable. Alonso had noticed it, too.

Cabello was now directing Iago to provide a stool for the man he referred to pointedly as "His Excellency," having the monk place it to one side between the crowd and the altar. When Alonso was seated, Cabello blessed the congregation and bid them be seated on the ground. Then he turned his back to the crowd, crossed himself, knelt, and kissed the altar cloth.

"*In nomine Patris, et Filii, et Spiritus Sancti, Amen,*" he intoned.

Alejandro had not been allowed to assist the priest at the celebration of the mass: his punishment for speaking out of turn. He now made himself as inconspicuous as he could, drifting towards the side and rear of the crowd where he would be out of Father Cabello's line of sight. As he looked over the congregation from behind he saw an incongruity: a person he had taken to be taller than the rest was not. The Africans and Niguas were seated on the sand, cross-legged or with their legs tucked under them, but this one was actually standing. But this person, a Nigua, was not much taller standing than some of the sitting men.

Alejandro was behind and to one side of the anomaly, who stood at the far back of the crowd, intently watching Father Cabello as the priest went through the ancient forms and phrases of the mass. He was giving it all the solemnity of tone and gesture of an archbishop when the King comes to the cathedral to receive the body and blood of Christ.

Alejandro was a more educated monk than many. He had been tutored and had even attended some classes at the university in Seville before he heard the call. So he knew that vision involved emanations from the eyes and knew also that some persons were able to feel the weight of those emanations. This diminutive Nigua must have been one of those sensitives, because he now felt Alejandro's gaze upon him and turned to regard the monk.

The eyes that regarded Alejandro were old, in experience if not in years. It also struck him as odd that the Nigua was watching him instead of the priest, who was putting on a performance that should have been far more interesting than a monk trying his best to be unobtrusive.

Alejandro dropped his gaze, folded his hands in the sleeves of his borrowed habit, and moved farther away. He angled his path towards the beach, where the stream entered the sea. He stood and gazed out over the waves to where the sky met the ocean and let his mind do nothing but register the sounds and sights his senses were taking in: the susurration of the surf gently stroking the beach, the measured tones of Father Cabello's mass, the almost imperceptible movement of a cloud far out in the offing, the patterns visible on the water.

His meditations were interrupted by the clearing of a throat. He turned and saw that the small Nigua had followed him and was now studying him closely. Alejandro spoke softly. "You should be back with the others, hearing the mass."

The little person glanced back towards the shrine and the black-robed figure before it, then dismissed the priest and his ritual with a twist of the small lips. To Alejandro, he said, "Do the colours white and blue have meaning to you?"

The monk was surprised to hear good Spanish, albeit in a strange, raspy voice. "You speak Spanish very well," he said.

"I have a good teacher," the *Indio* responded. "But what about the colours?"

"White and blue?" After no more than a moment's thought, he answered his question. "They are the colours of my habit."

"Habit?"

"To do with my . . . profession. We wear clothes of a certain colour. Mine is white with a red and blue cross on the breast."

The little head cocked to one side, studying his brown robe. "You are not wearing them today."

"No. This robe is borrowed. My order's robe is heavy wool, made for colder lands."

"Ah." The little chin went up and down in a confirmatory nod. Then the small Nigua turned to retrace his steps.

"Why do you ask?" Alejandro called after him.

The person stopped, half turned, and protruded a lower lip while considering a reply. Finally, he said, "To do with *my* profession."

He turned and walked on. Alejandro could not raise his voice for fear of disturbing Father Cabello at the altar, but he said, "Would you wait? I would like to talk to you."

Another pause and turn. He waited while Alejandro caught up to him. "About what?" he said.

The first answer that came to Alejandro's tongue was, *About what you are,* but he managed to make it come out as, "About your profession."

"We'll have plenty of time to talk about that." He gave him a knowing look and added, "And the things you're truly interested in. But not now."

"Why not now?"

He looked up and Alejandro followed his gaze. A large grey bird, its wing feathers spread wide like fingers, hovered high above them, circling. While they watched, it dipped one wing and glided out over the sea. At that moment came a shout from the crowd before the altar.

The gangly boy who had carried Alonso's scabbarded sword was standing and pointing out to sea. Alejandro turned and shaded his eyes against the sun's glare off the water. Far out, just above the horizon, he made out a tiny fleck of white against the blue. He blinked, wiped from his eyes the water that the glare summoned up, and looked again. The fleck had taken on a definite rectangular shape.

"A ship," he said.

The mass had come to an unexpected end. The Africans and Niguas were getting to their feet and streaming towards the tree-shaded stream where they had left their canoes and the raft.

Father Cabello was calling after them. "Come back! Please, come back!"

But only Alonso Illescas paused to look back at the priest, and the pause was only long enough for the African to shake his head. Then he turned and went with the rest. In only a little time, they had all disappeared from view. One of the last to go was the odd little Nigua, who made a last survey of the shrine, the priest, and Alejandro. Then he was gone, too.

Alejandro looked seaward again. The patch of white had disappeared. The ship must have tacked too far to leeward and hove up over the horizon at just the wrong time. He made his way back to the shrine, where Cabello was ordering the altar. The lump of gold gleamed in the shade and the priest stared at it for a long moment—before he rounded on the Trinitarian.

"What happened?" he said. "What did you do?"

"I? I did nothing. There was a ship out on sea, a flash of sail. The boy saw it and shouted."

Cabello blinked. He was clearly having trouble understanding what he was hearing. "A ship? There's not supposed to be a ship. They were supposed to go south and not come back for a month."

Alejandro said, "Sergeant Avila said they would stay out of sight, but would come in if we lit a smoky signal fire."

"Avila? Avila said? What does Avila have to do with anything?"

"He's friends with the captain of the *Guadeloupe*. They're both Portuguese."

Cabello had the face of a man who hears words he understands but that, put together, convey no meaning. "What has that got to do—" He cut himself off with a chop of his hand against the air, then took a deep breath and let it out.

"You're saying Sergeant Avila prevailed upon his friend, the captain, to disobey my explicit orders and remain up here, but out of sight beyond the horizon?"

"Yes, Father."

"And you did not tell me that?"

"No, Father. I thought—"

The priest's face was livid, two spots of red on his cheeks accentuating the pallor of his rage. "Never mind what you thought! Why did he do it? Tell me!"

Alejandro did not want to have the say the words. He realized now that it would provoke an explosion. But he could not lie.

"Sergeant Avila … cares about me. We are friends. He did not like to think of me … of us … stranded here on what might be a hostile shore. So he spoke to the captain and …"

Father Cabello said nothing. But his face seemed to change shape, and Alejandro realized that it was because the priest was grinding his teeth so hard that the muscles at the hinges of his jaw stood out like chestnuts under the skin.

"You," he said. He was not looking at the Trinitarian. He was looking around: at the ground, at the roof of the shrine, at the altar. "You stupid, fatuous, interfering …"

He took a shuddering breath and as he did so, his gaze fell on the palm-sized nugget of gold. He snatched it up, stared at it as if seeing it for the first time, clutched it to his chest. Then his eyes came back to Alejandro, and though the monk had never before seen murder in a man's gaze, he knew he was seeing it now. He turned and ran.

The sound that followed him was not a word. Yet it articulated the wrath of Miguel Cabello de Balboa to perfection. And as Alejandro fled, his robe hiked above his knees, his sandals finding little purchase in the sand, the roar of rage reached a crescendo just as a blinding white light filled his vision. He had a brief moment of pain in the back of his head, then all was black, and he was gone down into it.

Eighteen

Alonso Illescas

"The ship did not come," Poquito is saying. "It disappeared over the horizon and did not show itself again."

"But it is there," Anton says.

Poquito says one of his click words and shrugs.

"What did they do?" the chief says.

"There was an argument. The priest shouted at the tall monk, who ran away. The priest threw something and hit him in the head. He fell and lay still. The other monk would have gone to him, but the priest shouted at him, too. They just left him lying there."

Anton's eyebrows rise. "That is rather violent. Is he really a priest?"

Alonso says, "He told me he used to be a soldier."

Anton looks at him. "You didn't tell me that."

"It didn't seem important."

"What else didn't you tell me?"

"I don't know." Alonso thinks for a moment, and something occurs. "The tall monk did not seem to be impressed by the priest. I had the impression he was not the priest's man, if you know what I mean."

Anton gives that a nod. "I know what you mean."

"What I am saying is, whatever the plan, the tall fellow was not part of it." He thinks again. "And from the priest's reaction to our leaving, maybe he blames the monk."

"Huh," Anton says. There is silence in the council chamber. Finally, the chief says, "We will stay as we are for now. They cannot do anything tonight, even if the ship comes back and unloads soldiers."

He drinks from the wooden cup he has been holding throughout the session. Alonso can smell the rum on the chief's breath. Anton has not offered any of the liquor to the other men seated on stools, nor to Miriam, standing beside his chair. Nor does he even look at Expectaion, standing next to Chilianduli.

"Poquito," Anton says, "go down the river and tell Juanito to keep the ambush ready, but let the men sleep in watches."

The little brown man makes a gesture and leaves. Anton says to the rest of the council, "We'll meet again at first light. Everybody go get some rest." He drinks from the cup again and belches fumes.

Chilianduli looks as if he wants to say something, but the chief is now staring into the cup, seeing something only he can see, so he gives up and follows the rest out of the presidio. In the plaza, he catches up to Alonso.

"What do you think?" he asks in Nigua.

Alonso stops. "It makes sense to lay an ambush downstream," he says. "That is the way they must come if they send soldiers to take us." All of the *arcabuceros* and almost all of the Nigua bowmen are hidden in the trees on one side of the river where it makes a narrow bend half a league downstream from where the smaller stream meets it. If the Spaniards come in boats, they will be slaughtered.

"Not the ambush," Chilianduli says. "The ... situation."

Alonso shrugs. "We don't know the situation. We may know more tomorrow."

Chilianduli's face is hard to see in the dim glow of the lamps from the presidio's entrance and a few other huts. "If the offer is genuine," he says, "we govern ourselves with no forced labour—"

"If," says Alonso.

"Yes, if." says the Nigua. "It would mean no more hiding in the forest. We could live in a town again, trade with people along the coast as well as the Yumbo up in the mountains." His eyes catch light from the presidio. "Have you thought about it?"

"I have thought about it," Alonso says. "If it is an honest offer, we could benefit from it. We could take the Cayapas under our protection, maybe even convince the Campazes to make peace."

"That would be something," Chilianduli says.

"The Spaniards are not going away," Alonso says. "We need to find some way to live with them."

"But …" says the Nigua, looking at the presidio. He leaves the rest of his thought hanging.

Alonso glances back at the big house. "Yes," he says. "But." He takes a long breath and lets it out. "I am tired," he says. "Let us sleep and see what the morning brings."

Chilianduli makes a sound of agreement. He pats Alonso on the arm in what feels almost like a fatherly gesture, turns, and walks away. Alonso yawns and stretches before turning towards his own little home. The prospect of being within its walls with his wives and child has never been more comforting.

A voice speaks softly beside him. "It would be better if any conversation with Chilianduli took place away from the presidio."

Alonso stops and looks down. "Expectation. I did not see you there."

"But you and Chilianduli were seen. Anton was watching from the doorway." She tugs at his sleeve. "Come."

Alonso shrugs and walks on. "I cannot help what Anton does. He knows I do not want to be chief. He knows I advise him honestly."

"Your problem," the Nigua says, "is not what Anton knows, but what he suspects."

"I will speak to him."

"But will he listen?"

Alonso stops. It has been a long day, and fatigue envelops him. His eyelids feel gritty against his eyeballs. "What are you trying to achieve?" he says. "Why do you say these things to me?"

"I am trying to keep you alive," she says. "You are like a man who walks in darkness along the edge of a sheer cliff. At any moment you may fall to your death, but you don't even know the danger is there, right beside you."

"Anton will not harm me. He knows I am useful to him."

"You are also a threat."

Alonso suppresses his anger. His neck is stiff and throbbing. He wants only to go home and have Xinbu rub warm oil into the aching flesh. "I have told you. Anton knows I do not want to be chief," he says.

He can only dimly see the small, wizened face looking up at him, but he catches a glint from Expectation's eyes as she blinks. She says, "What makes you think it's just a matter of what *you* want?"

He makes a gesture of exasperation and walks away. He hears her footsteps behind him and says, "No more. Leave me alone."

The footsteps cease. A moment later he knows she is walking away, going to her own hut.

Alonso makes a wordless sound of relief. He is lying on his back, his head on Xinbu's knees, and she is kneading the tension out of his neck. He lifts his head and rotates it for a moment, hears the crack of vertebrae moving against each other.

On the other side of the hut, Kepepahta sits cross-legged, rocking Sebastian in her arms. The child is almost lost to sleep, murmuring softly.

"He will be talking soon," Xinbu says.

"I look forward to it," Alonso says, speaking in Nigua as he usually does now when he is at home. "We will have good talks together. I will teach him."

"He will need to learn both languages," his mother says.

"That shouldn't be hard."

"No," she says, "he will be like you. Maybe someday a chief."

Alonso sighs. "Not you, too."

She digs her strong, hard fingers into the place where his neck meets his shoulders and draws them slowly up to where the muscles attach to the skull. He groans.

Xinbu says, "The women talk about you. They say you would make a good chief. We are proud to hear it, aren't we, Kepepahta?"

His other wife looks up from the child. "Very proud."

"Well, tell them to stop saying it. Anton is chief and will remain chief."

The women say nothing for a while, then Kepepahta says, "Anton is a war chief—a good war chief. But everyone knows that you are the peacetime chief. When we no longer have to worry about fighting the Spaniards, then we can move into the … into where Anton lives."

Alonso sits up. His neck is throbbing again, the sensation reaching up into his brain. He can feel his pulse in his ears and his temples. "You cannot say that," he says. "Not even here and in Nigua. We do not have wartime and peacetime chiefs. Just Anton. And he will not allow anyone to challenge him."

"Come and lie down again," says Xinbu. He reclines and puts his head on her knees again. She begins to work the stiffness out of his nape. After a while, she says, "It's silly to have just one chief. He would have to be good at everything, and—"

"Enough!" says Alonso, sitting in one convulsive movement. Both women look at him in surprise. He has never raised his voice to them before. Little Sebastian jerks awake in Kepepahta's arms and begins to cry.

"Now see what you've done," Xinbu says. She wipes her oily hands on a piece of fabric then slips the collar of her shirt down to expose a breast. "Give him to me," she says, and a moment later the child is noisily sucking at her.

"Good appetite," says Kepepahta. She pats her swollen stomach. "I hope mine is the same."

"He will be," Xinbu says.

"I am sorry I shouted," Alonso says. He touches the child's head, runs his hand over the curly hair. "Let us not talk anymore about … that thing."

Xinbu and Kepepahta exchange a look. Kepepahta says, "Even if we don't talk about it, the women—"

"No," says Alonso, "please."

And then there is only the sound of Sebastian drawing nourishment out of his mother.

"In the morning, they built a smoky fire," Poquito says, "and they watched out to sea. In the afternoon, the ship appeared on the horizon, and by sunset it was anchored in the bay."

"Then what?" Anton says.

"I could not see too well. They lit torches on the land, and the men in the boat had lanterns."

"Did they land soldiers?"

"No. It was like before," the little brown man says. "A few sailors to bring the boat in and load their things into it. The man with the sword also came ashore. Then there was an argument."

"About what?"

But Poquito was not close enough to hear. All he knows is that the priest and the soldier argued, and the priest flew into a rage, shouting at the sailors to do something. But the soldier drew his sword, and the sailors had no stomach for a fight.

"So the priest and one of the monks were rowed back to the ship, while the soldier and the other monk—I think he was injured—stayed. Then the ship went away."

Anton gives a thinking grunt and looks around the half-circle of his councillors seated on their stools in front of his throne. "So what was that all about?" he says.

"The priest did not like the monk," Alonso says. "He threw the nugget of gold at him, and they just let him lie where he fell."

Poquito says, "The soldier is the friend of the injured man. He would not let the priest take him to the ship."

"I think the priest," Alonso says, "is not just a priest. He is an ambitious man, a climber. I saw his face change when he saw the gold we brought. The tall monk must have done something that interfered with the priest's plan."

"May I speak?" Expectation says.

"You are only here to translate," Anton says.

"But I know something."

"Let us hear her," Miriam says. Alonso looks at her in some surprise, but Miriam does not look at him.

"Speak," Anton says.

"I don't know about the soldier," the Nigua says in Spanish, "but the tall man will be useful to us."

Chilianduli says in Nigua, "I understand enough Spanish to know what you said. Does that mean you have *seen* this man?"

"Yes."

Anton says, "What? What's he saying?"

Expectation turns to the chief. "He is asking me if I have seen the tall monk"—she taps the side of her head—"in here."

Anton swears. "I've told you, keep your demons out of it!"

Expectation looks down at her hands and says nothing. Chilianduli says, "What does that mean, 'your demons'?"

Speaking softly, the healer begins to explain in Nigua. Chilianduli listens and looks at the chief with surprise that turns into irritation. He says in Spanish, "Expectation knows things. We should listen to her."

Anton's eyes grow large. He leans forward in his chair, and his hands grip the arms. His voice is hard and thin as a sword blade. "She deals with evil spirits! She is a witch and a sorceress! Listen to her? We should cut off her head!"

Chilianduli begins to protest, but now Anton raises his voice. "Silence! I am chief here! I will decide who advises me!"

The Nigua headman's face grows stark. He gets up and, without a word or a rearward glance, leaves the big house. Expectation follows him out.

Miriam says, "Anton— "

"Shut up! Who is chief here?" He glares at her and at all the others, his angry gaze lingering finally on Alonso, who keeps his own eyes focused on the rush-matted floor. No one else speaks or looks at him. The presidio is silent. From outside they can hear the sounds of the women talking and laughing as they make beer in their house across the plaza.

Then the women fall silent. Alonso knows it is because they see Chilianduli walking with stiff dignity towards his hut. After a moment, their voices come back, but now there is no laughter, no bantering tone. He hears an old woman saying, "What has happened?" But the answer, if there is one, is too soft.

Alonso looks up. Anton is leaning back in his chair. He has the figured cup in his hand and is drinking from it. Miriam is looking down the length of the presidio towards the doorway and the plaza beyond, where the women's voices are now a constant buzz, like bees in a disturbed hive.

Anton lowers the cup. "So," he says. "What do we do about the two on the beach?"

Alonso says, "If the monk is— "

But Anton didn't ask the question to elicit answers. He already has the answer ready. "We capture them and question them. Hot coals between the toes." He moves his lips against his teeth. "The sons-of-whores Spaniards taught me that."

Alonso waits to see if any of the others will speak. Juanito is looking away. Pahta is looking from Anton to Alonso. Poquito has the aspect of a faithful hound whose master has shouted at it. Miriam's face is tight, her mouth pursed, the lines at the corners of her eyes deeply etched.

It is up to Alonso, though he does not want to do it. "If the monk has quarrelled with the priest, he may face charges if he goes back to Lima. That could be what Poquito saw: the priest telling the sailors to seize him, and his friend the swordsman defying them."

Anton shrugs. "We'll find it all out. Don't worry." He belches, and rum fumes waft through the still air.

Alonso presses on. "It may be that the offer of peace is genuine but the Viceroy picked a too-ambitious envoy—a man who likes gold too much."

"Doesn't matter. What they want is a port. We're not giving them that."

"But we could," Alonso says. "If we have royal authority, we could have peace and prosperity. Live in stone houses instead of huts, drink wine instead of corn beer. We could be like dons."

Anton enunciates with the care for clarity of a man whose tongue is thickening from drink. "We're not doing it."

"Why not?"

For answer, Alonso receives a look he has trouble interpreting. Anton's face is framing a question set in mockery. Alonso says, "I don't— "

Miriam interrupts. "The offer is to you, not to Anton. You will be the governor. Then what will Anton be?"

Alonso is taken aback. "But that's just a fiction," he says. "I don't want to be governor any more than I want to be chief."

Anton has leaned forward again. "You think I'm stupid?" he says. "You think you just have to say, 'Oh, I don't want it,' and I'll believe you?"

He lifts the cup and drinks, his Adam's apple bobbing up and down. When he's finished, he looks in the bottom and makes to hand it to Miriam. "More."

"No more," she says, pushing the cup back towards him. "We have important things to do."

Anton stands up. His eyes have grown large again, as if pressure is building in his head and forcing them out of their sockets. He shoves the cup into the woman's chest, and she winces from the pain. "More!" he says. "Now!"

For a long moment, she looks at him. Alonso thinks it is as if she has not really seen him before but now she is taking a full evaluation. Then she goes behind the screen and he hears the sound of liquid pouring. She returns and hands Anton the cup. He takes a good swallow and sits down, belching.

"Now listen," he says. "Juanito, you take some men down the river. Take the raft and some matchlocks. Grab the two of them and bring them back. Tied up and blindfolded. They don't see where we are. Got it? Good. Now get out of here, all of you."

The others get up and leave, but Anton calls Alonso back. He lets the younger man stand before him while he drinks more of the rum. Alonso sees red veins in Anton's eyes.

The chief's voice is gruff. "I don't want you to argue with me anymore. Show respect."

"I'm trying to show respect," Alonso says. "I'm trying to do what is best—"

"Did you not hear what I just said? No more arguing! I'll decide what's best!" He slams the base of the cup down on the arm of the chair. Rum spills over the rim and splashes his shirt. He wipes at the wet splotch with his free hand, looking up at Alonso as if it's the younger man's fault. "If I want your advice, I'll let you know."

Alonso is at a loss. "What do you want from me?"

"I want you," Anton says, "to do as you're told. That's what I want from all of you. And, by God, I will have it!"

Miriam has been hanging back. Now she comes forward, takes Alonso's arm, and moves him towards the door. "He's got things to do," she tells the chief.

"Sure," says Anton, bringing the cup to his lip. "You go and do things." His voice drops almost to a mumble, but Alonso hears him. "You're so good at doing things." He drinks some more and shouts after them, "And bring me something to eat!"

Miriam and Alonso descend the steps. Across the plaza, they can see the women in the open doorway of their big house and hear the anxious murmur of their conversation. Alonso sees Expectation in there, standing back, watching him. And his wives, Xinbu with the baby in its cloth sling. Then Miriam says, "Go to your house," and gently pushes him in that direction.

As he moves away, he sees Miriam crossing the open space, heading for the women and the beer-making. And he realizes that Expectation was not watching him. She was watching Miriam. She is waiting for the African woman, has been waiting for her a long time—and now that time is over.

They bring the two captives just after midday, using the butts of their matchlocks to push them through the gate and towards the plaza. The monk and the soldier are blindfolded, their hands tied behind them, and they stumble. A purple bruise is spread over the soldier's cheek. Juanito carries the man's belt with his sword and dagger.

Alonso has been sitting in the doorway of his house, looking out onto the plaza. The women have finished the beer-making and have left the liquid to brew in the clay pots. But they have not left their big house, and there has been a constant susurration of conversation, softly spoken but occasionally punctuated by loud voices. Not long ago, the matriarch of the big noses, leaning on her stick and attended by two of her middle-aged daughters, left the beer-making and crossed the plaza, disappearing between two huts into the alley that leads to where Chilianduli and his clan have built their houses. No Nigua men are to be seen; they have retired to their homes.

Juanito and the others drive the soldier and the monk towards the broad ladder leading up into the presidio. Anton appears in the doorway. He is weaving, blinking as he comes into the light, and has to raise his hand to the lintel to keep from pitching down the steps. Now he pulls himself together, stands with fists on hips, looking down on the captives as they haltingly approach.

Juanito gives the monk a final push. The man trips, falls to his knees, and cries out in pain.

"Leave him alone!" shouts the soldier. "He is injured!"

Alonso can see that blood stains the back of the monk's robe. On his knees, he sways and has to catch himself lest he topple forward. Juanito puts a hand on the soldier's shoulder and pushes with his foot against the back of the man's knee. Now the soldier is kneeling, too. The ironsmith jerks the blindfolds off both of them. The monk winces as the harsh light strikes his eyes.

Anton nods. To Juanito he says, "Heat the forge. I want hot iron. Red hot."

Juanito obeys. The soldier turns to watch him go and says, "You don't need that. You didn't need to tie us. We would have come willingly."

Anton looks as if he has tasted something sour. "You're telling me what I need? You're used to telling people like me what we need, aren't you? And it's always less than you need, isn't it?"

"I am just saying—" the soldier begins, but a sudden lift of Anton's chin tells the African behind him to do something to shut the man up. The something is a hard punch to the back of the neck that drives the prisoner forward. He twists at the last moment to land on his shoulder instead of face first in the dust. At a gesture from Anton, hands seize him and pull him upright again.

The monk appears dazed, but the soldier is twisting his torso again, turning to look around in every direction. Finally, he sees Alonso sitting in the doorway to his hut, and his head lifts as if to say, "There you are!"

But Alonso does not move.

Anton sees and laughs, drawing the soldier's gaze back to him. The chief says, "You think that one's the leader here?" He laughs again, a sound without humour. "He is nothing. He is my dog! He comes when I call, fetches when I tell him to fetch."

Anton looks directly at Alonso now. Alonso looks back. Something in him stirs, but something else pushes the restive part down into the cellar of his being. He hears the Nigua women's voices rising in volume again. He looks towards the big house, sees in its shadows faces turned his way. He shakes his head at them, a stolid negative, and receives a louder response from the women: some angry, some urging him to rise. But he shakes his head again and looks back towards the scene before the presidio.

The soldier is no longer turned towards him but is speaking to Anton. "We are not your enemies. This one"—he nods his head towards the monk—"is as innocent as a lamb. He wants only to serve God and do good."

Alonso recognizes the expression that comes over Anton's face: it is the same mocking disbelief the chief showed him in the council meeting. "You like 'this one'?" Anton says, looking down on the monk. "He is your friend? Your special friend? Your catamite?"

"No," the soldier says, "he's just—"

"Then maybe we start with him," Anton says. "Singe his toes a little, or maybe those parts of him a monk is not supposed to need?"

"No!" the soldier cries. "You don't need—"

"Juanito!" Anton calls across the plaza to where the smith is stoking the forge's charcoal. Pablillo, his helper, is working the tapir-skin bellows. "How long?"

The smith holds up an iron bar, spits on the end, the saliva disappearing in a hiss of vapour. "Not long!" he shouts back.

"For the love of God!" cries the soldier.

"Whose God?" says Anton and laughs. He turns and shouts into the presidio, "Bring me drink!" When he receives no response, he shouts again, "Miriam! Bring me drink!"

Alonso looks towards the beer-making. He sees Miriam there among the Niguas and the few African women. He sees Expectation and his wives. Xinbu meets his gaze and gestures with her head towards the presidio.

Her meaning is plain, but Alonso only shakes his head and remains where he is. He looks away from her. But something is building within him. There is fear, an old familiar chill in his stomach, but there is something else: a roil of energy that he can only name as excitement. Abruptly, he remembers the moment on the swaying suspension bridge when it felt as if Anton was calling him forward, as if the motion was not of his own volition, but as if he were possessed by another's power.

All the more reason not to defy Anton, he thinks. But even as he is forming the thought, another part of him doubts its truth. This time, it is not Anton who is inside him. It is something of his own, a power that comes from within him.

Still he resists its force. *I do not wish to oppose Anton. It is not what I am for.*

Anton has disappeared into the former men's big house and now he returns. In one hand is his figured pewter cup, a little rum splashing over its rim as he moves with the exaggerated care of the drunkard. From the cord around the wrist of his free hand dangles the bloodstained club that bespeaks his authority. He pauses at the top of the ladder stairs and takes a drink, his head back, rum dribbling down into his beard. He wipes his chin with the back of his other hand, the club swinging loose, and calls again to Juanito. "Well?"

"Very soon," says the ironsmith. He holds up the bar, and Alonso sees its end glow dull red in the shade beneath the forge's roof. Juanito shoves the iron down into the coals and tells Pablillo to keep on opening and closing the skin bag.

As Alonso watches the scene before him, it is as if the figures in it shrink in size, as if they have drawn away from him into the far distance. But he knows that is an illusion. It is he who has drawn away. He knows what his wives want of him, what Expectation expects of him. They want him to be someone he is not, someone he has never been—at least not since he was that untended child they called Enrique, who learned that being useful would see him fed, get him a corner to sleep in, a rag to cover himself.

And it was not just being useful, in general, that Enrique learned would save him for a day: it was being useful *to the man who held the whip,* the man who could fill the bowl with millet porridge, the man who could, if he chose, keep the child safe from those who would use a child as no child should ever be used.

Far back before he can remember, Alonso developed the ability to identify the man to whom he must show himself to be useful. He has refined that ability ever since. Every map begins with one fixed point of reference, be it Jerusalem in the old maps Alonso studied in the Illescas family library, or the compass rose in the corner of a modern chart. Alonso's map always centres on the man in charge. And in this place and this time, it is Anton.

He blinks and comes back to the here and now. Juanito is holding up the heated iron, and Alonso can see it glows red. The ironsmith nods to himself, tells Pablillo to cease working the bellows, and begins to cross the plaza towards the presidio. Anton descends the steps from the big house, holding his cup precariously in two hands lest it spill the rum. The head of the club strikes his thigh with each step.

Alonso sees motion to his left. Expectation has come down from the women's house and is walking towards her dwelling. Her small mouth is downturned in an almost perfect bow of a frown, her shoulders hunched forward, her fists clenched—a portrait of determination, thinks Alonso, albeit in miniature. She looks once at him, and her expression does not change. Then she is climbing into the hut.

And now there is motion to his right. Chilianduli enters the open space from the alley that leads to his clan's quarter. He is carrying a feathered staff, and he is followed by the old matriarch and a dozen Nigua men of his lineage. His face is also set. The clan chief's features are larger and more regular than the healer's, but the expression is the same.

Juanito has reached the place where the prisoners kneel, and he stands behind them, awaiting Anton's order. The tall monk still seems to be in a daze, but the soldier has twisted around and seen the heated iron. He says something to Anton that Alonso is too far away to hear, but it must be a plea, because the chief dismisses it with a sneer. He takes hold of the club and uses its stained end to prod the soldier in the chest, pushing him backwards. The motion causes some of the cup's contents to spill onto Anton's hand and wrist. He licks the liquid off then looks to Juanito.

But now, Chilianduli and his men are nearing the scene. Anton turns his head and sees them. He is clearly drunk, and it takes a moment for him to understand what is happening. Then his face clouds, and he turns and steps towards the Niguas. Chilianduli stops no more than an arm's length away. The silence in the plaza seems immense. Alonso can hear his own breathing and realizes that his breath is coming fast. His neck has stiffened again, and it is almost an effort to hold up his head.

Suddenly Expectation is standing on the ground below him, her face upturned towards him. She looks like a child trying to solve a difficult problem in arithmetic. He does not want to see her, but his head has become so heavy it is easier to look at her than to turn away.

"It is your time," she tells him, her voice quiet and firm. "Take this and do what you need to."

From behind her back she brings out an object Alonso cannot at first recognize. The incongruity is too great between the diminutive Nigua hermaphrodite in her oversized shirt and the polished wood and dull steel of the crossbow.

"Where on earth did you get that?" he says.

"Never mind," she says, offering it up to him. A leather harness with three quarrels set in loops hangs from a strap wrapped around the stock. "Take it and do what needs to be done."

"No," he says. "It is not for me to do anything like that."

Expectation's features tighten. "It was always for you," she says. "It is what you are for. It is why you were shown to me."

Alonso shakes his head. If he did not know this was real and not a dream, he would be trying now to wake up.

There is a quiet rush of feet on dry earth, the sound of cloth in motion. Without a word, the Nigua women have come down from their house, flooding into the plaza with their children, those too young to walk carried in their mothers' arms. The African women have remained up in the women's house. Alonso sees Miriam standing at the top of the steps. She returns his gaze for a moment, then moves her head towards Anton and Chilianduli in a way that says, *Go*.

She turns and says something to the women behind her and descends the steps. One of the African women follows her, then another, then all of them. Miriam begins to make her way through the crowd of Niguas to where Chilianduli and Anton stand face to face. Neither has yet spoken.

The entire community is now gathered in the plaza except for Alonso and Expectation. She looks up at him again and says, "You must."

It still seems like a dream to Alonso. There is a high-pitched ringing in his ears. But though he cannot say why he is doing it, he finds himself rising up then descending to the ground. The healer offers him the crossbow again, but he waves it away. Between him and the front of the presidio now are the backs of the people, mostly women. Gently, he insinuates himself among them. As they turn and recognize him, they step aside, speaking softly to those in front, who turn and see him. A clear path appears before him; at the end of it he sees Anton and Chilianduli, the two kneeling captives, and Juanito with the hot iron.

All are still, like figures in a Christmas tableau, brightly lit and shadowless in the equatorial noon. Alonso goes forward while a part of him stands back, watching, still trying to make sense of what he is doing. He comes level with Chilianduli and hears the clan chief speaking to Anton in a firm but quiet tone, like a teacher explaining a Pythagorean theorem to a dull student, knowing that eventually the explanation must sink in and the truth become self-evident.

Anton is peering at Chilianduli, blinking, not understanding. He has not bothered to learn much of the other's language. There has always been someone to translate for him. At his best, sober and paying close attention, the chief might understand one word out of five. At this moment, Alonso realizes, Anton is hearing only odd sounds.

Chilianduli finishes. He stands with his chin up, meeting Anton's bleary-eyed stare and waiting for a response. Alonso steps forward and says, "He is telling you how things are among the Nigua, how they arrange leadership."

Anton switches his focus to Alonso, blinking slowly in the brightness of noon. He raises the cup and takes a swallow. "What?"

"In a time of war," Alonso says, "they are led by a war chief. In a time of peace, a different chief takes over."

Anton takes this in. He looks to Chilianduli and back to Alonso, and his face hardens. "He is saying he wants to be chief?"

Alonso raises his hands in a mollifying gesture. "No, no, no. When they all lived together in the old town, his father was the war chief. Pidi was the peacetime chief. But that way of living broke down when they split up into different villages."

Anton grunts. "So what is he saying?"

Alonso knows he has to tread carefully, even though he still feels as if he is watching himself from somewhere outside his body. "He is saying that, now they are all living together with us and the Spaniards have offered to make peace, the time for the war chief is coming to an end. It is time for a peacetime chief to ... take over the reins."

Anton's expression does not soften. He makes his thinking noise and takes another drink of rum, then runs the tip of his tongue across his moustache to catch the droplets trapped there. "And who does he think this 'peacetime chief' should be?"

Chilianduli has not said, though Alonso knows what the Nigua will say if he is asked. To Anton he says, "It's not for Chilianduli to pick somebody. This is something we should talk about in council, when everybody is ... calm."

"I'm calm enough," says Anton. "Now, who does he want to be chief?" He gestures with the hand that holds the cup. "Who do they want?"

Chilianduli has been trying to follow the exchange between the two Africans. Now he asks Alonso, "What is he saying?"

And now the moment is here. Alonso is also here, but at the same time he is far away, watching from a distance as his mouth opens and he hears himself put the question to Chilianduli. He does not have to translate the answer, because the Nigua puts his hand on Alonso's shoulder—it feels warm because Alonso is unaccountably chilled in the noonday sun—and says, "Alonso."

Again there is silence, broken by a fretful sound from an infant somewhere in the crowd, the mewling quickly ended when the child's mother clucks to it and puts it to her breast. It occurs to Alonso that it might even be his own son, Sebastian, disturbing the solemnity of the tableau, and the thought abruptly makes him feel absurd—absurd and trapped in absurdity.

He must have let something of his thoughts show, because in the next moment he feels a warm liquid strike his face, stinging his eyes, and the reek of over proof rum fills his nostrils and causes him to choke.

He raises his hand to wipe his face, and that is when the first blow lands, a hard backhand that rocks him and makes his own teeth gash the side of his tongue.

He is blinded by the liquor thrown in his face, shocked by the force of the blow. He scarcely has time to register the taste of blood in his mouth before the next one lands, and this time it is Anton's hard fist striking him in the mouth, loosening teeth and propelling him backwards. He takes two steps, and his knees buckle. He feels himself sitting down in slow motion, like an old bear worried by dogs in a pit.

It is another absurd image. He shakes his head to clear the thought and the white noise and dizziness clouding his mind. Somewhere he hears Anton's voice, swearing, and another voice—a woman's, he thinks—speaking urgently. But he can't make sense of it and, besides, there is now a babble of voices, shouts, cries of anger and protest from men and women in Nigua and in Spanish.

A part of Alonso is still observing all of this from a distance, and now it is as if he is a bird hovering high above the village. He sees himself on his knees, Anton stalking towards him. The chief has thrown away his cup. The bloodstained club no longer dangles from his wrist but is held firmly in his right hand. He reaches for Alonso, seizes him by the hair, and pulls him forward.

Alonso feels the chief's grip, the pain in his scalp, even as he looks down on the scene from on high. Anton pulls him forward until he is on his hands and knees, his palms striking the dusty hard ground—and, again, he feels the sensations while the business remains remote.

The noise of protest is louder. Alonso looks up, though his neck is as hard as old wood. He can see the men who brought in the prisoners, all Africans, move up behind Anton, raising their matchlocks. Juanito still holds the hot iron, his face irresolute.

But someone is pushing through the crowd from the rear. It is Miriam, with Expectation just behind her. The African woman is shouting, but Alonso cannot make out the meaning over the general noise of the crowd.

And then Anton releases Alonso's hair and instead takes a firm grip on his neck, raising the club to strike. And at the moment Alonso feels the chief's grip, the distanced part of himself rushes back into his mind and into his body. He feels an actual shock as his selves collide and merge, and now the remoteness is not even a memory.

He is here and it is now, yet at the same time he is somehow conscious of every moment of his existence. And then it is just one of those moments, the one when the hard hand gripped his neck to hold him helpless while the terrible thing was about to happen.

Later, when he thinks about it, it will seem to Alonso that he crouched like a great cat, bunching his leg muscles before springing forward.

Anton's fingers slip backwards on his sweat-slick neck, and then Alonso is free and moving through the air like a missile. His hands come up, and the heels of his palms strike the chief in the chest and send him stumbling backwards, just as Anton's punch did to Alonso.

But Anton does not fall. He crashes into the men with matchlocks behind him. They bear him up, steadying him with their weapons held at the port arms across their chests. Anton's face has registered surprise, but now that his feet are steadier under him, Alonso sees only murderous intent in the chief's eyes. He has not lost his grip on the club, and he rolls his shoulders like a wrestler going into a match and readies the weapon again.

"This is not necessary," Alonso says. The moment of action has passed. He takes a step back, raising his hands. "We can—"

But Anton is not listening. He comes methodically forward, no longer affected by all he has drunk, his face and form full of cold anger, with just the smallest of smiles beginning to show itself. He raises the club.

There is a sound from behind Alonso: a harsh, incongruous *clack*, as if someone has clashed two wooden plates together, followed by a thrumming sound that comes and goes quickly. And now a peculiar object appears to have sprouted on Anton's bare chest. It looks to be made of squares of stiff brown leather, each no more than the width of two fingers. Anton stops as if he has run into an invisible wall, and he looks down at the thing on his chest as if it is a puzzle he must solve. Then he looks up at Alonso and then at whoever is behind the younger man.

Alonso sees the surprise leach out of Anton's face, along with all emotion. The mouth goes slack and the eyes become dull, and a last sigh of air issues from the stilled lungs before he topples forward, knees, chest, face striking the dust. The weight of the club, its cord still looped over his wrist, pulls the corpse's arm down to its side to lie impotent. From the middle of its back protrudes a four-sided point of iron smeared in blood.

Alonso turns and looks behind him. He sees Miriam, the crossbow in her hands, her face working in a mix of feelings. Then she lets the weapon drop, and her expression becomes that of a woman who has attended to one disagreeable task and now squares herself to handle the next. She steps up beside Alonso, gives Anton's corpse a brief glance, and speaks to the younger man out of the side of her mouth, just loud enough for him to hear.

"Take charge. Now."

There is still no sound in the plaza. No one but Miriam has moved or spoken since Anton fell lifeless. Alonso sees faces turning his way, especially that of Juanito, still holding the hot iron. The smith is raising his eyes from his leader's corpse towards the young man. The shock is leaving Juanito's face, and Alonso sees a new intent forming there.

Somehow that makes it easy. For Alonso, it is as if there is only the smith to be dealt with. He steps forward, past the corpse, to place an open palm on the bar. His voice is low and calm but not soft as he says, "They will all be against you."

Juanito blinks. His gaze shifts from Alonso's stern face to take in the crowd: men and women, Africans and Niguas, all poised on a cusp.

Alonso says, "It is over. Your skills are needed. We don't want to lose you."

To himself, Alonso is thinking, even as he speaks, *It is not just what you say. It is what you don't say.* Had he threatened the smith, he might have forced Juanito to act. But an appeal to bring the man back into the circle …

He sees Juanito waver, take one last look at the crowd. Then the smith makes his decision. Alonso's open hand closes on the iron, and he receives it gently. He hears a soft sound from behind him and realizes that most of the people have been holding their breath.

He thrusts the hot tip into the ground then turns and addresses the crowd. "It is done," he says. "We will have peace. Will you have me as chief?"

There are no triumphant shouts, no cries of victory. The assent comes from a hundred mouths. Chilianduli steps to Alonso's side and puts an arm around his shoulders. In his own language he says, "This one is young, but he is wise. We will talk with him and follow his decisions." Another general murmur of approval comes from the crowd, and Chilianduli says in Spanish, "Good man, good chief," which raises a sympathetic laugh from those Africans who have not yet learned much Nigua.

Then the clan leader says quietly, "Time to give orders." A flicker of a finger indicates Anton's corpse.

Alonso feels curiously light, as if his chest is hollow. It is a good feeling, though: not a lack, but an enrichment. It is as if he has never quite known how to breathe before but now, somehow, has mastered the knack. Every breath he takes fills him with the energy of life. He wonders briefly if this what the religious mean when they talk about being filled with the Holy Spirit.

But there is no time for idle speculation. Chilianduli and Miriam are right. He will take charge, give orders. To Juanito, he says, "Put the weapons back in store and carry Anton's body out to the burial ground. Wrap it in some of the sailcloth we got from the ship."

The smith hesitates—but only for a moment, and in that moment the change is fully made. "Yes," he says and calls the matchlock men to order, telling them what to do.

The prisoners are still on their knees, their hands still tied behind them. Alonso turns to the crowd. "Who has a knife?"

Several appear in the hands of Nigua men. Alonso does not let his recognition of what that means show in his face. He takes the blade that Pahta offers, goes to the soldier and the monk, and cuts them free. As he hands the knife back to the Nigua, he looks for Expectation and finds her standing quietly behind and off to one side of Miriam. She is still holding the harness with the crossbow quarrels.

"This man is injured," he tells the healer in Nigua. "Take him to your house and do what you can for him."

The soldier has got to his feet, looking with wary hope at the crowd and at Alonso. He is helping the monk to rise. The new chief says in Spanish, "This small person is a healer. She will help your friend. You will come with me, and we will talk." He indicates the steps to the presidio.

Four men are carrying Anton's corpse around the rolled-up side of the big house, where one of the Africans is passing out a folded length of heavy cloth. Alonso watches it go and signals with a motion of his head to the soldier.

"What is your name?" he says.

"Gonzalo de Avila."

"Portuguese?"

"Yes."

"I am Alonso Illescas. I am— "

"I know," says Avila. "You are the Governor of Esmeraldas."

They climb the steps.

"That remains to be seen," Alonso says.

Nineteen

Expectation

Pallu had learned the skull-cutting technique from his own mentor, Unbeeruka, who was said to have learned it from the Quechua speakers in the highlands. It was a useful skill back when we used to fight the Campaze head-breakers. In the old days, before the Spaniards came with their *arcabuzes*, it was the mark of a Campaze warrior to engage an enemy at close range, delivering the death blow with a stone club to the head.

I had only seen Pallu perform the operation once, but he was always generous to me with his knowledge, and he not only let me watch but had me assist as well. He believed, as did Unbeeruka and the Quechua speakers, that a spirit could become trapped in the skull, and when that happened the healer had to cut a hole in the bone to let the spirit escape. My own studies had shown me that this was not so. Spirits were breath, and breath could go in and out of the skull by the nostrils or the mouth, as was obvious. They could be blown in through the top of the skull, but only because there was a portal there.

But there was something that could be trapped in the skull: blood. It sometimes happened, though I did not know why, when the bone was bruised by a hard blow. The impact did not even have to break the bone. Somehow, if the blood was trapped, it made the sufferer first grow dizzy, then lose consciousness, then show convulsions. Then die.

I supposed it was the convulsions that made the Quechua speakers conclude that a spirit was trapped in the skull. When an unwilling spirit is truly trapped inside a person and wants to escape, it flings itself around violently, the motion generating heat inside the body. If the heat is great enough, it can make the spirit uncomfortable, like a man sitting too close to a fire. The spirit becomes confused and thinks it must move the body to safety. The convulsions are an unsuccessful attempt to move the person. Spirits are good at motivating but cannot control arms and legs very well.

When I examined Alejandro Espinosa in the spirit hut, I already knew he had suffered a blow to the back of his head. I had the men who carried him in put him on his stomach, and I carefully probed the injured area. I found swelling and tenderness but no depression. The bone was not driven in.

That was good, but his condition was not. He had lost consciousness, and his breathing was shallow. I went to a basket I rarely opened and dug down into the layers of materials for Pallu's skull-cutting instruments. I was carefully shaving the back of his head when Alonso came up the ladder and into the hut.

He wanted to know what I was doing, so I told him.

"Can you really do that?"

"I think so. I have seen it done and assisted."

He shrugged and said he wished me success. "I believe this monk can tell us things that will be useful to us. The soldier says he has been the confidant of a powerful man in Quito."

"Ah," I said, continuing to scrape away hairs with a stone blade. "That is probably why he was shown to me."

"Shown?"

"By my guide. The eagle shows me things that are important to us."

Alonso blinked at me but waved the subject away. He was silent for a while, the only sound in the place the soft scritching of the shaving blade. Then he said, "I should have taken the crossbow when you offered it. I am sorry."

I paused then and thought about it. "No," I said, "I was wrong about what had to happen. You could not take the weapon until you had completed the journey. And for that, you had to return to where it started. I should have seen that."

He said, "I don't know what you are talking about."

"It doesn't matter. It was good that Miriam did the killing. I had hoped she would find her way to it."

"Why was it good?"

"First, it was good because she is an African, not a Nigua. Then it was good because she is a woman, so no one can say she did it because she wanted to be the chief. And, finally, it was good because she was his woman, with no relatives, so no one will talk in a way that could make trouble." I scraped away the last of the hair, revealing the bruised skin. "It all worked out just the way it should."

I probed at the injury again, then took a burin and pierced the skin, letting fluid run out and flattening the bump. Then I ran my fingers gently over the site and satisfied myself that there was no motion in the bone. I looked up at Alonso and said, "I'm going to start now. The sooner the better. Do you wish to watch?"

"No, I have several things to do."

"Call a council meeting as soon as you can," I said. "Give Chiliandúli a chance to speak in your favour."

"All right," he said. "But I will wait until you have finished here. Is there anything you need?"

"Send Pablillo in. He can assist." As he turned to go, I added, "And tell him to bring some water."

He left, and I used a stone knife to cut three-quarters of a square in the bruised skin, drawing it back in a flap to reveal the bone beneath. I took three long breaths to centre my powers, spoke briefly to my monkey-eagle guide, and took up the burin again. I was surprised how easily the bone cut, but I took it for a good sign.

By the time Alonso called the council meeting, my patient had regained consciousness. Enough thick blood had come out of the hole I made in the back of his skull to fill the palm of my hand. I heard voices and the sounds of people filling the plaza outside and asked Alejandro Espinosa to sit up and take some water. As he did so, I saw that his eyes moved together properly and that his pupils were the same size.

"You're doing well," I said. "Do you feel hungry?"

"I don't know," he said and raised a hand to touch the back of his head.

I gently stopped him. "Don't touch that just yet. It needs to heal." I did not want to tell him yet that there was a hole in his skull, the cavity filled with honey and the skin flap put back over it and pinned with some small thorns. From Alonso's response earlier, I knew that Spaniards were not familiar with the procedure.

"What happened to me?" he said.

I told him about the man in the black robe throwing the lump of gold. "He went away on the ship, but your friend the soldier stayed to take care of you."

He could almost remember that, and being brought up the river, but it was just a scattering of impressions interrupted by stretches of blankness.

"Your spirit may have been driven from you," I suggested.

"No," he said, quite firmly. "The spirit is always with me." He seemed to notice the noise and motion outside for the first time. "What happens now?"

I began to explain how he would need to rest and sleep a lot, but he interrupted and asked what would become of him and his companion. "Is he all right?" he said.

"He is fine, and you will be too," I told him. "There has been a change in our leadership."

He looked concerned. "I liked him—Alonso Illescas, the man who brought the gold."

I was surprised. "Alonso has two names?"

"Of course. Is he still your leader? I think he should be."

I would have been interested then to know about this business of having two names. I thought it might be a mark of spiritual distinction. I later discovered that having two was universal among the pale Spaniards, and many of them had three. Only the dark ones had single names, but even some of them—like Alonso Illescas, it now appeared—had two.

But Alejandro was tired and needed rest, and I wanted to get to the council meeting. I said, "Alonso is the leader, and he thinks well of you. If you want to stay and be part of … what is happening here, you and your friend will be welcome."

He sipped some more of the water and looked thoughtful. "I think," he said, "I am finally where I was meant to be."

"Yes," I said. It was what I thought, too.

"While I was unconscious," he said, "I had a vision."

The people had gathered outside. The council meeting was about to start. I wanted to be there, though I would not be needed to translate anymore.

But when a man has a vision, it is an important event. "Tell me of your vision," I said.

I listened carefully as he told me that he had come out of darkness into a golden light that surrounded him completely. He saw no walls or ceiling, no sky, no path before him, yet he had a sense that he was moving towards something.

"Something good or bad?" I said.

"Oh, good, very good. I think it was the presence of God."

I let that go and encouraged him to tell me what else he remembered. He said he came to a barrier. He could not see it, but he knew it was there, restraining him. And somehow he knew that he was not supposed to cross over. "I did not hear a voice," he said, "but I knew it was not my time, that I had to go back and do things."

"Hmm," I said. "Did you see any animals, or perhaps people you have known who are now dead?"

"No, just the light and the feeling of being stopped and sent back. But it was very gentle. I felt ... loved." He sipped some more of the water and said, "I think it was God telling me that my work for him was not completed and that I should return to the world and carry on."

This was surely a very peculiar man. I remembered the cool blue flame that rose out of his being when I first saw him through the eyes of my guide. When I had finished getting the thick blood out of him and he was sleeping normally, I had sat beside him and made my way into the spirit world, searching for his spirit.

Gliding along the river between its green banks, I saw many different animal spirits. But none of them showed themselves to me more than once or twice. None of them was this man's guide. It was as if he had no guide but still behaved as if there was a spirit at his centre—a strong spirit, even a benevolent one.

"It was a good vision," I told him now, as I would any of our people who had had a positive encounter with the other world. "Keep it within you and take strength from it."

He made a wordless sound of agreement. I said, "You need to rest. I can give you an herb that will help you sleep. It will also ease the pain of your wound."

"I want to see Gonzalo."

"Is that you friend's name?" When he nodded, I said, "He will need to be part of the council meeting, but I will bring him back after, and I will tell him that you are getting better."

He acquiesced to the herbs then, and I mixed them up in some corn beer. He drank it, belched discreetly, and lay down to sleep. When I saw him settled, I went out into the plaza. I saw that Alonso had assembled the councillors not in the presidio but on the ground before the entrance. I saw that they all sat on stools—no throne for the new chief—and that he intended to conduct the discussions openly, before all the people seated on the ground in a great crescent moon around them.

That's better, I thought, making my way towards them. I saw an empty stool waiting and Alonso lifting a hand to beckon me forward. *Much better.*

The Spaniards lived differently from us, in houses made of white-plastered stone, standing four or five times the height a man, roofed in tiles of fired red clay, with iron-braced wooden doors leading onto streets of cobbled stone. Rectangular windows shuttered in brightly painted wood over bars and grills of black iron, and yet more iron above enclosed ledges where people could step out of an upper floor and look down on the street below. It took me a moment to recall the Spanish word. *Balcones,* I said to myself, looking up. There were several of them on the steep street we were climbing on the slopes of the fire mountain the Quechua speakers called Pichincha. We were in the city they had named Quito—a name the conquering Spaniards had kept.

I had been hearing about these things and this place since my childhood, tales told by Nigua men like Hupuka, who had been conscripted to labour for the conquerors but, unlike so many, had managed to make it back to our land without dying in the mines or from the highland sickness. But to hear is one thing. To see is another.

It was morning, the air chill on my coast-reared flesh. The skin of my bared arms showed bumps like those that used to appear when, as a child, I sat and listened to tales of ghosts and malevolent entities, like the Old Deceivers, that haunt the borders of the underworld. When we arose just after dawn, in a village a little more than an hour's walk from Quito where we had spent the night, I had been fascinated to see my own breath issuing from my mouth when I breathed out softly. Yet it did not appear when I blew with more energy or breathed out my nostrils.

I would have liked to stay to study the phenomenon, but the four of us had to change out of the travelling clothes we had slept in and put on the finery we would wear to meet the Quitenos. Chilianduli was resplendent in a shirt of bleached-white cotton whose collar and cuffs were intricately embroidered with multicoloured threads in complex repeating patterns. Ditmar, the Cayapas chief, wore a simpler shirt but had put over it a short cape of soft wool woven through with small feathers of brightly plumed birds. I wore a new shirt Alonso's wives had made for me, well sewn but without ostentation. Hupuka wore his usual clothes, but he had been included in our company because he alone knew the way.

We entered Quito through a gateway guarded by steel-corselleted soldiers armed with halberds. A flow of people—mostly Quechua speakers and mostly women—were passing through, all going into the city, carrying baskets and bundles, some driving sheep or alpacas before them. But when we approached, the soldiers barred our way. It had been agreed that Hupuka would speak for us, but when the guardsmen crossed the staffs of their weapons and one of them gruffly said, "State your business," Hupuka's throat dried up.

So I stepped between him and Chilianduli and said, "We have come to see Don Rodrigo de Ribadeneira. We have a letter for him from his secretary, Fray Alejandro Espinosa." I drew the letter the monk had written from the satchel over my shoulder.

The soldier took the square of folded and sealed paper and scrutinized what was written on it. Alejandro had said not to expect the gate guardians to be able to read, and I doubted this one could, but he had also said that the mention of de Ribadeneira's name would open the way, and it did.

I asked for directions and received instructions to go up this street and turn that way at such and such a plaza, then more turns. We set off but soon found ourselves lost—the city was laid out in an orderly grid, but the deep ravines and stream courses that cut up the slope of the fire mountain meant that traversing it was not a simple matter of lefts and rights. Finally, a Quechua-speaking woman in a woven cloak and felt hat pointed out the big building with the two towers and said in Spanish, "Go there. Ask."

As we got closer to the landmark, the streets filled with more and more people, and we were carried along to a vast open space in which a great number of men and women—Quechua speakers, pale Spaniards and dark ones, and people who seemed to be mixtures of the different types—were walking, talking, standing, sitting, hawking cloth or pots or leather wares or items I could not recognize. I realized that I was seeing more people here and now than the sum total of all the people I had ever seen in my whole life.

The effect was daunting, as was the sheer wealth I saw casually displayed on the persons of those we passed: gold and silver and jewels, to be sure, but also steel and iron and fine cloth and beautifully tanned and dyed leather. I looked up at my companions: Hupuka was bearing up, holding himself together as he led us through the crowds; Chilianduli and Ditmar were more strongly affected, but they were chiefs and they had their dignity to uphold.

Coming down the steps of the building with two towers was an older man dressed in the same kind of simple robe Alejandro wore. I met him at the bottom of the stairs and said, "Sir, can you please direct us to the house of this man?" I showed him the name written on the letter.

He read the name then paused for thought. After a moment he said, "Yes, it is not far, and I am going that way myself. I will guide you."

I thanked him and translated for the others, and we set off. We had only gone a few steps when the Spaniard said, "May I ask from whom is the letter?"

When I told him, he clapped his hands in pleasure. "Is he well? I have not seen him in a long time—in the two years since he left Quito. I heard he had become ill down in the forest. Where is he?"

I assured him Alejandro was well and living near the sea. "He was not ill," I said, "but injured. A blow to the head."

The man's brows drew down. "By the savages?"

"No, by the priest he was helping."

At that, the man stopped and put out a hand to stay us. He looked up and down the crowded street, then leaned down to speak to me softly. "You should not say that to too many people," he said.

"It is the truth," I said. "I, myself, nursed him through the recovery." I did not think it wise to mention the hole I made in Alejandro's skull.

"Then I bless you," the man said, making the Christian sign in the air. "But that was not the tale the priest told upon his return. And in Quito, Father Miguel Cabello Balboa is not a man to offend. Do you understand?"

I assured him I did. He nodded. "Come, then. De Ribadeneira's house is not far from here." After a few steps, he said, "My name is Fray Geronimo. I am the Hospitaller of the Mercedarians." My face must have shown him I did not understand, because he said, "The building where we met. If you have need of anything, come and ask for me." He paused to think. "In fact, come and see me when you can. I would like you to take a letter from me to Fray Alejandro, if you are going back to him."

"We are. I will," I said.

We rounded a couple of corners and came to a strong door set into the wall of a tall house whose shutters were open, revealing barred windows. "This," he said, "is the house of Don Rodrigo. I will knock and speak to the porter on your behalf. Otherwise, you might not be listened to."

"Thank you," I said.

A few moments later, Fray Geronimo was telling a short, squat Spaniard in a greasy leather vest that his master had visitors and they bore a letter from his secretary. The porter nodded and beckoned us to enter. We went into a long space, floored, walled, and roofed in stone, that led to a wider space open to the sky. Walls rose on all sides, with windows whose shutters were open, and in the middle of the space was a structure of stone. Water spouted from its middle. *That must be convenient,* I thought.

The man in the leather vest told us to wait here. There were stone benches to one side, but Chilianduli and Ditmar remained standing, and thus so did Hupuka and I. It was only then that I noticed that Fray Geronimo had come with us into the house.

He saw the question that formed on my face and said, "Two reasons: I wish to hear news of Fray Alejandro, and you may need some help dealing with Don Rodrigo."

We stood and waited. Time passed. I heard voices from several parts of the establishment and edged over to peek around the door the servant had gone through. It led to a another large open space, this one not open to the sky, where I could see men—some of them Quechua speakers—toiling among large bales of wool and cotton cloth. Against the far wall were stacked barrels and wooden crates. To one side, a Spaniard stood behind a tall, narrow table with a slanted top. He used a quill the way Alejandro had when he wrote the letter I carried.

It was all most interesting, and I understood that what we used to consider riches were nothing compared to the wealth a Spaniard could command. I wondered what that might do to the way they saw themselves and the world. And, of course, us.

The porter came down a flight of stairs against the far wall. Behind him came a man I recognized. I went back to where Chilianduli and the others waited. A few moments later, the porter passed through the courtyard—I learned the word later—without looking at us. Then from the door emerged Father Miguel Cabello Balboa. I heard Fray Geronimo say something under his breath in a tongue I didn't understand, the one Alejandro sometimes spoke to himself: *Dicere diaboli et apparebit.*

Cabello gave the monk a brief quizzical glance and strode over to Chilianduli and Ditmar.

"Who are you and what do you want?" he said.

He had not noticed me. Now I stepped forward and said, "We have a letter from Fray Alejandro Espinosa for Don Rodrigo de Ribadeneira." I showed it to him.

He put out a hand. "Give it to me," he said.

"It is for Don Rodrigo de Ribadeneira."

"He is not here at the moment. I am waiting to see him myself. I will give it to him."

The Spaniards might have had a different way of saying no, but Nigua do not. "No," I said. "We will wait, too." I turned then and translated for the others.

I saw anger flash across the priest's face. He opened his mouth to say something then seemed to recall that we were not alone. "Fray Geronimo, what do you know of this?"

"Nothing," said the monk. "I wished to hear news of my friend the Trinitarian. He has been gone a long time." Then he added, "Since he accompanied you on your … mission."

There was something going on between the two of them that had nothing to do with us. Cabello met the monk's stare for a few heartbeats then put whatever it was aside and came back to me. "I have seen you, haven't I? You came to the mass on the beach." His expression darkened as memory came. "You were talking to Fray Alejandro."

"Yes," I said. "We have since become friends."

The priest's eyebrows went up. "Oh, really? Has he taught you your good Spanish?"

"No."

He waited for more, but I did not supply it.

"What is he saying?" Chiliandulı asked me.

"Nothing important," I answered.

"He does not like us."

"No, he doesn't. And he wants the letter." I used the Nigua word for message so Cabello would not know what we were talking about. I still remembered the colours I had seen in him through my guide's eyes. He was not to be trusted.

"It is not for him," the Nigua said. "Ask him when his chief will come."

"The man we are waiting for is not a chief," I said. "He is a man who can bring us to the chief."

Chiliandulı shrugged. "You have said this before. It does not matter. Ask him when the man will come."

I did so, I thought politely, but the priest did not take it well. He said, "I have wasted enough time on this. Give me the letter. I will see that Don Rodrigo gets it."

Among our people, if someone has said no to a request, it is very bad manners to repeat it. I dropped the letter down the collar of my shirt and looked away.

I sensed that things might get difficult, but Fray Geronimo stepped in then. "I could take our visitors to the monastery. They have come a long way and would surely like some rest and refreshment." From the way he said it, I understood that Cabello was being a less than perfect host. "Then, when Don Rodrigo returns, you could send a messenger and they could come back."

Cabello had a small mouth, but now it grew smaller still, and the wrinkles at the sides of his eyes deepened. But whatever he was about to do or say remained undone and unsaid. A fist hammered on the outer door and a voice said, "Open!" in a tone and volume that brooked no delay. A moment later, from the corridor that led to the outside, in walked three men, only one of whom counted for anything.

I had seen Alonso dressed in the garments he called doublet and hose, with buckled shoes on his feet. I had thought them rather fine. Now I saw the same items and knew I was seeing the difference between a slave's garb and a rich man's. Don Rodrigo de Ribadeneira's legs were clad in yellow silk, his torso in a doublet of some material that resembled fine black fur, the sleeves slashed vertically to reveal an under layer of deep-red cloth that actually managed to reflect light. His shoes were elegantly stitched, the buckles made of gold, and on his head he wore a hat like a round cushion studded with round stones that I later learned were pearls—which I'd heard of but had never seen. Over his shoulders was a sleeveless, open-fronted garment of some rich, dark fur, its edges stitched with what must have been more gold spun into a fine thread.

The two men who trailed him also wore better clothes than Alonso's, but not that much better. That would have told me they were underlings even if I hadn't seen the way they kept back and waited to be called.

De Ribadeneira looked at us, at Fray Geronimo, and finally at the priest. "What's all this?" he said.

Cabello was putting together his response when the monk spoke. "They are from Esmeraldas. They bring you a letter from Fray Alejandro."

I saw that de Ribadeneira was a man who could take in information and know immediately what to do with it. "Where is it?" he said, his eyes going from Chiliánduli to Ditmar and back again, dismissing me and Hupuka as inconsequential. But when I stepped forward and held out the folded paper, he took another look at me and I saw him reassess his first impression.

"Thank you," he said. He broke the seal, read the letter quickly, and spoke to Cabello. "What is on de Canaveral's agenda today?"

I could see that the priest's first impulse was to ask why, but he smothered it at birth and said, "He is meeting with a delegation from the street merchants society and another from the mine owners of Potosi."

"So he will have some time before supper?"

"I suppose. Yes." Now the priest asked the question. "Why?"

De Ribadeneira refolded the letter and put it into some inner part of his fur garment. "Because these people have come from Alonso Illescas to see the judge. And I think they should do that as soon as possible." When Cabello just blinked at him, he said, "So you will please go and arrange that, Father. Now."

"But I was waiting to talk to you about—"

"This is more important. Go. Now." De Ribadeneira pointed towards the passageway to the outer door while the expression on his face asked why Cabello was still here.

The priest went, his face carefully frozen, though I expected he would wear a different expression in the street. De Ribadeneira turned back to me and said, "Would you care to make introductions?"

Pedro Venegas de Canaveral was Judge of the Court of Quito. Alejandro had tried to explain how the land was governed, and I had tried to put it into terms that Chilianduli and Ditmar could understand. The best I could do was to explain that the Spaniards did not have war chiefs and peace chiefs. They had one grand chief called the King, far over the water in the land where the Spaniards came from. The King had named a man in Lima to be sub-chief over all the lands of the Quechua speakers, and that man had found it too hard to govern Quito and its lands from so far away, so he had appointed more sub-chiefs, called judges, to rule in his name. And this was the chief of all those judges.

"The important thing," I reminded the Nigua and Cayapas chiefs as we waited for Canaveral to enter the room where we had been asked to wait—at least it was a room, not a courtyard—"is that he can be war chief or peace chief, whichever he decides is best."

"It is a strange way to organize things," said Ditmar, looking around at the polished sheets of wood that covered the walls, the remarkably lifelike paintings that adorned them, and the well-made furnishings and fittings, including plush-seated chairs and lamps of glass and shining metal. "Still," he continued after making his survey, "we have to admit it works for them."

A door opened, and in walked a man whose fine garments and proud bearing immediately identified him as the wielder of power. Behind him, in the midst of whispering some remark into the judge's ear, came the priest Cabello, followed by Don Rodrigo and a man in doublet and hose of simple black cloth whose demeanour said he was trying not to be noticed. This man went to a tall slanted table like the one I had seen in the de Ribadeneira warehouse, though of more polished wood. He took up a quill and stood ready to write.

De Ribadeneira said, "Your Excellency, these are"—he did his best to pronounce Chilianduli's and Ditmar's names—"the envoys of the *cimarrones* of Esmeraldas." When I had translated this into Nigua, he added, "And their translator and guide."

From his expression, I concluded that Canaveral was not unused to seeing people of the lands the Quechua-speaking kings had ruled. But he was not used to meeting men like Chilianduli and Ditmar, who looked him in the eye in a way that said they were willing to entertain the notion that he was their equal. Cabello whispered something else I could not hear but the judge could. His mouth turned down at the corners, and he folded his arms across his chest.

"What is your purpose here?" Canaveral said.

It had been agreed that Chilianduli would speak. He began to now, in Nigua fashion. That is, he started with his personal history, described his ancestry, and touched upon some of the notable deeds of its more illustrious members. Then he told of his own exploits and how they had won him the rank of headman of the big nose clan and war chief of the Nigua when Pidi was peace chief.

Canaveral interrupted my translation to ask, "Did he say 'big noses'?"

"Yes, sir, he did. It is an important clan."

The judge made an untranslatable sound and, with a peremptory gesture that needed no translation, said, "Tell him to continue."

Chilianduli made his own sound then, deep in his large chest. "Agreed," I told him. "He does not have good manners, but we still need to do this."

The Nigua headman decided to overlook the man's condescension and continued to speak. He shortened his remarks, leaving out the history of the Nigua and Cayapas peoples since the beginning of the world and concentrating on the events since the Pizarros had arrived on our shores and begun forcing our men into servitude. It did not take him as long as it might have to get to the point when the Africans arrived, but he noticed the judge's tapping of his fingers against his elbow.

Chilianduli stopped talking. Canaveral looked from him to me, and when no more words were forthcoming, he asked me, "Is that all? Has he come all this way to give me a history lesson?"

"No, Your Excellency," I said, having noted the term of respect though it was clearly not merited. "Those were ... the normal preliminary remarks. I will now state the message we have been asked to bring."

He interrupted again. "Whose message?"

"That of the people of Esmeraldas."

Cabello whispered something. Canaveral nodded and said, "You mean of the *cimarrones* who have enslaved you."

"What is he saying?" Chilianduli wanted to know.

I was feeling a little beset from both sides and spoke more bluntly than diplomatically. "Do these men look to you like slaves?"

Canaveral might have taken argument from a de Ribadeneira. He was not going to take it from a half-sized peculiarity in a cotton shirt. His face tightened further than it already was, and over his shoulder I saw the smallest of smiles in the corners of Cabello's lips. "Speak your message," the judge said.

I did so. I reminded him that the priest at his ear had brought an offer of amnesty and manumission for the fugitive Africans and of a governorship for Alonso Illescas if we assisted in establishing a port near the mouth of the Esmeraldas River. "We are still willing to talk about that if you are. But you must stop sending soldiers against us."

"Is that it?" the judge said.

"It is."

"We will take it under advisement." He turned towards the man with the quill. "See that they have some gifts: knives, hatchets, hats, whatever's usual." To me he said, "Go with God," which I knew was the Spaniard way of saying one of us was leaving. It turned out to be him and the priest.

De Ribadeneira remained behind as Cabello and Canaveral left the room, the priest closing the door behind them and now making no attempt to hide the smile on his lips, even when de Ribadeneira turned his way.

"Not so good," de Ribadeneira said, "but I will speak for you."

Chilianduli said several things, then, and Ditmar added his heartfelt concurrence. I did not want to translate, but de Ribadeneira asked, so I summarized. "You can send soldiers. Those that disease does not kill, be assured we will."

The merchant sighed. "Eventually," he said, "the lesson will be learned." He put his hands together in a way that said we were moving on. "Come with me. You can stay the night at my house."

"I have heard you sleep on platforms high above the floor," I said.

"Not too high," he said, "but we will make you comfortable." To the little man in black, he said, "Bring the gifts to my house in the morning."

He turned to lead the way out, but Fray Geronimo stepped into his way and said, "Don Rodrigo, I would be remiss if I did not inquire into the state of our visitors' souls. Perhaps you would let me take them to the monastery for a little while and bring them to your house in time for the evening meal?"

The merchant gave him a peculiar look but said, "Of course, Brother." He smiled at me. "That will give us time to saw the legs off the beds."

When we were out in the street, de Ribadeneira went off in one direction and we went in another. "Saw the legs off?" I said to the monk.

"That was humour," he answered. "The beds are only this high." He stooped to put his hand at his knee. "You need not fear broken bones." He looked at de Ribadeneira disappearing into the distance and said, "And I will have to confess a lie and do penance. It is not the state of your souls that I wish to inquire into but the condition of my friend Fray Alejandro."

"He is well," I said, "and I think happy. He is well regarded by the people, and his counsel is listened to."

"That is good to hear. He struck me as a young man who has been searching for the place where God wishes him to be."

"I cannot speak for your god, but I think he has found what he was looking for."

Fray Geronimo said something in a language I did not know and made the crossing gesture on his head and torso. "Thank you for telling me. When you see him, please give him my blessing."

"I will," I said, "but do I have to do the magical motion?" I sketched the gesture in the air.

"No," he said, and I saw that I had amused him. "Though it will do you no harm."

"It's just that I was afraid it might not be effective if I did it."

"I think," said the Spaniard, "that most everything you do is effective."

Chilianduli broke in. "What are you talking about?"

"Spirit matters," I said.

"Oh." He waved away any participation, and we went on.

"There are other things to speak of," the monk said, "but we will wait until the only ears to hear are ours."

The monastery was much larger than de Ribadeneira's house or that of the judge but less impressive in its decor. The walls were plain—Fray Geronimo explained what plaster was, which I found interesting but not practical for our own dwellings—and the furniture was simply made. He led us to a room with an unshuttered window made of small squares of glass, which I'd heard about but hadn't seen. It let in light but kept out sound and biting insects. *Very useful,* I thought.

We sat on benches, and he had another monk bring us Spanish beer that he poured from a pitcher into wooden cups. Chiliandulі and Ditmar thought well of the drink. It seemed a little strong to me.

When the other monk had left and closed the door, Fray Geronimo said, "Here is what you need to know. Canaveral is allowing another military *entrada* against you. It is being put together now."

I translated this for the others. Chilianduli's face turned to stone, and he said, "We will kill them where we find them. They will not find us."

"I agree, it is foolish," the monk said when I had translated. "Don Rodrigo has spoken against it, but he is hampered by the fact that the man chosen to lead it is Lopez de Zuniga, who is of Don Rodrigo's wife's family."

"Ah," I said. "So women *do* have influence among you."

"Some women," he said. "This one certainly does."

Chilianduli wanted to hear more. The monk said, "There is talk about enlisting a hundred soldiers."

"That is a lot of mouths to feed," Chilianduli said. "Your people are not very good at finding food in the forest."

Fray Geronimo spread his hands. "The *entrada* is being planned and conducted by men who have not been in your forest."

I translated this for the two chiefs. "What do you wish to say?" Chilianduli said.

The monk said, "You will withdraw into the forest and make it hard for them to find you."

The Nigua nodded. "Yes. And we will ambush them and set traps."

"I ask you not to do that," Geronimo said.

I sensed this was as clever a man as de Ribadeneira, though he lived much more simply. "Why?" I said.

"Because if you do not kill any of them, it will be easier to make peace after the *entrada* fails and they come straggling home."

Chilianduli looked at Ditmar and at me. I said, "People who come into our land from the high country have the wrong spirits. They often get sick and die."

Chilianduli said nothing for a few moments, thinking. Then he asked for more of the beer and drank off a second cup. "Will they bring any of this with them?" he said.

"Probably."

The Nigua belched. "Good," he said and held out his cup again.

The next morning, having survived elevated beds and carrying bags of sturdy cloth containing the gifts from the judge, we set off for home. In my shirt I carried another letter, this one from Fray Geronimo and addressed to Alejandro. By the time we had descended far enough to encounter the highland forest, we were certain that two Quechua speakers were following us.

"Shall we kill them?" Chilianduli said.

"Not in their own land," I said. "It would make trouble for us."

He grunted. "Yes," he said. "Perhaps that is what they want us to do."

Hupuka said he knew a path he could lead us along that had a place where we could divert without being noticed and leave our trackers behind. We followed where he led, and by late afternoon we were on our own once more.

When it was safe to talk again, Chilianduli said, "They are strange people, these Spaniards. They keep doing the same thing even when it does not work."

"They are not used to failure," I said. "Look what they did to the Quechua speakers."

"That is just what I mean," said the clan chief. "When we saw what they did to them, we made sure we did not let them do the same to us."

I thought about it for a while. Then I said, "It may have something to do with the three-faced spirit they believe in. They think it is all-powerful, and so they expect it to bring them victory."

"If I had a spirit that could not do what it said it could," said Chilianduli, "I would find a new spirit. That's just common sense."

I agreed it was. "They are a puzzle, these Spaniards. But if we kill enough of them, eventually they'll have to leave us alone."

*T*WENTY

ALEJANDRO DE ESPINOSA

"What good did they think horses would do them?" Alonso said. He was surveying the wreckage of the fort the Spaniards had rebuilt near the mouth of the Esmeraldas River. Fray Alejandro supposed the chief was only musing to himself, but he answered with the thought that came to mind.

"Everywhere they have fought the natives, men on horseback have been invincible."

Alonso gestured to the thickly wooded banks of the river, upstream from where the invaders had cleared a killing ground around the log fort. "But it's a forest. You can't see ten feet into it on either side of the trail, and sometimes you can't see that far in front of you."

He turned and pointed the other way, to where the river widened as it neared the sea. "And that's a mangrove swamp."

"I suppose horses give them confidence," the monk said. "Perhaps they also helped keep the natives from the highlands in line. After all, those poor souls have experienced a cavalry charge, or their relatives have."

The Spaniards had sent a hundred soldiers down from Quito along with two or three hundred Quechua speakers from the uplands. Some had come on foot and in wide canoes. The horses had come by ship, lowered into the water on canvas slings swaying from a yardarm then towed to shore by boats until they came up, terrified and shaking, onto the mud flats.

Poquito and Pahta had watched the operation and reported back, shaking their heads at the folly. When the first soldiers and highlanders had come down the river, the word had gone out to the Cayapas to join the Niguas at the little *palenques* scattered throughout the impenetrable forest. By the time the Spanish fort had been built and stocked with men and materials, there was no one within a day's walk of the site except for the two scouts.

And then the weeks had turned into months. The Spaniards and their bearers had struggled into the forest, carrying the weight of their weapons and armour and supplies. It was an alien environment, a green gloom, often with sight lines shorter than a man could throw a rock, cut across with small streams and occasional ravines choked with vegetation.

Under their steel and padded jerkins, the soldiers sweated. The rain came, sometimes in steady drips from the canopy above, sometimes in drenching torrents that broke through the green roof and reduced visibility to less than an arm's length. When they tried to ride horses along the narrow trails, the animals slipped on the muddy slopes, caroming into each other, breaking their legs in the ravines.

"Ridiculous," Alonso said. They were crossing the open ground. Seventeen crosses marked the graves: fourteen Spaniards had died of coastal fever; three more were killed in the mutiny that finally ended the *entrada*. No one knew how many of the Quechua speakers had died. Though they were nominally Christian, their remains were dumped in a common grave.

Alejandro paused to offer a brief prayer for the souls of the dead. When he was finished, he followed after the chief and the mixed party of Africans, Nigua, and Cayapas who had come to see what might be salvaged from the abandoned fort. He passed through the gap where the Spaniards had torn the gates from their pillars. They had tried to burn parts of the stockade, but it was the rainy season, and the wood had been too wet to stay lit.

Juanito the ironsmith saw what he was looking for and made his way across the compound. The invaders had built a forge using fire-bricks they had hauled down from Quito. Someone had made a half-hearted effort to break it up, but much of what remained could be salvaged.

There were also ingots and scraps of iron, some broken tools and weapons that could be mended, and—so the smith said—what had once been a nicely balanced hammer that needed only a new handle to be put back to work.

The rest of the foraging party found other treasures to take away. In a corner of a now-roofless building that had housed the expedition's commissariat, Alejandro found a leather folder that contained thirty sheets of good paper, and in a cupboard was a half-filled bottle of India ink. He tucked the folder into his robe against the rain that was threatening to come in from the sea and kept the bottle firmly in his hand. He would need it to fulfil the next phase of Alonso's plan.

They were making a heap of their finds in the middle of the compound. One of the Cayapas had found a jug that sloshed when he shook it, but Gonzalo de Avila shouted a warning when the man lifted it to his lips: the Spaniards could be spiteful in defeat and might leave poisoned drink behind.

In the open-fronted stables, Alonso found a spur with a broken strap. He held it up and shook his head. "Horses," he said. "What were they thinking?"

It took a while to bring everyone back to the village and get the Cayapas resettled in their own places along the Esmeraldas. When all was again as it should be and people were feeling at peace again, Alonso called a meeting of the grand council that now included the Cayapas headmen as well as the Niguas and Africans. It was a dry day, and they all sat on stools in front of the big house—it was no longer called the presidio—while the rest of the Nigua and Africans, along with a few Cayapas, sat on the ground around them.

"The question is," Alonso said, to open the discussion, "what do they want?"

"A port," Alejandro said. "Don Rodrigo and the Quito merchants don't want to have to send and receive everything by mule train through Guayaquil. It costs them money." He smiled. "They like money."

"Yes, they want a port," Alonso said. "What else?"

Alejandro spoke again. "They want all of you to become Christians."

Now it was Expectation who spoke. "Why? What business is it of theirs?"

"We've been through this before," Alonso said. "It is how they think. But," he said, and here he raised a placating hand to the monk, "they will be satisfied if we just do the things that Christians are expected to do: the prayers, the masses, not eating meat on a Friday."

"What is a Friday? How often does it come?" the healer said.

"Every seven days."

She shrugged. "That's not so bad. We don't eat meat every day anyway."

"All right," said Alonso. "A port and Christianity. What else?"

"People," said Hupuka. He was not one of the council, but he spoke from the front of the crowd. "They want people to carry things and tend fields and animals and, worst of all, go down into the mines and die."

"Yes," said Alonso. "They want workers. It's how their soldiers get wealthy, making others work for them."

"We will not do it," said Chiliandulì. "Those they took, in my father's time, most of them never came back."

Alonso said, "We are not talking yet about what we will or will not do. We are still trying to get clear in our minds the situation we have to deal with. So, what else do they want?"

Ditmar, the Cayapas chief, spoke. "Gold. They think there is gold in the river. They've seen the gold we got from the tombs of the people who lived here before we came down from the high country to get away from the Quechua speakers. They think it came from here, because we are here and we have it. We do not know where the old people got it from. Maybe by trading sea shells to the highland people."

Alejandro rubbed the back of his head where the hole had healed but left a permanent indentation. "Gold, for certain," he said. "And I remember Father Cabello talking about emerald mines."

Ditmar laughed. "There are no emerald mines. We told them there were some upriver so they would go away and leave us alone. They never found any, but they still believe the emeralds are there. They even named the river after them."

"Anything else?" Alonso said. When no one said anything else, he said, "All right, what do they have that we want?"

"The beer is good," Chiliandulі said. People laughed.

"Steel," Juanito said, "or iron if we can't get steel."

"We've always traded for cloth," one of the old women said, plucking at her cotton shift."

Expectation spoke. "To be left alone."

"I don't think we can get that," Alonso said. "But we can set the terms for how they deal with us." He waited for more suggestions. Then he said, "So they want a lot from us, but we don't need much from them."

Alejandro said, "That is not a bad position to be in. But if we give them the port, they're going to bring soldiers, and the soldiers are going to want to steal people to work for them—no matter what the Quito merchants say."

There were murmurs and mumbles in the crowd. Alonso waited until they died down and said, "There is a way we could give them people."

Now the sounds from the crowd intensified: "No!" "Not my man!" "They never come back!"

Alonso raised a hand and the protests subsided. "I wasn't thinking," he said, "of giving them any of our people."

Chiliandulі voiced the question. "Then who?"

Alonso looked above the heads of the people, off to the south. Many heads turned that way but saw only the stockade and the forest beyond. But when they turned back to the chief, he said, "The Campazes."

"The head-breakers?" Chiliandulі said. "They are hard. I have fought them."

"So have I," Alonso said. "It will be different with *arcabuzes,* iron spears and halberds, iron on our bodies and heads."

Alejandro said, "I am not a fighter, but Gonzalo and I went with Carranza's *entrada* against the Campazes. They had all those things you listed. It was still a disaster."

Alonso turned to the Portuguese soldier. "What do you say, Gonzalo?"

Avila thought before answering. "Carranza fought the way Spaniards fight. The Campazes fought the way the Campazes fight." He pulled his nose thoughtfully. "If we fought the Campazes the way the Campazes fight, but with better weapons …" He spread his hands and nodded his head. "Maybe so."

Alonso turned to Ditmar and Chilianduli. "What do you think?"

Chilianduli said, "They watch Guayaquil. When their scouts see boats assembling in the port, they pull back into the forest and set their traps." He paused, thinking it through. "After Anton led the raid south, they sent scouts to watch us. We caught them and killed them, but we never went south again. After a while, they stopped sending scouts. They may have heard that our war chief is dead."

Ditmar added a thought. "We could send scouts. If our scouts were not seen …"

There were more sounds in the crowd now, but the tone was no longer fearful. The Campazes had broken a lot of Nigua heads, and Anton's raid had not even come close to evening the score.

Hupuka spoke. "Last time, I had a long spear with a steel point. I said to a Campaze warrior, 'Come, let us dance.' But I danced longer than he did."

There was more laughter. One of the younger Nigua men got up and did a few steps of a comical dance.

"So, are we agreed?" Alonso said. "Do we tell them they can have their port, we will not eat meat on Fridays and they can send priests to say mass, and we will deliver them Campazes to work for them?"

It was agreed. Alonso said he would send the judges in Quito a letter. Alejandro would help write it.

"And I had better deliver it, too," the monk said. "They will pay more attention to me than they did to Ditmar and Chilianduli."

"Perhaps I should take it," Avila said. "I am just another vagabond soldier. You, my friend, have made an enemy up there."

Alejandro said, "I do not fear Father Cabello. Don Rodrigo will see to my safety. And if he cannot manage it, God will."

Avila said, "My experience with God is that sometimes He needs help."

In the end, it was decided that Alejandro would take the letter, but first Avila would go to Quito to see how the land lay. He would be just another unemployed soldier drinking in a tavern or lounging in a plaza, hearing the gossip and weighing the mood of the place.

Before he left, Alejandro begged him to visit Fray Geronimo at the Mercedarian monastery and tell the hospitaller that the young

Trinitarian was safe and well. Expectation was close by when Alejandro made the request—she and the monk now regularly spent time together, comparing and contrasting spiritual practices. Alejandro was beginning to wonder if the spirits with which the Nigua and Cayapas routinely dealt were not fallen angels in thrall to the Prince of Darkness but a separate order of spiritual being afforded to these people by a merciful God until they could eventually be brought the true revelation of the Resurrection.

When Expectation heard Alejandro ask Avila to seek out Fray Geronimo, she said, "He was a good help to us when Ditmar and Chiliandul went to Quito. His advice not to kill the soldiers was wise."

"Not all Spaniards are hungry for gold and workers," Alejandro said. "Some want only what is best for all."

"Like you?" the healer said.

"I hope so."

"And some want only what is best for them," Avila said. "Like Father Cabello."

"I have prayed for him," the monk said.

The soldier laughed. "I doubt he has prayed for you. Though if he ever takes hold of you, you'll need all the prayers you can get."

With that, and with Alejandro's blessing, the Portuguese settled the straps of his pack squarely on his shoulders and set off with Hupuka to show him the way beyond the headwaters of the river. Alejandro said a brief prayer for him.

"He will come back," Expectation said. "My guide has shown it to me. Years from now, he is still among us."

The original plan to marry African men to Nigua women and African women to Nigua men had created a rising generation of mixed bloods. The Spaniards called them *mulattos,* but the young people themselves referred to themselves by a native word: *zambaigo,* which had lately been shortened to *zambo.* The adults had picked up the term from their children, and now it was common for everyone of all ages to refer to themselves as the Zambo people. Even Avila and Alejandro could say 'we Zambos' without feeling self-conscious and without anyone correcting them.

"It has worked," Alonso said, "and we should keep on doing it." The matter had come up during a council discussion of what to do with the occasional black fugitives who found their way into the forest either after a shipwreck or after fleeing servitude up in the high country or down at Guayaquil. They were taken in and quickly married to Nigua or Cayapas of the opposite sex.

"It is because," Expectation said, "you Africans have not just gained spouses. You have married into families, and the families are connected to clans. And we all help each other."

The only time an issue arose out of the rule was the day a slave couple were brought in by a hunting party who found them splashing their way downriver in a derelict boat that had no paddles. But it turned out that the man and woman had been arbitrarily joined together by their Spanish owner and both were happy to be paired off with new spouses.

When Alejandro and the healer spoke together, the monk said the fact that many Zambos had three or four wives would be a problem for the Church. "One man, one woman. That is the rule."

Expectation peered around the hut the monk had been given. "And where is your woman?"

"Monks and priests do not marry. We devote ourselves to our vocations."

"So there are exceptions to the rule?"

Alejandro moved his head from side to side, like a man sizing up a new thought. "You could say that, I suppose."

The hermaphrodite poured them a little more corn beer. "Then we will just have to be another exception," she said. "If, that is, they want their port and all those Campaze workers."

Gonzalo d'Avila was gone several weeks. When he came back, Alonso called a meeting of the council. He told the Portuguese to rest and wait until the farther-flung councillors could gather.

"Don't you want me to tell you first?" Avila said.

"I want to know," the chief said, "but it is better for us all to hear the news together. We need to avoid divisions."

Avila shrugged and went to his hut, where his wives had begun preparing food and beer the moment they'd heard that he was back. After hugging his children and kissing each one in turn, he sent the oldest to find Alejandro. The monk was somewhere out in the gardens, where he helped with the crops but told tales from scripture during the rest times. The Nigua loved tales, and all of his were new. Even Expectation would sit and listen. Sometimes she asked questions afterward.

Alejandro came running and smiled when he saw his friend tired but in good condition. He hiked up his robe and sat on the stool Avila offered, taking a cup of corn beer from the younger wife. "It is good to see you safe," he said. "You were gone longer than I thought you would be."

"It is a complicated situation up there," Avila said. "It took me a while to make sense of it all."

"Have you told Alonso?"

The soldier laughed. "He wouldn't let me."

When Avila explained why not, Alejandro said, "Then don't tell me. I'll wait, too."

But his friend's face grew serious. "There's something I will tell you. Cabello's influence has grown, and he has a particular dislike of a certain Trinitarian monk."

Alejandro threw up both hands and shrugged. "He has no authority over me."

"He has the ear of the Bishop of Quito."

"The Bishop is another matter," Alejandro agreed. "But Don Rodrigo is not without influence."

"Cabello also has the ear of Judge Canaveral."

"That's quite a collection of ears for one priest," the monk said.

Avila put down his cup and leaned forward, his face a map of concern. "I don't think you should go up there. Write the letter, but let someone else carry it."

Alejandro shook his head. "There are things I must say to Don Rodrigo that cannot be put in the letter to the court—things that will stir him to action."

"Then write him a separate letter."

"No. That would be the kind of letter I wouldn't want intercepted. Neither would Don Rodrigo."

Avila wore the look of a soldier who knows he is losing a fight. "I worry about you," he said.

"God has shown me to this place and put my work before me," the monk said. "He will not let anyone keep me from its completion. Not even a priest who has the ear of the Bishop of Quito."

"I think," Avila said, "it has to be a combination of the carrot and the stick. Offer them something they very much want, but let them know things could go badly if we don't get what we want."

"The important thing is to get the tone right," Alonso said. "We cannot come across as supplicants. It is a partnership we are offering, a partnership of equals."

Chilianduli said, "I remember that chief, Canaveral. He will not see us as equals."

"Then he must be brought to a new understanding," said Alejandro. "They have tried their way over and over again, and it has always failed. Now they must learn a new way."

Alonso nodded. "Our way," he said. "What have we got so far?"

Alejandro read from the paper on which he had been writing, while the rest of the subcommittee sat on their stools and listened. He had to raise his voice against the sound of the rain striking the layers of interwoven palm branches that roofed the big house.

"I'll skip the opening and summarize," he said. "We promise to assist in establishing a port at the mouth of the river, to offer aid to shipwrecked travellers — "

"As we have done before," Alonso said.

The monk added a few words above the line. "All right. And we undertake to reduce hundreds of Campazes 'to the service of God and His Majesty'."

"Meaning," said Avila, "that God will get their souls and His Majesty's officials will get their labour, which they will dole out in batches to their favourites."

Alejandro looked at him. "That does not sound very diplomatic," he said.

"Better leave it out, then," said Avila.

Alonso said, "But make it clear that we do not want them sending settlers. Especially not soldiers."

Alejandro made a note. "We should say why, I think. Put them on the back foot."

"Put down this," Alonso said. "'I am fearful because your captains have always broken their word to us.'"

"Good," Avila said. "Put the blame on the soldiers, not the authorities who commissioned the *entrada*."

"But they'll know we mean them," Alonso said.

"Oh, certainly. But the bastards all like to pretend they're honourable men. Now give them some of the stick."

"How is this?" Alejandro said, jotting down a few words. "'We would no longer see it as incumbent on us to do everything possible to procure and pacify the natives of this province.'"

Avila said, "Try to work in the term 'smoothing of the land'. I hear the Bishop of Quito prefers that to 'conquest'."

Alonso smiled. "They're getting very civilized up there, aren't they?"

"Oh, yes," the Portuguese said. "Although when they smile at you, you're not supposed to notice how long and sharp their teeth are."

"What else?" Alejandro said, his quill poised.

"The usual about our desire to be brought into conformity with the rites of the Church that our souls may be saved."

"Though not the marriage rites," said Avila.

"We won't discuss that," said the monk. "But I think we should ask them to send us a Mercedarian friar to instruct converts. It is not really my … speciality."

"All right," said Alonso, "but no priests. And especially not that Cabello."

The monastery's porter was a Quechua speaker novice. He showed Alejandro to a small room where three of the walls were lined with a continuous bench. Hupuka, who had been the Trinitarian's guide up the river and trails, went off to an inn in another quarter of Quito where visiting natives were accommodated.

Several minutes went by. A stern-faced monk Alejandro did not know put his head in the open door, studied the visitor for a moment, gave him a perfunctory, "Good day, Brother," and left. A short time later, another member of the cloister did the same, though this one dispensed with the greeting. More time passed before Fray Geronimo appeared, and Alejandro stood to greet him.

"Have you spoken to anyone?" the hospitaller said, after they had embraced.

"No, why?"

"Yours is a name to conjure with in Quito, that's why. Word has spread that you undermined Captain Zuniga's *entrada* and advised the natives to resist."

Alejandro's face showed his surprise. "There was no resistance. The people just went into the forest and hid until the soldiers got tired of dying of fever and mutinied. Certainly, no one needed my advice for that. After so many failed *entradas*, the Zambos are experts at the tactic."

"Zambos?" the older man said.

"It's what they call themselves now."

"Well, Don Canaveral is calling them 'savage sons of Satan', and his opinion is dominant."

Alejandro sighed. "I had hoped the merchants would by now have been able to convince the *Audiencia* that conquest must give way to diplomacy."

"Eventually," Geronimo said, "it must. But soldiers still outrank merchants in the eyes of the judges, and the captains cannot believe that what has worked so well in every other part of the New World will not work in Esmeraldas."

His face took on a worried cast. "Then there is Father Cabello. He has laboured very hard to make himself agreeable to the Bishop, and the Bishop is even more listened to than the soldiers."

Alejandro drew the carefully folded letter from the leather wallet attached to his belt. "So this is wasted?" he said. He briefly described its contents.

"At the moment, yes. Give it to me, and I will see it gets to Don Rodrigo."

Again Alejandro was surprised. "It is addressed to the *Audiencia*. I thought to deliver it myself in the morning."

"To the *Audiencia*?" Geronimo said. "If you go in the door, you can expect to come out in chains."

The Trinitarian blinked, too taken aback to form any other response.

The Mercedarian took him by the arm. "Cabello has talked the Bishop into laying charges against you."

"Charges? What charges?"

"Treason, apostasy. For all I know, they're accusing you of simony and dancing with the Devil." He looked about. "You're not safe here, probably not even at Don Rodrigo's."

He took the letter from the young monk's nerveless grasp and said, "We need to get you out of here, out of the city, before Cabello learns you are here. He has little helpers even among my brethren."

Alejandro said, "Two of them looked in on me while I was waiting for you."

"Describe them."

Alejandro did so, at which Geronimo tucked the letter down into the neck of his habit. "Then you have to go now. Right now."

"The man who showed me the way has gone off to an inn. We agreed he would come by tomorrow morning."

The older man shook his head. "No time for that. Find your way to the gate, go down the road towards Riobamba, and spend the night in a field. When your guide comes, I will tell him to look for you."

"I can't believe this is real," Alejandro said. "I did nothing to earn Father Cabello's enmity."

"You stood between him and what he considers his destiny," Geronimo said. "That was more than enough."

As he spoke, he drew the younger man out of the room, along a warren of corridors, and through colonnaded courtyards, finally bringing him to a wall with a small, barred door. The Mercedarian lifted the thick, squared timber and looked out into a narrow alley, unpaved and lined with high, blank walls.

"That way," he said. "Don't go through the grand plaza. If they're coming from the Bishop's palace or the presidio, that's the way they'll come. Go by narrow ways to the south gate and get as far away as you can before nightfall."

He looked again, saw the alley was empty, and said, "And don't talk to anyone."

With that, he pushed Alejandro through the small portal—the young man had to duck to clear the lintel—and with a final blessing and a consignment to God's keeping, shut the door. Alejandro heard the bar fall back into place.

It was well past noon and the passage was in shadow, only a bright strip of blue sky high above. The Trinitarian set off in the direction Geronimo had indicated, head bowed, hands joined in the robe's sleeves, the image of a religious contemplating as he walked. He came to another alley, estimated that it trended towards the south, and turned into it.

A few minutes later, he came to a wider street, its surface cobbled, and passed a few doors, some of them wide enough to admit a cart. He realized he was in a back road that brought deliveries to houses or businesses that fronted on a higher-status thoroughfare. After a while, the road turned and angled downward; looking ahead, Alejandro could see a wooden bridge that crossed one of the ravines that ran down the mountain on whose lower slopes Quito was built.

Just across the bridge, the backstreet connected to a wider avenue lined by houses with iron-barred windows and ornately carved doors. The monk recognized the place from his time in de Ribadeneira's service. Two more turnings would bring the south gate in sight. Head still bowed, sweating hands still folded in his sleeves, he hurried on.

There were some pedestrians here, and a man on a horse, but none of them paid him any heed. He turned a corner. A little ways on, he negotiated another, and there it was: the gate, not yet closed against the sudden night that the lowering sun would soon bring. He saw guards with swords and halberds, but no more than the usual number, and their attention was turned to the outside world.

He did not cross directly to the gate but went instead to the city wall and followed it towards the portal. That way, the guards would not see him until he was right upon them. With any luck, he would slip past them without a challenge and be gone down the road towards Riobamba.

He deliberately slowed his pace; a hastening monk might be an unusual sight. Ten paces to the gate, then five, then two, then he was turning into the gateway, brushing past the guards, and out into the space beyond the wall.

He lifted his head to scan the road ahead. A hand took a strong grip on his arm, just below the elbow. "Stop there, Brother," said a voice used to being obeyed.

There were three of them: two soldiers in breastplates and morions and a man in the clothes of a notary, the badge of the *Audiencia* on a chain around his neck. They had been waiting outside the wall, and now the second soldier came up on Alejandro's other side and took an equally uncompromising grip.

The notary came around to peer into the monk's face. "Fray Alejandro Espinosa?" he said, in a voice as dry as parchment.

The idea flashed through Alejandro's mind to deny his name, as Patya had denied his Saviour. Then he put aside cowardice, secure in his faith that God still had plans for him. "I am," he said.

The cell was not quite a dungeon, but the *Audiencia*'s jail was barely a step above. Alejandro had a rough wooden bed, a straw pallet, and a pot in the corner. Fortunately, the pot had a lid.

They fed him, bread and beans and plain water, then left him for the night. In the morning, there was some kind of porridge with a lump of lard in it. He said his prayers and sat on the bed until the steady movement of a shaft of light from the small, high window told him noon had come and gone. No one brought him a midday meal.

He prayed again. After that, he thought the lack of distraction might mean this was a good time to practise the meditation techniques he had been learning from Expectation. He sat cross-legged in the bed, crossed himself, and began the process of controlling his breathing and stilling his mind. He was in the early stages of clarity when the chain that held the door shut on its outer side rattled.

Alejandro opened his eyes and looked towards the entrance as the door swung inward. He was still within the placid state when he recognized the black-clad man in the doorway.

"Father Cabello," he said.

"Stand up!" said the priest.

Alejandro did so, but without the fearful humility the priest must have been seeking. As he brought his gaze up to meet the other man's, a stinging slap to his face broke his peaceful state of mind. The blow took him by surprise, and he saw that his shock brought satisfaction to Cabello.

"Now, we'll get somewhere," the man in black said. He pushed the monk backwards so the bed caught the back of his knees. Alejandro was sitting again, and Cabello loomed over him, his hand raised for another slap.

"Are you a *converso*?" the priest said. "Speak the truth!"

"I was born into the faith."

Cabello made a contemptuous sound. "But were your parents?"

"They are good Catholics."

The hard hand swung again, struck the same cheek, and this time the pain was worse. "Were they born so?" When Alejandro did not answer, Cabello nodded in triumphant confirmation. "I thought so. What are they, Jews? Not Mohammedans—you're too fair to be a Moor."

"My father's father was a Jew," Alejandro said.

"And so was your father, and so are you!" Another slap brought involuntary tears to the monk's eyes. "If I have you stripped, I will see the truth of it!"

"I am not circumcised. I am a good Catholic."

"Liar!" Cabello raised his hand again and laughed when Alejandro could not keep from flinching. "I have worked you out, Jew!" he said. "I wondered why a Trinitarian should come to Quito—"

"God called me here."

That earned another slap. "Silence! The Trinitarians have no house here, nor in all the New World. You came without the authority of your order because the Holy Office had smelled out your iniquity. You fled before they could question you!"

It was partly true. The Inquisition had been taking a particular interest in the Trinitarians that year. The order was popular with *conversos*. Alejandro knew some of his brethren had been questioned, imprisoned, even tortured—especially, as was always the case with the Holy Office, if they came from *converso* families that had wealth that could be extorted.

Alejandro's grandfather had been a lawyer at the court of Ferdinand and Isabella and had invested in the first plantations on Hispaniola.

He had converted to keep his rank and his wealth, and, because he was useful to them, the King and Queen had kept him in his position.

But times had changed. Alejandro had feared the Inquisition, but mostly he had wanted not to be caught up in its tedious bureaucracy. God had been calling him to cross the ocean, and he had hurried to answer.

There was no point explaining this to Father Cabello. The priest was subject to another calling altogether. Now, with cold glee, he was doing the explaining: laying out what would happen next.

"The Bishop has brought charges against you. You will be tried by an ecclesiastical court." At Alejandro's frown, he barked a humourless laugh. "Yes, that's right, there is no one from your order to take part in the proceedings. So you won't be tried here, nor even in Lima. You're going to Madrid. In chains."

Alejandro's voice was soft. He was speaking to himself. "No."

Cabello heard him. "You defy our Holy Mother Church?" Another slap, but Alejandro scarcely noticed it. "Jew pig! For you, it will be an *auto-da-fé.* I wish I could be there to see it, to smell your charring flesh, to hear you scream." He straightened the sleeve of the arm that had done the slapping. "But my duty is here. Still, I will send a letter asking someone to write me a description."

Alejandro looked up at him. "God will not let me be diverted from my task," he said. He spoke as if mentioning an obvious truth and did not react when the assertion earned him another slap. "Nonetheless, He will not."

Did a tiny doubt cross Cabello's face? If so, it was extinguished by a grimace of renewed anger. The muscles in the priest's jaw bulged as he delivered a final slap. Then he spat on the monk and left the cell.

Alejandro wiped the spittle from his cheek. For a moment, no longer than Cabello had spent in his uncertainty, the thought came that perhaps he had been mistaken about his vocation. Then he remembered the people he lived among, the sense of belonging, of being where he ought to be, and his faith was renewed.

He crossed his legs as before and began again the process of stilling and seeking. The shaft of light climbed the wall, and the cell gradually darkened, but Alejandro did not notice.

On the morning of his third day in prison, the jailer who brought his porridge told him to eat it quickly. Before Alejandro was finished, the man was back. The monk upended the bowl and used his fingers to scrape out the last bits of softened grain even as the jailer was lifting him from the bed and hustling him out the door.

He was marched down to a courtyard where two soldiers waited along with a smith who had brought fetters and leg irons. These were fitted around his wrists and ankles and hammered closed. When that was done, one of the soldiers said, "Right, let's go," and they took him by the elbows and forced him towards the gate.

The edges of the leg irons scraped against his flesh, and the chain between shortened his steps. The soldiers did not try to hurry him but moved him along with a disinterested firmness. Fortunately, they did not have to go far to reach their destination: the yard of a freight storage, where a train of mules was almost loaded and ready to depart.

Alejandro was marched to where a man was standing, his hat pushed back on his head, his finger tracing a line in a piece of paper he was studying. He looked up when the monk and his escort reached him.

Alejandro smiled. "Juan Hernandez, it is good to see you."

The muleteer glanced up. It took a moment for recognition to arrive. "Ah, so *you're* the troublesome monk. I should have known."

He looked Alejandro up and down then spoke to the soldiers. "He can't keep up the pace in those things. Get them off him."

The senior of the soldiers said, "Then let him ride."

The muleteer shook his head. "No one has paid his haulage. You can carry him if you want. Or you can travel at his speed on your own."

The senior man took only a moment to decide. He sent the junior man to fetch the smith.

"Better hurry it up," Hernandez said. "As soon as we're loaded, we're leaving."

He looked at the monk and shook his head in a manner that said life was once again confirming his lowest expectations.

"Thank you, Juan," Alejandro said.

The muleteer gave him a neutral look. "I do no favours. I attend to my business and expect others to do the same."

But in the calmness of Hernandez's gaze Alejandro thought he saw another statement.

They walked south: eight muleteers, two soldiers, a miscellany of travellers who sought comfort or security in numbers—some disappointed fortune seekers had taken to brigandage—and one Trinitarian. Alejandro's escorts did not see their role as tormentors; as long as he kept up the pace, they walked behind him and attended to their other interests, which centred on wine, women, and a sergeant named Garcia for whom they had no fond regard.

When the sun was overhead, they stopped at a stream to water the mules and eat bread spread with a paste of beans and flecks of green the monk could not identify—it did not matter, since the only taste was of garlic. As night approached, they stopped again, this time at a corral that Juan Hernandez had had built, with a well and a trough for the animals. The mules were unloaded and rubbed down, their cargoes piled in a heap around which the travellers slept after a meal of more beans and salt pork boiled together in a copper pot over an outdoor fire pit topped with an iron grill.

In the morning, they rose, ate, loaded the animals, and set off south again. An hour along the trail, Hernandez came down the line of mules, checking that each one's cross-tree saddle and burdens were properly seated. A galled mule could not bear its load.

When he came near where Alejandro walked at the end of the train, the monk said, "Are you prospering, Juan?"

"Well enough," said the muleteer, tugging on a strap to check its tightness.

"What will happen to your business if the Quito merchants get their port on the Esmeraldas River?"

Hernandez shrugged. "The river can carry boats only so far upstream. There will be a need for mules." He gave Alejandro a considering look. "What has happened to you, Brother?"

"I found my vocation."

The muleteer looked down at the iron on the monk's wrists. "Are you sure?"

It was a fair question, and Alejandro gave it some thought as he followed the mules through the morning towards Riobamba. Before coming up to Quito, he had prayed to be spared an encounter with Father Cabello. That prayer had been answered in the negative. So now he would have to go to Madrid and face an ecclesiastical court. But in Madrid he would not be confined; his order would support him. Thus he would have an opportunity to speak for the people of Esmeraldas—his people, now—and perhaps accomplish more than he had been able to by writing letters to the Viceroy and the *Audiencia*.

There were many within the Spanish Church, some of them highly placed, who saw the forced labour of converted natives as a grave sin. They were fellow Christians, yet they were as ill-used by their Spanish conquerors as were the poor Christians stolen by the Moors of North Africa—the corsairs who boarded ships in the Mediterranean Sea and raided coastal towns and villages as far east as the Adriatic and as far north as Ireland.

Those who spoke up for the *Indios* would welcome Alejandro's first-hand testimony as an aid to their cause. When he reached Guayaquil, he would ask for pen and paper so he could make some notes. He could already imagine himself addressing a group of senior prelates, describing the plight of the Zambos as they were forced to flee into the forest to escape the depredations of invading soldiers.

When God closes one door, he thought, *he opens another.*

Nightfall found them south of Riobamba and beginning to descend the trail through the upland forest. Among the pine trees, Juan Hernandez had built another barebones station. Alejandro helped with the unloading and care for the mules, not much hampered by his fetters.

"Thank you," said Hernandez, "though I cannot pay you. This shipment is precisely costed."

"I do it for the exercise," said the monk. "And because I knew an old Irish Trinitarian who always used to say, 'What are we here for, if not to help each other?'"

The muleteer looked at the soldiers, sitting with their backs against the lower rail of the corral. Somewhere they had acquired a well-filled wineskin and were passing it back and forth. "Some of us are here for less charitable purposes," he said.

He went off to supervise the cooking of the evening rations. Alejandro went to sit beside the soldiers, who regarded him neutrally but did not offer him any of their drink.

"Where did you get that?" he asked.

The senior man said, "Esteban here went to make water among the trees and there it was, hanging from a branch."

The other man belched wine fumes and said, "A miracle, Brother."

"Of some kind, perhaps," Alejandro said. "God does provide for our needs."

He ate with the others but drank water from the well. The muleteers and other travellers cast meaningful glances towards the wine drinkers, but these bounced off without registering. Finally, he lay down near the fire—he had been permanently relieved of his cloak at the prison in Quito—and went to sleep.

He awoke in darkness, the fire reduced to mere embers. Nearby, the soldiers snored. He looked up into the bright splash of stars for a moment—there were so many more here than down at the coast—before he thought to wonder at what had awakened him. He realized it had been a shaking of his shoulder only when it came again and a voiced whispered close to his ear, "Don't make a sound. We've come to take you home."

The words were in Nigua. He recognized the voice. He whispered back, "Hupuka?"

"Hush." A dark shape interposed itself between the monk and the stars. He felt motion and realized that the man was doing something to the chain that connected his wrists: binding the links in cloth so they would not clink together.

"Good," came the whisper after a few moments. "Now, get up and come with me."

In the distance, a mule snorted and stamped. Alejandro, by now on his knees, froze. Then the animal blew out its breath and went back to sleep.

"Come."

Away from the glow of the dying fire, Alejandro's vision adjusted to the starlight. If he looked out of the sides of his eyes, he could make out trees. Hupuka seemed to have a more feline sense and led him unerringly a hundred paces. Then he paused to listen before leading him a hundred more. They came to a trail that sloped gradually downward and followed it. After a while they came to a level spot, and the monk saw more dark shapes.

"Is he all right?" said a voice.

Alejandro said, "I'm fine, Gonzalo. And glad to see you."

"Then let's go."

Or sometimes, Alejandro thought, *God keeps the same window open, though others try to close it.*

Soon after Alejandro's liberation, the Spanish sent another *entrada* down the river. When the Cayapas brought word, Alonso called a council meeting. Chilianduli suggested they try Anton's strategy: attack them while they were still establishing their base, kill a lot of them.

"We did that," Alonso said, "but they still came back."

"They are slow learners," Juanito said. "Still, I would not mind acquiring some iron and steel."

"How about this?" Alonso said. "When the Spaniards come down from the mountains, we will move south."

"Into Campaze lands?" said Chilianduli.

"Yes. It is time we taught them another lesson. And they always have weapons and armour taken from the Spaniards."

Chilianduli thought for a moment. "I like fighting Campazes. Let us do that."

More time passed. The Spaniards came, suffered, achieved nothing, and finally went back to Quito. The Zambos moved back into their old haunts. Over the next year, several more escaped Africans found their way to the settlements.

"Let us try sending them another letter," Alonso said.

Alejandro saw that the chief's hair had grown greyer. There were lines around his eyes and mouth, though they mostly came from smiling.

"Maybe we should fight them first," Chilianduli said. "We could raid them for a change. I have heard that some people on the far side of the mountains have killed thousands of Spaniards. Maybe if we killed more of them, they would change their minds."

Expectation spoke. "No, I have seen this. Their war chiefs are too proud. They think if they keep doing what has worked in other places, it will work here."

"If they don't learn from failure," Chilianduli said, "when will this ever stop?"

Avila tugged on his nose, thinking, and said, "If you have a war chief who does not win, what do you do?"

The Nigua did not need to think. "Get a new war chief."

"And if the war is not worth fighting?"

"Follow a peace chief."

"The Spaniards are no different. Their war chiefs are failing. The merchants want a peace chief who will help them get richer. It is but a matter of time."

"Do we have the time?" Alejandro said, with a glance towards Alonso.

Alonso caught the glance. "Yes," he said and smiled with one corner of his mouth. "At least most of us."

"Is he ill?" Alejandro asked as he and Expectation walked back towards her hut.

"He had a fever while you were up-country. It comes back from time to time."

"Can you not heal him?"

The small face drew inward. "So far, yes. There are herbs that strengthen his spirit. But eventually …"

The monk said, "It is not good for him to have to move deep into the forest. The air is bad there."

They had come to the ladder leading up to his hut. Expectation looked back towards the space where the council had met, and Alejandro followed her gaze. Alonso was watching his wives gather up the stools to take them back inside. They were matrons now, broad of hip, strong of arm. His sons, Sebastian and Alonso, arrived to help their mothers. Their father said something to them, and they all laughed.

Alejandro had a brief moment of longing: it would have been good to have had sons—or daughters, for that matter. Then he put the thought away. If God has given you what you wished for, to wish again for something else bespeaks a lamentable ingratitude.

He asked Expectation, "What happens to us when ... ?"

She shrugged her small shoulders. "He and Miriam are raising Sebastian to take his place."

"And the people are happy about that?"

"Yes. Sebastian is a proper Zambo. We just need to get him wives from the different clans."

*E*PILOGUE ONE

EXPECTATION

The Spaniards had come again. We had moved south, deep into the forest. They were still tramping about, futilely hunting for us as the year moved into the season of the long rains. Xinbu came to me and said, "Alonso has the coughing sickness again. I think he may break a rib."

I took my bag and went to see him. It was as I had expected, and I spoke to Xinbu and Kepepahta outside their house, where the constant drumming of the rain gave us privacy.

"His chest is filling with the water of death, squeezing out the breath of life."

"Is it an evil spirit?" Xinbu asked. "Can you take it from him?"

"No, it is Alonso's own spirit. It has decided it is his time."

Their faces took on the calm dignity that is the Nigua way, though Xinbu's mouth could not keep a firm line. Kepepahta said, "Is there anything we can do?"

I said I would give them a tea that would calm the coughing and let him go on without pain. At that moment, Alejandro came hurrying across the open space.

"He is dying, isn't he?" he said.

I saw the shock on the women's faces and said, "We don't use that word at a time like this. It draws … bad things."

He blinked as he often did when confronted by reality and said, "All right. But there is a … ceremony that I must perform." When my brows drew together, he said, "He was baptized a Christian. It is our way."

Xinbu and Kepepahta looked to me, their shock having given way to worry. I asked the Spaniard, "Will you mention … that thing that mustn't be mentioned?"

He put up both hands. One contained a little glass bottle. Someone had found it washed up on the beach, and he had asked to have it. It seemed to contain water. "No," he said. "I just have to make the sign of the cross on him with this water. And I will speak only in Latin."

I could have quibbled at that. Spirits understand all languages. But I was sure he would do no harm. I bade him go up into the house. A few moments later, I could hear him speaking softly in that other language: "*In nomine patri, et filii …*"

I said to the women that they should bring Alonso's sons to the house. They left to find them. I needed to go and prepare the tea, but on the way I would stop and speak with Miriam.

Epilogue Two

Alonso Illescas

The coughing has ceased. The taste of the tea is bitter in Alonso's mouth, but the fiery ache in his lower ribs fades, fades, and then it is gone. He takes a shallow breath, lets it out, then takes and releases another—and realizes that was the last one. He cannot get another; his chest is still; it is all gone from him.

He feels light. He is rising towards the grass bundles that roof the house. His wives and his sons are there, looking down at him as he looks down at them. Then suddenly he is rushing upward. The roof disappears. He shouldn't be able to see stars for the rain but he does, thousands of them. They fly towards him then disappear like a shower of cold sparks.

He has broken free. He is filled with an exhilaration that makes him feel as light as breath itself. He is floating in darkness, serene, neither happy nor unhappy, and for a long time—or so it seems—that is all he wishes to do.

Now he becomes aware of a presence near him. It has power, yet he has no cause to fear it. It is not friendly towards him, yet he knows it wishes him well. He reaches out, not with his hand but with his being, and encounters … he does not know. He has no senses as he used to know them, cannot see or hear or touch or taste or smell.

Yet he knows there is something with him. *I will open my eyes,* he thinks, *and see.*

He opens his eyes and there is light: soft, diffuse, a pale gold. But it illuminates nothing, not even himself. It is everywhere yet at the same time far off, though he cannot tell in which direction it lies.

He floats in the light as he floated in the darkness. Time passes. Or it doesn't. He cannot tell. The presence is still there, but now somehow he knows that it will not always be so. There is something he must do, though he cannot think what.

The knowledge bothers him. He does not wish to be bothered. Perhaps if he ignores the knowledge it will go from him, leave him to float, leave him his serenity.

But now another presence makes itself known. A voice from somewhere in the light says, *There you are.* Then, *I am with you.*

The voice is familiar. He has heard it often and, indeed, very recently, though he thinks it used to have a raspy quality. He cannot place it. That also disturbs him, and he tries to settle back again into the peace.

Come along now, says the voice. *Give me your hand.*

I don't have a hand, Alonso says.

You do if you want to. Stop being difficult. There is not much time.

Alonso says, *There is no time.*

The voice is calm but firm. *Give me your hand.*

Alonso knows he will get no more peace until he does as he is bid. When he reaches out a hand, he finds that he does have one after all. Someone's fingers take hold of it, guiding it, and suddenly there is sensation: his hand has been placed on something both soft and hard—softness over hardness, fur over muscle, he realizes, warm and full of life. Feeling it is like learning touch all over again.

What is that? he says.

Open your eyes and see, says the voice.

They are open.

No, you closed them when you tried to go back to sleep. Now, hurry up.

He opens his eyes again. The diffuse glow is still there but now, under his hand, is a long, lithe shape, pale gold like the surrounding glow but marked with darker shapes like … he cannot remember what the shapes remind him of, and the voice interrupts his musing.

You've seen this before.

Have I? Yes, I think I remember.

This is not a time for thinking or remembering, the voice says, *but for looking forward to where you must go. Keep your hand on the companion. It knows the way.*

Alonso feels motion under his hand, as if muscles flex and release. He is being drawn forward and now it as if he is standing—no, walking—beside an animal, his hand resting lightly on its back.

Good, says the voice. *Keep going. One last difficulty.*

He walks. It feels right. But then, ahead and off to the side, he sees dark shapes, huddled things, and he knows they are aware of him. Now they are speaking to him, hissing vileness, spreading their sourness towards him.

The animal keeps walking and so does Alonso, though their path will take them past the whisperers. The creature turns its head and growls at them, and Alonso is suddenly fearful.

The firm voice comes from beside him, though when he turns his head he sees no one there. *Pay no attention. They are sad liars and without power over you.*

Now he cannot hear the evil voices. Their darkness becomes paler, and then they are gone like shadows fading under light, taking the fear with them.

Look ahead now, says the voice.

Alonso looks. The glow is brighter in front of him, a deeper, warmer gold. There are other shapes now, dim at first but becoming clearer. The animal beneath his touch moves away from him and is gone, but that is as it should be. Ahead, he sees bodies taking form. A hand is reaching out to him, eyes and smiles and …

Oh, he says. *Of course.*

Behind him, the oddly familiar voice says, *There you go. All right now.*

And he is.

Afterword

This is a work of historical fiction. That means that, unlike the twenty-some other novels I have written, it is not entirely made up by the fellow who occupies the back of my head. The key events—the shipwreck, the mission of Father Miguel Cabello de Balboa, the *entradas*, the coming of Avila and de Espinosa to the Zambo state, the final resolution—all happened more or less as I have portrayed them.

Many of the persons involved—especially Alonso de Illescas, dons Alonso and Alvaro, Miguel Cabello de Balboa, Anton, Rodrigo de Ribadeneira, Gonzalo de Avila, Pidi the Nigua chief—really existed and played roles that I have adapted into the narrative. The Trinitarian monk Alejandro de Espinosa also existed, though his Christian name was Alonso, apparently a very common nominative in sixteenth-century Spain. I changed it because we already had two Alonsos in the story; one more would have been too confusing. Juan Hernandez, the muleteer, also had a real life, but it was lived in Mexico. I moved him south, but I am sure there would have been someone like him in Guayaquil. Somebody had to move those goods up into the high country.

I first came across a mention of these people and what they went through in a brief footnote in a book I read (and cannot remember the title of) back in 1971 or 1972, when I was in the process of dropping out of university to begin a career in journalism. As a teenager, I'd had an ambition to be a historical novelist, inspired by the works of Robert Graves, Lionel Sprague de Camp, Cecelia Holland, Zoe Oldenbourg, and a slew of authors who wrote tales of Vikings and ancient Greeks for juvenile readers. I had even started to write one of my own but had given up after one chapter.

As years went by and I got busy being a speechwriter, husband, and father, I put aside my fiction-writing ambitions—which had since broadened to include science fiction, fantasy, and crime fiction—but I always kept the story of the Zambos somewhere among the furniture in my mental attic. Occasionally, I would attempt to research the history—a difficult task, since there was little information to be found in English and I was not proficient enough in Spanish to read the academic papers published in South American journals.

But a few years ago, and more than forty years after that footnote caught my imagination, the Canada Council for the Arts gave me a substantial grant, and I set out to gather what information I could. It turned out that since the turn of the century, a number of academics had written in English about the Zambo state. I was able to get a better picture of what had happened and to whom.

But back to my first sentence above. It is a work of historical *fiction*, which means I have used real events and persons of the past to tell a story—my kind of story. And, as readers of my speculative and crime fiction will recognize, my stories tend to be about social outliers who are a bad fit for their environments, who have to struggle to make a place for themselves. I write about people like that because I am one, and because I suspect many of my readers share some of the same traits.

I took liberties in the pursuit of storytelling. The Nigua language no longer exists, so I borrowed words from their neighbours, the Cayapas, to make up most of the Nigua names. No one knows what the shamanistic practices of those long-disappeared people may have been, so I imported the techniques and visions of other cultures. How Anton ceased to be the leader of the Africans, and how Alsonso took his place, is not recorded, so I conceived of a dramatic situation. And I may have been grossly unfair to Miguel Cabello de Balboa by painting him as an ambitious schemer, but a story needs an antagonist and he fit the part.

So, to those far better versed than me in the history of the Kingdom of Quito and the struggles of the Zambos, I beg your indulgence. I am no historian. I am a fictioneer, a tale spinner, and I ask that you judge the novel for what it is trying to be: a story about people who did their best with what they had in a less than hospitable world. And won through.

I won't name the learned academics whose books and papers I consulted to find the framework for the story. They might not approve of the embroidery I wove around their findings. But I am grateful to all of them.

I do express my sincere gratitude to the Canada Council for the Arts, the British Columbia Arts Council, and the Speculative Literature Foundation for their faith in me. And I am grateful to my old friend, Janet Battison Lazare, for digging through the academic databases and finding rare gems.

About the Author

Matthew Hughes writes science-fantasy and science fiction. An alter ego, Matt Hughes, writes crime fiction. A personality fragment, Hugh Matthews, writes media tie-ins.

His novels are *Downshift* (Doubleday Canada, 1997 and Five Rivers Press, 2013); *Fools Errant* and *Fool Me Twice* (Warner Aspect, 2001); *Black Brillion* (Tor, 2004); *Majestrum* (Night Shade Books, 2006); *The Commons* (Robert J. Sawyer Books, 2007); *The Spiral Labyrinth* (Night Shade Books, 2007); *Template* (PS Publishing, 2008 and Paizo Publishing, 2010); and *Hespira* (Night Shade Books, 2009); *The Damned Busters* (Angry Robot Books, 2011); *Costume Not Included* (Angry Robot Books, 2012); *The Other* (Underland Press, 2011); *Song of the Serpent* (Paizo Publishing, 2012); *Hell to Pay* (Angry Robot Books, 2013); *Old Growth* (Five Rivers, 2013) ; *A Wizard's Henchman* (PS Publishing, 2016), *One More Kill* (PS Publishing, 2018), *A God in Chains* (Edge SF and Fantasy Publishing, 2019), and *Ghost Dreams* (PS Publishing, 2020).

His short fiction has appeared in *Alfred Hitchcock's, Asimov's, Blue Murder, Fantasy & Science Fiction, Postscripts, Lightspeed, Storyteller, Interzone,* and a number of bespoke anthologies, including the bestseller *Rogues.* Night Shade Books published his first short story collection, *The Gist Hunter and Other Stories,* in 2005.

He has self-published collections of his novels and short fiction backlist as *9 Tales of Henghis Hapthorn,* (2013), *The Meaning of Luff and Other Stories,* (2013), *The Compleat Guth Bandar,* (2014), *Devil or Angel and Other Stories,* (2015), and *9 Tales of Raffalon,* (2017).

A series of novella chapbooks featuring Hughes's far-future master criminal, Luff Imbry, began appearing as limited editions from PS Publishing in 2010. The first title is *Quartet & Triptych*, the second is *The Yellow Cabochon* (2012), and the third is *Of Whimsies and Noubles* (2014). The fourth, *Epiphanies*, appeared in 2015, and all four will be published in a paperback omnibus in 2019.

Hughes also edits fiction and hires out as a "book doctor" for publishers and individual authors.

From a working-poor background, he became a journalist then a staff speechwriter to the Canadian Ministers of Justice and Environment in the Pierre Trudeau government of 1974–79. After that, he spent more than twenty-five years as a freelance speechwriter for Canadian corporate executives and political leaders. At present, he augments a fiction writer's uncertain income by housesitting. He has lived in twelve countries and passed through a half a dozen more.

He has won the Arthur Ellis Award from the Crime Writers of Canada and has been short-listed for the Aurora, Nebula, Philip K Dick, Endeavour (twice), A E Van Vogt, and Derringer Awards.

His web page is at http://www.matthewhughes.org.

For a complete bibliography, see www.matthewhughes.org/matthew-hughes-bibliography/.

www.ingramcontent.com/pod-product-compliance
Lightning Source LLC
Chambersburg PA
CBHW020604310726
48979CB00008B/1342/J

* 9 7 8 1 9 8 8 8 6 5 1 5 7 *